ABOUT THE AUTHOR

Christopher Taylor is married with three children and lives in Surrey. A graduate from London's City University, he was an Investment Banker for over thirty years before embarking on his second career as an author. He is an accredited psychometric evaluator and believes that this keen interest in how people interact and his experiences in the hair-trigger world of financial trading have helped to ensure his writing remains original.

www.cctaylor.co.uk

THE RULE OF 72

C. C. Taylor

Matador
9 Priory Business Park
Kibworth Beauchamp
Leicestershire LE8 0RX, UK
Tel: (+44) 116 279 2299
Fax: (+44) 116 279 2277
Email: books@troubador.co.uk
Web: www.troubador.co.uk/matador

ISBN 978-1783063-826

British Library Cataloguing in Publication Data.
A catalogue record for this book is available from the British Library.

Typeset in Aldine by Troubador Publishing Ltd
Printed and bound in the UK by TJ International, Padstow, Cornwall

Matador is an imprint of Troubador Publishing Ltd

To my wife, Julia

"We are a plague on the Earth. It's coming home to roost over the next fifty years or so. It's not just climate change; it's sheer space, places to grow food for this enormous horde. Either we limit our population growth or the natural world will do it for us…"

Sir David Attenborough

"The danger is that global warming may become self-sustaining, if it has not done so already."

Stephen Hawking

"Food production must increase by 50% by 2030 to feed the world's growing population or there will be civil unrest."

United Nations

"…Nature, the biggest bank of all could go bust."

HRH The Prince of Wales

PART 1

CHAPTER 1

A shrill of brakes heralded the arrival of yet another underground train. Arthur Withers – 'Arf wiv us' to his friends – raised a battered harmonica to his cracked lips and, after delicately setting down a half-empty can of Carlsberg Special Brew, started to blow and suck an unidentifiable tune from the instrument. The usual throng of early evening commuters and theatregoers rounded the bend in the tunnel and streamed busily past him as he stood unsteadily with his back against the tiled wall. They hardly noticed him and he them. Their minds were elsewhere whilst his was frozen, paralysed by years of loneliness and abuse. He played on, his senses numbed by drink. All that registered through the fog was the occasional chink of change as coins dropped into the tatty cardboard box at his feet. A sign, written during a rare venture into full consciousness, declared: 'due to fine weather, all music half-price!'

Uncannily, Arthur could instinctively tell the value of every coin that dropped into his box. The tinkling sound of coppers would cause his face to contort and he'd squeeze his eyes shut as if the act caused him actual, physical pain, whereas when he detected the clinking of heavier metal that signified a one or two pound piece, he would reward the unknown donor with an especially energetic display of gratitude, accompanied by a manic, see-saw rocking of his head.

They soon passed by on their many different ways, like so many before them. All, that is, except one who lagged behind the others as they disappeared around the next bend in the subway tunnel. Arthur turned towards his unexpected audience and drew back his cracked lips as he fixed a smile on his worn face. Then he clasped his harmonica between the rotting stumps of his teeth, ready to give a special rendition.

Arthur glimpsed a momentary glint of steel as the blade tore effortlessly through his throat. Air wheezed from his lungs and he heard an odd gurgling sound as blood began to flood his chest cavity. Throughout his last moments, he remained strangely detached from events, as if he were a spectator at his own death. Shocked and disorientated, his mind struggled to keep pace with events. He lurched sideways against the wall, his hands fumbling urgently at his neck whilst his legs started to kick spasmodically, before he crumpled to the ground.

Arthur's last moments were spent staring glassy-eyed at the new leather soles of a pair of expensive shoes as his departing executioner walked away, unhurried, up the tunnel. He was dead before the next train disgorged its unsuspecting passengers to happen upon the gruesome scene.

CHAPTER 2

Caroline dabbed at her eyes one last time, before expertly reapplying her make up. She'd been crying again; the third time in as many days. She cursed her weakness, but most of all she cursed Tom Beresford. Ever since his arrival three months ago, her working life had steadily deteriorated. It wasn't that he set out to slight or belittle her. He was simply one of those people who was incapable of understanding how their words and actions affected others. From now on, she resolved, she wouldn't let it get to her. She'd be strong. But she'd said that yesterday.

Deep down, she knew things wouldn't improve. She would never be able to accept him and could certainly never forget the way he had been brought in above her, with not a moment's warning.

The sting of betrayal stiffened her resolve. With a final glance in the mirror, and an indignant toss of her head that sent her blonde hair swirling round her shoulders, she turned for the door. After one last deep breath, she jerked it open and strolled casually out of the washroom, a smile of false confidence painted on her pretty face.

Any hope that her tearful dash for the Ladies had passed

unnoticed evaporated in an instant. Over by the water dispenser, she noticed Laura the graduate trainee and Stephen from group advertising deep in conversation. Upon spotting her, both darted separate, concerned glances in her direction. She set her jaw and straightened her back, hating their sympathy.

But their attention was fleeting, and as she approached her workstation, she noticed Kelly, her PA, sitting perched on a desk, the obvious centre of attention. As she drew closer, she heard Kelly's voice piping out loudly.

'It was disgusting. There was blood *all* over the shop.'

As she stressed the word 'all', Kelly made a sweeping arm movement that took in half the open-plan office and her eyes widened in mock horror.

'I nearly puked my guts up on the spot,' she continued.

Just then, a loud and authoritative voice boomed out from behind them. 'I, Tom Beresford, declare this meeting of the Eastcheap women's knitting circle *closed*!'

Caroline could hardly believe that he actually clapped his hands as he delivered his patronising rebuke. Kelly stopped mid-sentence, glanced once at Tom then skulked back to her desk. The others did likewise. Caroline stood her ground though, determined not to be ushered away like an errant schoolgirl, but her gesture of resistance passed unnoticed.

'Oh and *Caroline*,' Tom muttered over his shoulder as he walked nonchalantly away, 'Leo Brooks wants to see us upstairs immediately, there's a flap on.' Then raising his voice just loud enough for everyone to hear, he added, 'Some juicy scandal brewing if my spies are to be believed.'

Half-running to keep up, she followed Tom to the lobby, the journalist in her eager to find out what this was all about.

Emerging from the lifts, Tom strode confidently past Phyllis Clapham, Leo Brooks' trusty PA.

'He's expecting us,' he muttered.

Caroline felt an involuntary stirring of admiration at this fearless act. Phyllis was what all senior executives needed: a veritable Rottweiler if her master's territory were ever violated.

But Caroline noted that Phyllis seemed as impotent as everyone else when exposed to Tom's boorish manner, her impassive eyes betraying the merest flicker of disapproval before her thin mouth creased into a smile of recognition when she saw Caroline. They'd always got on. Or, put another way, Caroline had never done anything to provoke Phyllis's legendary ire, so they'd never fallen out.

'Morning, Phyllis,' Caroline said, conjuring up her most friendly smile.

'Oh! Hello Caroline. I like your outfit, very smart! Whose is it?'

It was her new Vivienne Westwood suit. But as she was about to answer, she noticed Tom tapping his foot impatiently.

'No time for gossip, ladies. There's work to be done.'

For a split-second, Caroline and Phyllis' eyes met. In that instant there was absolute solidarity between them. They were united in animosity and disdain.

Phyllis then took them through into Leo Brooks' exquisite domain, where he was studiously reading one of the bank's many daily research reports. He had built his formidable reputation by being well informed and was revered in investment banking circles as one of the few CEOs who remained 'in touch' with the business. Indeed, it was this hands-on management approach that had enabled Montagu Steinhart to navigate the credit crunch with minimal bad debt provisions and its reputation untarnished.

As they entered, Leo marked his place precisely on the page before carefully laying the report to one side of his highly polished, walnut desk – impressively uncluttered, save for three neatly stacked piles of paper, a notepad and a miniature Daniel Quires antique carriage clock. No gauche In and Out trays or executive toys for Leo Brooks, a man of renowned taste and style, one of the youngest and most respected investment banking chiefs in the City.

He stood and warmly shook Tom's outstretched hand. 'Thanks for popping up, old chap. Caroline, nice to see you. I trust this reprobate hasn't been working you too hard?'

This last comment was accompanied by a playful mock punch to Tom's shoulder. Their obvious familiarity disappointed her. How could Leo Brooks, so polished and refined, like this thick-skinned oaf? she wondered.

Leo led them into an expansive lounge to one side of his office.

'Please, take a seat,' he said, gesturing towards a generously upholstered cream sofa.

He then ran a hand through his neatly styled grey hair ensuring it was, as always, smoothed perfectly into place.

Caroline had always found him an attractive man, although at five eight he was a little short for her usual taste.

Leo projected an impression of fitness and health, and certainly didn't look the forty-eight years attributed to him in the most recent edition of *Fortune* magazine. A prize catch, you would have thought. But there was no Mrs Brooks and never had been. In fact, there were no stories or even rumours of any romantic liaisons at all – of any persuasion – which Caroline had always thought was strange.

Tom slumped heavily on the sofa, his trousers stretched tightly over his thick, splayed thighs. Caroline settled herself in an armchair at the other end of the low rosewood table that conveniently separated them. She allowed the niceties of the meeting – coffee, biscuits, a quick summary of the mood 'down in the trenches' – to wash over her, only really plugging in when Leo looked rather earnestly at them both and said: 'I have every confidence you two can help rectify a rather irksome little problem that has arisen.'

He paused and leant further towards them, as if about to divulge a great secret.

'You both know Hubert Dunwoody who ran our Equities Division up until a month ago.' This was a statement rather than a question, but they both nodded anyway. 'Well, it appears Hubey ... er, Hubert has become a little too friendly with his secretary over the past few years, if you follow my meaning.'

Leo steepled his fingers together as he looked over to gauge their reactions. Like Tom, Caroline kept her expression impassive.

Truth was, Caroline had often come across Hubert in her duties as Corporate Communications Director. It was quite obvious he was what could be described as an opportunist flirt. He constantly sought eye contact whilst invariably wearing an irritatingly superior half-smile on his face. His conversation was usually a clever tapestry of suggestive double-entendres, so this news was more predictable than surprising.

Caroline and Tom remained silent as Leo continued talking in his characteristically clipped and rather staccato manner. Caroline had noticed before that whenever Leo addressed more than one person, he resorted to this formal way of speaking, almost as if he were giving a military address. It was an odd but effective way of communicating, since although Leo's voice was not loud, this technique ensured that his words received full attention at all times. With Leo Brooks, fact was followed by fact with little embellishment or digression. For a man like this, Caroline acknowledged, time was always of the essence.

'The Management,' he continued, 'was made aware of this state of affairs six weeks ago and the matter was discussed at length. Although Hubert had displayed a singular lack of judgement, we decided to take no action, since we expected matters to run their course. And in any case, we believe a person's private life should remain, just so. '

'Quite right,' said Tom, with an approving nod. 'Hubey gets caught dipping his pen in company ink. So what? None of our business!'

'Quite obviously we don't usually waste our time discussing the indiscretions of our staff,' Leo continued, an edge of impatience creeping into his voice. 'But Tom, you will no doubt remember that Hubert Dunwoody was recently promoted to head up our North American operations, an extremely senior position for someone of his age.' There was silence again as Leo drew breath. 'It transpires that this relationship was serious and not just a passing dalliance.'

Caroline's feminist antennae twitched at this rather quaint description, but she said nothing. Leo's expression was fixed in concentration and Caroline sensed he would soon reveal the reason behind their summons.

'In order to take up his new position, Hubert was forced to make an important decision: whether to take Sarah, his wife, and their three young children to the States with him, or whether to take Miss ... Miss…' He excused away the missing name with a dismissive wave of his hand. 'Wisely, he chose his wife and family. The other young lady in question was understandably upset.'

Tom nodded and pushed his bottom lip forward childishly.

Caroline was beginning to feel mildly irritated by the impassive, matter-of-fact delivery of this real-life drama. She could well imagine the emotional turmoil of the situation, even if he could not.

'Regrettably, when it was obvious that their relationship was over for good, the woman decided to go public.'

'Hell hath no fury, and all that,' exclaimed Tom, shaking his head knowingly and noisily sucking in air through his teeth.

'Quite, quite,' agreed Leo stiffly, eager to continue without interruption.

'For a week, it was all everyone talked about in the

trading room. Soon enough, the whole of the equity market was buzzing with tittle-tattle.'

Serves Hubert right, Caroline thought. She was beginning to enjoy this part of the story.

'We hoped it would die down, and for a while it did. Yesterday, however, things took a rather worrying turn for the worse. I received a call from a *Sunday Times* journalist who asked if I had any comment on allegations that Hubert Dunwoody was recently promoted to a senior post overseas to extricate him from the fallout of an extramarital affair. He also suggested that this move was designed to protect Hubert from criticism of the way he ran the Equities Division, which, as you both know, turned in a loss last year.'

Caroline did know this. It had been the first time Equities had ever done so. *A scandal in itself*, she thought.

'The journalist has also discovered that Hubert was in the same house at Harrow as Donald Champney, our head of corporate finance, as well as myself.'

That's it, thought Caroline. This wasn't about saving Hubert from public ridicule. This was about the old school tie, the reputation of Montagu Steinhart, the integrity of its management and, ultimately, the judgement of its CEO. Leo was not going to allow the shabby extramarital activities of a junior member of his management team to tarnish his carefully crafted public image and that's why he needed her and Tom. Their job was to make it all go away.

There was no doubt this was an ugly and potentially explosive situation. Caroline knew only too well that once the press had the scent of scandal, it was difficult to put them off. The story would smack of a clumsy cover-up to protect one of the firm's golden boys. 'Jobs for the boys,' the journalists would cry, scrambling to highlight the public school angle, dredging up the decadence of the investment banking world. That would doubtless hit a nerve in recession-blighted Britain. Hubert's Ferrari and his penchant for nights out at Spearmint Rhino were perfect tabloid fodder. There was certainly enough for a juicy story to savour over Sunday's fry-up, to be followed no doubt by a special feature on how nothing had changed in the world of 'casino banking'. Yes, this was trouble and represented the sort of publicity no City firm wanted in these days of austerity.

'Where's the girl now?' asked Tom.

'Yes, what happened to *her*?' blurted Caroline a little too quickly.

She regretted her words immediately. Whereas Tom's enquiry was a call for more information, hers screamed 'forget Hubert, what about the real victim of all this?' There was a moment's silence as her words hung in the air. Leo turned to face her, clearly nettled.

'No need to worry about her. She was well looked after. Landed on her feet, by all accounts.'

He looked straight at Caroline now. She could hear his foot tapping on the base of the table leg in irritation. Unsettled by this sudden change in mood, she tried to act as if her question had been asked purely from general interest and smiled weakly. Leo, however, was not to be appeased.

'Hubert paid her handsomely, so much in fact that people assumed she was some sort of high flyer. She's now

PA to Joe Schwartz, Chairman of Kravits and Sons. An excellent position and well beyond her ability, I would imagine. No, don't worry yourself on her account,' he added tersely.

As Leo stared at her, Caroline saw a coldness in his slate grey eyes. She blanched inwardly, but nodded appreciatively at the explanation, still trying to project a relaxed manner. Was he annoyed with her personally for focusing on the plight of the secretary? Or was he just angry at the whole Hubert Dunwoody mess and its potential to damage his reputation?

'Don't worry, Leo,' said Tom confidently, breaking the uncomfortable silence. 'We'll sort this out in a jiffy.' He turned to Caroline. 'You know a hack at *The Sunday Times*, don't you?'

'Yes,' she replied keenly, desperate to be seen as useful.

In actual fact, she knew their Special Features Editor, Jonathan Daniels, affectionately known by all his friends as 'Jack'. They'd been at college together and had been close friends, very close at one time, she remembered with an unexpected pang of regret.

'Well,' Tom continued, 'get him on the blower and see what you can find out. Tell him it's not much of a story really, etcetera. You know the form. I'll give Smyth, Jenkins and Wilkes a call to warm them up. If all fails, we can slap an injunction on the paper.'

Although a little theatrical, the display had the desired effect. At the mention of the bank's legal advisers, Leo nodded his head enthusiastically. His mood lightened.

'Right, we've got work to do,' Tom said, struggling clumsily to his feet.

Then, with his friend at his side, he strode purposefully to the door. Caroline followed a few paces behind.

'Been fishing recently?' Tom's voice was jaunty as they stood waiting for the lift to arrive. Leo was a keen salmon fisherman, a passion that he indulged to the full at his extensive estate in Scotland, whenever his punishing work schedule permitted.

'Simply haven't had the time recently, what with the AGM last week. But you know what, Tom? I think I'll pop up this weekend.'

'Yes, you do that,' boomed Tom. 'It will do you the world of good. Forget this grubby business. We'll snuff this one out in no time, won't we, Caroline?'

He tossed his head in her general direction, but Caroline stood there in silence. In the last few minutes she had glimpsed another Leo Brooks: a cold, angry and brittle man.

The lift arrived and the doors opened silently.

'By the way,' Tom said, thrusting his foot between the doors to stop them closing. 'That Edward van der Linden fellow would like lunch with you.'

'Interesting,' replied Leo, nodding his head slowly as he took in the information. 'I heard he was in town. He's been doing the rounds of the major hedge funds and private equity houses, I understand. Ask Phyllis to find a date in my diary. I would certainly like to meet this character.'

'I'll get Caroline to prepare a briefing paper for you,' offered Tom.

Tom turned her way to ensure Caroline had registered this instruction. She nodded acknowledgement, now very much the obliging employee.

As the lift doors slid shut, Tom prodded the control panel with his stubby finger, hitting the button for the second floor at the third attempt.

'Dirty old bugger, that Hubey,' he muttered as if to himself, though obviously intent on goading Caroline. 'Actually, she's a good-looking filly.' He was unable to resist a sideways glance. 'So, change that to: lucky old bugger!'

Caroline maintained her silence. She was in no mood for another verbal sparring match. But Tom was not to be deterred.

'A word of friendly advice, Carol.'

She hated her name being shortened, and he knew it.

'It's generally regarded as a career-limiting move to suggest to the big white chief that he's a sexist. I should keep your feminist views to yourself if I were you.'

They'd reached the second floor and Tom sauntered out of the lift without another word.

CHAPTER 3

Gayle Stourbridge had always been a pretty girl and by fifteen she was well on the way to becoming a beautiful woman. With a quick brain and an impish sense of mischief, she had been a popular and well-adjusted teenager. Stewart Stourbridge, her father, adored her. She was his jewel, his hope for the future. When she won the East Sussex 'Gymnast of the Future' prize, he had videoed the competition from start to finish. How the family had laughed when he replayed the film and they heard him sniffing and gulping throughout as he struggled to stifle the welling tears of pride. But that was before she met Sammy Assif, before her life had been derailed by crack cocaine.

Two years on from winning her gymnastic prize, she lay slumped in a shop doorway just off The Strand, every fibre of her body crying out for the drug that was daily leeching the life from her. Dirty, lank hair framed gaunt, hollow cheeks. Gone was the sparkle in her eyes that had so enchanted her friends and given her father's mundane life a purpose. Gone too was the slim, young body of a blossoming teenager. Now her skinny frame was angular and emaciated, her bones clearly visible under her ill-fitting, stained clothes.

The girl in the doorway stared ahead of her, at nothing. She didn't mind what she looked like; she was way past caring about that. Pride had departed, along with the last of her treasured possessions which had either been pawned to feed her addiction or else pilfered by others who shared her nightmare world. All that mattered to her now was how she could find the money to buy her way to temporary oblivion. This was her routine, a torment that she woke to every day.

The day had already turned bad. She'd spent the morning begging in a subway tunnel near Kings Cross station.

'Spare some change, spare some change,' she'd bleated over and over again.

Wrapped in a grubby pink blanket, she wore her most pathetic expression. But few had been moved enough to dip into their pockets. To most people she was invisible, a blemish on their day to be blanked out and ignored. Eventually she'd been moved on by a self-important Community Policeman, resplendent in his shiny uniform with its many gadgets and pouches.

So far she'd made about six pounds, well short of the twenty she needed to sate the pains now gnawing at her stomach. This was just the start though, she knew they would only get worse unless she secured her fix. She'd have to sell herself if things didn't pick up soon. It was always a last resort but one that had become all too frequent of late. She scratched her arms and looked around her furtively. When she needed her hit she always felt more vulnerable. Sleeping rough, she had learnt to be wary of those with whom she shared the streets – the drunks, addicts and the mentally deranged – as many of them were predatory. In fact, the majority were downright unpredictable and dangerous. If they caught her alone, the men would often pester her, pawing at her clothes as part of some kind of haphazard, sluggish sexual overture. The women would simply scream threats and if they got close enough, attack. That's why she had chosen this particular spot. It was public enough to keep them at bay, but private enough for her to do what she had to do. In fact she'd spotted another girl she recognised from the streets in a doorway two shops down who was obviously thinking along the same lines. So here she sat in a dark, dank alcove, observing that other world of bright colours, sweet-smelling perfume and laughter. A world to which she longed to return, but knew she never would.

Gayle was busily raking her fingernails up and down her arms in an attempt to quell the itching when a shadow fell on her. Someone was standing in front of her, blocking the glaring yellow and red lights from the pizza restaurant opposite. The world snapped into sharp focus, her self-preservation instincts kicking in as she became aware of a potential threat. Her first thought was that her father had finally tracked her down. She knew he was looking for her because she'd seen him a few times from afar, but had so far managed to avoid detection. An involuntary sob caught in her throat at the thought of him. He mustn't find her. Not like this.

The motionless spectre standing over her wore a heavy dark-coloured winter cape. Slowly, the figure bent forward, momentarily touching her outstretched hand. There was perhaps the hint of a smile and the sparkle of excitement in a pair of staring eyes deep in the dark cavern of a hood, but before Gayle could see more, the apparition silently moved on. The encounter was so unexpected and fleeting that, in her ravaged condition, it assumed a dreamlike quality. Only when she rocked back into the pile of refuse sacks stacked behind her did Gayle become aware of the silver foil package in her upturned palm. The mysterious figure must have dropped it in her hand before leaving.

She stared at it for a full twenty seconds, hardly daring to believe what it could be. It appeared to be a two gram twist of crack cocaine. But why? Why would a stranger simply give her what looked like four days' supply? At that moment though, the answer to the question became far less important than discovering what the packet actually contained. With busy fingers she urgently unwrapped the silver package, taking special care not to spill any of its contents. She then let out a sharp gasp, for in the sparse light available in the doorway, she could just make out a small pile of white-coloured powder. She licked her finger and dabbed the substance before tentatively tasting it. It fizzed on her tongue and then yielded that familiar sweet metallic taste. It was the real deal. It tasted good and very strong, far better than what she had been putting up with lately, which she knew was bulked out with baking powder.

She rummaged through her remaining belongings in the tatty holdall next to her, in search of the special tin which contained her treasured drugs paraphernalia. She found it, prized open the lid and three minutes later, Gayle was dragging deeply on her worn clay pipe, making the yellow and blue flame dance on its bed of tobacco and crack. The familiar sweet, sickly smoke filled her lungs, warming her torpid body. Almost instantaneously, she felt an unstoppable wave of pleasure sweep through her whole being as the narcotic raced along her synaptic connections, igniting a million neurons in her brain. She relaxed and slumped deeper into her nest of waste paper, content at last.

At first she thought someone had hit her on the back of her head with a club. But they hadn't. Her mind burst into a kaleidoscope of colours. The poison was ruthlessly efficient. The moment it entered her body, the outcome was inevitable. First of all, it attacked the cranial nerves, inducing immediate and irreversible paralysis, before steaming through the entire central nervous system, shredding every sensory nerve along her spinal-cord as it went. The agony was beyond description, beyond comprehension. White-hot pulses of liquid pain coursed through every fibre of her young body before her consciousness evaporated, granting her a merciful release.

A shadowy figure passed by and paused momentarily as she toppled backwards, melting gracefully into her cardboard grave.

The early morning refuse collection team uncovered her lifeless body at six in the morning, lying cocooned in a blanket of newspapers and pizza cartons. Two doors down they found a similar scene. Two bodies in one morning, in one street alone. They weren't surprised though; such discoveries were becoming increasingly common-place on their shift.

CHAPTER 4

Caroline pulled hard on the steel handle of the heavy door at the main entrance of the police station known as West End Central, an ugly 1970's concrete block awkwardly attached to the end of a Victorian terrace in Savile Row. Bland and nondescript, like so many buildings of the era it had been designed to be functional rather than stylish. Although she was tired and desperate to put the day behind her, there was no way she would let Kelly down and when she had implored her to accompany her there that evening, there was really only one response.

The desk sergeant looked up slowly as they approached the counter. Years of clerical tedium had sapped the life from him. Those same, dulled eyes, Caroline thought, had probably viewed murderers and rapists with the same dispassionate gaze.

'Detective Chief Inspector Cavey will be with you shortly,' he informed them in a predictably monotone voice.

The sergeant then turned and introduced them to a small, plain girl in her early twenties with an acne-scarred face and hair scraped back in an unfashionable bun.

WPC Jenkins smiled pleasantly, before leading the way

through a pair of battered swing doors. They followed her in silence down the corridor beyond. The only sound as they walked was the rhythmic squeak of WPC Jenkins' sensible shoes on the polished lino floor.

They passed a number of closed doors before being shown into an oppressive little room, with scarcely enough space for a battered Formica table and four plastic chairs. Caroline noticed immediately that there were no windows and no source of natural light. Instead, the room was lit by a single fluorescent tube which cast its sickly, flickering light onto shiny pea green walls. A lone poster featuring an unknown cartoon character with huge binocular-shaped eyes urging the reader to 'Watch for crime ... all the time' was the room's sole gesture of decoration.

Kelly pulled a face as they traded looks across the table. Caroline replied with a deep sigh. Neither one spoke. The room was uncomfortably warm, made so by a heavy tubular radiator on the far wall pumping out a suffocating heat, thick with the smell of hot gloss paint. The desk sergeant had said that someone would be with them 'shortly'. As she waited, Caroline found herself wondering how far her idea of 'shortly' would differ from his. She began drumming the table with her fingers in mild irritation. She was starting to feel a little queasy and loosened the collar of her blouse.

To the outside observer they were an odd match. Kelly, with her brassy manner and no nonsense approach to life seemed a world apart from her erudite boss. But it was their differences that bonded them together. Kelly was fiercely loyal to Caroline and Caroline repaid this trust by providing support to her less educated colleague at times when she was forced out of her comfort zone, such as their current circumstances.

By now Kelly too was wilting. A flush of pink slowly crept up her cheek from underneath her neatly tied Burberry scarf. She wasn't what you would call a classic beauty, but she was definitely pretty: a small, well-proportioned face with a button nose peeping from below a cascade of blonde curls. The impartial observer would say that she was attractive and well turned-out, but there was something decidedly overstated in her obvious and conspicuous glamour. Kelly was certainly not short of admirers, but she was as choosy in her flirtations as she was direct in her response to uninvited advances. Neither Caroline nor Kelly had managed to establish a lasting, meaningful relationship of late, but Caroline hoped this situation would soon change. Although she was still technically going out with Richard Thorn, a Fixed Income Trader at Montagu Steinhart, she had lately developed a strong interest elsewhere. It was all quite out of character for her and had also come from a rather unlikely direction.

Just then, the door clattered open, knocking against the back of Caroline's chair as Detective Chief Inspector Cavey entered the room. He was smartly dressed in a checked sports jacket and a crisp buff, button down shirt but his appearance was otherwise unremarkable. His tawny brown hair was neat, with the precise slash of a straight parting to one side but at medium height and medium build the Inspector was eminently forgettable. Cavey introduced himself in a soft, even voice and then sat in silence studying the two women in front of him. There was something almost forensic in the way he looked at them.

'Kelly Owen?' he asked as he continued to observe them.

'That's me.' Kelly instinctively raised her hand as she replied.

'And you are?' His eyes flicked from Kelly to Caroline as he fired the question at her.

'Caroline, Caroline Hartley. I came with her. I'm her friend. Well her boss actually. We work together…'

Caroline heard herself blathering her answer, but there was something unnerving about the detective. He watched her struggling to make sense for a moment and then, with a slight shake of the head, switched his attention back to Kelly. Her turn was over.

Everything Cavey did seemed economical and driven by a desire for efficiency. His movements were measured and definite. The overall impression he gave was of a man with a job to do, who knew how to do it with the minimum of fuss or distraction.

'I understand you were the first witness on the scene following the fatal stabbing of a vagrant at approximately 19:37 in a subway tunnel in Leicester Square tube station last night.' The statement was delivered in an emotionless tone as if he had been reading from a train timetable. 'Please tell me, Miss Owen, what you saw, in as much detail as you can remember.'

Kelly swallowed hard before launching into a faltering account of her discovery of the tramp's bloody body. DCI Cavey listened attentively, stopping her frequently with questions or to gain clarification of what she had just said.

Caroline watched in fascination. The Detective Inspector was meticulous in his interrogation. Every point of significance was established beyond any doubt. He took notes throughout the interview in a standard issue, black police notebook with the letters 'JC' embossed in gold script at the bottom. His pen, however, was anything but standard issue: it was a rather beautiful antique-looking Yard-O-Led ballpoint. He absent-mindedly stroked and fiddled with it in between questions, extending and retracting the ballpoint as he twizzled the end backwards and forwards. His handwriting was small and well-formed, the words perfectly legible, almost as if they had been typed. Some were underlined, whilst he drew strange symbols next to others, a code no doubt known to DCI Cavey alone.

By now, Kelly's skin gleamed with perspiration due to the combined stress of the grilling and the stuffy atmosphere in the little interview room. Caroline noted that her statement had not really amounted to anything of substance. She hadn't seen anything of significance except of course the bloody aftermath of the killing, and the police had been able to view this for themselves.

At that moment, the door crashed open again and a young, good-looking police constable poked his head into the room.

'Sorry to interrupt, ladies,' he started politely.

'What is it, Hargreaves?' challenged DCI Cavey.

'Sir, if you have a sec, I think we have another one,' replied the young constable deferentially.

Cavey stood up sharply, with a muttered 'excuse me', as he hurried from the room but offered no further explanation.

When they were alone again, Kelly puffed out her cheeks and exhaled loudly.

'I'll tell you what. I'm bloody glad that's over. Halfway through I thought I was in the frame myself!'

'What now?' asked Caroline, desperate to escape the suffocating little room and return to the real world.

Not long afterwards, she received her answer. The young WPC with the sensible shoes informed them that DCI Cavey had finished with them and proceeded to escort them off the premises.

They left by a different route this time. Rather than taking them back down the corridor, the WPC led them through a large open-plan office furnished with standard issue, grey metal office furniture. Over at the far side of the room, a crowd of about twenty police officers were gathered around a large map of Greater London covered in red dots. Their full attention was on DCI Cavey, who stood at their centre addressing them and intermittently gesturing towards the map.

Ever inquisitive, Caroline slowed her stride and strained to hear what the detective was saying.

'... two already today. That brings the tally to thirty-four and ...'

Here the discussion became a little muffled and the squeak of the WPC's shoes drowned out the few words that were audible.

'...all over London from Hammersmith to Canning Town ... no pattern ...'

She couldn't hear any more, so she stopped and peered over a large filing cabinet in DCI Cavey's direction. He abruptly stopped mid-sentence and stared directly at her.

'Is there something I can do for you, Miss Hartley?' he shouted sternly from the far side of the room.

She recoiled and took a step backwards in shock. The whole group had turned around and were now looking in her direction.

'No, nothing thanks,' she stammered, then grasping at her foot, mumbled something about the strap on her shoe coming loose.

The Detective Chief Inspector raised his eyebrows. 'Jenkins!' he shouted to the red faced WPC, 'Can you see our guests out? Immediately please.'

Two minutes later, they had been ushered out through a small steel door at the rear of the building into Old Burlington Street, where they both savoured the refreshingly cool evening air.

Caroline said nothing for a few moments; she was still digesting what she had just heard.

'Did you hear what they were saying?' she asked her friend, who shook her head in response. She didn't seem particularly interested though.

'It looks like this is just one of a number killings they are investigating'.

'Really? You sure?' replied Kelly, still showing little real interest.

'Yes. That's what he was saying back there. Thirty-four murders.'

The girls parted company shortly afterwards, by which time Caroline was looking forward to the home comforts of her flat in leafy Parsons Green, which would tonight involve a very large gin and tonic with plenty of ice. *Strange*, she reflected as she walked into Green Park Underground station: *if there had been well over thirty murders, why hadn't the papers picked up on the story?*

CHAPTER 5

'I'm at my wit's end, dear!' shrilled Janet Hartley, once again close to tears. 'I really don't know what to do.'

'Just calm down, Mother, I'll sort this out,' soothed Caroline, desperate to ward off another bout of hysteria.

The phone had been ringing when she'd entered the flat an hour and a half ago and she'd been on it ever since. *A fitting end to the day*, she thought wryly. Here she was, playing a substitute for Samaritans to her distraught mother! Unfortunately, it was a role she was all too familiar with these days.

'All I want is to be left in peace … in my house. In the house you were brought up in. The house your father and I bought with our hard-earned money.'

Caroline detected the tremor in her mother's voice at the mention of her father. He'd died suddenly a year ago, leaving Janet Hartley desolate and helpless. Overnight, Caroline had become the head of the family.

They had both struggled to come to terms with the loss. Whilst Caroline had immersed herself in her work, poor Janet had no such distraction. So she had never come close to filling the cavernous void that had opened up in her life.

As an only child, Caroline had always been conscious of her dual role as loving daughter and emotional crutch, but never more so than now. This was a real crisis and one that would not be easily resolved.

That morning, out of the blue, a letter had dropped through Janet's letter box that had turned her life on its head. She had been waiting for almost a year for her solicitor to grant her probate but due to the complex business affairs of her late husband this had not been forthcoming. It now appeared that there was a very good reason for this delay. Michael Hartley's architect partnership was bankrupt. And worse, its debts were secured against his primary asset – Janet's home. According to the letter, in two weeks' time the bank intended to seize the cottage and Janet would be homeless.

'It's all that Vernon Cartwright's fault,' raged Janet, 'I never liked him. Your father was just too trusting ...'

Caroline cut her short, she could see where this particular line of conversation was going, 'Now don't get worked up, Mum. Trust me, I'll fix this.'

Her father had mentioned his business problems to her some months before his death, confiding too, his reservations about his business partner. She hadn't appreciated though, quite how bad things were.

Her feelings towards Vernon Cartwright however, predated this discussion. She'd never liked him. There was something quite unsavoury about the man. He oozed false charm and Caroline had always suspected that under his obsequious façade, lurked a deeply dishonest individual who would stop at nothing to further his own interests. Sadly her ever-trusting father had never seen this and it now looked like her instincts had been correct.

When Michael and Vernon Cartwright first went into partnership five years ago, they seemed like an ideal combination. Michael was a talented architect, tired of working for a large practice, whilst Vernon, the ex-head of planning at Oakdene Borough Council, was keen to move into the private sector and make some serious money. Initially business was brisk. The practice appeared to flourish, driven on by Michael's considerable architectural flair and Vernon's contacts. Vernon devoted all his time to business development, which largely involved lavish entertainment and the schmoozing of local companies. He became particularly close to a number of leading property developers. Too close, according to local gossip which muttered increasingly about back-handers and shady dealings. The first signs of trouble had occurred two years ago, when Michael had been shocked to discover that the practice had racked up significant debts despite the strong revenue generated by his own hard work. Vernon could not explain the massive shortfall nor could he account for a number of large withdrawals from the practice's account. The relationship descended into acrimony and remained so up to Michael Hartley's untimely death.

'He's a crook, you know,' Janet railed.

'We don't know that Mother,' Caroline replied, trying to keep the discussion away from emotional subjects.

'Well, where's all the money gone then?' Janet replied sharply, 'He's still living the high life up in that private estate with its big gates and swimming pool, whilst I'm... I'm going to lose everything!' her voice cracked and the tears came again.

Caroline knew she would need all her resourcefulness if she was to find a way out of this one. The partnership's debts were in excess of half a million pounds and well beyond her meagre savings. Her mother was right though, Vernon Cartwright had probably embezzled a great deal of money from the partnership, but how to prove it? Fraudsters like Vernon were clever; he'd have covered his tracks, that's for sure.

'Just go to bed, Mum, take one of your pills and have a good night's sleep. I'll get onto this first thing in the morning.' She finished, sounding far more confident than she actually felt, 'Don't you worry, no one's going to take your home from you.'

Caroline slowly replaced the receiver in its cradle. She had no idea what she was going to do. After all, she was a communications specialist, not a forensic accountant. She really didn't need this additional problem on top of the Hubert Dunwoody saga and her deteriorating relationship with Tom Beresford.

CHAPTER 6

Just as Caroline was finishing the first draft of her briefing paper for Leo Brooks the next afternoon, the phone rang. It was her old friend Jack Daniels from *The Sunday Times*.

'Hi Jack, how are you?' she said with the warmth she felt for her old friend.

But Jack was anything but friendly.

'We'll run the story, Caroline,' he said without preamble. 'Even your ten grand a day lawyers won't stop us. They can slap an injunction on us if they like, but it won't stick.'

She had warned Tom that involving the lawyers at this early stage ran the risk of inflaming the situation. But he wouldn't listen. He liked the idea of showing that 'the bank has teeth'. Besides, he had pompously told her, 'he wasn't going to be pushed around by a bunch of teenage scribblers'.

Caroline sensed Jack's simmering anger and braced herself for an outpouring of scorn.

'You really have sold out, haven't you, Caroline?' he continued. 'Big company, big salary, flash car and all it has cost you is your integrity.'

'Now that's not fair Jack!' she replied sharply.

He had nettled her. She was simply doing her job and

he knew it. The fact that he was working eighteen hours a day in the bruising world of investigative journalism for a pittance was his choice, not hers. But Jack wasn't listening. He was in full flow now, giving vent to his pent-up frustration.

'Anyway, leaving aside your conversion to the cult of Mammon, this whole thing became a load more interesting this morning. Before, I couldn't quite work out why you guys were getting so heated about it. After all, it's just another over-promoted, upper-class twerp living the high life and cheating on his wife. Most firms would have booted him out without a second thought. But you didn't and I found myself asking why. So I continued to dig and I found out your CEO went to the same school as Hubert Dunwoody. Are you aware of that little fact?'

'Yes I am, actually,' she replied, her voice sounding a little too starchy for her liking. 'So what, Jack? So did hundreds of others in the City. Anyway, they're years apart.'

'Yes, you're right, they are. That's why I thought it a little odd that Leo Brooks acted as Hubert Dunwoody's referee when he applied to Montagu Steinhart.'

It was news to Caroline. 'That's no big deal, Jack.'

'Not on the face of it Caroline, no. But I've actually seen the reference and I can tell you that your Mr Brooks was quite effusive in his support for Hubert St. John Dunwoody, who, as you may or may not know, didn't attend university and only managed to amass a mediocre collection of GCSEs and A-levels despite being given the best education money can buy. Strange – don't you think – that with all the highly educated and talented people out there, Leo Brooks would choose to patronise an under-achiever like Hubert Dunwoody?'

'Where's this going, Jack?'

'He owns a large estate in Scotland doesn't he, your Leo Brooks? Evidently he's got some of the best salmon fishing in the country. Correction, he *now* has some of the best salmon fishing in the country. When he first bought it, the salmon stream was actually owned by the neighbouring estate.'

Jack paused for dramatic effect and Caroline was forced to wait but she knew something big was coming.

'Would it surprise you, Caroline, to learn that that neighbouring estate is actually owned by one Lord Carnegie of Strathmore? Or Mr Dunwoody senior to you and I. Hubert's father. According to Land Registry records, the title to the land was transferred to Leo Brooks twelve years ago. Coincidentally, around the same time that Hubert joined Montagu Steinhart. Funny old world, isn't it?'

Caroline could think of nothing to say. It was now obvious to her why Leo had been so agitated. He knew that if the connection was made between himself and Hubert, he would be dragged into this sordid affair. Well, the connection had well and truly been made. Jack had done a good job. Now it would be open season on Leo Brooks himself. They'd look at his remuneration – an eye-watering bonus of fifteen million pounds last year alone as far as Caroline could remember – as well as his career and personal life. They wouldn't stop until they had unearthed something unsavoury to feed the scandal-hungry masses.

If it had not been for Tom Beresford's pugilistic

approach, this might all have died down. But no, he had to threaten and bully. Caroline knew you didn't do that with Fleet Street and expect them to back off.

'Careful Jack, you are straying into very dangerous territory now. This is pure conjecture. If you make any unsubstantiated claims, we will sue your arse and you know it.'

'We'll run the full story by you before we go to press.' He managed to make it sound as though he were doing her a personal favour. 'But I can tell you now, it won't make for comfortable reading with your Sunday morning cornflakes.'

CHAPTER 7

The City looked spectacular as the early evening sun glistened on the gilded spires of a hundred ancient churches. A surprising number had survived the rigours of a thousand years of history and now those that remained nestled practically unnoticed in amongst the towering office blocks that characterised the twenty-first century City of London.

The evening was pleasantly warm. A fresh breeze gently ruffled the pleats of Caroline's skirt and toyed with her fringe as she strolled past the iconic green Gherkin building. She crossed the road at the junction with Gracechurch Street, nimbly sidestepping a black cab performing a nifty U-turn to pick up a fare on the other side of the road. Still in the shadow of the Gherkin, she passed one of London's less fortunate churches, St Andrew's Undershaft, which had just reopened after many years of refurbishment. The ancient building had survived the Great Fire of London and the Blitz only to have been destroyed some years ago by an IRA bomb.

As she strolled along the historic streets, Caroline's mind replayed the conversation with Jack Daniels. It had rattled her. She knew that Jack's revelations heralded a massive escalation in the whole affair since the bank's CEO was now firmly centre stage. Leo Brooks had known that this was a risk all along and he should have told them about his close links with Hubert. What else had he not told them? she wondered.

She recoiled at the thought of telling Tom of the latest developments in the morning. There was no doubt that he would fly into a rage when he heard what Jack had unearthed. He had been putting her under increasing pressure to exploit her personal relationship to help quash the story. Characteristically unencumbered by propriety, he had well and truly crossed the line at their last meeting with his suggested solution.

'I'm not going to take this lying down!' he had dramatically proclaimed, then winked at her. 'But it would help if you would, Caroline, if you get my drift!' The comment had sent her storming from the room, much to Tom's obvious amusement.

But he wouldn't be amused tomorrow. Without doubt, he would see the deteriorating situation as her personal failing. She just hoped Leo Brooks wouldn't share this view. Perhaps she'd get fired. It was a thought that had never occurred to her before in her entire career, but now caused an icy spasm in her stomach. People disappeared all the time from their posts in investment banks; it was very much part of the employment landscape. Of course, she wouldn't actually be sacked; they'd have to have proper grounds for that. Anyway that was generally too drawn-out a procedure for the hair-trigger culture of the modern-day City. No, it would most likely be dressed up as a departmental 'restructuring' and her job would simply become redundant. She would be paid, of course. The HR people knew exactly how much to pay to keep an employee from making a claim for unfair dismissal at an employment tribunal. Not that many would ever go down that route, as that was the road to oblivion. The Market talks and no one wants to employ a troublemaker.

Whether it would be a sacking or plain redundancy, it all amounted to the same thing: if they didn't want you around, you're out. Tom didn't want her around – she was sure of that – and who knew what Leo Brooks would think in the morning.

Five minutes later, after a brisk stroll up Gresham Street, Caroline reached her destination, London's magnificent Guildhall, the ceremonial headquarters of the City of London since Roman times. The sun was still high in the sky and warmed her back as she approached the arched entrance, following in the footsteps of royalty, Lord Mayors and countless other dignitaries.

Once inside, out of the bright sunlight, it took a while for her eyes to adjust to the dim light. She found herself at the end of a short queue of people waiting to register at the front desk. She waited her turn, happy to be anywhere rather than back at the office attempting to deal with the festering mess she had left behind.

Nevertheless, neither the pleasant walk here nor the prospect of listening to Edward van der Linden could dispel the feeling of dread which continued to gnaw at her even as she stood in line.

Reception was manned by an arrestingly handsome

young man in his early twenties and a young woman of similar age. They looked like models. Caroline was attended to by the young man, whose name, according to the badge on his lapel, was Seb.

'Ah! Welcome, Miss Hartley,' he said, as if he had been waiting expressly for her.

Then, with a melodramatic flourish, he ticked her name off a list on his clipboard.

'If you'd like to come through with me, we have reserved a seat especially for you at the front.'

He flashed her a practised smile, which revealed impossibly white teeth, as he manoeuvred himself to her side from behind the reception desk.

Impressed and a little flattered, she followed him into the vast Great Hall with its historic ribbed ceiling and five-foot thick walls. It smelt musty and damp as ancient stone buildings often do, which added to the overall atmosphere of grandeur and antiquity.

Seb marched confidently ahead. When they reached the front of the hall, he snatched a 'Reserved' sign from a seat in the second row, then twisted an adjacent chair to one side, lifting it clean off the ground to make a space for Caroline to take her seat. As she sat down, he gently pushed the chair forward underneath her as if she was sitting down to dinner and he was an attentive date.

'Mr van der Linden will start speaking at seven sharp.'

He fixed her with azure eyes. They twinkled, conveying supreme confidence – he knew he looked good and enjoyed the power it gave him.

'I hope you will have time to stay for refreshments

afterwards. This will give you the opportunity to meet our team and ask any questions you may have. Thank you for attending this Eleventh Hour Corporation event. We greatly value your interest.'

It was interesting, she thought, that Seb repeatedly spoke in the third person plural. He obviously regarded himself as a part of the company, which was the mark of an inclusive organisation. So far, she definitely liked what she saw.

At the centre of the stage, in front of the burgeoning audience, there stood a large LCD screen. It was the largest that Caroline had ever seen. It was at least three metres wide, but no more than an inch thick, obviously the very latest in audio-visual technology. Across the screen scrolled the message: 'Sliding ever faster to the edge'. This was clearly the title of the evening's talk. At the bottom of the screen was a simple black and white clock face transposed onto a globe. Its hands were at the five to twelve position – a very simple, but effective corporate logo for the Eleventh Hour Corporation.

The room filled quickly. As she discreetly scanned the audience, Caroline picked out numerous leading figures in the world of finance and the odd City dignitary. Someone waved from a few rows back. It was Fabien Blenck, Chief Investment Officer of a leading fund management company and a frequent visitor to Leo Brooks' office. She nodded back politely just as Walter Steiner, the Chairman of AG Schneider and Sons, one of Montagu Steinhart's fiercest competitors, slumped down heavily onto the seat next to her.

'Good evening, my dear,' he wheezed, his breath catching uncomfortably at the back of his throat as he sought to recover his composure after the short walk from the street outside. Walter certainly fitted the profile for this event, she thought. For starters, he was fabulously wealthy. *Forbes* placed him in the top 100 in its Rich List and this only took account of his declared assets. People like Walter Steiner were by nature, and also in his case by profession, masters in the art of secretive investment. They had a network of accounts in offshore banking centres and so-called tax havens designed to operate beneath the taxman's radar. Yes, Walter was very rich. He was also grossly overweight and a little sparing with the deodorant, as Caroline couldn't help noticing. He may have been fat, rich and a little smelly, but he nevertheless had good manners and made polite small talk up until the time the event was scheduled to commence, even though Caroline suspected he had no idea who she was.

At exactly 7.00pm, Edward van der Linden strode purposefully onto the stage with the confident air of someone well within his comfort zone. The hum of conversation died immediately at the sight of him, for Edward van der Linden, affectionately known to all as the 'Green Giant', was simply enormous. He wasn't just tall, he was super-size in every respect. He stood and regarded them all, his eyes scanning every face in the audience. Then he clasped the sides of the lectern in his massive hands and bowed his head for a full thirty seconds, as if in prayer. One hundred and fifty faces stared up at him in palpable anticipation. No one moved. No one made a sound.

His voice, when he finally spoke, was not deep and gravelly, as you would have expected. It was clear and rich with more than a hint of his native South Africa in its inflection.

'Let me share something with you,' he began, beckoning with his hand as if to draw them closer. 'A few years ago, I read a story in the newspaper that had a profound effect on me. It concerned a group of boys on a school ski trip in the Alps.'

Van der Linden then started to speak more quietly, moving adeptly from the voice of a bold orator to the more intimate timbre of a storyteller.

'It had been a perfectly normal day, the snow was good and they'd just said adieu to their ski instructor. The lads were bored as they waited for their teacher and the rest of the school party, when one of them suggested a very good way of passing the time. Why didn't they have a sliding contest? Well, that sounded like a great idea, it appealed to their competitive nature and anyway what eleven-year-old doesn't like skidding down an icy slide? So they set about building the mother of all slides with the steepest possible gradient to guarantee maximum speed. They stamped the snow flat, then rubbed and polished it icy smooth. When it was complete, they raced each other to the top of the slope, slipped off their heavy boots and in stocking feet launched themselves fearlessly down that slide one after the other, each determined to be the fastest.'

There was absolute silence in the vast room. No one spoke, no one coughed, no one fidgeted. They all wanted to know what happened next.

'Such was their industry and competitive spirit,' continued van der Linden in the same engaging manner, 'that no one realised that they had not thought things through properly. Unfortunately they had overlooked the more practical aspects of the enterprise, like how to stop before the mountain's edge.'

Still the room was silent as he paused.

'The slide worked well. Very well indeed. It was slippery and exceptionally fast, just as intended. One after the other, they slid down that slide and one after the other they tumbled over the cliff face to certain death. In reality, the moment they had launched themselves down that slide, they were doomed.'

He paused at this point and shook his head, as if trying to rid himself of the distressing visual image of the boys' last moments as they wriggled in mid-air, seconds before death.

'When I read that story, what stayed with me, and has continued to haunt me since, was not the needless waste of young lives, which of course it was, but the thought that each one of them must have realised their mistake as they hurtled down that slope. They must also have recognised that it was too late to do anything about it. Some no doubt dug their heels in to try to slow down, some perhaps fell over in a desperate effort to reduce their momentum. All to no avail. Try as they might, they could not defy basic physics. It was futile. They were locked onto their fate, sliding ever faster to the edge.'

Then, like a vicar in his pulpit on a Sunday service, Edward van der Linden looked down at the expectant faces and delivered his message.

'Let's not be like those boys. Let's not get on that slide!'

He paused again and looked inquiringly at his audience, scanning their faces to gauge their reaction to his story. They looked back at him as one, all understanding the analogy and eager to hear more.

Satisfied with the reaction, he started to speak again.

'Look around you,' he said, 'what do you see? You see a world choking for breath. You see a planet wilting by the hour, its beauty fading, its energy being literally sucked from its core. This is our doing: you, me ... everyone. We are despoiling the planet. Like junkies hell-bent on self-destruction, we seem unable to break our addiction to excess in spite of the fact that we see its consequences all around us. And every day we slide closer to the edge. And every day that slide accelerates. Let me just pause here and ask you a question. Is there anyone here who genuinely thinks that mankind is not doing serious damage to this planet?'

He stopped again and, with his hands planted firmly on his hips, stared accusingly at them all. There was an uncomfortable silence punctuated by the odd shuffling of feet and nervous throat-clearing. No one spoke and he paused for what must have been a minute before accepting their silence as confirmation that indeed no one did believe this.

'Good!' he all but shouted. 'Because it is absolutely unequivocal and beyond dispute. Did you know?' he continued, 'that seventy percent of the world's coral reefs are either dead or dying and that in the middle of the Pacific Ocean there is a massive floating garbage dump of discarded plastic bags twice the size of France.'

The information drew a disapproving grumble from the audience.

'But it's our doing,' he chastised, 'we are desecrating our planet whilst at the same time plundering its natural resources. Humanity already consumes forty percent more than the Earth is able to regenerate. And with the world population growing exponentially, this situation will only get worse.' He paused and looked heavenward as if seeking guidance. 'So where to from here eh?' His eyes raked the rows of attentive faces in front of him, daring someone to answer.

'I'll tell you where to,' he whispered, leaning towards them as if about to divulge a great secret. 'Oblivion and complete annihilation. That's what lies at the end of this particular road. At the current rate, polar bears, black rhinos and tigers will be extinct by 2020 and we, mankind, will follow shortly afterwards if we do not take immediate action.'

There was a buzz of conversation in the Great Hall as the audience reacted to this last incendiary statement. Caroline looked around her and noted that some delegates were decidedly less engaged than others. Although the content of the speech was fascinating, she could tell that van der Linden's direct and very personal style was not to some people's taste. One or two people were looking uncomfortable whilst others sat stony-faced, glancing surreptitiously at their wristwatches. The big man behind the lectern raised his hand in an appeal for silence before continuing.

'We exist in an orderly society as individuals, insulated from macro-level problems by our governments. That's why we elect them – isn't it? To manage the big picture and ensure we live in safety and comfort. If there was real danger to us, they'd tell us wouldn't they?'

He let the question hang for a moment, before giving them his answer.

'Wrong!' he boomed.

The word was said with such force that Walter Steiner, sitting next to Caroline, who had clearly let his mind drift off, started in his chair.

'Bloody hell,' he muttered as he embarked on a fresh bout of wheezing. 'It's like being back at school. Not sure I'm going to stay to the end if he carries on like this.'

Despite his complaint, he was now giving the Green Giant his full attention.

'Saving humanity is not a vote winner,' he said, stabbing an immense finger at them all. 'Telling your electorate that they must learn to do without will not get you re-elected. That's why politicians will never grasp this particular nettle. In any case, we know their vision is limited to the next election in three, four or five years. Any duration longer than that is simply of no interest to them. No, we're on our own. All of us … together. Forget state, forget government. We have to fix this mess ourselves.'

Another pause. The big man stood and observed them again as they considered his words.

'And that,' he announced triumphantly, 'is where Eleventh Hour comes in.'

At which point, the screen on the stage behind him burst into life with a fanfare of music and a starburst of colours. The Eleventh Hour promotional film that followed was produced to perfection. For five breathtaking minutes, the audience were transported around the world, from the snow-capped summit of Mount Kilimanjaro to the arid deserts of Outer Mongolia, from the twinkling inky-blue depths of the deep Cayman trench to the steaming jungles of Brazil. The feelgood factor was overwhelming. By the end of the film, as a group of native children waved a laughing goodbye, the audience were duly in awe of their wonderful, diverse planet.

The film faded. The lights came back on. There was a moment of mesmerised silence, the kind often experienced in concert halls or theatres after a virtuoso performance. Then the hum of excited conversation as people felt compelled to share their immediate thoughts on the experience with their neighbours.

'I particularly liked the shots of those magnificent waterfalls in Africa,' Walter said, leaning towards Caroline, with a blast of mint-tinged coffee breath. 'Spectacular, absolutely spectacular. I've seen the Victoria Falls, went there with my late wife on our silver wedding anniversary, but not the other two they showed though.'

He was suddenly far more enthusiastic and engaged. She couldn't really remember the scenes he referred to. In any case, her mind was still lingering on the vivid image of humpback whales leaping majestically out of the water amongst towering icebergs in the Arctic Ocean. She, like all the others, was moved by an overwhelming sense of elation, which she could not explain.

'As I said, that's where Eleventh Hour comes in,' said Edward van der Linden, his voice intentionally softer now, unwilling to break the spell cast by the masterful cinematography. 'It's all so worth saving, isn't it?'

The muttered agreement became a little louder now.

'Eleventh Hour is not a charity. We don't run appeals. We don't shake buckets at railway stations. Every penny pledged to us is used. We never give money to others. We don't aim to make things generally better. Our objective is to solve problems. And when we solve a problem, it is solved for good.'

This string of bold statements struck home and Caroline saw people nodding their approval. She liked his method of delivery. One minute painting a picture, the next peppering his audience with quick-fire facts to hammer home his point.

'At this moment,' he continued, 'we have dedicated teams throughout the world, working on key tasks. Each team is managed to a strict set of objectives, just like all of you here run your own businesses. We know what success looks like and we don't have the word failure in our vocabulary.'

More enthusiastic nods. They liked it, he was one of them.

'We have specialists from every field: engineers, doctors, chemists, psychiatrists, financiers, lobbyists ... any discipline you can think of, Eleventh Hour have expertise in spades! We pride ourselves on our ability to influence. We make it our business to be close to government and state at every level in all countries. Let me give you an example of how we operate. You remember I mentioned the vast floating plastic rubbish dump in the Pacific? This swirling garbage vortex is responsible for the deaths of a million fish and one hundred thousand birds and sea mammals each year. Well, we're going to clean it up! All of it.'

A flutter of light applause greeted this statement.

'A month ago, we took delivery of two specially modified ex-factory fishing ships. These vessels are literally going to suck the debris out of the water then process and compress it into blocks which will be used as building bricks. These have been earmarked for our extensive disaster relief projects in Bangladesh, Pakistan and the cyclone corridor of Asia. Our scientists estimate that we should be able to build over a quarter of a million new dwellings in the area, all of them highly water-resistant because of the nature of the building material. And that's the essence of this company: we turn bad into good!'

The room erupted into rapturous applause at this lesson in ingenuity.

'Thank you for your appreciation.'

He raised his hand in acknowledgment of the continuing applause, more like a tennis player who has hit an ace than a public speaker. Eager to capitalise on the mood, he gestured for them to quieten down before continuing.

'That's what we do. We identify a problem. We evaluate it and then we tackle it. Now, you all have causes that are close to your hearts. I certainly do. Some of them big, some of them not so big. But whatever their scale they are important to you. I want to hear about the things you care about and I want to help. But I also want you to be involved.'

He smiled with satisfaction at his audience and all but a few smiled back at him.

'This is Eleventh Hour's unique proposition. We don't simply want you to fund us, we want you to work with us to deliver the solution. Right now we have donors camping under the stars in rainforests, diving on reefs and sailing the oceans. They are running what we call direct action squads.'

Caroline looked around her at a remarkable scene, more

reminiscent of an evangelical Christian gathering than an evening presentation to business leaders and top financiers. The whole atmosphere had changed after the film. In fact, she couldn't help wondering whether they hadn't been subjected to some subliminal jiggery-pokery, so comprehensive had been the transformation.

Edward van der Linden raised an immense hand and a hush fell on the room.

'Thank you for being so attentive and showing your appreciation for the massive strides being made by this company. Now, let's break up the formal proceedings. I'd like to invite you to join us for refreshments in the crypt of this magnificent building, which will give you the opportunity to ask us more about our work. We can then help you decide how to get involved. I sincerely hope you do join us in solving whatever problem is closest to your heart. Together we will win the fight, whatever your personal cause. Just remember that the sum total of all your efforts and your invaluable funding will ensure that we never get on that slide.'

Edward van der Linden didn't stay to enjoy the applause. With two massive strides, he descended the four steps down from the stage and walked smartly along the central aisle of the hall, stopping only momentarily to shake the outstretched hands of delegates on the way.

'You know,' said Walter, hauling himself awkwardly from his seat, 'I came here expecting to be bored rigid by some bleeding heart talk on climate change and a plea for me to reduce my carbon footprint, whatever the hell that is. But I have to admit, I've rather enjoyed myself. Clever chap.

There aren't many people who can keep me interested for that long. Certainly not at this end of the day, anyway.'

'Are you staying for drinks?' asked Caroline, by now quite relaxed in Walter's company. There was something quite endearing about the old buffer.

'No, my dear. It's not really my thing and in any case, I have a very important prior engagement with a large glass of Bowmore 1957 malt at my club, which is an engagement that cannot be broken. Be sure to pass on my regards to that rather smooth boss of yours,' Walter continued, 'and tell him I hope that we can get some fishing in together later in the season. He has the most wonderful streams up there in the Highlands, you know. Last time I visited, I swear a six pound salmon virtually jumped into my pocket. I'll never forget it. Wonderful spot!'

He then bade her a warm goodbye, accompanied by an awkward, slobbery kiss on the cheek.

As she watched him making his way towards the exit, stopping every few steps to shake hands with people he recognised, Caroline made a mental note not to underestimate people like Walter Steiner. He had forged his career through dedication, hard work and, above all, a razor-sharp intellect. He had known who she was all along. She should never have doubted that.

CHAPTER 8

A gentle throb of conversation greeted her as she descended a stone staircase into the crypt. Under its low, vaulted ceiling, there was already a throng of delegates talking excitedly to one another. Seb, his female colleague and an assortment of other similarly beautiful people were weaving their way through the crowd and dispensing flutes of champagne to grateful recipients.

Caroline located Fabien Blenck. 'That was something else,' he said as he nimbly relieved a waitress of two glasses of champagne as she swished past. 'What a powerful speaker and what an impressive event!'

'Yes,' replied Caroline taking the proffered glass. 'But what now?'

Something had been niggling at her since the end of Edward van der Linden's talk. She now knew what it was.

'What do you mean? We drink his champagne!'

Fabien took a large swig from his glass to illustrate the point.

'You're right, it was a fantastic presentation,' continued Caroline. 'One of the best I've heard, but all that rhetoric … the impact is simply lost because there was no follow through.'

Fabien had fallen silent as she delivered her harsh assessment and had a rather strange look on his face.

'There's no point in a sales pitch if you don't clinch the deal. He definitely didn't do that at all. I mean, where do you sign up?'

Fabien still looked odd. 'A very shrewd observation,' said a deep, and by now familiar, voice.

Caroline froze as she realised Edward van der Linden had been standing behind her whilst she delivered her critical verdict.

'But you have misunderstood the object of today's meeting,' he continued. 'That wasn't an appeal for money. It was an introduction to Eleventh Hour. There is no hard sell. It's simply not necessary for an audience like this. You're a communications expert, aren't you, Miss Hartley?'

Caroline's surprise that he knew who she was, made her momentarily forget her embarrassment, and she turned fully to face her host.

'Of course I know who you are. I was delighted that you accepted the invitation in place of Leo Brooks, who I look forward to meeting next week.'

Caroline was getting used to people she hardly knew knowing all about her.

'I find it interesting that you only see this in your own terms, as if I am pitching a deal. Take a step away from your world and don't judge me by your rules.'

'I'm sorry,' Caroline spluttered, a tinge of pink colouring her cheeks. 'I didn't mean to be disrespectful, it's just that—.'

'Don't apologise, Caroline. You have a point. I'm

genuinely interested in what you thought of the talk, that's why I came over to talk to you.'

He chuckled good-humouredly and winked at Fabien, who still looked a little bewildered.

'I thought the talk was exceptional,' Caroline started, keen to make amends for her unguarded comments. 'It was paced just right and you can see from the audience reaction that the message was received loud and clear.'

Van der Linden held up his hand to stop her.

'I wasn't fishing for compliments. I actually felt a lack of buy-in from some people out there today, it didn't quite gel if you know what I mean. You're a specialist in the spoken word, what do you really think. Constructive feedback is crucial to me.'

Caroline was flattered that such a masterful orator should ask for her opinion. His presentation had been first rate and the content obviously carefully selected and crafted with phrasing designed to deliver maximum impact. She suspected that even the pauses had been choreographed. However, she too had noticed how some people in the audience had become disengaged.

'My opinion is that perhaps your direct style and interrogation of the audience may have alienated some people.'

As she said it, she wondered about the use of the word 'interrogation'. It was a little strong. However, he didn't seem bothered.

'Hmm, really. Interesting, perhaps that's why I didn't feel a strong connection at the beginning today. Was that because I put them on the spot?'

'Yes, exactly,' she replied. 'It was a predominantly English audience out there today and generally speaking we have an aversion to being singled out in public.'

'I get it,' he replied, 'the Americans love that punchy, audience participation stuff but you Brits absolutely loathe it. I should have remembered that. I really appreciate your candour, Caroline. Right, I'll cut it out in future.' He stopped talking and stroked his jaw for a few seconds with his massive hand. Before adding, 'I wish I had people like you on my staff who could guide me on such matters. Now, tell me Caroline ...' he continued, fixing her with a searching look. 'What's your passion? What is it that Caroline Hartley really cares about in this wonderful world of ours?'

The question was rather unexpected and it wrong footed her. For a second or two, her mind went into a spin. The vivid images imprinted on her memory by the film seemed to block her ability to think straight and she struggled to visualise anything beyond the sight of a massive whale rising out of the water.

'The preservation of the creatures in our seas,' she blurted.

'That's a very noble cause. What makes you care about that?'

Fabien Blenck, who had been standing quietly spectating on the exchange, took this as a cue to depart. The Green Giant watched the Frenchman leave and then he took Caroline completely by surprise.

'You care greatly about a lot of things, I am sure. Caroline, I'm an intuitive being. I love to understand the human mind and whenever I talk to people I find myself wondering what is behind the façade they throw up to hide their real self.'

Caroline remained silent; she was unsure where this rather odd line of conversation was going.

'When I look at you,' he continued, fixing her with an unfaltering stare, 'I see a very presentable and personable young lady who possesses the rare gift of sharp perception.' He paused for a second or two before adding in a softer tone, 'But underneath this veneer I detect a restlessness. You have a distracted air about you that suggests to me some inner turmoil. Something's bothering you, Caroline.'

She looked back at him, unsure what to say next. Was it really so obvious that she had problems? Or was this simply a clever technique designed to entice someone to open up and bare their soul? Whatever the answer, with her tongue loosened by champagne, she took the opportunity to unburden herself and seconds later she found herself inexplicably telling him about her mother's predicament and the pressures of balancing her working and private life. He listened attentively, asking questions when he thought it appropriate and when she had finished he smiled sympathetically.

'Caroline, you're a delightful young woman and I am certain that you will be equal to the challenges in your life. My advice to you is: don't give in. You must be strong, resolute and determined – that's what I tell all my activists. And specifically on your mother's predicament though, I would recommend that you—'

But he didn't finish. At that moment, a thickset individual with a bland, expressionless face and closely cropped hair walked up to Edward van der Linden and tapped him on the shoulder, interrupting him in mid-sentence. He then took hold of an arm and tugged him gently towards a neighbouring huddle of delegates.

'Ah! Aleksei,' said van der Linden breezily. 'Before you launch me off to another part of the room, can I introduce Caroline Hartley? She has been very helpful today. Caroline, this is Aleksei Lubov, my Chief of Staff. He looks after me and ensures, amongst other things, that I circulate properly at these functions.'

Lubov nodded and drew back his lips in an attempted smile. There was no warmth in the dark eyes as he checked Caroline over before unceremoniously manoeuvring his boss over to the next group of champagne-quaffing guests.

Weaving a path through the dense crowd, Caroline made her way towards the exit. En route, she was intercepted by Seb, who elegantly took her hand and guided the way to the reception desk.

'I hope you've enjoyed yourself today and found the meeting worthwhile,' he gushed insincerely.

But Caroline was hardly listening, she was still thinking of her conversation with Edward van der Linden.

'I saw you talking to the big man himself,' he said, then paused. Having deviated from his script, he immediately realised his faux pas.

'I mean, the man himself,' he corrected swiftly.

'He is pretty big though, isn't he?' replied Caroline, in the mood for a little fun.

Seb looked flustered but then realised she was playing with him and gave her the full intensity of his Colgate smile.'

'Ms Hartley, I have a special gift for you in gratitude for you giving up your valuable time to be with us today. Also, we hope this token of our appreciation will help you remember us in the future.'

He was back on script now and much more comfortable. Caroline took the small, neatly wrapped package he held in his hand and left. Once outside, she decided to walk to the tube station, rather than take a cab home. She needed time to think.

*

A small crowd was massed outside St Paul's underground station. As she approached, Caroline could plainly see that access to the station was blocked by a ribbon of blue and white tape.

'What's the problem?' she asked a middle-aged man in front of her in the crowd. He looked anything but amused; no doubt someone working late who just wanted to get home after a long day, she thought sympathetically.

'Station's closed,' he snapped, unable to contain his irritation. 'Evidently there's been "an incident".' The last words were laced with heavy sarcasm and he shook his head in disgust.

Caroline craned her head above the crowd and stared towards the station entrance where two uniformed police officers stood with their arms clasped firmly behind their backs. From where she stood, she couldn't see very much really, as her line of sight was obscured by a forest of heads, so she moved around the angry commuter and slowly weaved her way towards the front of the melee. When she reached the police tape she looked up and was surprised to spot a familiar face amongst the onlookers just to the right of the entrance. It was Leo Brooks. He hadn't seen her yet, so she waved her hand in an effort to attract his attention. He still didn't notice her as his attention was fixed on what was happening in the station. She started to move towards him, manoeuvring herself sideways through the crowd, which wasn't easy. This could turn out to be a very fortuitous encounter, she thought, as it would give her the opportunity for an informal chat with Leo. She may even be able to get back into his good books. Just then her attention was distracted by the sound of a siren as an ambulance pushed its way gingerly through the crowd. When it reached the two policemen guarding the entrance the vehicle stopped and two paramedics in green overalls hurriedly dragged a stretcher through the back doors and headed for the station platform fifty feet below street-level. When she looked back Leo Brooks was nowhere to be seen. He'd disappeared into the crowd.

'Damn,' she said out loud, making an about face and pushing her way more forcefully back though the throng in an effort to follow him. She knew that Leo lived in a penthouse flat in the nearby Barbican complex, just to the north of the City and she guessed he would probably be making his way there now down St Martins le Grand, the street just behind them. If she hurried, she reckoned she could still catch him. But unfortunately by the time she was free of the crowd, there was no sign of Leo Brooks in the deserted streets beyond. Their personal one-on-one wasn't to be she ruefully acknowledged as she hailed a passing black cab. It was odd seeing him like this though, as he was usually driven to and from work by his bank chauffeur.

CHAPTER 9

A grey early morning mist blurred Detective Chief Inspector Cavey's view of the ugly concrete network of walls and walkways that surround the Imax Cinema in the centre of the Hungerford roundabout. It was a dismal, dank place, even on a summer's day. Back in the '80s, these same tunnels spawned what came to be known as 'Cardboard City'. Here hundreds of down-and-outs and ex-mental patients, evicted from mental homes, had taken refuge underground and out of sight. The honeycomb of subways was colonised by the least fortunate members of society who had erected a shanty town of makeshift homes made of anything they could scavenge. It was a foul smelling, crime ridden area and an enduring image of life for the 'have not's' in Britain in the Thatcher era. A Britain where well-to-do theatregoers leaving the National Theatre after a night out were forced to run the gauntlet of drunks and muggers as they made their way home via Waterloo mainline station.

Subsequent governments, realising the negative PR effect of this squalid public encampment, cleared the site and attempted to re-establish the network of subways as a safe, public thoroughfare. Recently however, with austerity and unemployment very much back on the agenda, 'Cardboard City' had made a comeback.

'Anything?' asked Cavey, as always economical with his words. DC Hargreaves had been attempting to take statements from some of the residents of Cardboard City. He had just finished with a grizzled old man who was still shouting incoherently as he climbed the steps to street level and approached DCI Cavey.

'That guy says he thinks he remembers something. Says he saw the angel of death. Swears it looked like a beautiful woman in a big cape and a hood. Trouble is he's not exactly a reliable witness. Freely admits he was out of his skull at the time. Could have been Count Dracula for all he'd have known.'

Cavey nodded pensively, listening intently to the young policeman. Hargreaves had the makings of a very good detective. He was on temporary secondment from the Cyber-crime unit and already Cavey was planning to make his stay permanent. He had excellent analytical skills, a penchant for all things technical and most importantly, he possessed an understated 'no nonsense' nature that was ideal for a job that required good old-fashioned graft and no attitude.

'Funny thing though, sir,' he continued, thumbing through his notebook to find the relevant page. This was good practice, Cavey noted. Always write things down and refer back to your notes. Never trust to memory, you will invariably miss out the important, peripheral facts through recall alone.

'There's a bloke in walkway three over there,' said

Hargreaves, still reading from his notes and gesturing towards the south side of the tunnel network. 'He claims he saw a big black bird or a bat hovering around near where the first body was found. He's absolutely barking but there could be something in it. It may have been the woman in the cape.'

Cavey tilted his head to one side quizzically, then held up a finger to stop Hargreaves from continuing. A simple and economical gesture.

'We don't know it was a woman though, do we? The first witness merely thought it looked like a woman. Remember the state these people would most likely have been in. Imagination plays a big part in what they think they remember. The first witness mentioned a cape with a hood. The hood would most probably have hidden the face. In that case, it could have been a man or a woman. It could even have been a priest for that matter!'

'Yes, sorry sir. You're right. I'll go back and talk to him again. At least I know where to find him,' added the young detective. Cavey didn't reply but looked at him quizzically.

'He's bedded down next door to one of the victims who for some reason had put a house number on his cardboard box, very helpful: Number 72, written in black marker pen six inches tall.'

'Bizarre,' remarked Cavey, stroking his chin pensively, 'but who knows what's in the mind of these poor tortured souls. Perhaps he thought a house number brought an element of normality to his life.'

'Sad,' remarked Hargreaves, 'we know his address but not his name.'

They had two suspicious deaths here. One stabbing and one suspected strangulation. Cavey's team had received the call at around 6.30am when an early morning commuter had raised the alarm after spotting a pool of blood seeping from underneath a makeshift cardboard enclosure. His team of three PCs and two WPCs had immediately set about rousing the other residents – not an easy task by any means – and that was when the second body had been discovered, still with a thin wire ligature wrapped around its neck.

Cavey surveyed the scene below and couldn't help reflecting that it had something of a medieval leper colony about it. Shadowy figures wrapped in filthy blankets limped into the tunnels then disappeared from view whilst others, similarly attired, emerged from the gloom and lurched awkwardly into the open. In the centre of the roundabout, just by the Imax building stood a motley cluster of Cardboard City residents. Some stood in silence whilst others muttered conspiratorially as they drank warm tea from Styrofoam cups and wolfed down the greasy bacon sandwiches provided by Cavey's team. It was a pathetic sight. These sad, ravaged human specimens were huddled together more for safety than companionship. Fear was beginning to sweep the streets. Panic would follow. The street dwellers knew what was happening even though the general public were still in ignorance.

How long before the story was out? Cavey wondered.

'Still no real pattern,' said Hargreaves, articulating a thought that was very much on Cavey's mind.

Cavey shook his head slowly and the two men fell silent once again. Including the two bodies from St Paul's underground station the previous night and the two down below, now lying under crime-scene white tents, there had been forty-two killings in less than two months. There may actually have been many more because the type of people being targeted were rarely missed and the authorities generally paid little heed to unexplained fatalities amongst this community. Even using the official figures, this was the most prolific homicide in London's history and miraculously they had managed to contain the story. But surely, not for much longer.

Of course, Fleet Street knew about it. Well, some of it. Enough anyway to provide the headlines for weeks. But they had been muzzled. The Home Office had placed a draconian news embargo on the story on the pretext that it might encourage copycat killings. The blanket ban was helpful as, remarkably, the police had no definite leads. They had plenty of information of different sorts but frustratingly, it all seemed to point in different directions. Cavey had never known a case like it. The absence of a suspect was a source of extreme embarrassment within both the Met and Scotland Yard and the longer they could keep their lack of progress from 'Jo Public' the better!

'There's a pattern, Hargreaves. We just haven't spotted it. There's always a pattern and killers always make mistakes,' said DCI Cavey, looking at his watch. It was now 9.00am, by now news of the killings would undoubtedly have reached both the Police Commissioner and the Home Office. He should expect a call very soon. It was likely that things would become awkward. He knew that the Home Secretary wanted someone else appointed to head the investigation and had already briefed the head of the serious crimes unit in Scotland Yard and strangely MI5 too; a typical politician's solution to a problem – change the team. But his boss, Duncan Gravelle, Head of the Murder Squad would know that this wasn't the answer. And certainly Gravelle's superior, Sir Geoffrey Collins the Police Commissioner, an old friend and colleague of Cavey's, would want him to remain in situ. They had worked closely together on two major investigations and shared a strong mutual respect. Collins knew Cavey was the best man for the job and had the best crime solving stats in The Force by a long chalk.

But Cavey also knew one thing for sure: he had to deliver something soon or else he'd be side-lined, irrespective of Sir Geoffrey's loyalty to him.

His phone rang and he plucked it from his pocket and looked urgently at the caller display. It wasn't the one he dreaded, not Head Office. He relaxed and took it, listening quietly for a few minutes with just the occasional nod and grunt of acknowledgement. Finally, with a polite 'thank you for phoning to tell me', he closed off the call and slipped the phone back into his pocket, deep in thought.

DC Hargreaves had been watching him intently throughout the conversation, no doubt trying to work out what it was about.

'Sir?' he asked expectantly.

Cavey fixed the constable with a practised interrogatory stare. 'So … let's not look at what we don't know, Hargreaves. Let's look at what we do know. Can you run through the facts for me?'

This was a technique he had used on numerous occasions to great effect. If someone else presented the details of a case as they saw them, it often showed things from a completely different perspective.

'Start off with the witness reports. Go!'

'OK, sir,' said Hargreaves, obviously a little apprehensive at being put on the spot like this but at the same time rather relishing the opportunity to run through the details of the case with this renowned detective.

'Witnesses at the Kings Cross and Bermondsey killings claim to have seen a man of around thirty years of age acting suspiciously; he was rather plump, wore a cap and was carrying a sports bag. At Angel, Lambeth and Clapham people at the scene mentioned a wiry, thin man with shoulder-length hair wearing a dark overcoat. The only CCTV footage we have been able to obtain at any of the crime scenes, although grainy and distorted, appears to show an older man in say his mid to late fifties with a slight limp and a walking stick.'

'This was at the Canons Park incident wasn't it?' said Cavey.

'Yes, we had hoped to get a much better image after the Charing Cross murder but the cameras there were not operative.'

'Have we got an answer from Transport for London on why this was?

'No, sir, not yet. I'll get onto it straight away.'

'Good. I don't like the fact that we have so little CCTV evidence. London is the electronic surveillance capital of the world, and it's unnatural that so many cameras haven't been working at these locations. I don't like things out of the ordinary. It makes me suspicious.'

'And finally, we have today's witness statements suggesting a figure in a hooded cape. Er, could be male, female or even someone from Transylvania,' concluded Hargreaves. A grin flicked across his lips as he added the last part of his description but his attempt at levity fell flat. John Cavey was not known for his sense of humour.

'So, what do we conclude from all of this?' said Cavey, so deep in thought that Hargreaves was not really sure whether he was actually asking him the question or just thinking out loud.

'We could be looking for more than one killer?' answered Hargreaves hesitantly, the inflexion in his voice making it more of a question than an answer, betraying his lack of conviction.

'Unlikely,' replied Cavey, still visibly distracted. 'Mass murderers are generally solitary. They are driven by a twisted sense of injustice or a burning hatred. Very rarely is anyone else involved.

'Also, serial killers are usually insane. It is highly unlikely that you would get a number of mad people working together in an organised way, unless of course they are members of a cult.'

'So, in that case perhaps we are looking for someone who disguises himself?'

'Or herself,' added Cavey without a trace of humour in his voice. He looked long and hard at the young PC, replaying his synopsis of events.

'That doesn't sound much like the maniac we've been

looking for though, does it? Remember our killer's profile: a madman who preys on the most vulnerable members of society and kills indiscriminately whenever the opportunity presents itself. He skulks in the shadows waiting for his opportunity and when he strikes he is savage and quick. He kills because it gives him power. He enjoys killing. There is no pattern because the killings are random and opportunistic. He...'

Cavey's speech slowed and it was apparent to Hargreaves that he was speaking whilst actually thinking about something else. Finally his words petered out altogether and he stood staring intently at the pavement in front of him.

Then he jerked his head up and pointed a finger at Hargreaves.

'We may have something here.' Then he exploded, 'I think we've been looking for the wrong type altogether.' He was suddenly energised.

'The call I just took was from pathology. They've identified the poison used on the young drug users found near the Strand. It's an extremely rare and sophisticated organic toxin. A derivative of a rare star fish found in the Indo-Pacific region called ...' here he flicked open his note book and read from it, 'Tetrodotoxin; it's as deadly as ricin and just as difficult to detect. Almost impossible, in fact. The Hospital for Tropical Diseases finally came up trumps on this one for us. They say they have no record of this poison ever being used before.'

He leant towards the young detective.

'DC Hargreaves, I don't think our killer is a maniac; far from it. I think he's clever and calculating. He plans each crime meticulously, he chooses his victims, does his homework – CCTV locations, likelihood of being disturbed – that kind of thing and yes, he dons a different disguise for each crime. He intentionally changes his modus operandi so there is no pattern. He does that to throw us off the scent. He wants to kill and he also wants to avoid being caught, which, by the way is atypical for a serial killer. They generally court danger; they often enjoy the notoriety and the attention, sometimes even trying to form a relationship with us, their pursuers. Our killer doesn't do that, though.'

'So, what's his motivation then? Does he just enjoy killing?' asked Hargreaves, scratching the stubble of his unshaven jaw.

'No, I don't think so,' said Cavey very slowly, choosing his words carefully. 'We are not dealing with a serial killer.'

He had Hargreaves' full attention now.

'For our murderer, the killing is a means to an end and not an end in itself. Hargreaves, we are hunting an executioner, someone who is hell-bent on mass extermination.'

'Extermination of who?'

'Whom,' corrected Cavey, his instinct for exactness as acute as ever.

'By all appearances, 'he', or, I should add 'she', wants to kill anyone who lives rough on the streets.'

'Why would someone want to do that?' said Hargreaves in a quiet voice, as if asking himself the question.

'When we find an answer to that, we will be close to catching our killer. In the meantime, I am sure of one thing; this will not end until we stop it.'

Cavey's mobile phone trilled once again. This time it *was* the call he had been expecting.

'Good Morning, sir,' he said, raising the device mechanically to his ear.

CHAPTER 10

Caroline took a long drink of her extra shot cappuccino and savoured the bitter taste as she scanned the morning headlines.

The day had started well. She had received a particularly warm 'good morning' from Simon at front entrance security. There was definitely a connection there. She couldn't be imagining it. The whole thing was ridiculous and adolescent, but she felt real excitement whenever she thought of him.

Tom wasn't in yet. He was a late riser, choosing to put his work in at the other end of the day when the best politicking was to be had. In any case, the traditional dawn start for traders in the financial markets was not to everyone's taste, particularly someone like him who was used to Civil Service hours. He usually sauntered in at around 8.30am, which gave Caroline plenty of time to decide how she'd explain why she'd not alerted him to the nature of Jack Daniels' call last evening. It would no doubt be this fact that he would zero in on rather than the dramatic revelations themselves. Of that she was certain.

As she weighed up her options, she spied the package

from last night, her Eleventh Hour gift. It was poking unopened out of her Mulberry bag, where she had stuffed it when she had jumped into the taxi.

Eagerly tearing off the elegant wrapping, she was intrigued to discover a very stylish electronic tablet inside. The device was about the size of a paperback book, but wafer-thin and very light. A sumptuous Buckingham Green colour with a matching velvet case with gold trim and a small gold engraving of the distinctive Eleventh Hour clock logo in the bottom corner.

'Wow, someone's been splashing out!' said a chipper voice from behind her.

It was Kelly, bright and breezy as always first thing in the morning. She dropped her huge handbag onto the desk with a thud and leant over to examine the gift more closely.

'It's bloody smart,' she continued. 'Never seen one like that before. Where'd you get it?'

Kelly was hardly able to contain her curiosity as she extended her hand towards the device. She was good with technology and generally sorted out all the IT issues in the office for Caroline.

'Switch it on then,' she said impatiently, taking it from Caroline and gently tapping the 'on' button at the base of the screen.

With a flash of electric blue, the screen erupted into life for a second then went blank. Just as Kelly was about to give it another poke, a message flashed up in crimson: 'Thank you for supporting the Eleventh Hour Corporation. To activate the tablet, please answer the following questions.'

What followed was a short questionnaire formulated to

gauge attitudes to everything from conservation to climate change to recreational interests. Finally, came the prompt: 'What is the issue you care about most passionately? When you have answered, press the activate button and your tablet will be validated. Enjoy!' Below was the scrawled signature of Edward van der Linden.

Caroline smiled and shook her head appreciatively. 'What a brilliant way of following up. Quality, real quality,' she muttered.

'You what?' said Kelly, now perched on the side of her desk, busily filing her nails in ritualistic preparation for the day ahead.

They then heard a loud ringing sound coming from the tablet.

Caroline stared at the device in surprise.

'Press the app,' said Kelly, peering over her shoulder at the tablet which was now displaying a flashing green telephone icon on its screen.

Caroline tapped it tentatively.

The ringing stopped and the screen display melted away and was replaced by what looked like a video link. Next, the screen was filled by a large smiling face.

'Thanks for completing the questionnaire, Caroline,' said Edward van der Linden, obviously enjoying the fact that he had taken her by surprise by suddenly appearing in this way.

'I am sure it will make interesting reading. Also, your suggestions for improving the presentation were spot on. Thanks for being so candid. I like people who aren't afraid to tell it the way it is.'

Caroline just stared at the screen, not really sure what to do next. Although she was well used to Skype and Face Time conferencing it still seemed strange that Edward van der Linden had arrived in the room with them so unexpectedly.

'Will I be seeing you next week at Leo Brooks' lunch?' he continued.

'I'm not sure,' said Caroline, somewhat hesitantly, before remembering her manners. 'But thank you so much for this marvellous contraption.'

'Don't mention it. This is our technology though, so we would ask you not to let it fall into enemy hands. And by that I mean Microsoft and Samsung, not Al-Qaeda!' He laughed at his own remark. 'We'll be in touch soon. By the way, I haven't forgotten about your mother's problem. Good luck with that and if you need to talk any time, you now know how to do it! I'm only ever a click away!'

The screen went blank as the call ended. Caroline looked at Kelly, who was speechless, a rare occurrence in Caroline's experience.

'Very interesting, I'm sure,' said the voice of Tom Beresford who had been standing silently behind them. Caroline instinctively looked at her watch. Tom was early. 'I would strongly recommend you declare your little gift to Compliance, otherwise you may be in breach of the Bribery Act, which would lead to instant dismissal,' he added haughtily.

That was a good point, Caroline conceded. It was mandatory that any gift with a monetary value of over forty pounds had to be declared.

'Of course,' she fired back tersely.

Tom fixed her with a stern look. 'I'd like a word with you, Ms Hartley. In my office, please.'

He then left without waiting for a response.

*

Tom was comfortably ensconced behind his generous desk when she entered. Rather than speak, he simply pointed to the chair opposite. She sat as instructed.

'Do you have anything you'd like to share with me?' Tom began.

She opened her mouth to speak, but a response was obviously not required.

'Like, for example, any major developments in the Hubert Dunwoody matter?'

Caroline felt a thud in her head as a surge of adrenalin coursed through her body. He knew. She had no idea how he had found out, but now it was patently obvious what this meeting was about. She braced herself for a drubbing.

'You see, Caroline, you're not the only one with contacts. I know people in newspapers who make your boyfriend look like the office boy, which he probably should be anyway! In fact, they wondered why I hadn't been in touch about the 'new developments'. Well, of course, I would have been, if I'd bloody well known about them!'

He bellowed this last statement at the top of his voice. His face went a livid beetroot red from his thick neck upwards and his eyes bulged. Caroline shrank back from him as he leant towards her menacingly.

'Listen carefully,' he continued, 'there will be a parting

of the ways, my dear girl, if you carry on like this. And I'll give you a hint. I'm not going anywhere!'

He was calmer now and intentionally spoke in a slow and precise way as if he were lecturing a young child.

'Consider this a verbal warning. I will notify HR accordingly.'

This twist shocked her to her core. He was actually taking disciplinary action. It was a simple procedure and he was following it: verbal warning, written warning, then dismissal. Tom wanted her gone, she now knew that beyond doubt.

Caroline opened her mouth to protest, but thought better of it when she saw the look on his face. The aggression was still there, barely concealed behind tiger-like eyes. She chose the next best option and stared at him. He stared back, defying her to speak. It was an unequal contest, so she got up and walked towards the door in cold silence.

'So what's wrong with your mother?' he said to her back.

'What?' she exclaimed.

She was confused at this unexpected question and annoyed that he should even mention something in her personal life. It was almost an act of defilement in her mind.

'It's just that I heard ... what's his face, him on that tele thingy ... mentioning that she had a problem.'

He held his hands in front of himself in a defensive gesture as if he were bracing himself for a strong rebuttal.

Caroline didn't know what to say. The sudden change in tone after their explosive exchange wrong-footed her. She was bewildered.

'Is everything OK with her?' Tom continued. 'We've all

got mothers, you know and what with her being on her own and all …'

Caroline took a deep breath as she wondered whether she should continue the discussion at all.

'She may lose her house due to some dodgy dealings by my late father's business partner and she's very upset about it.'

She knew her voice was tart and actually didn't quite understand why she was telling him this at all. It would have been far better to have left his prying question hanging in the air and marched out of office. But at that moment she just wanted an end to the conversation and this seemed like the simplest way to achieve it.

'Where's that, then?' Tom asked.

'Where's what?' she said, impatient now to leave this absurd exchange behind her.

'Where is it that she lives?'

She'd had enough. She really didn't want to discuss family matters with this vile man.

'Oakdene in Buckinghamshire,' she replied coldly and stalked out of the room.

'Hmm, shame,' she heard from outside the door. 'Pretty little village.'

★

Kelly was waiting at her desk.

'That was quite a bollocking!' she exclaimed as she watched Caroline approaching. 'He really bawled you out. I reckon the whole office must have heard.'

This observation didn't exactly help Caroline's confidence. She could certainly do without her humiliation becoming public. One or two people were looking over in her general direction, so Kelly was probably right. Tom Beresford's words were still fresh in her mind. Then a thought stopped her in her tracks: how did he know her mother lived on her own?

CHAPTER 11

The first thing you noticed about Harold Butterworth was his enormous, bulbous nose. It was a massive protuberance, flecked with a network of broken veins and stuck between two ruddy cheeks. But at seventy-four years of age, he was well used to double-takes from passers-by and the occasional shouts of abuse. They were the least of his problems. Life was hard for this ex-merchant seaman of no fixed abode, with no money and no one to care for him.

Every day at 6.45pm, he could be found in the same place. The daily food hand-out from the Christian Mission at Vauxhall was a lifesaver for him, as it was for many others like him who found themselves down on their luck.

There had been happier times, when he and his late wife, Vera, had lived in a comfortable flat in Penge, southwest London. But that was before Vera was diagnosed with dementia. He simply couldn't let her go into one of those state-run institutions, so he'd been forced to re-mortgage the flat and cash in his paltry pension to pay for the private care home. Sadly, by the time it was all over, he had lost everything, including his much-loved wife and soul mate.

He didn't mind the waiting. Time was the one thing he

had in abundance. In fact, it gave him an opportunity to socialise with others who, like him, were willing to queue in all weathers for a mug of soup and a dry bread roll. Today the wait was longer than normal. He and Seamus O'Keeffe, a leather-skinned fifty-something labourer, who favoured drink to working on building sites these days, had been standing patiently for over an hour now. Seamus wasn't one for conversation. The drink had taken its toll on his health and he found it difficult standing for long periods, so he decided to squat down on the cold pavement rather than continue to lean up against the redbrick wall of the Mission. Harold flopped down beside him in sombre silence, sitting awkwardly on his rolled-up coat. They expected to see the battered Volvo that delivered the food come chugging around the bend any moment now. Tommy and Drew, the affable Californians who ran the 'Soupa Time' charity hot food delivery company, were late. Very late, indeed.

However, on this particular occasion, they would not be making the daily soup run. At that precise moment, five miles to the east of the Mission, in a shabby backstreet in New Cross, Tommy was shaking his dreadlocked head in disbelief as he surveyed their battered vehicle. All four tyres had been slashed and the rear window smashed in for good measure. They were going nowhere today.

Back at the Christian Mission, there were developments. The majority of the ragtag gathering, who had been queuing so patiently, had taken Seamus and Harold's lead and were now lolling all over the pavement, much to the consternation of two young policemen summoned to the scene. The hungry band was getting quite agitated. Their daily routine was very important to them: it was all that many of them had left in their empty lives. Things would turn ugly if they weren't fed soon. Two volunteers from the Mission were moving slowly down the queue, good-humouredly attempting to calm the more excitable characters in the group. Thankfully, they knew most of those waiting quite well. For the majority, the next stage in their daily routine would be an evening inside the centre, playing cards or watching the antiquated television that seemed to be permanently stuck on full volume, followed by a bed for the night in the linoleum-floored dormitory. All they had to do to earn this privilege was stay the right side of sober and mouth The Lord's Prayer before lights-out at 11.00pm. A small price to pay for warmth, comfort and companionship.

To everyone's relief, at that moment a smart silver transit van swept around the bend and slowed to a halt at the kerbside. The doors at the rear slid open to reveal a large urn and two columns of cardboard cups. A cheer went up from the ragged group, grateful that the wait was over. Forty-two shambling old men struggled to their feet.

'Where's Tommy. What've you done with him and Drew?' asked Seamus as he took a cup of the thick yellow liquid that was offered to him.

The soup smelled fishy and had a greasy film on its surface. It was an unwelcome departure from the usual fare of tomato, mushroom or minestrone dished up by the affable Americans. Still, the buttered roll and currant bun filled with jam more than made up for this break with tradition.

Seamus slurped loudly before wrinkling up his nose in an expression of distaste.

'Your soup's crap,' he said gruffly. 'What is it?'

'It's called Fugu,' was the polite response. 'It's Japanese. Would you like some more?'

'No thanks,' replied Seamus recoiling at the suggestion. 'I think I'd heave me guts up if I did. I don't like foreign muck,' he continued, an edge in his voice. 'What's wrong with good old English grub. Eh?'

With that, he downed the dregs of the soup. He then crushed the cup as a sign of displeasure and tossed the crumpled remains into the rubbish sack provided. Seamus seemed to consider this act of defiance earned him the right to double rations of everything else and without waiting for an invitation he crammed two rolls and a couple of buns oozing strawberry jam into his bag before tottering off towards the park behind the Mission. Once there he planned to have a lie down on a bench and to enjoy the half bottle of supermarket whisky in his pocket.

★

The blowfish of genus takifugu rubripes *– or 'fugu' as it is generally known – is a Japanese delicacy. In Japan, the preparation of this dish in restaurants is strictly controlled by law. Indeed, only chefs who have completed rigorous training are allowed to handle the fish. The reason for this is that this dish, although greatly prized, is also lethally poisonous. In fact, a fully grown man would die from a single dose of the tetrodotoxin contained within it, a dose that could fit on the head of a pin. The toxin is a thousand times more deadly than cyanide, and one of the most toxic substances known to man. The poison is a sodium channel blocker which paralyses the muscles* *while the victim remains conscious, unable to move or speak, eventually dying from asphyxiation. There is no known antidote.*

The progression of fugu poisoning is gradual. The toxin systematically shuts down the electrical signals in nerves. Initially, this causes numbness in the lips and tongue one to two hours after ingestion. Next to feel the effects are the fingers and toes. Painful headaches follow, accompanied by stomach cramps. The final phase is rapid: anaesthesia, motor paralysis, speech disability, fall in blood pressure and, finally, inability to breathe.

★

Harold first suspected something was wrong when his roll-up cigarette kept falling from his lips. Then, when he stooped to pick it up for the third time, he found it impossible to grasp. His fingers felt like a clump of twigs. Seamus was affected sooner. The alcohol in his body made his blood thinner, which helped the poison flow around his body more rapidly. He collapsed in an awkward heap an hour after the meal. At that stage though, most people thought he was just drunk as usual.

★

Detective Chief Inspector Cavey answered the phone on the third ring. The bedside clock showed 23:18. He hadn't really been sleeping deeply anyway. These days he had trouble switching his mind off. Even when he was semi-conscious, he found himself ordering and then re-ordering facts, looking for the vital clue they had overlooked; the illusive detail that would unlock this baffling puzzle.

'DCI Cavey?' said a faint voice. It was DC Hargreaves but he sounded anything but his usual, confident self.

'Speaking,' barked Cavey, now fully awake.

'You'd best get down here, guv. We've got a major incident on our hands.'

'What do you mean, Hargreaves? What's happening?'

'There's people dying all over the place, sir.'

In Hargreaves's thin voice, Cavey could detect an edge of panic.

'Where are you, Hargreaves?' DCI Cavey asked, already slipping into his clothes.

*

Dispatched from nearby St Thomas' Hospital, a fleet of ambulances was already at the scene when Cavey jumped from his car. He noted with some relief that the local police had had the foresight to cordon off the area. This was no mean feat given that Vauxhall Cross incorporated a number of major road intersections. However, it was essential at this stage to keep the area free from inquiring eyes. There were nevertheless already a couple of journalists pacing around outside the 'Police Incident' tape. It is said that bluebottles can detect putrefaction from a distance of five miles or more. Journalists, Cavey thought, seemed similarly equipped.

Bodies were everywhere: on the pavement, in the alleyway beside the Mission, even some sprawled in the park around the back. Doctors and paramedics were working frantically, bending over the victims or kneeling alongside them in a bid to stop their lives from ebbing away.

'It's no good, sir,' said Hargreaves, crouching down nearby and holding a saline drip whilst a paramedic pumped and thumped the chest of an inert body lying on the ground.

'Most of them are dead already and I reckon those that aren't soon will be. There's nothing we can do to save them.'

A young doctor rushed by, hurrying over to assist DC Hargreaves and the paramedic. He was too late. Cavey grabbed the doctor's arm just as he was about to dash over to a group of medics clustered around another victim over by the Mission entrance. He looked like a typical junior doctor: gelled hair framing a young face that had lost its fresh glow due to the long hours and stress of the job. He was tired, that much was apparent from the deep black rings around the eyes, but he also had an energy that was equally evident. Cavey's expert eye identified this at a glance. He was a man worth talking to.

'Doctor, what do you think it is?'

'I just don't know,' he said. 'This isn't like anything I have seen before. They have definitely ingested poison of some sort, but it isn't behaving like the usual toxins we come across. There are no convulsions or signs of abdominal spasm. They don't even appear to be in any great pain. The victims seem to just slowly fade away.'

He shook his head despairingly and was about to move on when Cavey tightened his grip.

'But what is actually killing them?' he asked insistently. 'Is it heart failure?'

'No, definitely not. They stop breathing, but there is no cardiac arrest. It's …'

The doctor cocked his head to one side thoughtfully '…

paralysis. That's it. They stop breathing because their muscles cease to function.'

'So, the poison is not actually killing them?' said Cavey, speaking faster now as an idea formed in his mind.

'Not that I can see. In fact, if any of them could actually continue breathing long enough for the effects of the poison to diminish, they would probably make it. But that's not going to happen,' he said, as his fleeting look of optimism evaporated.

'Yes, it is,' shouted Cavey in reply. 'An iron lung! What they need is an iron lung.'

'Maybe,' replied the doctor tentatively and then more urgently as the idea took root, 'yes, that at least would give them a chance.'

Cavey leapt into action. 'Hargreaves!' he yelled. 'Find anyone that's not too far gone. And you ...' He pointed at the nearest paramedic '... get onto St Thomas' and tell them to have respirators on standby for anyone that's still alive.'

The paramedic scurried off to radio from his ambulance, leaving DCI Cavey, Hargreaves and three other police officers to search out anyone that had not yet succumbed to the deadly poison.

Minutes later their efforts were rewarded: a man had been found alive, sitting on the cold pavement with his back resting against the wall of the Mission. He hadn't been noticed before because he was tucked away by the side of the building. A doctor fumbled urgently with his wrist, searching for a pulse, whilst a nurse held a mirror to his nostrils to check for the mist of exhaled breath. He was still breathing, but only just. Unlike the others, Harold had drawn the line at drinking all the lukewarm fishy brew. Forty years at sea had taught him to avoid fish that didn't taste right. He'd taken just a few sips before surreptitiously pouring the remainder into the nearby shrubbery. Then, like his now deceased mate Seamus, he'd loaded up on the buns as compensation. Harold's dose, although small by comparison to others, was still potentially fatal. It had simply taken effect much more slowly. Nevertheless, the poison continued its progress remorselessly. The central nervous system was gradually being switched off, branch by branch. His vision was blurring and shapes now swam before his eyes. There was no longer any colour in his world, all he could sense were sepia shapes and muffled sounds as all sensation was being dimmed.

Cavey watched helplessly as the old man struggled to snatch another precious breath then his attention was drawn to something else: written in chalk on the mission wall just to the right of Harold's head was a number, 72.

'Get him to the hospital, fast,' Cavey commanded the assembled throng of medics.

But they continued fussing over the old man, monitoring his pulse and administering drugs.

'Stop doing what you're doing,' Cavey shouted. 'It won't do him any good. Just put him in the ambulance, *now*!'

For a small, quietly-spoken man, DCI Cavey had an unexpectedly loud voice.

CHAPTER 12

As expected, Leo Brooks had not taken the news well.

'I thought you were going to fix this, Tom,' he said icily.

'We're trying Leo,' Tom ventured, 'but it would have been helpful if we had known about this additional personal connection with Hubert.'

'OK, OK. I suppose so,' said Leo testily. 'But it was a while ago and I'd virtually forgotten that I was Hubert's referee. Harrow seems like a different lifetime, you know?

Caroline pitied Leo. This intensely private man was finding it difficult giving others access to the details of his personal life. Unable to bear further interrogation, he started to pace up and down the length of his magnificent office.

'I'm probably going to sell the place in Scotland anyway you know,' he said despondently to no one in particular.

'What do you mean, Leo?' Tom asked, with what looked like genuine concern on his face. 'You love it up there.'

'They're going to build a thumping great hydroelectric plant upstream, apparently. The salmon simply won't be able to make it past the dam to spawn.'

'When did you find this out, old chap?' asked Tom.

'Last weekend. I went up there, as you suggested Tom,

to try to escape this shambles. Hamish, my gamekeeper, told me all about it.'

'Are you sure? It could just be local tittle tattle or scaremongering. Or perhaps someone's trying to trick you into selling up?'

Leo held up his hand to stop Tom from continuing with his conspiracy theory.

'I checked, Tom. I got straight on to Elgin Council last Monday. It appears plans for a "pumped storage empoundment hydroelectric plant" on the River Findhorn are now well advanced. They already have preliminary Department of Environment approval. I understand they've also had the informal nod from the Scottish parliament. I checked that out with a chum of mine at Holyrood. It's virtually a done deal.'

'Sorry to hear it, Leo,' Tom said softly, putting a sympathetic hand on his friend's shoulder. 'I know how much your fishing means to you. What a bummer. I still can't believe it.'

Caroline watched the exchange in silence. The mention of local authorities and planning had been an unwelcome reminder that she was no closer to resolving her mother's problem and time was short. She had drawn a blank when she had contacted the bank. They simply refused to discuss the matter with her on the grounds of confidentiality. This was to be expected but she had met the same resistance from the accountants handling the partnership's bankruptcy proceedings and their solicitors. No one would talk about it and all referred her instead to the only person authorised to do so – Vernon Cartwright and she wasn't going to discuss the matter with him! The whole situation was impossibly frustrating and she wondered what she should do next as time was running out and failure was definitely not an option.

In front of her, Leo stood silently staring at the Oberson Rug in the middle of the office, lost in his own tormented thoughts. To Caroline, he suddenly cut a rather pathetic, lonely figure. He seemed to have shrunk in stature and had lost his air of natural authority. The sullen figure standing in front of them was certainly a far cry from the suave, confident CEO that Caroline had always admired. All of a sudden, it was as if he had read her thoughts and remembered himself. He straightened up and turned to face them. The self-pity had gone and in its place was a look of icy determination.

'One problem at a time,' he said crisply. 'Let's get this business with the newspaper sorted first.'

Caroline watched the Jekyll and Hyde transformation with fascination. Leo really was a mercurial character – one minute reserved and dejected, the next determined and clinical. Which of his two personae was his true self? she wondered.

'That's the spirit, Leo,' said Tom, back in familiar guise as a kind of supportive school-chum figure. 'We'll lick 'em yet.'

His show of bravado did the trick and within a matter of minutes they were chatting away happily on far less emotive matters. Tom had expertly turned the conversation to the forthcoming Formula One season, Leo's other great passion. This year, Montagu Steinhart had decided to take a hospitality tent at Silverstone, the venue for the British Grand Prix, with an estimated total outlay of close to a million pounds. This was to be their biggest public relations spend since the financial crisis and Leo and his fellow board directors were keen to ensure that it was money well spent.

'It will be a roaring success,' Tom pronounced confidently. 'We've sent out invitations to all the bank's top clients and acceptances are already rolling in. I reckon you're on to a winner here.'

Leo listened politely but said nothing, which Tom seemed to take as a sign of doubt.

'Look Leo,' Tom continued. 'I'll go up there myself this Thursday if you like. I'll check out the arrangements and kick ass if I need to. How about that?'

Leo smiled and nodded appreciatively. 'That would be first-class, Tom. I want this to be a slick affair with no hitches. A lot of people will be watching. We have to pitch it just right. Too lavish and it will look gauche, too sparing and we'll look cheap.'

'Damn!' Tom suddenly exclaimed, slapping his thigh in a show of frustration. 'That means I'll miss lunch with ... what's his face ... that van Lindenburg chap. Still, never mind. Caroline, you can step into the breach can't you? You already know him, anyway.'

'Of course,' she said, attempting to sound as casual as she could.

In actual fact, she'd started to resent the fact that she was doing all the preparatory work for a lunchtime meeting that Leo and Tom would attend without her. This unexpected twist of fate was perfect. She really wanted to meet Edward van der Linden again, he was an intriguing character involved in a fascinating enterprise.

Leo seemed back to his friendly, affable self, the man she had known before this whole thing had blown up and it suddenly dawned on Caroline that it was the Hubert Dunwoody matter alone that was blighting her career. It was souring her working relationships and stunting her promotion prospects. She had to do something about it. As she returned to her office on the second floor she made her mind up; she would call Jack immediately and try to persuade him to drop the story.

*

'Hi Jack, don't hang up, we need to talk,' she entreated when he picked up her call.

'I'm listening,' he snapped.

This wasn't the kind of conversation she wanted to conduct from her desk, so Caroline found herself pacing up and down outside Montagu Steinhart's main entrance trying to find somewhere private to talk. She paused for a second then walked on again as a group of smokers huddled by the building's wall looked over at her suspiciously.

'Jack, what if I give you another story? Something big, ' she whispered, cupping her hand around the phone in an effort to keep her words as private as possible.

He laughed humourlessly.

'What are you on Caroline? You must be insane to think I'm going to barter with you like this.'

'Just hear me out Jack. I know this is unorthodox but I think you'll be interested in what I have to say.'

He fell silent for a moment or two as he deliberated on her proposal.

'OK, shoot. I've got nothing to lose by listening.'

'Before I start, Jack, I want your word that you'll drop the story if what I'm about to give you is bigger and you decide to run with it.'

'I can't promise, Caroline, but I won't stitch you up, you know that.' His voice registered more than mild interest now.

At that moment two figures pushed through the swing doors on their way out of the building. Caroline recognised them as two of the Managing Directors from the M&A Division. They both turned to look at her, one nodded a greeting but neither spoke. She realised that she must look extremely suspicious, walking up and down outside in the street. Generally speaking, people who exhibited such furtive behaviour were speaking to either headhunters or lovers. She wondered which the two of them thought it was in her case.

She composed herself, took a deep breath and went for it.

'Jack, I think people are being murdered on the streets of London and no one knows about it. It's not being reported anywhere.'

'That's it,' said Jack scarcely able to hide his distain. 'Sorry to burst your oh so naive, middle class bubble, Caroline, but there's murder and violence out there on the streets every day. We don't report it because it's not interesting or newsworthy.'

'I don't mean that Jack. Just listen before you judge me,' she snapped back. 'What I'm telling you is that there have been thirty, possibly even forty by now, murders of homeless people in London and no mention of it at all in the papers.'

'You sure?' Jack replied, definitely more interest now. 'How do you know this?'

'My PA at work discovered one of the bodies and we went together to the police and I overheard them talking about it.'

'So what are you saying? There's mass murder on the streets of London and somehow the press are complicit in covering it up?'

'I simply don't know what I'm saying. It makes no sense to me. All that I do know is that the police are investigating a large number of killings and none of it is mentioned in the press.'

Jack fell silent as he considered what she was telling him. 'And you're sure of this?'

'One of the detectives said it. I heard his exact words and the other night St Paul's Underground Station was cordoned off. Then an ambulance turned up. It was another murder, I'm sure of it, but once again there was no report of it on the news

Jack fell silent for ten seconds or so before continuing in a slow and measured tone.

'OK Caroline, here's what I'll do. I'm going to check with our crime desk to see if they've got wind of this. If it's got legs, I'll see what I can do on the other story...'

His voice tailed off as he said this and Caroline instantly zeroed in on his lack of conviction.

‘Jack, you promised,’ she said, trying hard not to sound desperate.

‘I know, and I’ll do what I can. It’s just that my Editor really wants to go to print on the Leo Brooks story.’ Then he added, ‘It’s your own fault really. He wouldn’t have taken such an interest in it if you hadn’t got your lawyers involved. No one likes being threatened, Caroline.’

The line went dead and as she slipped her mobile back into her pocket she noticed someone standing with the group of smokers nearby, staring in her direction. It was Hubert Dunwoody.

‘You’re looking foxy today Caroline’, he shouted, which drew a murmur of agreement and a lascivious chuckle from his mates.

Caroline stared back coldly then walked towards the entrance. Hubert made another comment which she didn’t quite catch, but she assumed was personal, judging by the way his acolytes sniggered. How ironic, she thought, that she was trying desperately to keep this smirking prig’s name out of the papers, when he so deserved to be exposed to public censure.

CHAPTER 13

DCI Cavey had personally telephoned his boss, Duncan Gravelle, from the crime scene in Vauxhall as he watched the remaining bodies being unceremoniously loaded into a fleet of ambulances. There had been no further survivors. Gravelle had taken the news badly. Whether this was because he was not at his best when woken from his slumbers at 3.00 am or because he realised he was now obliged to break the news to the Police Commissioner who in turn would have to tell the Home Secretary, Cavey was undecided. He suspected the latter. As he weighed this up in his mind, he had scanned the growing knot of reporters chatting furtively behind the hastily erected police cordon. Duncan Gravelle and for that matter, Sir Geoffrey, had his sympathies. The Home Secretary, the Right Honourable Arthur Winterbourne, would not take the news well, he was sure of that. This was a dramatic development and he knew that it was imperative that the police were seen to be on top of the matter.

Lurid, uncorroborated reports of a mass poisoning in central London were already doing the rounds on the internet and if they didn't take prompt action he knew that the story would run out of control. Their hand had been forced. They had to go public.

Six hours later, Cavey could be found seated alone in a small office in New Scotland Yard, watching the Media Room down the corridor slowly filling with journalists through a video link. He, more than anyone, wanted to retain the cloak of silence around the street killings, but could not see how this was now possible given recent events. The Home Secretary though did not agree and had been quite emphatic on the issue. He maintained that until there was actual proof that the Vauxhall poisoning and the street killings were the work of the same murderer the two were not linked and the news embargo must remain in force. But Cavey knew he was clutching at straws. One piece of evidence linked them both beyond reasonable doubt – the number 72. He himself had seen the number written on a makeshift cardboard shelter in Cardboard City and again on the wall of the Vauxhall Christian Mission. The killings had been committed by the same hand, he was certain of it.

DCI John Cavey would not be a party to a lie, so he had respectfully declined to attend the press briefing in person. Meanwhile, the Home Secretary, who was less ethically constrained, had personally ordered the fabrication of a credible story around the Vauxhall slaughter at a hastily convened early morning meeting, so that no connection was made by the press to the street killings. It was a desperate and highly risky strategy. Cavey suspected that the public may forgive them for supressing the news but there would be a savage backlash if they discovered that they had been lied to.

Although they were polls apart morally, Cavey and the

politician nevertheless agreed on one point: they had to bring the matter to a conclusion before too long as both their careers depended on it.

The deaths the previous night had brought the total to eighty-three known victims, and still they had no firm leads. The frequency of the killings was accelerating and it was apparent that the killer was becoming more audacious, moving from the piecemeal murder of individuals to wholesale slaughter on an almost industrial scale. Cavey's position was perilous. He knew how vicious politicians could be when they were under threat themselves and he couldn't rely on help from within the force. If he didn't deliver soon, he'd be out.

One consoling fact was that now at least he had a witness, if barely. He also had the mystery number. What did 72 mean? he wondered.

Cavey stared at the screen in front of him, keen for the briefing to finally get under way. The sooner it did the sooner he would be able to get back to real police work. He had an intense dislike of this sort of gathering but naturally he understood that it had to be done. After all, he, the Commissioner and all the other officers were public servants and owed a duty to the man in the street. In the conference room, there was a hum of animated conversation. Forty journalists and news cameramen were crammed together in the room, all vying for the best seats and most favourable camera angles, all hungry for information. So far there had been frustratingly little detail made available to them. This was a big story and they wanted a comprehensive and detailed briefing. Nothing else would suffice.

The excited buzz died away as the Police Commissioner,

Murder Squad Head, Duncan Gravelle and the Met's Head of Communications, Simon McAlister, filed solemnly into the room. The procession had something of the school assembly about it. A hush fell over the audience as the senior figures solemnly took their seats.

'Ladies and gentlemen, thank you for coming here today,' said Sir Geoffrey in a strident voice full of authority. He cut a distinguished figure in his Commissioner's uniform with its pocket fringed with decorations and its braided cuffs.

'Last night,' he continued, 'London witnessed its greatest loss of life in a single incident since the 7/7 terrorist bombings of 2005. As many of you may already know, forty-one people were fatally poisoned at a soup kitchen in Somerville Street Vauxhall SE1.'

It seemed most present had not realised the extent of the tragedy, there was a murmur of surprise and then a general hubbub as they all tried to ask questions at the same time.

'Hold on, one at a time please!' shouted Simon McAlister, leaping to his feet in an effort to restore order and stamp his authority on the meeting. 'Let the Commissioner finish. There'll be plenty of time for questions.'

'Any idea yet who killed them, Sir Geoffrey?' shouted the Sky News reporter from a seat near the front. 'Have there been any arrests?'

'Morning Angus,' replied the Commissioner, straining to be heard over the din. 'I can't say anything yet except that you should expect developments imminently.'

'Who's leading the enquiry?' asked the man from CNN.

'We have put one of Duncan Gravelle's top men, Detective Chief Inspector John Cavey, on the case.'

On cue, a photograph of a young DCI Cavey flashed onto a large screen behind the panel.

'Where is he then?'

The question came from a bull-headed individual dressed in a creased beige suit. He was leaning against the wall with an impertinent expression on his face. They all knew him: his name was Stuart Heyworth, the lead investigative reporter for a down-market tabloid. It was difficult to conceive of a more repugnant individual. He was renowned for his general rudeness and abrasive manner. Other journalists gave him a wide berth, as they knew he would stop at nothing to secure an exclusive. Stuart Heyworth was friendless, but it didn't seem to bother him.

'I'm sorry,' fired back the Communications Director, who had risen slowly to his feet again when he saw who it was asking the question. 'Where's who?'

'Cavey. You know, Inspector "haven't got a Clue-so",' sneered the journalist as he chewed busily on a mouthful of gum.

The comment drew a ripple of laughter.

'Unfortunately, DCI Cavey is unable to be with us. He is pursuing his enquiries in an effort to bring this matter to a swift conclusion.'

The Director of Communication's lie was said in the kind of clipped tone that did not invite further questioning.

'So what can you tell us?' shouted the man from Sky.

'Our initial inquiries suggest that a volunteer worker at the Vauxhall Christian Mission, who we understand had long-standing mental health issues, laced last night's soup with poison. Paraquat to be precise.'

'Is he in custody?' shouted a reporter from one of the regional newspapers.

'No. The suspect fled the scene before he could be apprehended,' replied Sir Geoffrey. 'However, we are optimistic that we will make an arrest very soon.'

'Let him get away then, did you?'

It was Heyworth again.

'I was there last night, at Vauxhall. You had it sealed off as tight as a duck's arse. He must have been about the only person left alive besides you boys in blue and the medics! And still you let him escape. How'd you manage that?'

A hush fell over the audience. The Commissioner and Heyworth locked eyes as Sir Geoffrey's face reddened with anger before he replied acidly, 'Mr Heyworth, we will have to ask you to leave if you don't behave. Any further outbursts and I'll have you ejected.'

The rebuke was unexpectedly firm, and was accompanied by a finger jabbed directly at the journalist.

Heyworth smirked and gave a self-satisfied snort. Getting under people's skin was his speciality.

'It's your show, old chap,' he replied in an exaggerated upper class accent, holding his chubby hands aloft in mock surrender. 'I was just wondering though, whether this particular individual *was* actually responsible.'

'What do you mean?' the Commissioner replied curtly.

'Well,' continued Heyworth, savouring his moment in the spotlight. 'The question I have is: are you sure this whole thing isn't connected to the recent string of killings throughout London?'

Silence weighed heavily on the room. Cavey closed his eyes and waited.

'What other killings?' Sir Geoffrey challenged in a foolhardy attempt to face him down.

'The three dozen or so unexplained homicides involving people living on the London streets. Those killings, Commissioner. Had they slipped your mind?'

Sir Geoffrey's mouth opened to make a reply, but he thought better of it.

'It looks to me like there's a dangerous psychopath out there,' continued Heyworth to a hushed room, 'and I think it's high time the public knew about it.'

Panic showed on Simon McAlister's face as he leapt to his feet. 'That's enough now, Stuart. This briefing is about the Vauxhall poisonings. Nothing else.'

But the words had been spoken publicly and the connection made.

Cavey shook his head in disapproval. He was powerless to help as the press conference descended into a state of uproar. Time and time again in his career, he had witnessed fabricated stories unravel in front of him. Normally, however, those responsible for the deceit were criminals. As of one minute ago, the news blackout he had negotiated with the media on the vagrant killings was null and void. For the press, a big story had just become huge. A murderer was on the loose in London. Someone had killed more than eighty people, forty-one of them in a single mass poisoning.

Thanks to Stuart Heyworth, the genie was now well and truly out of the bottle.

★

Back in the hospital, Harold had noticed the figure in front of him twist in his seat and crane his neck sideways. The television in the corner was on; he could see the flickering of the screen. The unknown person was obviously watching it. Harold couldn't make out the picture though. Everything was a blur to him. He couldn't focus because the ciliary muscles in his eyes, like most other muscles in his body, were not operating properly. He could make out the sounds though if he concentrated hard. Someone was talking about… poison… people dying… the Vauxhall Mission. They were talking about what had happened last night. Someone had survived; *him*, they were talking about him! He was under guard in hospital. The man in the chair was a police officer. As these thoughts bounced around his mind, the television screen suddenly came into focus and Harold found himself staring at the photograph of a serious-looking policeman: Detective Chief Inspector John Cavey.

He was obviously in danger. Harold's heart rate quickened, tripping an alarm on the monitor. A nurse hurried into the room and the policeman sprang to his feet and stared him in the eyes. Harold could see his features clearly now: a nice-looking young man with a carpet of thick stubble on his jaw and dark rings framing lively, enquiring eyes.

'He's OK,' said the nurse as she guided the detective back to his seat, out of her way. 'Looks like he just got a bit excited. It's probably a good sign actually. Shows he's aware of his surroundings.' She then spoke directly to Harold. 'You're alright, Mr… old …'

She then glanced back at DC Hargreaves.

'I'll just give him something to help him relax,' she said softly.

Harold was scared. Terrified in fact. Someone had tried to kill him. In the past few weeks, he'd heard the rumours circulating on the streets about how people were being bumped off virtually daily. Word was it was the authorities. The Government was behind the whole thing. They'd obviously tried to kill him, but failed. Now here he was, a sitting duck until someone finished the job. He couldn't speak and he couldn't move and all the time he was being watched. That was what the young detective was doing, watching. He was keeping an eye on him, just waiting for the right moment.

The nurse swabbed his skin with cotton wool before gently easing a needle into his arm. He felt a mild sting as it punctured his flesh. Then it dawned on him. He'd felt it! He was slowly recovering his senses, but he wasn't going to let on. No, he'd bide his time. Then he'd make his move and escape.

CHAPTER 14

For the day of her much anticipated lunch with Edward van der Linden, Caroline chose to wear her favourite Stella McCartney. The outfit always drew admiring looks: from men, because it accentuated her curves, and from women, because it was simple, elegant and very stylish. Anyway, she felt good in it and that was important. Simon on security seemed to like it too.

'Good morning, Ms Hartley,' he beamed as she entered the foyer through the revolving doors. 'Special day, eh?'

So, he was perceptive as well as handsome. She said nothing, but made sure she gave him a particularly warm and friendly smile.

'That's a neat little package,' he muttered as she walked by.

She was shocked. It was an unexpectedly personal and inappropriate remark; not what she would have expected from him at all. Caroline turned to voice her disapproval, but noticed he was actually looking at the electronic tablet given to her by Edward van der Linden, which was sticking out of the top of her bag.

'Oh, that. Yes, it's incredible.' She took it from the bag.

'Wasted on me, though, I'm afraid. I'm a complete klutz when it comes to technology.'

It was their longest conversation to date and she found herself instinctively moving closer.

'Can I see?' he asked.

She handed it to him.

'I've never seen one like this,' he said, dextrously flipping the tablet over in his muscular hand to examine its underside.

'It's beautiful. So light, it feels like it's made of aluminium or something like that,' he enthused, before adding; 'I bet it has amazing functionality.'

'I wouldn't really know. Look, why don't you keep it for a while? Have a little play and give it back to me before I leave tonight.'

'Oh no, I couldn't do that.'

'Believe me, I'm very unlikely to be using it today,' she said, gently pushing the device back to him as he tried to return it.

'Thanks. That's really good of you. I'll get it back to you later on and that's a promise. Enjoy your day.'

He walked over to the reception desk and placed the tablet in a drawer while Caroline waved and headed for the lift.

Kelly's eyes were sparkling with excitement as she grabbed hold of Caroline's arm and pulled her towards her.

'What were you two talking about? Tell me.'

The lift doors slid shut and it began to ascend.

Caroline didn't want Kelly and, no doubt thereafter all the other secretaries, to know about her little infatuation, so she decided to play the whole thing down.

'He just asked me about my tablet, you know, the one that did the video conference the other day all on its own. He saw it in my bag. So I let him borrow it. That's all.'

'Oh, right,' said Kelly, obviously a little disappointed, 'I thought he was asking you out or giving you his 'phone number or something. Perhaps when he gives it back...'

'Kelly! I'm already in a relationship. Richard. Remember?'

'Sure thing,' she replied sarcastically before adding 'we both know it's only a matter of time before he's toast.'

Kelly was right, as usual. Caroline felt no real attachment to Richard, and doubted she ever had. It was, and always had been, a relationship born of convenience. She, like so many career girls, didn't want to live a solitary home life, so it was good to have someone to go out with in the evening. Anyway, he wasn't bad-looking and he was good company when he wasn't drinking too much, although such temperance was a rarity these days she had to admit. Yes, Kelly had a point. Richard was history. She just hadn't got around to telling him yet.

'I suppose he is quite good looking,' said Caroline, trying hard to feign indifference.

Kelly had made another good point, she thought, with a flutter of excitement. She would indeed have to meet Simon again later on when he returned the device.

*

The bank's suite of client dining rooms was situated on the ninth floor of the Steinhart Centre building. Lunch was to be in the Buckingham Room. Each of the ten dining rooms was named after a former bank chairman and decorated to a different level of luxury. This variation enabled the bank to entertain its guests in a setting that was appropriate for each client, taking into consideration the purpose of the meeting. There was invariably a rationale behind the room chosen for a particular meeting. If the surroundings were too lavish, some clients would be prompted to question whether their fees were not too high. Whereas others would respond positively to an obvious show of luxury, happy, if not flattered to be associated with an overtly successful organisation

The Buckingham Room was at the top of the luxury scale and as such was an exercise in sheer opulence. The walls were panelled in oak, each panel having been painstakingly transplanted from the bank's previous headquarters in Lombard Street. Although Montagu Steinhart had transformed itself from an old City merchant bank into a modern global investment bank some years ago, these oak panels symbolised its longevity and sound English banking values. They were also phenomenally expensive.

The Chippendale table in the centre of the room was a magnificent piece of furniture which stood ten feet in length and was capable of comfortably seating a dozen diners. It was resplendent with silver cutlery, two towering antique candelabra at each end and a forest of lead crystal wine glasses. To finish off the room's decoration, and to leave guests in no doubt as to the institution's financial prowess, an original Canaletto masterpiece hung on the far wall behind the host's chair. The painting showed a view of St

James's Park and the Horse Guards Parade and had been painted during one of the celebrated Venetian master's frequent visits to England. It was insured for £100 million but was, in reality, like all such masterpieces, priceless.

Caroline heard Edward van der Linden well before she saw him. With its strong accent, his voice was as clear and confident as ever. Leo Brooks had met him at the lifts. As ever the consummate professional, Brooks always insisted on extending this courtesy to his guests, recognising how much people responded to the personal touch.

'I think you already know Caroline Hartley, our Director of Corporate Communications,' Leo said, gesturing towards her as he strode into the room accompanied by the massive South African.

'Ah, yes, of course,' van der Linden said, unexpectedly hugging her to his broad chest before placing his massive hands on her shoulders and kissing her loudly on each cheek. She didn't really know what to do after this warm greeting and felt suddenly very small as she tried in vain to extricate herself from his embrace.

A third person had entered with them and stood watching van der Linden's clumsy greeting with a look of apparent amusement. She was a tall, angular woman in her early fifties. Her straight grey-blonde hair was cut a little severely in the kind of pageboy style fashionable in the late 1970s. She wore a smart, if somewhat drab, chocolate brown suit over a cream silk blouse with a high collar. Her unremarkable appearance was however rescued by a pair of pearl earrings and a spectacular matching necklace made with some of the most perfect pearls Caroline had ever seen.

They were natural not cultured, she could easily tell by their metallic, mirror-like lustre that made them glisten as if wet. As an admirer of classic jewellery, Caroline was transfixed by these magnificent pieces. The necklace was comprised of three bands, fixed in the centre by a shimmering, finely-cut emerald.

'Sorry, Caroline,' boomed the Green Giant. 'Can I introduce Sue Baxter? Sue heads up Eleventh Hour's Direct Action Unit. I thought you and Leo would be interested in meeting her and hearing about her marvellous work. Sue has been with me from the start and essentially translates our words into action.'

Van der Linden put a comradely arm around Sue as he spoke these words and pulled her closer.

'Direct Action, that sounds fascinating. What exactly does that mean?' asked Leo, eager to make his guests feel at home.

It was Sue who replied. She was well-spoken but Caroline immediately noticed that her London working life had not managed to squeeze out her Mancunian roots. A hint of Moss Side still remained.

'We choose to do things to change people's minds rather than naively trying to spend our way to Utopia.'

This rather obtuse answer didn't really leave them any the wiser, so Leo pressed her further.

'Like what, Sue? Do you mean mass demonstrations and the like?'

'No, not at all,' she said, disdainfully. 'They're just political stunts and actually rarely change anything. No, what we do is use our brains.'

'How so?' asked Leo politely.

Caroline sensed Leo's frustration. It wasn't a difficult question after all, but Sue was being annoyingly non-specific.

'*Well* ...' she said, drawing out the word. 'Let's put it this way. Imagine you want to kill me.'

'Right,' said Leo hesitantly, shooting Caroline a look that said, 'where's this going?'

'Rather than setting about me with a machete,' Sue continued, swishing her hand from side to side by way of illustration, 'it would be better to gently slide a skewer between the fifth and sixth ribs. Far less messy, much less effort and infinitely more effective. Brains over brawn, you see. That's the way we operate. We always plan our angle of attack before executing our strategy.'

'Figuratively speaking, of course,' Edward van der Linden added, and they all laughed. He helped himself to one of the exotic-looking shellfish canapés being offered by the steward before continuing, 'Sue, perhaps if we give a real life example of your projects, Leo and Caroline will realise just how exciting your work is.'

Caroline wondered what lay in store for them. Sue was a supremely confident person and apparently free from any social inhibitions. There was little doubt she would say whatever was on her mind. Her eyes glinted with the energy of a fearsome intellect, Caroline observed, but like so many super-intelligent people she was a little off the wall. Lunch was likely to be a rollercoaster and Caroline was preparing herself for a bumpy ride.

Leo placed Edward van der Linden at the opposite end

of the grand table to himself and put Sue and Caroline between. Caroline noticed how, ever the attentive host, he pulled back Sue's chair before sliding it gently under her as she sat down.

Sue launched into an explanation of her latest campaign hardly pausing even when presented with their delicious starter of grilled scallops in clam minestrone. Evidently her group planned to site posters showing graphic photographs of the slaughter of dolphins at major airports throughout the world. The campaign was designed to specifically target the Japanese who are prolific travellers but also still indulged in this barbaric practice and hence the strap lines under each image would be written in Japanese as well as English.

When she had finished, Leo puffed out his cheeks.

'Well, that's a pretty forthright approach and it's bound to be highly controversial,' he exclaimed.

'I know,' replied Edward van der Linden, 'but sometimes you have to shock people to their senses. Hit them between the eyes.'

'I like it,' interjected Caroline. 'Putting the message in Japanese as well as English is a clever way of pointing the finger without actually saying: "It's you we're talking to!"'

'Absolutely right Caroline. I thought you'd see its subtlety,' interjected Edward van der Linden enthusiastically.

'Subtlety?' exclaimed Leo. 'I'm not sure that's the word I would use!'

'Well, like it or not Leo, that's the essence of Direct Action, Sue Baxter style,' replied Sue.

'Yes, and as you can see, Ms Baxter doesn't exactly take prisoners,' added her boss proudly.

'No petitions, no lobbying, no demonstrations,' Sue continued, making small chopping motions with her hand as she said each word. 'We just identify the pressure points and squeeze until they submit!'

Sue looked directly at her boss as she said this, giving Caroline the distinct impression that she wasn't just talking about the current campaign, but that this was a continuation of a previous discussion between the two of them.

Caroline was a keen student of body language and had developed a useful talent for interpreting unspoken gestures. On the surface, van der Linden and Sue Baxter made a good double act – an accomplished verbal tag-team – but beneath the surface there seemed to be a less harmonious relationship. Sue appeared excitable and, at times, obsessive. Although van der Linden encouraged her to talk, he watched her carefully and whenever her emotions looked in danger of boiling over, he would intervene to rein her back or take the conversation in a different direction. He was very much in control, the master puppeteer. She sometimes resisted or shot him a look of disapproval but always in the end acquiesced to his will. The interaction was subtle and almost telepathic but quite apparent to Caroline's expert eye. As they talked on about conservation, climate change and other Eleventh Hour causes, this ringmaster characteristic became more apparent. He loved her passion, and probably also her money (she confessed to being a multi-millionaire early on in the proceedings) but he made sure she behaved as he wanted.

Coffee was served after lunch. Sue, predictably eccentric, requested ginger tea, which they didn't have, and then surprised them all by producing a tea bag containing the brew from her pocket. Leo was unfazed by her antics and despite his starchy exterior seemed to be thoroughly enjoying her company. He and van der Linden had really gelled over lunch and chatted away over coffee like long-time friends. But they hadn't agreed on everything. Indeed, Leo's strident views on energy policy had nettled Sue, coming close to igniting a temper that Caroline was sure lurked behind the occasional cold silence. Montagu Steinhart was a leading provider of corporate finance advisory services to the energy sector and a major player in international project finance. In addition, the chairman of the UK's largest oil and gas company was a non-executive director of the bank, so Leo's pro-fossil fuel stance was unsurprising to Caroline.

'Fossil fuels will eventually suffocate this planet,' Sue railed. 'The Chinese have a five-year economic plan based solely on coal as their main energy source. Did you know that lorries taking coal to the docks from their mines in Inner Mongolia, along the Beijing to Tibet Expressway, have to queue for nine days? It's the world's worst traffic jam. A line of eight-wheelers, nose to tail, just imagine how much coal they are shipping. And after the Fukushima disaster, other major industrial nations like Japan and Germany are turning from nuclear power to gas. It's like we've gone back two hundred years to the Industrial Revolution!'

'But what's the alternative?' countered Leo, folding his arms.

'Well, natural power such as wind and wave power. Not forgetting hydroelectric power of course, one of the oldest sources of power generation.'

Leo flinched and swallowed hard. 'Yes, well I'm not the person to talk to about hydroelectric power generation.'

Ever sensitive to changes in mood, Edward van der Linden spotted Leo's reaction and was quick to probe for more information.

'Why's that, Leo? Has the bank lost money on a hydro project or something?'

'No, Edward, it's a private matter.'

Leo's face reddened slightly and his lips tightened. For the first time in their company, he looked stern and unamused. This change in mood was all too apparent to van der Linden's experienced eye.

'Tell us more, Leo. You're amongst friends here. It's obviously something of great importance to you personally.'

His voice had become soft and entreating, like a counsellor, as he encouraged Leo to open up. Caroline watched carefully, enjoying this master class in subtle interrogation.

'Well,' Leo ventured, 'it's just that they plan to build a socking great hydro plant up river from my salmon stream in the Highlands. It's a magnificent unspoilt part of the world, downstream from Aviemore and the high Highlands. This new facility will decimate the salmon population in the river. Unless, that is, they learn to jump over a dam,' he added sarcastically

'That's sad, Leo. Very sad. I can see your fishing means a great deal to you. Scotland is such a naturally beautiful country. I've fished there myself. Heaven, absolute Heaven!'

Van der Linden's face was etched with genuine concern as he delivered his words of sympathy. He rocked back in his chair and stared thoughtfully at the ceiling for a few seconds before continuing.

'One of the primary tenets of Eleventh Hour is to preserve the beauty of our planet and to prevent environmental destruction of any kind. Hydroelectric power is clean, there's no doubting that. But it is often highly controversial. I can assure you that we are no strangers to this problem. It's somewhat incongruous, I'll admit, as you would expect a group like ours to be wholly behind this kind of power generation. But we're not. In fact, Sue's currently closely monitoring a situation in eastern Siberia, aren't you Sue?' He added nodding in his colleague's direction before continuing.

'A vast three kilometre dam is being constructed on the Angara River and the local population of ten thousand has been compulsorily resettled.'

Sue then took up the story in a seamless baton change.

'Our people have already detected a change in water quality since the ancient forests upstream have been flooded,' she said excitedly, 'they've transformed thousands of acres of previously productive agricultural land into stinking marshland.'

'I can assure you that there's going to be some plain talking with the Russian government and the oligarch running the project in the next few weeks,' interjected van der Linden vehemently.

None of them doubted his words, especially since he pounded the table with his immense fist to emphasise the point.

'That's good to know,' said Leo, still a little subdued. 'I

wouldn't have thought you'd be in favour of fishing, though.'

'Far from it, Leo,' boomed the South African. 'We find that people who derive pleasure from the land – hunters and fishermen – are often the greatest supporters of the environment. They care, you see. And that's what it's all about, isn't it – looking after our world for generations to come?'

Sue remained silent and watched Leo intently. Caroline was a little surprised, given the diametrically opposed views expressed in their previous, good-natured disagreement, to see a look of sympathy on her face.

'There may be things we can do here, Leo,' she said softly. 'Even if we can't halt the project we can probably force changes – a run off, rather than a standard dam design, for example that will minimise the impact on fish stocks. We know about these things. I'll call Caroline tomorrow to get more detail if I may and we will get involved on your behalf.'

'Would you?' Leo said. 'That would be kind. I'm grateful to both of you for your concern.'

'Don't mention it, Leo. We really want to work with you. Who knows? Perhaps this will be the start of something more permanent in the future.'

Caroline, who had been quietly sipping her coffee and watching the exchange, didn't at first notice one of the girls from reception slip into the room and discreetly approach her.

'Miss Hartley,' the receptionist whispered in her ear. 'Sorry to interrupt, but I have an urgent telephone call for you.'

Caroline was taken aback. Who could possibly be calling her in the middle of this important meeting? And why had Kelly put the call through?

'It's your mother,' the receptionist continued apologetically. 'She insisted.'

Caroline felt a rising panic. Something serious must have happened. Her mother rarely called her at work.

'Everything alright?' Leo asked, reading her expression.

'I think so,' she replied with more confidence than she felt. 'If you will just excuse me, I must take an urgent call.'

With that, she hurried from the room.

'What is it, Mother? Are you OK?' she said as soon as she was handed the phone.

'I couldn't be better. Wonderful news, dear,' Janet Hartley replied. 'I just had to tell you. Vernon Cartwright's been arrested. Evidently he's been taking bribes from developers for years, just like I always said.'

'Are you sure, Mum?'

'Absolutely certain, dear. Everyone is talking about it.' And, you'll never believe it, they've found the money. The money he stole from your father. He had it in a secret account in Jersey.'

'So that means—'

'Yes, it does,' interrupted her mother excitedly, 'the bank's not going to take the cottage. I can stay put. Isn't it marvellous?'

Caroline was stunned by the unexpected turn of events.

'Thank you so much,' continued Janet, 'your father would be so proud of you. You've obviously got friends in high places.'

'No, Mum. I can assure you, it was nothing to do with me,' Caroline protested.

'Oh come on… you're too modest, but thank you anyway. I must be off now. Some of the neighbours are coming round for a little celebration. Goodbye.'

Caroline slowly replaced the receiver, as she digested this wholly unexpected news.

Back in the dining room, Sue was pointing a well-manicured finger at the Canaletto.

'… and for the price of that piece of wall decoration, you could provide permanent, clean drinking water for twenty million people in the Developing World.' Caroline noticed how relaxed and at ease Leo was as he indulged in good humoured banter with his guest. Gone was any sign of tension.

'Yes, that's as may be,' Leo said, taking a long sip of coffee before continuing. 'But how would you ensure that the money reaches the needy and doesn't get diverted into the pockets of corrupt government officials? Believe me, if I thought every penny would be put to good use, I'd personally package that painting up for you to take home with you today.' Then he added with a smile, 'It's a particular favourite of our Chairman, mind you, so I'd have some explaining to do.'

'Well said, Leo,' van der Linden replied, laughing. 'I think we may well take you up on that offer. Corruption is a massive problem to others, but not to us. I run Eleventh Hour and every payment has to be authorised by me personally,' he said patting his huge chest earnestly. 'But perhaps this is a subject for another day. I think we should now take our leave as I am sure you have important work to do. I've so enjoyed our lunch today. Thank you!'

'Likewise,' replied Leo, smiling broadly.

He rose smartly from the table to pull back Sue's chair. She gently placed a hand on his arm as he did this and smiled up at him.

'I can't remember being so looked after. Leo, you may be an absolute philistine when it comes to the world's energy problems, but you're a very charming host.'

They all laughed. Sue and Leo left the room together, with the other two close behind. The lunch had been a great success. Although no actual business had been discussed, Leo and the Green Giant had enjoyed an easy rapport. Caroline liked van der Linden's style: he didn't push, he didn't demand and, most of all, he didn't try to sell. That was refreshingly different from the *modus operandi* of investment bankers, who were all driven by a simple maxim: 'you eat what you kill'. Whatever they said and whatever they did was always about a deal they wanted to do.

Before the visitors left, van der Linden met Caroline's eyes and smiled.

'Everything OK?' he asked.

'More than OK, Edward. That call was from my mother. She can stay in her cottage. Everything has been sorted.'

A smile lit up his massive face.

'I told you it would work out, didn't I? Never give up on these things, Caroline.'

As he said this, he patted her on the back in a gesture of solidarity. But he didn't ask for any more information, which seemed odd. Caroline smiled back and said no more. What a welcome turn of events. Perhaps her luck had changed.

CHAPTER 15

The young detective was deep in conversation with a doctor, who kept looking over his shoulder. The detective on the other hand was trained to be discreet and just shot the occasional glance in Harold's direction. Harold, for his part, was pretending to be asleep as he strained to hear what they were saying.

They were talking about him. He knew that. He had been drifting in and out of consciousness for a few hours now and every time he awoke, more feeling had returned to his muscles. He still had a thumping headache, but there was little doubt that he was well on the mend. They'd taken him off the ventilator some time ago when it became apparent that he could breathe unaided. He'd tried wiggling his toes five minutes previously, but the movement had attracted the detective's attention so he'd stopped. The poor lad had been struggling to stay awake for the last hour or so and had it not been for the doctor's unexpected appearance, Harold was sure that he would have finally succumbed.

He cursed the doctor under his breath. He needed the detective to fall asleep and then he would make his escape. He was pretty sure he could walk and he had caught a glimpse of his clothes in the cabinet next to his bed when the nurse had put something away. So he planned to grab them on his way out. He was determined to get away, before someone came to finish him off.

The doctor looked over again to check he was still asleep.

'I'm puzzled,' he whispered under his breath. 'He doesn't seem to be recovering uniformly. His iris reflex and pupil dilation are perfectly normal. So I can't understand why his limbs are still not functioning properly.'

Hargreaves darted a suspicious look at the patient, instinctively alert to anything out of the ordinary. Something wasn't quite right. He had seen the old man's eyelids quivering as if he was trying to watch them without fully opening his eyes. Also, he was sure that he had seen his legs moving under the blankets a few minutes ago. The old man was faking it. He was pretty sure of that. But why?

As he mulled this over, the bank of monitors behind the bed, with their undulating lines and flickering green numbers, caught his eye.

'Doc, does the heart rate change between sleep and full consciousness?'

'Yes, generally the heart rate will fall to around fifty-two in standard non-REM sleep from seventy-two beats a minute when someone is fully conscious and alert.'

They both looked at the monitor. It showed sixty-eight beats and rising.

'And when someone is anxious, the heart rate increases, right?'

The monitor jumped to seventy. Yes, the old man was definitely awake.

At that moment the door swung open and in marched DCI Cavey.

'Everything OK?' he asked, on seeing the two of them in deep conversation.

Hargreaves moved close to his superior and lowered his voice to just above a whisper. 'Yes, fine sir, except Grandpa is pretending to be asleep and seems to be trying to fool us into thinking he isn't getting better.'

'Probably scared,' said Cavey in a barely audible mumble.

'Or trying to prolong his stay in a nice warm bed?' added Hargreaves, noting that the heart monitor now read a very wakeful seventy-two beats per minute.

Cavey approached the bed, before turning back to his detective constable and the doctor.

'Do we have a name?'

They shook their heads. Cavey turned back to address the old man.

'You're probably a little scared and confused,' he said slowly. 'You're in hospital. The soup you drank last night was poisoned, but the doctors and nurses here have saved your life.'

No reaction. The heart monitor clicked up to seventy-three.

'I know you can hear me. We all know you're awake.'

The old man screwed his eyes up more tightly in a childlike effort to emphasise that he was in fact fast asleep. When he realised he was fooling no one, he slowly opened one then another bloodshot eye and looked sheepishly up at the three faces staring down at him.

'Thank you,' said Cavey. 'You have absolutely nothing to worry about. First of all, what's your name?'

"Arold.' His voice came out hoarse. "Arold. But… but… tterworth.'

Cavey looked at the doctor enquiringly, who nodded his consent for them to continue.

'Take it slowly, Harold,' said Cavey. 'Have a drink; it will help.'

The detective constable filled a plastic cup with water from the jug on the bedside table, but Harold decided not to reach out to take the drink. Perhaps it suited him to keep them guessing as to the extent of his recovery. Perhaps he simply didn't trust them.

Hargreaves reached down and, putting a hand behind the old man's head, gently lifted it and tipped the cup to his dry lips. Harold took two gulps and managed to swallow, but some of the water dribbled out from the corners of his mouth, since he still hadn't regained full muscle control.

'What 'appen'd to Seamus?' he croaked.

They didn't understand.

'Seamus … he was with me …'

Now Cavey knew what he was asking. 'I'm sorry, Harold. He didn't make it. You're the only one who did.'

The heart monitor moved up another notch to seventy-five.

'Who did this, Harold? Did you see their face?'

Harold nodded submissively. Tears welled up in his eyes and ran down his cheeks and the length of his bulbous red nose before dropping onto the starched white sheets.

'What did they look like, Harold?'

Cavey's voice was gentle and cajoling, but Harold did not reply. He just sobbed pathetically, his eyes tightly shut in an effort to blot out the brutal world that surrounded him.

The doctor moved protectively to his bedside and pressed the buzzer for the nurse.

'I think we should leave it there for now, gentlemen. The patient needs some rest.'

'Just a couple more questions?' replied Cavey urgently, raising his hand in the air. He was close to a breakthrough. Harold had seen the killer and could give them a description and he needed that information. But the doctor was emphatic.

'Sorry Inspector, you can continue later on but you must appreciate that this man is still very sick.'

Cavey conceded with a nod. He wasn't going to win this argument.

'Stay with him and don't let him out of your sight for a second,' he said to DC Hargreaves as he headed for the door. 'I want to know what he saw!'

A meeting with the Commissioner awaited; following the shambolic press conference, Sir Geoffrey was unlikely to be in good humour.

★

Back at the bank, Caroline met Kelly moving fast up the corridor in the opposite direction to her desk. She had a scared rabbit air about her, as if she did not know where she was going but was not comfortable remaining where she was before. This proved to be very much the case.

'Tom's back,' she said, a little breathlessly.

'Why?' asked Caroline uneasily. Tom was scheduled to be up at Silverstone all day and Caroline couldn't think why he would return to the office so soon. Kelly shrugged and shook her head as she shuffled past, quite obviously not wanting to stop.

'I dunno,' she said over her shoulder as she headed for the sanctuary of the staff restaurant. 'But he's going ape at the moment. Someone was getting a proper ear bashing on the phone when I left. I'd stay away if I were you. You know what he can be like.'

As Caroline approached the office, Tom's voice was clearly audible. He sounded very angry indeed. The rest of the corporate affairs team – those who were brave enough to remain at their desks, that is – looked uncomfortable. Tom was a renowned bully and they knew that there was a good chance that when he finished his telephone rant, he would come looking for a victim and would regard them all as fair game under the circumstances.

But Caroline's confidence was still buoyed by her lunchtime meeting. After all, she and the bank's CEO had just jointly entertained one of the world's most renowned philanthropists, a man who ran a company reputed to hold liquid assets well in excess of US$25 billion. She wasn't going to cower at her desk outside Tom's office like the others. She was a senior member of staff and at that moment felt like one.

With a final flurry of curses, Tom slammed the phone down, which Caroline took as her cue to walk casually into his office.

'Tom. You're back.'

'Yes, of course I'm back,' he snapped. 'What's this? A stating-the-bleeding-obvious contest!'

His jaw jutted forward aggressively. He was usually scruffy but today, even by his own low sartorial standards, he was a dishevelled mess. Whenever he was on the phone, in the midst of a 'difficult conversation', he had a habit of rubbing his hair and scratching his flaky scalp. This had the same general effect on his coiffure as a ride in an open-top sports car. Today, he had also undone his shirt's top button and loosened his tie. Half rolled-up sleeves and dark sweat stains under the arms completed a look that was pure Detective Colombo.

Caroline kept her cool. Seeing Tom's 'morning after' appearance only bolstered her confidence.

'Yes, but why are you here?'

She kept her voice steady, but her tone was a little patronising and subtly entreated him not to be difficult, which was a futile plea in his current frame of mind and only served to fuel his simmering rage.

'Well,' continued Tom. 'There I was minding my own business up at Silverstone as planned when I received a call from an old journalist contact. He's a good sort and owes me large, so he wanted to tip me off that a certain newspaper is trailing an explosive story about corruption and nepotism in high places at Montagu Steinhart.'

Caroline felt her spirits sag. Her attempt to have the story shelved by Jack had obviously failed. It was still going ahead. She must have shown her disappointment in some unconscious way, as Tom instantly went on the offensive.

'So I hightailed it back here to do what you should have done a while ago and—'

'What do you mean by that?' interrupted Caroline, still willing to fight her corner.

'I mean, Ms Hartley, that I called someone senior at the paper and told them that if they did not desist from rumour mongering I would be compelled to sue them for every penny they have and then for good measure, I'd sue them again.'

Tom moved ever closer as he spoke, so that the last few words were shouted directly in her face. She felt his spittle on her cheeks, but stood her ground. It had been an intentionally threatening act, but she refused to be intimidated. They stood in silence, staring at each other, their faces six inches apart for what seemed like an age to Caroline, but must in reality have been no more than twenty seconds.

To her relief, Caroline noticed that they were no longer alone. In the doorway stood Simon from security. One look at his fixed jaw and unblinking stare told her he had witnessed their fiery altercation.

'What do you want?' sneered Tom.

'I was just returning this to Miss Harley,' said Simon, holding up the electronic tablet for him to see.

'Really. Well, I'm sure it hasn't been missed. What did she do, leave it in the khazi?'

'No, she lent it to—'

But Tom didn't want to listen. 'Just leave it on the desk and get out.'

He waved his hand dismissively. But Simon didn't go. He looked over at Caroline and smiled.

'I'll leave it on your desk, if that's OK? Thanks a lot.'

He spoke as if they were the only two in the room. As if, as far as he was concerned, Tom didn't exist. He was as charming as ever and seemed totally indifferent to Tom's rudeness. Caroline smiled back, fortified by his goodwill. Then, with a polite nod, Simon turned around and walked from the office without so much as a glance in Tom's direction.

'Arrogant bastard,' muttered Tom when he was sure Simon was out of earshot. 'Don't know who he thinks he is, but someone should remind him of his place in the food chain. Not far above bloody plankton, that's where he fits in.'

'And you're the man to tell him, are you?'

Caroline was surprised at her own boldness, but it seemed to do the trick. Tom stared back, with the air of a petulant schoolboy, for once unsure of what to say. Caroline took this as her cue to leave too. There was no point in hanging around when Tom simply wanted to fight.

'We'll finish this later,' he yelled after her.

But she didn't acknowledge his words, didn't even break her stride, she just kept going. The tablet was on her desk with a yellow post-it note stuck to its screen: 'Call me if you need a chat. I'm a good listener. Simon.' And underneath the message he had printed his mobile number.

*

DCI Cavey had never seen Sir Geoffrey Collins so angry. The meeting was brief and the message simple. Find who did this and arrest them – fast! Sir Geoffrey was still smarting from the press conference fiasco. He had already personally telephoned the newspaper to complain that Stuart Heyworth had broken the reporting embargo on the London killings. But his mood had not been improved by the proprietor's implicit support for his maverick employee. No doubt he had sensed the Commissioner's job was on the line, which gave him a coward's courage.

'John, before you go,' Sir Geoffrey added as Cavey was preparing to leave. 'We've known each other for what, fifteen, sixteen years?'

'Near on twenty,' interrupted the detective, knowing where this conversation was going.

'My goodness, is it twenty years? Anyway, you know that it doesn't get much bigger or uglier than this one. I'm sorry, but if you don't deliver, I will have to instruct Duncan Gravelle to appoint Greg Simpson as head of this enquiry. The Home Secretary is already pushing for an expanded team under Greg's control.'

'Understood,' said Cavey, noticing that his friend and, up until that moment, his main sponsor within the force, was finding it difficult to look him in the eye. He hoped the decision hadn't already been made. In his distinguished career, he had rarely failed. This case, with its tangle of conflicting leads, frustrated him more than he cared to admit. He didn't feel betrayed, he felt sympathy for Sir Geoffrey. He knew how humiliated he was and could well imagine the remorseless pressure he would be experiencing from the politicians.

'How long have I got?' he asked, without turning to look at his superior.

'Not long. A week maybe. Perhaps two if we keep up this charade that one of the hostel workers was responsible for the poisoning. But after this morning, we both know that the press can now go the whole hog and report on the other murders, linking the two.' Sir Geoffrey's voice was hollow and he was finding it difficult to disguise his wretchedness.

'There is one thing, Sir Geoffrey,' added Cavey. He hadn't intended divulging it, but decided to offer a crumb of comfort before leaving his friend.

Sir Geoffrey didn't answer but just raised his eyebrows as an invitation to continue.

'At the scene of at least two of the murders, the killer has left a sign, a kind of calling card.'

'What do you mean, "sign"?'

'Well, we've found a number, the number seventy-two, written nearby.'

Sir Geoffrey digested this fresh information in silence, he may have been Police Commissioner but he was first and foremost a policeman and one with an enviable crime solving record at that.

'Whoever they are, they're flagging it as their work,' he said, deep in thought. 'But it's a strange development. Why now? Why start to label your crimes in this way at this stage in the game?'

'Quite,' added Cavey, 'unless it's an indication of their mental state.'

'Meaning?'

'Well, things are escalating, as we have seen. It's almost as if there is an extra urgency to the killings. Like time is running out and they are becoming more cavalier.'

They both fell silent as they considered his words before the Commissioner asked the inevitable question:

'What does it mean though, seventy-two; seventy-two what?'

'We don't know, sir, but we're working on it.'

'Perhaps it refers to a year, something that happened in 1972,' offered Sir Geoffrey, before suggesting, with mild excitement, 'golf, par is seventy-two strokes...'

'We're looking at everything, sir,' interrupted Cavey, who had been through numerous suggestions with his team already. He was now keen to get on with his day and return to the hospital where he could continue questioning their valuable witness.

He left Sir Geoffrey at his desk, still running through an increasing list of possibilities for the mystery number. As he passed through New Scotland Yard's reception area, he noticed, on a large plasma television suspended from the ceiling that Sky News was reporting on the incident. His own face flashed on the screen as did a much younger version of the man he had just left. The sound was turned down, but it was easy to tell what was being said. Now the cameras switched to the park in Vauxhall where the anchor-man was interviewing local residents. The park appeared much bigger in the daylight and looked familiar. Then Cavey remembered why. It was from here in the 1990s that the IRA mounted one of its most audacious terrorist acts: a mortar attack on the modern MI6 building just across the road. He stopped in his tracks. The MI6 building was simply bristling with surveillance equipment: cameras, CCTV, sound-activated microphones and heaven knows what else. The building was just down the road from the Christian Mission. They must have picked something up!

Cavey dialled Sir Geoffrey's number on his mobile. He needed his clout to ensure that the spooks co-operated. He'd had dealings with them before and remembered how reluctant they were to help and how ready they were to retreat behind a wall of secrecy when they wanted out of an inquiry. This time should be different, though. They were, after all, dealing with the most prolific serial killer in Britain.

The news report was now showing a female reporter, microphone in hand, standing outside another building. It too looked vaguely familiar to DCI Cavey. Sir Geoffrey was unavailable, so he started to leave a message. Then, with a jolt, he realised where she was. He looked more closely. Yes, there was no doubt about it. She was outside St Thomas' Hospital! Newswire text, scrolling slowly across the bottom of the screen, confirmed his fears. They read 'Police hunting hostel worker. Over forty dead in mass poisoning. One survivor'. There had been a leak. Now everyone would know of Harold's lucky escape.

CHAPTER 16

Harold had just finished a hearty lunch. Hospital food may not be to everyone's liking, but to a street dweller like him every mouthful was like the finest Beluga caviar. He drained a cup of tea – with four sugars – and felt something close to physical contentment. Mentally though he was still on edge and definitely wary of the policemen who were watching him constantly. The young, friendly detective had been replaced by a rather grim-faced man in his late thirties, who smelt of stale tobacco and hadn't even attempted conversation. He also had a rather annoying habit of constantly clearing his throat as if he was about to speak but never did. Harold didn't like him at all.

'So how are we this afternoon?' asked the nurse in a strong antipodean accent.

Probably a New Zealander, thought Harold. He'd been there once when he was in the Merchant Navy. Lovely place. A bit wet though. The people were friendly but a little quiet and reserved. The nurse started to examine him, pulling up his eyelids and then slapping his cheeks to check his sensitivity.

'Feel that?'

'Too bloody right I did! Steady on dear!' Harold protested.

'Sorry mate,' she replied.

Australian, he thought. *Definitely Australian!*

The nurse bustled out into the corridor leaving the two men alone in the room together. Every time Harold looked up, the policeman was staring at him and after a while even when he closed his eyes he imagined he could still feel the detective's eyes on him. They were watching him closely. How long before they made their move? he wondered, feeling the panic rising within him. They were obviously just waiting for the chance to bump him off. It was the government behind the killings, they all knew that. They'd killed Seamus and they wouldn't rest until they did for him too! He needed to come up with a plan, and fast. It would be a good idea, he decided, if he were to take his clothes and hide them somewhere outside the room. Then, during the night, or when an opportunity presented itself, he could slip out, get dressed and make his getaway.

He half opened one of his blood-shot eyes and watched the sour-faced copper yawn again. Like Hargreaves before him, he was fighting hard to stay awake. Harold watched him shake his head in an effort to rid himself of the tiredness that threatened to overwhelm him and then he settled back in the comfortable chair with leaden eyes. Harold feigned sleep and listened to the rhythm of the policeman's breathing, just waiting for his cue. It wouldn't be long now, he sensed. Minutes passed. Five, ten, fifteen and still the policeman resisted. Then he heard a shuffling noise as his guard, drunk with lethargy, struggled to his feet. Risking a surreptitious glance to find out what was happening, Harold saw the policeman plunge his hand into his jacket pocket, pull out a packet of cigarettes and then head for the door. This was the moment he had been waiting for and without wasting any time, Harold slid out of bed, grabbed his clothes and with an unsteady step, followed the detective out of the door.

Wearing his outdoor shoes and dressed in an orange towelling robe with no belt that he'd found hanging by the door, he cut a rather comical figure as he padded down the corridor. He wasn't really sure where he was going but it was good to be out of the room and away from watchful eyes. The gown kept gaping open, so he was forced to hold it closed with his left hand whilst his right arm clamped his clothes to his body out of sight, underneath the gown. He looked furtive and awkward and it must have been quite obvious that he was hiding something under the garment but no one noticed. Everyone he passed was too busy or preoccupied to give a second glance to an old man with a big nose in an ill-fitting orange dressing gown.

When he had gone some thirty paces from the room he spied the Gents toilets to one side of the corridor and decided to head there. Perhaps he could find a cupboard in which to hide his clothes somewhere in the washrooms, he thought. Looking up he noticed a nurse approaching, dressed unflatteringly in a green blouse and loose grey slacks and carrying a bag of saline. 'She looks like a man in those trousers,' he muttered to himself, 'what's wrong with a nice starched uniform like nurses used to wear?' He stared at the floor, keen not to attract attention but as they passed by each other he darted a quick sideways glance. The nurse did likewise and for a second their eyes locked. Harold froze, and then shrank back against the wall. He'd looked into those eyes before and they had haunted his every waking moment since. The nurse carried on walking in the direction he had just come from, unhurried and without missing a step. But Harold knew. He had seen recognition in those cruel eyes. He'd also detected a look of something else: excitement. An icy fear gripped him. He had to get away. He had to leave immediately, otherwise...

*

DCI Cavey hurried towards the hospital's main entrance. As he crossed the car park a growing sense of foreboding made him break into a gentle trot. He needed to reach the old man before any harm came to him. The moment he had seen the news report filmed outside the hospital he had realised that his only witness was in jeopardy. If he had seen the report, so too most likely had the killer. How the press had found out that someone had survived the poisoning was at this stage immaterial, he would look into that later, at that moment Harold's safety was his prime concern. A call to the network had ascertained that the footage had been shown on all the channel's news bulletins since 07:30. He looked at his watch. It showed 13:35; there'd been ample time for the killer to plan their next move.

Harold had seen who dispensed the fatal brew at the Mission, which made him a vital witness. He just had to be encouraged to talk. But that would be difficult if he was dead, thought Cavey as he sprinted up the steps outside the hospital entrance.

As he reached the top he was confronted by the sight of a man in blue overalls, balancing precariously on a stepladder, examining the CCTV camera over the front doors.

'What's the problem?' snapped Cavey, instinctively whipping out his police ID card as he spoke.

'Camera's on the blink,' was the puzzled reply. 'The whole lot went down twenty minutes ago.'

CCTV cameras mysteriously not working. *This had an all too familiar ring to it*, thought Cavey, barging through the doors without another word.

A security guard blocked his path, attracted by his sudden burst of energy.

'Police,' he yelled, flashing his ID again. 'Sound the alarm.'

'What alarm? We don't have an alarm!'

Cavey pushed past the guard and stuck his elbow through the glass of the nearest fire alarm. A second later the air was pierced by a penetrating siren.

He decided to take the emergency stairs, rather than waiting for the lift to take him to the first floor. Once there, he dashed along the corridor, narrowly avoiding a collision with a nurse in ill-fitting grey trousers moving purposefully in the opposite direction. DCI Cavey trusted his instincts and he knew before he reached the room that all was not well. He barged shoulder first through the door, sending it crashing against the wall and then stood incredulous as his eyes swept the empty room. A second later, the door flew open again and in rushed the sour-faced detective.

'Where is he?' shouted Cavey at his stunned subordinate. 'My orders were to stay with him at all times. So, I'll ask you again, where is he?'

'I don't know, sir,' was the bewildered reply as the man frantically scanned the room in the desperate hope that he would somehow discover his charge hiding somewhere.

'He can't have gone far. I only nipped out for a moment.'

The Australian nurse had joined them in the room.

'He's probably gone for a walk or something,' she offered matter-of-factly.

Then she picked up the end of the drip which was lying loose on the bed and tutted loudly.

'He shouldn't have taken this out by himself. He could get an infection.' Then her expression changed to one of puzzlement.

Cavey saw the look. 'What is it?'

She squeezed the saline bag, without replying, turning it around on its stand.

'I don't understand. There's no date.'

'What do you mean?' shot back Cavey, homing in on her obvious confusion.

'All bags have to have an expiry date printed on their side and a signature on a sticker on the back to show they've been checked. This doesn't have either.'

She stopped for a second then her eyes widened in surprise.

'What's going on?' she shouted. 'This isn't one of ours at all!'

'Leave it alone and stop touching it then!' commanded Cavey.

Cavey's eyes then alighted on the clipboard at the bottom of the bed which showed a record of Harold's treatment. There in large red script was scrawled a number; seventy-two.

'And you,' he shouted, turning his attention to the startled detective. 'Get out there and find our man!'

At the main entrance, the CCTV cameras crackled back to life, much to the satisfaction of the security technician who was convinced that it was the result of something he had just done. He folded away his stepladder and swung it around under his arm, narrowly avoiding an old man who had just tottered unsteadily through the swing doors.

'Mind yer back mate!' he shouted.

But the old man didn't so much as look his way. He just walked straight on out of the gates, turned left and headed in the direction of Waterloo Station.

CHAPTER 18

Caroline had been thinking about Simon's offer all night. He'd left his number and it seemed ungracious not to at least contact him to thank him for coming to her aid. He was an attractive man, and having witnessed the way he handled Tom Beresford she liked him even more now. She grabbed her mobile phone and punched in the number he had left the day before.

He answered immediately.

'Caroline, how nice to hear from you. What can I do for you?' he said in a clear, cultured voice.

'I just wanted to thank you for your support yesterday. Things were getting a little fraught as you probably noticed.'

'Yes, that was quite a barney you were having. Is he always like that?'

''Fraid so,' she replied, enjoying the luxury of discussing her problems with a sympathetic listener.

'You shouldn't let him bully you like that though. It's not right.'

'I know,' she replied flatly, 'but there's not much I can do about it really.'

'Hmm maybe. You know, I reckon he's afraid of you.'

She laughed.

'I can assure you that's not the way it is at all.'

'No, hear me out Caroline,' he replied defensively. 'I think he can see how good you are at your job and he realises that the only way he can score points is by asserting his authority over you. He's the new boy, remember and in my experience the people who shout the loudest are often the most insecure.'

Perhaps he had a point, she thought.

'So what should I do then?'

'Do what you're best at. Use your friends, use your network. Show him just how good you are at your job. This problem you've got, the one you were arguing about yesterday, find someone to help you sort it out. Believe me, Beresford will be all over you if you do something that makes him look good.'

It was a good plan but before they could talk further, she spied Tom lolloping towards her from across the office.

'Look thanks Simon, you've been a great help,' she said hurriedly, 'I've got to go now'. Then she ended the call and as Tom approached, picked up her electronic tablet and started to read the latest news headlines in an attempt to look casual.

'Still playing with our little toy are we?' was Tom's opening remark of the day. A straightforward 'good morning' would have been too much to hope for. He then walked past her desk and slammed his office door behind him without another word. She continued to read the news, and in particular an article about the mass poisoning at the Vauxhall Mission. The piece made reference to the killings she had alerted Jack to. This probably explained why he hadn't come back to her, she thought with a sinking heart. The story was out now, so she'd lost her leverage.

She hadn't actually planned to spend time reading the news but she was interested to know what was happening with the murder cases and anyway, at that moment, the last thing she felt inclined to do was stop doing something Tom objected to. He had riled her as he no doubt intended.

A minute later, he poked his head out of his office door.

'Are you actually going to do any work today?' he sneered. 'Just put it away and come in here. We need to talk.'

This sounded ominous; his tone was heavy with malicious intent. She walked into the room marshalling her courage, ready for another fight. As usual Tom was sitting behind his big desk. He waved her to a chair opposite him. She knew the game he was playing and turned her chair so she wasn't facing him directly and stretched her long slim legs out in front of her.

This momentarily distracted him, which pleased Caroline.

'So, let's start with yesterday.' He paused and fixed her with a cold stare. 'Don't ever walk out of my office until I say you can. Comprendez?' His tone was threatening as he growled the words.

'Tom, you can't bully people like this. It's illegal,' she protested. She was actually doing quite well she thought, but he cut her off in mid-sentence.

'Don't give me that PC rubbish. If you're not tough enough to play with the big boys dear, you should find something else to do.'

‘I am, I am tough enough,’ she protested lamely, her voice unhelpfully weak and high in pitch.

‘No you’re not. You’re a spoilt, middle class little girl who blubs whenever there’s a problem.’

She stood up to leave.

‘Where are you going?’ he said leaping to his feet and leaning towards her across the desk. ‘I haven’t finished.’

‘Yes you have Tom. Any further discussions will be in the presence of someone from HR.’

‘Have it your own way Caroline. “Back me or sack me” is that it? Go ahead. I can assure you that after the mess you’ve made of this Hubert Dunwoody business you’ll struggle to find supporters in this firm.’ He let the words hang for a few seconds before continuing, ‘I know for a fact that Leo Brooks is very disappointed with you. He told me so himself.’ Caroline felt winded. She couldn’t have answered him, even if she had thought of something to say. She just stared back at him.

‘In fact,’ Tom continued, taking full advantage of her stupefied state. ‘When his name is plastered all over the Sunday Tabloids he’ll probably want to dismiss you personally himself!’

Caroline sagged and put a steadying hand on the desk. He’d won. She was no match for a street fighter like Tom. If she complained to HR, he would tell them she was only complaining to avoid criticism of her bad performance. After all, he had already given her a verbal warning, which would be recorded by now on her HR file. He’d covered all bases; the time to protest had passed. Tom watched the realisation dawn, saw her submission and a crooked smile snaked its way onto his flabby, wet lips.

'Now go and get on with your work,' he said pointing towards the door. Then with a twinkle of sadistic pleasure in his eyes he added: 'I have to say though that this whole business will not look good on your annual appraisal, which if I am not mistaken, is due very shortly.'

Caroline trudged wearily back to her desk. She was beaten, finished. He would give her an 'unsatisfactory' rating in her appraisal which would have the effect of freezing her pay, cancelling her right to an annual bonus and effectively crippling her career at Montagu Steinhart.

The vindictive bastard had won. Then she remembered Simon's words and a spark of hope set her brain racing. Perhaps she could still rescue the situation. 'Solve the problem,' she muttered to herself. If she did that Tom couldn't touch her. 'Use your network,' Simon had urged and as she sat at her desk a plan germinated and took root in her mind. It was risky but she was desperate. She remembered how daunting her mother's predicament had seemed before it was miraculously solved. Perhaps this could be the same. So, picking up the tablet she walked casually towards the client meeting rooms at the far end of the offices, where she would be able to make a call in private.

After finding an empty room she sat down, positioning the tablet in front of her on the table. She paused for a second, steeling herself, then took a deep breath and gently pressed the Eleventh Hour icon on the screen. The device made a soft ringing sound before bursting into life and a second later she was faced with a beaming Edward van der Linden.

'Caroline, this must be telepathy. I was just thinking about you,' he said jauntily.

‘That’s nice, Edward,’ she replied hesitantly, instinctively uncomfortable with what she was doing.

‘Yes, I’m on a plane travelling to St Petersburg to meet with a group of environmentalists and I just can’t seem to strike the right tone in my speech. And I thought to myself “Caroline would know”. ’

‘Well, thank you for that,’ she replied, greatly flattered by the compliment.

‘You see Caroline, since the speech in London and your valuable insights, I’ve realised just how wrong I must have sounded to so many of the audiences I have addressed. I am so busy that I tend to use the same material in different places and now I know that that just isn’t right. Each audience in each country should be viewed as unique and deserve specially tailored material. ’

Caroline watched in silence as a stewardess placed a glass next to van der Linden. He really was on a plane.

‘So what can I do for you?’ he asked taking a sip of his drink.

‘Well, it’s a very delicate matter,’ she started, suddenly acutely aware of the sensitivity of what she was about to divulge. A week – a day ago even – this kind of conversation would have been anathema to her as it breached all the rules of confidentiality. Indeed since it centred on a scandal involving the bank’s CEO, what she was about to say had the potential to affect the bank’s share price. She was, she suddenly realised, about to pass on ‘inside information’ which was a criminal offence. She paused, took a deep breath, then spoke.

‘The *Sunday Times* are planning to run a highly damaging

article on Leo Brooks and I wondered whether you had a way of ...'

'Stopping them?' he interjected before she could finish.

'Yes,' she said weakly. All of a sudden not so sure this was such a good idea.

There was a moment's silence. Caroline could clearly hear the whine of the 'plane's engines. When the South African finally spoke his tone was more serious and business-like.

'Caroline, I'm not sure what I can do. I really like Leo but ...' his voice tailed off without finishing the sentence, before continuing: 'surely you and your mighty bank can handle unfounded allegations against senior management. That is, if they are unfounded,' he added staring intently at Caroline in an obvious effort to gauge her reaction. She didn't flinch.

'Look, you'd better explain exactly what this is all about.'

Caroline then told him the full story. Everything.

'Well, I can fully appreciate your problem,' he said when she had finished, 'but I'm still not sure how I can be of any help.'

At that moment another voice spoke out from within the room, directly behind Caroline.

'I think it would be a good idea to end that call now Miss Hartley.'

Caroline spun round in her chair and her eyes widened in shock when she saw who it was. Sylvia Hetherington, Head of Human Resources was standing by the door, staring at her with an angry look on her face.

'Tom Beresford said you wanted to see me urgently. But

first of all I think you had better explain what's going on here and who you are discussing such a sensitive matter with.'

Caroline cut the connection without saying another word, fully aware that she had probably just sacked herself.

PART 2

CHAPTER 19

'Yes, that's him!' exclaimed DC Hargreaves pointing his finger excitedly at the screen. 'That's Harold, I'm sure of it.'

The team crowded closer to the monitor to view the grainy image. They'd been at it for half an hour now and had viewed the footage shot from the reactivated camera at the hospital's entrance ten times already.

DCI Cavey stared intently at the screen as he watched a ghostly figure walk falteringly out of the hospital swing doors and allowed himself the rare luxury of a thin smile. Yes, Hargreaves was correct, it was Harold Butterworth. Now he could inform his superiors that their main and, as yet, only witness, was still alive and had not been spirited away from under their noses by the killer. He wondered what had led to Harold's sudden flight. Had he seen something? Or had he just seized the opportunity to slip away when he had been left alone? Whatever the reason, Cavey was glad he had not stayed where he was and become prey to a highly resourceful and brazen murderer.

There were still so many questions that remained unanswered, but Cavey was sure of one fact beyond a shadow of doubt: someone had come to the hospital that day with the intention of finishing off Harold Butterworth, the sole survivor of what was known by the tabloids as: 'The Mission Massacre'.

'OK, quieten down!' he shouted, rapping the table to get everyone's attention. 'Our man is alive and running. Hargreaves, I want you to start reviewing all the footage from cameras on his likely route after he left the hospital. Let's find out where he's going. The rest of you, continue questioning people at the scene. Someone saw something. I want to know who is hunting the old man. Go!'

The team then scattered to embark on their allotted tasks.

Half an hour later, Cavey once again walked through the busy hospital reception area and pushed the entrance doors open. A large camera protruded from the wall above him.

'The camera's fine, sir,' said a voice beside him.

It was Gary Johns, the Met's top communications technician. What Gary didn't know about electronic surveillance really wasn't worth knowing. Cavey had worked with him on a number of occasions and respected his professionalism and particularly liked his understated manner. He was the type of person who got on with the job in hand with the minimum of fuss or drama. Departmental gossip had it that he had learnt his trade in the army. He didn't talk much about that part of his life, so everyone assumed he must have been involved in covert military surveillance or even espionage. Whatever his past, the Met was lucky to have him, as his particular skillset was much in demand these days.

'I've found something. If you would follow me, sir, I'll talk you through it.'

He marched the detective up to a green telecoms box outside. The door was open, revealing the multi-coloured spaghetti of electrical wires.

'It's pretty straightforward really, sir. Someone simply shorted out the wires that carry the picture signal. There ...' He held up a couple of wires as he spoke '... if you look closely, you can see how the wires have been skinned.'

'So it's an easy job, then?' countered Cavey, crouching down to have a closer look inside the box.

'Well, not really, sir, you have to know what you're doing. Locating the correct wires would require a detailed knowledge of this type of system, plus some signal testing equipment.'

'So what you're saying is that I couldn't do this sort of thing?'

'Exactly. Whoever did this, knew their onions.'

'How long would it have taken?'

Gary stood in silent contemplation for a few seconds, gently stroking the stubble on his chin before answering.

'Five, ten minutes. But they had to come back of course afterwards.'

'What do you mean?' said Cavey, puzzled.

'Well, the system was immobilised and then reactivated.'

'Of course it was!' Cavey exclaimed, the detail of the plan now becoming clearer to him. 'They wanted it to look as if the victim had simply succumbed to the original poison. The lab tells me that the saline bag we found in the room was laced with adrenalin.'

'Adrenalin?' repeated Johns.

'Yes. It's a very subtle poison. Notoriously difficult to detect, in fact because it is a natural substance it is rarely spotted or even tested for.'

Johns then spoke, 'I get it now: so just in case we suspected foul play they needed to ensure that there was no footage of the mystery nurse, so they knocked out the cameras for just long enough to get into the hospital, fix up the contaminated drip and then once outside, they simply reactivated the system.'

'Clever,' said Cavey.

'Very clever. It's a good thing you were on the ball, sir, otherwise they'd have succeeded,' added Johns, closing the door of the telecoms box.

'Quite,' replied Cavey, looking at the ground pensively. 'The question is though, did the same person immobilise the cameras before entering the hospital to plant the spiked saline bag? Or are we looking for two people?'

'If I may, sir,' said Johns respectfully.

'Of course Gary, fire away.'

'Well, sir, as I said before, for starters, you would have to be an expert in electronics to take out the cameras. On top of that, you would also have to be a pretty cool customer to then slip into the hospital, find your target, make the hit then get out before reactivating the cameras and making your getaway. You're talking James Bond here or otherwise two operatives at least, maybe even a team.'

Cavey said nothing. Gary John's words had triggered a plethora of new possibilities in his mind, which at that moment was sifting through hundreds of what-if scenarios.

He'd considered the possibility that all the killings were not by the same person before. But a team? This suddenly made a lot of sense and went some way to explaining the widely varying descriptions of the killer, it was a shocking prospect.

The speed of response and the cleverness of the plan suggested that they were up against an organised and professional foe, but that did not in itself mean that more than one person was involved.

'What about ex-Special Forces?' he asked Johns.

'A definite possibility,' replied the engineer. 'They are all trained in electronics these days and the rest would be a walk in the park for an ex-SAS or SBS.'

So, were they up against a single killer who possessed the skills of 007 or were they hunting a well-organised team? As he walked slowly back to the entrance of St Thomas' Hospital, Cavey pondered these possibilities. Whichever it was, he concluded ruefully, he needed to find Harold before they did. The old man was undoubtedly in grave danger and he was also still their only useful lead.

By now Johns was carefully packing his tools away.

'Seventy-two, what does that mean to you?' said Cavey, turning back to address the engineer. He thought he might as well ask, as, given his background, he might have a different perspective from others in the force.

'Right, yes, I heard about that,' Johns shouted back. Cavey wasn't surprised he knew about the mystery number as his team had been discussing it all day, each one offering ever more obscure suggestions. It certainly introduced an intriguing new element to the case. Why, he wondered had the killer only started to leave the number at the crime scenes this late in the day? Was he scenting his territory – identifying it as his work? Or was he goading his pursuers with a gesture of patronising confidence that said: 'You're not doing very well, so here's a little clue!' Cavey didn't like that thought.

'Don't really know, sir,' replied Johns. 'Seventy-two killings?

'No we're well north of that figure already.'

Seventy-two degrees is room temperature,' continued Johns. 'It's also the limit for characters per line in computing.'

'No,' said Cavey, 'not personal enough. This number has personal significance.'

Johns shrugged to indicate he had no further suggestions. 'I'll keep thinking,' he offered, then picked up his bag and walked back to his van.

Seventy-two. What did it mean?

CHAPTER 20

Just as Caroline arrived home, carrying the iconic cardboard box containing the contents of her hastily emptied desk, Kelly called her on her mobile.

'What the hell's happening?' her friend whispered.

'I'll fill you in later, but first of all, what are they saying about me?'

Caroline was unable to hide the urgency in her voice. She was desperate to find out how her sudden departure was being explained. This information was vital as it would give her a good steer on her chances of survival.

'That you've decided to leave to pursue other interests,' Kelly replied.

Caroline's spirits sagged. There was no way back. In her imagination, she had hoped for a happy ending in which Leo Brooks, on hearing the circumstances of her breach of confidentiality rules, had intervened because she had been acting in his best interests. But now this seemed patently absurd. There was to be no redemption. If they were already telling people about her departure, she was gone.

'Oh Caroline!' Kelly whined softly. 'I don't know what's

going on, but I'm gonna miss you. Are you sure there's nothing I can do to help?'

Kelly's simple expression of loyalty and compassion unfroze Caroline's emotions, which had simply seized up in shock. She gently replaced the handset on its cradle, put her head in her hands and wept tears of total desolation. She now had nothing. Her job, her reputation and her career were all gone in the space of two hours.

A text message alert sounded on her mobile. It was Simon. She dabbed her eyes with a tissue and read: 'Just heard the news. Unbelievable! Call me if you need to talk.' His message made her feel a little less alone. But she knew he could do nothing to help her. This whole thing was actually his fault really, he'd told her to use her network and try to solve the problem herself. But she didn't blame him; neither of them could have anticipated how things would turn out. How would she break the news to her mother? she wondered. How would she explain that the daughter she was so proud of – whom she no doubt told all her friends was a 'high flyer' in the City – was now unemployed and most likely now unemployable. The problem with this kind of termination was that it always stained your record – '*Question*: Reason for leaving last employment? *Answer:* Dismissed for gross misconduct and contravention of insider dealing regulations.' A reference that certainly wouldn't appeal to many future employers!

Just then, her thoughts were interrupted by a low hum that grew progressively louder. The tablet was glowing orange through its green felt cover as she plucked it from her handbag. It continued to pulse in her hand and only stopped when she prodded the flashing Eleventh Hour icon. Edward van der Linden's face filled the screen.

'Just landed Caroline. We were cut off before. Hit some turbulence.'

'Me too,' replied Caroline.

'Perhaps we can continue our discussion. Is this a good time for you?'

She actually laughed out loud at the unfortunate choice of words.

'No, Edward. This is certainly not a good time for me, personally.'

She was unable to hide the emotion in her voice as she spoke, but she really didn't care. His expression changed from one of benign good humour to one of studied concern as he peered intently at her down the video link, looking for clues.

'You've been crying. Tell me what's been happening.'

So she did. After all, she had nothing to lose now. They couldn't fire her twice.

Her account of the explosive end to her employment at Montagu Steinhart didn't take long, though it was punctuated by moments where her emotions got the better of her. But soon enough he understood what had transpired.

'Would it be helpful if I called Leo?' he asked when she had finished.

'That's very kind Edward, but I don't think it would do much good at this stage. I'm afraid the dye is cast.'

'Yes, I suppose it is. I don't understand why you bankers get so hung up on technicalities like this when we all know your whole industry runs on the transfer of information. Don't they say that a grapevine grows best over a Chinese Wall?'

At that moment Caroline wasn't particularly receptive to humour and said nothing. As she continued to watch the screen van der Linden turned to talk to someone else out of view. She heard a muffled conversation but couldn't make out what was being said.

'Look Caroline, I have to disembark now, but let me leave a thought with you. I love your passion, your understanding of people and the intuitive way you operate. Montagu Steinhart's loss may be my gain. There's a job for you here if you want it. I need a Director of Communications. You can write my speeches and help maximise our impact. I was going to suggest this anyway. Think about it and come back to me.'

The offer was so unexpected that she took a few seconds before replying. In any case, she needed to replay his exact words in her mind just to make doubly sure that she was not mistaken. It was a dream outcome. The way things had been going she would have taken the job anyway and resigned from the bank without a second's thought.

'Edward?' she blurted.

His face was still peering at her enquiringly, but the volume of her response startled him and she noticed his eyebrows shoot upwards in surprise. She decided to tone it down a little, taking a deep breath before continuing.

'I can give you my answer straight away. I would love to work for you at Eleventh Hour. In fact, at this moment, I can think of nothing else I'd rather do.'

'Brilliant!' he replied. 'That's settled, then. I have to go now, Caroline. But if I was you, I would get onto them sharpish and resign before they sack you. I'll square it all with Leo Brooks. I need to talk to him anyway.'

The image of his face faded and the screen became blank and lifeless once more. Caroline sat staring at it for some time, afraid that any second the device would leap back to life and the Green Giant would withdraw his offer. He didn't, so a new life dawned for Caroline Hartley.

CHAPTER 21

It was an abnormally dark morning. A mass of slate grey cloud obscured the watery, late September sun which cast a feeble light over the majestic city. Autumn was on its way, there was no mistaking it.

The usual cacophony of engine noise, revving motor scooters and the impatient shrill of car horns greeted John Cavey as he descended the steps outside the Gare du Nord. Traffic chaos was as much a part of modern Paris as roadside cafes and the street artists of Montmartre.

After receiving a call from his old friend Alain Chazot, Capitain de la Sûreté Nationale in Paris, Cavey had gone directly to St Pancras to board the first available Eurostar train. Chazot was a first-class detective and the two of them had collaborated closely on a number of cases in the past with great success. Cavey trusted him implicitly, hence this unscheduled dash to the French capital.

Le Brigade de recherche et d'intervention, Chazot's department, which dealt primarily with serious cases of robbery, gang crime and kidnapping, was a unit of the French Ministry of the Interior. It was based in the historic Préfecture de Police building on Ile de la Cité. This imposing headquarters was also a tourist attraction in its own right and a far cry from the nondescript modern glass building that housed the UK's senior police hierarchy at New Scotland Yard.

The Frenchman was waiting outside the building when Cavey arrived. To Cavey's relief, he chose an enthusiastic handshake over the more traditional French greeting of a kiss on each cheek. He was a small wiry man with a thatch of wavy blond hair which, uncharacteristically for a Frenchman, was not fashionably cut. It gave him a slightly untidy appearance. Beyond that, there was nothing particularly remarkable about Alain Chazot apart from his trademark bow tie. Today he was wearing a bright purple specimen with large white polka dots. It shouted at his rather drab check sports jacket, but that was no doubt the intention. Here was a man of apparent contradictions: small and ordinary to look at, yet possessing the mental fortitude to head up one of the toughest departments in the French police force.

'Good to see you my old friend,' said Chazot, putting his arm around the British detective's shoulder as he guided him through the spectacular domed entrance of the Prefecture. Inside, Cavey noted that the building was unexpectedly modern as Chazot led him down a series of long corridors. There was not a trace of the civil service decor one would have expected upon entering this fine historic building, complete with its own museum and the actual prison cell that once held Marie Antoinette. But time had moved on, it looked, smelt, sounded and most importantly, functioned, as a modern office complex.

Chazot's department occupied a floor in the east wing of the building which overlooked the Seine with a view of Notre Dame in the distance. Not that that mattered one iota, because Chazot's team were unlikely to spend time taking in the view. The offices had a more lived-in look than those Cavey had just seen. Against one wall stood a stack of cardboard boxes and he noticed the carpet was spotted with coffee stains. There were twenty or so people in the immediate vicinity and a definite buzz that reminded Cavey of his own team at work. Chazot showed Cavey into his office. It was functional but nothing special. A large pile of paper all but covered the surface of a small desk over by the window and Cavey noticed a stack of files lying untidily on the floor nearby. His friend caught his gaze and threw his arms in the air in a very Gallic gesture of exasperation.

'Paper. Everywhere paper. Now we have computers, but what do they do? Produce memos, reports and analysis: more paper!'

Although his speech was heavily accented, Chazot's English was practically flawless, thanks largely to an English university education and the fact that he had completed a year of his police training at Hendon Police Academy.

'Sit, my friend,' he invited, gesturing towards a scruffy but comfortable-looking sofa against the far wall, below a dog-eared map of Paris. 'John, I am so glad you have come to see us today.'

Cavey sat down as instructed, although he was never particularly at ease reclining in comfy chairs, which seemed somehow at odds with serious business. His host meanwhile busied himself extracting two extra strong coffees from an espresso machine on his desk. It smelt good. The French took their coffee very seriously and, at that moment, John Cavey was pleased they did. Eurostar's offering had been worse than usual that morning.

'So, John,' said the French detective, savouring the bitter brew. 'You have a big problem, no?'

'Yes Alain, you're right, we do. Any help you can give us would be invaluable.'

The Frenchman had risen from his chair as Cavey was speaking and grabbed something from his desk. Cavey now saw that it was a series of photographs which the detective spread out on the table in front of him.

'These pictures were taken yesterday in the Bois de Boulogne. A young, as you would say, "courting couple" were looking for a quiet place, away from people and they were unfortunate enough to discover this.'

As he uttered the words, he swept his hand over the photos. Each one showed a corpse, the face hollow and empty in death, with milky, sightless eyes staring heavenward.

'There are five in all. We think they died two nights ago and, as far as we can tell, they died within hours of each other. Probably at the same time.'

'And the cause of death?' asked Cavey, bending over the table and examining the pictures intently with a small magnifying glass handed to him by the Frenchman.

'Two had their throats cut, two were asphyxiated with what was probably a wire ligature (which was not left behind at the scene) and the last was stabbed. It appears that he was trying to escape as there are two wounds, one in the back which punctured his aortic artery and was actually the cause of death, the other in the stomach and lower bowel.'

Cavey winced. A stomach wound was excruciating as it invariably resulted in gastric juices like battery acid flooding the abdomen.

'Who are they?'

'No one! Bums, winos, whatever you like to call them.'

'And the killer or killers?'

'We don't know for sure, but forensic evidence suggests this may be the work of a single assassin. John, you understand this would not usually be my type of case; there are no gangs or professional criminals involved. However ...' he paused, searching for the precise words to use. Cavey sensed a major revelation was about to be made.

'In the light of what is happening in London,' continued Chazot, 'one of our young gendarmes showed great initiative and checked our database for unexplained deaths amongst our city's homeless community over the last three months. There have been fifteen, John. He found fifteen similar cases!'

Cavey's expression was impassive save for a slight tightening of his jaw as he took in the news.

'It appears that without us realising it, your murderer is here, John. Your problem is now our problem too.'

*

Half an hour later, Detective Chief Inspector Cavey was on his way back to London. He dialled DC Hargreaves' number on his mobile. It rang once.

'Yes, sir,' came the familiar voice. 'Good trip?'

Cavey didn't answer the question; he wasn't in the mood for pleasantries.

'Hargreaves, I need you to do something for me urgently. Drop what you're doing. I want you to research all suspicious deaths of homeless people throughout Europe over the past six months. It looks like this thing is bigger than we thought. I need a report on my desk first thing in the morning. Can you do that?'

'On it already, sir.'

Cavey smiled to himself. He liked Hargreaves' keenness.

'Anything on the number?' he asked hopefully, although he knew that he would have been the first to know if Hargreaves' laborious trawling of the internet had paid dividends.

'I've got loads of facts, sir. But nothing that leaps out at you.'

'Try me!' challenged Cavey.

'Seventy-two degrees Fahrenheit is regarded as the ideal room temperature. It is also numerical radio shorthand for "Best Wishes"'.

'Next,' said Cavey dryly.

'It's also a number used to calculate how quickly something will double in size—.'

'Put them all on the list, Hargreaves,' interrupted his superior. 'The answer's there, I know it is and when we discover it, this whole thing will make more sense.'

CHAPTER 22

A liquid sun shot shards of midday sunlight onto a billion ice crystals. Below them, the immense glacier shone with a blue whiteness as it snaked its way between two mountain peaks in the far distance. The Aletsch Glacier was the largest ice sheet in the Alps. With a length of twenty-three kilometres and a thickness of one, it covered a total of 123 square kilometres of the Swiss canton of Valais.

A group of twenty-two spectators drank in the awe-inspiring sight. Beyond the observation platform was vastness, grandeur and space. So beautiful and precious was this ice field, nestling amongst the fairy-tale spires of the Alps, that it had been designated a UNESCO World Heritage site.

'Stunning,' someone whispered under their breath.

It was Matt Bristow, the thirty-five year-old technology mogul and television presenter who had become a household name in the UK, having recently sold his production company for £350 million. This had been the first word uttered by anyone in the group since they had congregated on the Riederfurka platform, two thousand metres above sea level.

'So, what does everyone think?' van der Linden said.

He had been standing behind the group observing their reaction. This was the third group of investors he had brought to this spot in the last two years and he knew that it was virtually guaranteed to have a profound affect. The grandness of the vista instantly reminded the observer of the vastness of the planet and, at the same time, their own insignificance. The sparkling white snow fields stretching to the horizon presented an image of breath-taking beauty and unspoiled purity. The silence enveloped them in a blanket of peacefulness, isolating them from the frenetic hurly-burly of modern-day life. They felt a connection with nature and a wonderful detachment from modern life that, once experienced, would be difficult to relinquish. No one answered his question. They just continued to drink in the atmosphere and enjoy the peace of this other world.

Half an hour later, the scene was very different. Back in the observation station, the room was alive with excited conversation. Waiters weaved their way through the throng, dispensing canapés and glasses of warm mulled wine, shots of schnapps and grappa.

Caroline was standing listening to Darren Wilkins, who had made his fortune in the storage business. Boastfully, he told her how he had started out with a lock-up garage in Dagenham and now owned the largest self-store business in the UK. According to *The Times* Rich List he was worth £125 million, but with a conspiratorial wink and a theatrical glance over his shoulder, he whispered that he was a lot richer than that. Darren wasn't a particularly interesting person to talk to, but Caroline did her best to listen as he continued his self-centred monologue. His newfound wealth had enabled him to indulge a passion for winter sports. He had three ski chalets, two in the Alps and one in Aspen, and he spent as much of his precious time as possible on the slopes.

'Trouble is, though,' he lamented in a gravelly taxi-driver drawl, 'it's too crowded. The whole world comes over here in winter these days. You can't get on the slopes for Japanese tourists, school parties from Brazil and God knows where else. And the Russkies ... well, they're buying it all up, they're everywhere. They've been banned from taking any more property in Verbier you know? The Swiss could teach us all a thing or two about preservation. They keep things nice for themselves and good on them!'

Try as she may, Caroline had been unable to keep Darren's focus on the beauty of the mountainscape he had just seen. He kept coming back to his personal gripe: there were too many people enjoying winter sports these days and they were ruining his personal enjoyment. It was a pathetically selfish point of view and she looked around for someone else to talk to.

Van der Linden was working the room expertly. It was, as usual, a masterfully staged event and guaranteed to succeed in its objectives.

'Show them that the world is worth saving and they will do it,' he had said to her beforehand.

It was a simple strategy but very effective. Each one of them had been specially selected by the Eleventh Hour's researchers. Behind the scenes, they had a whole team of data miners whose job it was to build personal profiles on the rich and famous. Caroline hadn't yet been allowed access to the database, but understood that it contained comprehensive information on all the world's richest people. Once the potential delegates for these events had been selected, Edward van der Linden himself reviewed the list and decided personally who to invite.

The clear chime of a wine glass being struck with a teaspoon sounded out above the hum of conversation. It was time for van der Linden's speech, the main event of this extravagant gathering. Caroline felt a little flutter of nerves. This was the first time she had written a speech for Eleventh Hour and although van der Linden had approved her work with characteristic gusto, she was still apprehensive. She so wanted it to strike the right balance. Indeed, this had been her greatest challenge: how to appeal to potential new members by pushing their 'hot buttons' without appearing to preach.

Her life now could hardly be more different from her final days at Montagu Steinhart. Working for the Green Giant, she was free from the gradual, systematic constriction she had experienced under Tom Beresford. Not to mention the bruising arguments that characterised their fractious relationship. Here, she was completely unfettered and free ... except, that is, for the close, ever present scrutiny of Aleksei Lubov, van der Linden's Chief of Staff. She didn't like him and she suspected the feeling was mutual. He was looking at her now from across the room with his cold, suspicious stare, so she moved, placing someone between them and blocking his line of sight.

The venue had been specially selected to support both the theme of the address and the particular audience invited.

Caroline had spent a full two weeks, fifteen hours a day, finessing the text and researching the background to Edward van der Linden's speech, entitled: "*Global Warming – a problem man can no longer ignore*". Now, armed with her words he set about convincing his highly malleable, extremely wealthy audience of this fact.

The evidence supporting the argument, all delivered with a combination of passion and immaculate timing by the accomplished orator before them, won the audience over without a problem. Afterwards, they stood as one to applaud. By now, they all wanted the privilege of being part of van der Linden's very exclusive club. This yearning owed a great deal to Caroline. She had advised van der Linden to stress the exclusivity of being a member of Eleventh Hour and appeal to the audience's desire to be part of an organisation that endorsed their status. Her time in an investment bank had taught her that the wealthy enjoy one thing above wealth and that is people knowing that they are very rich. Although many regarded conspicuous consumption as vulgar, they still wanted to be seen to be members of the most exclusive clubs.

Van der Linden discreetly winked at Caroline as he chatted easily with his company's new members. He looked pleased.

'Fantastic, Caroline,' he said when she was in earshot. 'It felt very good, very natural.'

She smiled back at him, delighted that her work was appreciated. But before she could answer him, Aleksei Lubov interrupted them.

'We have business,' he said, grasping his boss' arm and

steering him away to the other side of the room where they joined Darren Wilkins of all people. She was getting used to Lubov's rudeness, but was somewhat surprised at van der Linden's easy capitulation to his blunt instruction.

'What a superb day, Miss Hartley,' Serge Aleve said.

Serge was the multimillionaire owner of a chain of exclusive restaurants in top skiing resorts throughout Europe and North America. He was a good-looking man with close-cropped hair and designer stubble, and he had been following Caroline around since the previous evening in an attempt to impress her with his not inconsiderable charm.

'Yes, wonderful,' she answered.

He took their re-acquaintance as an opportunity to kiss her gently on both cheeks. As he did so, she noticed, over his shoulder, van der Linden and Aleksei Lubov, accompanied by a smiling Darren Wilkins, slipping discreetly from the room.

CHAPTER 23

A light drizzle had been falling all day. Harold looked forlornly at the run-down buildings and narrow streets that surrounded him. Portsmouth had been regenerated in the fashionable Gun Wharf Quays area with its trendy designer outlet stores but it was a different story here around the old naval docks. But that was ideal for Harold's purpose. He wanted to be off the beaten track and away from people. This was his old stomping ground and he drew comfort from its familiarity. He could even smell the sea when the wind was in the right direction and if he strayed near to the dockyards themselves he got the occasional whiff of diesel which usually brought on a wave of nostalgia. For him this was sanctuary. Surely no one would find him here?

Since his arrival some two weeks previously he'd been very careful not to attract attention. His general strategy had been to find somewhere out of the way and stay put. Night time was difficult though. Although the Merchant Seaman's hostel was comfortable and guaranteed him at least one hot meal a day he hadn't wanted to push his luck there. He reckoned it would be the first place anyone looking for him would go, so to date he'd only dared to spend three nights there. The rest of the time he had been sleeping rough and his aching, arthritic bones were beginning to rebel against the cold, hard pavement. Winter was definitely on its way.

The rain was falling harder now and a large black puddle was spreading from the pavement into the doorway where he was sheltering. He had no money; all he possessed in the world were the dirty clothes he stood in and a tatty great coat with no buttons he'd been given by a charity shop two days ago. He hadn't eaten properly for days and his strength was flagging. The day before he'd started with a cold which had already gone to his chest. His situation was getting desperate.

Harold hung his head and clasped his hands to his face in a gesture of total despair. Looking down he saw that the sheet of cardboard he had been lying on for the last few nights was now sodden and useless and all of a sudden the hostel seemed an attractive option, if he dared risk it.

Ever since his brush with death and his flight from the hospital he had been gripped by the icy hand of fear. He spent every waking moment looking over his shoulder, expecting to see a now familiar figure walking towards him. He saw that face everywhere – in shop windows, on mannequins, on passers-by – everywhere. Even when he closed his eyes he was not free from the vision. The killer was out to get him and he knew it.

Tears of despair ran down his ruddy cheeks and plopped one by one into the pool of water he was now standing in. He started to mutter his dear wife's name over and over again like an incantation as he stood sobbing in the dark puddle. But she was gone. There was no one there to hear him, no one there to help. He was alone; alone and terrified.

Just then he heard the tap, tap, tap sound of expensive shoes on the stone pavement. Someone was approaching. He had chosen this side street because it was quiet and out of the way. Suddenly, he wished it wasn't. He wanted people and cars. He wanted noise. The footsteps came closer. Harold shrank back into the alcove, his eyes wide with fear. A shadow passed by the doorway without hesitating and kept on going.

That was enough for him. His mind was made up. He pulled his coat tight against the chill of the dank night air and tripped off unsteadily down the road. Perhaps the hostel wasn't such a bad option! Five minutes later he saw the welcoming light of the lamp above its entrance and he quickened his pace. Almost there.

'Ello there mate,' said a cheery voice at the door.

Harold had seen him last time he was there. A nice young lad. He'd given him an extra helping of porridge at breakfast as he remembered.

'Was 'oping you'd pop back,' he continued jauntily. 'A friend of yours was here yesterday askin' after you. I said you were around an' about. Seems I was right. They said they'd call back.'

Harold's blood froze in his veins and without another word he turned and melted back into the darkness.

The killer was here. They'd tracked him down.

CHAPTER 24

Sue Baxter embraced Caroline extravagantly when they ran into each other in the lift lobby of the Eleventh Hour headquarters. A casual observer would have thought they were lifelong friends. But it was just Sue's nature. She didn't do anything by halves. That was why she had become a very rich woman and also why she was so valued by the company. In jeans and a t-shirt, she was dressed far more casually than the last time they had met. Her attire would have been the standard student activist uniform, except that she was wearing an elegant Hermes scarf. Sue noticed Caroline looking at it.

'I know, I know. Not exactly in keeping with your average tree hugger, but I simply can't resist a few luxuries. Anyway, I don't see why I can't wear something nice if I want to.'

She put on the face of a spoilt child as she said this and they both laughed.

'I think we are going to have great fun together,' Sue continued excitedly. 'Come down to the basement and I'll show you where the real action is in this place.'

She was holding Caroline's hand now and led her to the

lift. As they were waiting, Aleksei Lubov appeared in the lobby. He'd come through a door behind reception which Caroline hadn't noticed before.

'*Cave*!' whispered Sue, quaintly using the old Latin word for 'beware', which Caroline hadn't heard since school. 'On second thoughts, let's go this way.'

She pushed her way through the fire escape doors, dragging Caroline down the stairs behind her.

'It's quicker this way. In any case the Commissar and I aren't exactly seeing eye-to-eye at the moment. So I really don't want to stand around making polite conversation with him.'

'Oh?' Caroline said.

'Nothing serious. Slight difference of opinion on what I am up to, that's all. At the end of the day, I'm right and he's wrong. It's as simple as that!'

She cackled loudly, obviously finding her remark very amusing. She was really hyped up for some reason. A few minutes later, Caroline found herself standing outside a doorway in a rather dingy corridor. There was no signage to denote what was beyond; it was simply a plain door in a bare white corridor. Once again, Sue read Caroline's thoughts.

'I prefer it down here. We're left to our own devices and an added bonus is that that poisonous Russian can't get in.' She chuckled again as her fingers punched in a code on a keypad and then she swiped her pass in a device underneath.

'Wow, that's secure alright,' remarked Caroline.

'Just the way I like it,' said Sue, her eyes twinkling with mischief, 'we change the code regularly to make certain of that!'

Since joining the company three weeks previously, Caroline had been introduced to all the other heads of the business units, or 'cause cells' as van der Linden sometimes referred to them. There were four others, aside from Sue's Direct Action unit: Conservation, Preservation, Climate and Finance. Sue had been away on urgent business abroad, but the section heads of each of the other areas had made her most welcome. She had been quite stunned when she visited Finance, an area that looked after the corporation's vast cash resources. Jim Garman, the department's head, hadn't been able to hide his delight at her surprise when he opened the doors to reveal a state-of-the-art twenty-man trading room, complete with dealing positions with multiple widescreen monitors. There were dot matrix price displays and televisions hanging down from the ceiling. 'Home from home, eh?' he had smiled, before adding proudly, 'We've got a similar facility in Hong Kong and a bigger one in New York.' (But as far as Caroline could remember, none of the other units had key-pad security, even Finance.)

Beyond the anonymous little door, Sue's office was unexpectedly spacious. Despite the absence of any natural light, it was brightly lit, and they both paused momentarily for their eyes to adjust after the gloom of the corridor. There were seven others in the room, all dressed similarly in jeans and t-shirts. It looked a little like a university common room to Caroline, especially as the walls were covered in posters.

'This is Caroline everyone, our new communications guru,' Sue shouted to them all.

There were a few grunts but nothing more by way of welcome. They all seemed very busy and totally engrossed in what they were doing. A cluster of three men caught Caroline's attention. They had been in a huddle, deep in conversation when she and Sue had entered. All three were now looking over at her with less than welcoming expressions. They obviously didn't like being interrupted.

'What's up?' said Sue.

'We need to talk,' said one of them sternly.

This large, bearded individual wore a t-shirt with the words 'I know where you live' in bold lettering across the front. Underneath, in smaller print, the slogan continued: 'I live there too, so let's work together.'

'In a minute. Alright!' Sue snapped, before turning back to Caroline. 'They're like kids, always wanting your attention.'

Her response didn't go down well. The three went back in a huddle and Caroline could hear the irritation in their voices. Her attention was drawn to a huge map of the world on the wall behind them, covered in red stars.

'What do the stars mean?' she asked Sue, but didn't get an answer, for at that moment they were interrupted by a loud and persistent knocking on the entrance door. When it was opened, in barged Aleksei Lubov. He looked furious.

'Miss Hartley is not cleared for this area,' he said in his heavily accented English.

'She's here at my invitation,' replied Sue, looking down on the Russian, who was a full six inches shorter, with a definite air of aggression in her manner. 'I'll ask whoever I want into my department and I'll be buggered if I'm going to ask for your permission.'

It was evident that there was a fight brewing. Everyone

stopped what they were doing and watched the two of them squaring up to each other. Caroline, who detested confrontation, realised that she was the source of the problem and instantly tried to diffuse the situation.

'Look, I'm finished here now. I have to get back to my work anyway. Thanks Sue.'

Caroline walked towards the door. It seemed to do the trick. Lubov and Sue Baxter watched her go. As she closed the door behind her, Caroline heard the voice of the bearded activist.

'Sue we need to talk. There've been developments.'

CHAPTER 25

DCI Hargreaves was physically and mentally drained. His eyes were red and his back ached from being hunched over his computer for hours on end. A short, typed report lay on the desk in front of him. It contained the fruits of his night-long labours. And what a night it had been.

The rest of the team had been arriving one by one since 7.00am. When they saw him, each one of them commiserated, they'd been there too. One minute you have your coat on, looking forward to an evening of R&R, the next you're hauled back for a night of mind-numbing tedium to trawl through old records or scour the internet for something that proves in the end to be irrelevant. Except, in this case, Hargreaves had struck gold.

Cavey arrived at 8.00am on the dot as usual and walked straight up to DC Hargreaves.

'Well?'

'I think you had better read this, sir,' replied the young detective, handing the papers to his boss.

Cavey took the report and walked toward his office. Something in Hargreaves' manner alerted him to the fact that a matter of some significance had been unearthed. He quickened his pace, but before he reached the door, he remembered himself and turned around.

'Thank you Detective Constable, you'd best get off home now and clean yourself up.' Then he turned to the rest of the team. 'I have a meeting with the Commissioner and the top brass at 9.00am over at The Yard. Team briefing here at 11.00am. Read this, all of you.' He waved the report in the air. 'I have a feeling it's very important.'

*

The meeting at Scotland Yard convened precisely on time. Sir Geoffrey was flanked by the Home Secretary, the Right Honourable Arthur Winterbourne on one side and the Deputy Commissioner on the other. They all looked stern. DCI Cavey noted that Greg Simpson, Head of the Serious Crimes Unit at Scotland Yard had also tagged along. This sounded a warning bell because he knew that Simpson was the Home Secretary's preferred candidate to replace him as head of the investigation. It was the first time he had attended any of these gatherings and Cavey's keen political antennae alerted him to potential trouble.

'Good morning, gentlemen,' started Sir Geoffrey. His tone was polite, but his fixed stare and the stiffness of his expression betrayed an inner tension. 'As you know, this is the most high profile case in this country's history. Our actions are under the microscope and it is imperative that we can demonstrate progress. Detective Chief Inspector, could you give us an update on your investigation?'

It was a wooden opening speech and Cavey sensed that

the Commissioner was following instructions. It looked like an ambush. The others remained silent. All eyes were on him. He sat impassive and silent for a full ten seconds. So long, in fact, that the MI5 team began to fidget and exchange enquiring glances.

When Cavey finally spoke, he directed his words to Malcolm Wallace, the Deputy Commissioner.

'Could you pass me the coffee please, Malcolm?'

All attention switched to the large tray of cups and saucers on the table in front of Malcolm Wallace.

'Good idea, coffee first,' Wallace said, relieved that the awkward silence had been broken.

Then, aided by MI5, he proceeded to distribute cups and to pass around the coffee pot. Cavey started talking whilst they were still busying themselves with the refreshments.

'Examination of CCTV footage from buildings and shops around St Thomas' Hospital yielded a vital piece of information. We now have reason to believe that the main suspect, who was dressed in the medical uniform of a nurse, was not acting alone.'

'That's all very interesting, but are you any closer to catching the murderer?' interrupted the Home Secretary.

Since taking his seat, he had shown his impatience by drumming his fingers noisily on the table and doodling on the pad in front of him. Cavey threw a glance in his direction and then continued as if he had never spoken. Sir Arthur looked up from his doodling, an irritated expression on his face. He wasn't used to being ignored.

'We have identified a van that we believe was driven by

an associate of our main suspect.' Cavey took a black logbook from his inside pocket and opened it in front of him. 'This vehicle entered the hospital at precisely 12.53am and left shortly afterwards. During the time it was on hospital premises, the building's CCTV system became inoperative. The van then left the hospital complex and parked in Upper Marsh Street just opposite the main entrance for approximately fifty minutes and returned to the hospital shortly afterwards, whereupon the cameras started working again.'

'So we're now hunting two people, then?'

It was Greg Simpson who asked the question. Cavey didn't like the use of the word 'we' and he certainly didn't like Simpson's patronising tone.

'I am not sure.'

'And why is that?'

Cavey also didn't like being cross-examined, especially by someone who was not his superior and as yet, nothing to do with the investigation. He caught Sir Geoffrey's eye.

'I think that we can come on to that later, Greg,' said the Commissioner, coming to Cavey's aid. 'Please let the Chief Inspector finish.'

The Minister's face was taut with simmering anger. Politicians are generally masters at disguising their true feelings, but today the Right Honourable Arthur Winterbourne was struggling to hide his impatience. His small, piggy eyes flicked slyly over at Cavey, sitting opposite.

'One person, two people, I don't really care,' he said with scarcely disguised contempt, 'what Her Majesty's Government wants to know is ...' He paused here for effect

'... after two months of investigation, are you, Detective Chief Inspector Cavey, any nearer to making an arrest?'

Cavey could tell that the politician was trying to provoke him, so he sat in silence rather than fuelling the fire by proffering a response. Frustrated, Sir Arthur then turned on the Commissioner.

'How long are you going to let this go on? The PM wants positive action, not more theory and conjecture. There's a crisis of confidence out there, you know. People are afraid to walk the streets. It's intolerable!'

'I know you are frustrated, Arthur—'

The Home Secretary cut him off. 'No, Commissioner. It's gone far beyond frustration. We have nothing to say to people. Nothing at all!'

This last word was accompanied by a sharp rap on the table. Cavey, who had watched the exchange impassively, now spoke.

'Shall I continue?'

'If I had my way, you would definitely not continue,' the Home Secretary retorted.

'Really?' said Cavey, fixing him with an impassive stare.

'Yes, really! In fact, Commander Simpson here has some very interesting ideas on how this investigation should be conducted going forward.'

Greg Simpson's face reddened and he shrank back in his seat. Although the politician had no qualms about revealing to all present that they had held clandestine discussions, the policeman looked anything but comfortable at the revelation of his duplicity.

'Home Secretary, I think we are digressing,' said the

Commissioner. 'I would like the Detective Chief Inspector to finish the update before we discuss anything else,' he continued.

The Right Honourable Arthur Winterbourne looked at his watch as a way of signifying that he thought it would be a waste of his time.

'Fine. But perhaps the Inspector can limit himself to telling us what he *does* know rather than what he *doesn't*. That should save a lot of time.'

One of the MI5 men smirked at this clever sideswipe and the Home Secretary visibly puffed up in his seat.

There was silence as all present waited for Cavey's response. The policeman twizzled the top of his gold Yard-O-Led pen, retracting the ballpoint as he carefully put it away in his jacket pocket. It was followed a few seconds later by his notebook. Then, calmly locking his fingers together and resting his hands on the table in front of him, he looked directly at his tormentor. When he spoke, his voice was unemotional, his words measured and precise.

'What we know, gentlemen, is that at least eighty-three of the most vulnerable members of society have been murdered without provocation and without apparent motive in a matter of just two months. The perpetrator of these crimes remains at large and will undoubtedly kill again. At this moment, thirty experienced detectives are sifting through the mountains of evidence that we have collected at the crime scenes. We are examining hours, weeks, months of CCTV footage from around London, all in order to detect a pattern or to unearth a clue as to the identity of the killer. We have also flooded London, thanks to our colleagues in the Met and the City of London police, with over two hundred extra officers who patrol the streets each night.'

'But you are still nowhere!' interrupted the politician.

'On the contrary, Home Secretary, we are making steady progress. This is no ordinary case. These killings are carefully planned and meticulously executed. But each time we learn something new.'

'Hell man, how many more deaths do you need before you make an arrest?' the Home Secretary exploded. 'I can tell you this much, your job, the Commissioner's job and my job for that matter, are all on the line. Our careers are riding on this.'

His face was red and his eyes were angry.

'Something else I know,' continued Cavey, intentionally softening his voice to contrast with the rabid tone of the Minister, 'is that these killings are not the work of one person alone. These brutal murders are also not limited to London or the United Kingdom.'

'What do you mean?' said the Commissioner, an expression of surprise and apprehension on his face.

'Yesterday I learnt from a contact in the Sûreté that there have been fifteen similar killings in France.'

'Good God!' exclaimed the Commissioner, shaking his head in disbelief.

'Following on from this discovery, we have conducted further investigations to explore whether there have been other incidents outside London that may not have been linked to our investigation. We have found a further twelve deaths in the UK with similar features, in Manchester, Birmingham, Edinburgh and Leeds.'

The revelation provoked a collective intake of breath.

'Twelve more, on top of the eighty-three! This is quite unbelievable.' The Home Secretary was already imagining the Cabinet's reaction to this news. He had been struggling to maintain the PM's confidence with just the London killings. Now he was going to have to tell him that people were also being murdered throughout the country. That nowhere was safe!

'It doesn't stop there though,' continued Cavey, in the same measured tone he had used throughout.

He had their attention now. The hostility had gone. The floor was his.

'We have broadened our enquiries and have identified similar crimes in continental Europe, specifically in Marseilles, Nice, Berlin, Frankfurt, Madrid and Naples.'

'How many?' gasped an incredulous Greg Simpson.

'We don't know,' replied Cavey, and then turned to the Home Secretary. 'Apologies, Minister.'

'What we do know though, as of today, thanks to the excellent work of one of my officers, is that these killings are not even just limited to the UK and to Europe. We have identified homicides that share broadly the same characteristics in Sydney, Hong Kong, Brazil, Mexico and in a number of major cities in the USA.'

There was total silence as each one of them worked through the significance of these words.

No one knew quite what to say, such was the gravity of these unexpected revelations. All the Right Honourable Arthur Winterbourne could manage was a rather lame rejoinder.

'Are you absolutely sure?'

'Regrettably, yes,' Cavey replied. 'What you must understand though is that this is not mass murder or the work of a serial killer. What we are dealing with here is systematic extermination, the annihilation of people at the very bottom rung of society. Gentlemen, this is not the work of one or even two people, which explains why we have not managed to build a consistent description of the killer to date.'

'So, what in heaven's name are we dealing with, John?' asked Sir Geoffrey, half out of his seat as he leant across the table towards the detective.

'Apologies again, Minister,' Cavey said, nodding in the Home Secretary's direction before answering the Commissioner's question. 'I don't know, sir.'

Then he let his eyes sweep across the whole room.

'But you can be certain of one thing: I'm going to find out.'

CHAPTER 26

Next day, a sudden rain shower took Caroline by surprise as she was walking to work from the tube station. As she rummaged in her bag for an umbrella, a large, black limousine drew up to the kerb ahead of her. The door swung open and as she approached she was surprised to see the face of Leo Brooks peering out at her.

'Hop in Caroline and I'll drop you at your offices,' he said merrily. 'This is a lucky encounter; I've been meaning to call you to find out how things are going.'

Caroline was at a loss for what to say. They had last spoken before her dramatic departure from Montagu Steinhart and she didn't quite know what he had been told about the circumstances of her leaving.

'Well, it's all going very well, thank you Leo,' she replied.

'Good, good. Interesting chap, Edward. Fascinating business,' enthused Leo before adding: 'And Sue ... well, she's a one off! Remarkable woman. You're a lucky girl.'

The car drifted over to the kerb again, drawing slowly to a halt outside Eleventh Hour's main entrance and the driver came around to Caroline's side and opened her door.

'I'm so glad it's all worked out for the best,' said Leo once again smiling broadly. 'We will no doubt run into one another again soon.' And with that he bade her farewell and the car moved off effortlessly through the early morning traffic.

Caroline watched it go, it seemed strange seeing Leo in this part of town and she wondered what he had meant by his last comment. Another unanswered question to add to the many others she had amassed since joining Eleventh Hour.

She had aired her many reservations to Simon, a few days before. He had become a trusted friend and confident, but nothing more. Although for her part, she found him very attractive, there seemed to be a reluctance from his side to taking things further, which puzzled, and if she was honest, disappointed her. On the plus side though, having someone sensible and objective to talk to was a real bonus, as she sought to navigate through the initial teething problems of joining Eleventh Hour.

The spat between Sue and Lubov had set alarm bells ringing in her mind, which was odd as she was certainly no stranger to arguments. Indeed, during her investment banking career, she had witnessed many brutal disagreements, but somehow this was different. She had also detected a definite atmosphere of wariness from the staff in Sue's department, which she couldn't understand. Her presence hadn't been welcomed. But why? The behaviour made her feel like an outsider and this unsettled her as she so wanted to be accepted as a valuable member of staff.

Simon had initially helped quell her fears, pointing out that everything was simply very new to her and that she was probably being a little over sensitive. However, one thing they both agree on was that it was odd that anyone needed, as Lubov had referred to it, 'security clearance'. It also seemed strange that Sue's department, unlike all the others, had secure entry. Caroline decided to raise the matter directly with van der Linden. She didn't want the shadow of negativity in her new career at Eleventh Hour and was keen to dispel this feeling of disquiet. There was bound to be an opportunity for a quiet chat some time during their forthcoming trip to meet a select group of New York's mega-rich.

The theme of the speech she had been asked to prepare was: *dwindling world resources and what steps need to be taken to accommodate the world's growing population*. It had been a fascinating piece of research and she was somewhat shocked to learn that if the global population were to keep on growing as predicted, there would not be enough food or water to go round in less than ten years' time.

★

The O'Neil Tower Penthouse, with its panoramic view of the city, was perched on top of New York's most luxurious hotel. As the city's most expensive hotel suite, it made an appropriate venue for Eleventh Hour's meeting with the super-rich of America's first city.

The Green Giant had delivered his speech with an intensity and passion Caroline had not witnessed before. He had captivated his audience with well-crafted words before jolting them with a series of dramatic statistics as was his way. The force of his delivery and his sheer presence simply compelled them to listen. As he left the raised dais and stepped down three shining marble steps, a smile of satisfaction lit up his face – he knew it had gone well, very well. With beads of sweat plainly visible on his brow, he raised a hand to acknowledge the applause. He had put a lot into this one and this was his reward.

The audience was comprised of forty or so of America's richest industrialists, entrepreneurs, hedge fund managers and financiers; every one of them a billionaire with more money than they could ever spend in a lifetime.

Caroline stood to one side of the room, her back to a marble pillar, holding a copy of the speech she had laboured so hard over in her hand. She was both puzzled and irritated in equal measure. In the excitement of the moment, van der Linden had decided to deviate from her skilfully-written script. She had actually taken great care to strike the right balance. But his passion had been such that he had elected to put it in his own words in an effort to drive home the message. Unfortunately though, by ad libbing in this way, he had actually changed the emphasis, and in some cases the very meaning, of what was being said. For example, rather than saying there was not enough food to feed the people of the world, he had said that the population of the world was too large for the current food resources. It was the same thing really, but a subtly different underlying message. To make matters worse, he had missed out the section that gave details of proposals to boost global food production and change resource distribution. Instead, he chose to emphasise the speed of global population growth and the widening age disparity between the 'Old World' in the West and the youthful emerging markets in the East. Where he had got his information from, she didn't know, but it was high impact stuff.

He may have provoked a strong reaction from the audience, but it was for the wrong reasons entirely. If she had been one of them, standing out there listening to him today, she would have come away thinking that he was advocating population control, not a radical overhaul of the system to distribute food. She would have to take this up with him. There really was no point in employing her to write for him if he then did his own thing.

The buzz of animated conversation reverberated around the marble and gold reception room. Caroline liked the way it was modelled on Ancient Rome, with its statues, ornate balustrade and magnificent fountain at the centre. It all seemed most fitting for today's audience. This level of luxury came with the price tag of eighty-five thousand dollars per night. The sum bought the use of the reception room, a vast lounge and state-of-the-art office, four bedrooms and the penthouse master bedroom, complete with a huge sunken bath and Jacuzzi. All the rooms had panoramic views over the city, forty-eight floors below. A butler and maid were thrown in for good measure. But those attending tonight expected no less; this was how they lived their cosseted lives.

Edward van der Linden was over the other side of the room by the fountain, deep in conversation with an elderly man with yellow teeth. The old man wore a shabby-looking brown tweed suit with shapeless, above the ankle-length trousers. Caroline made her way over to them, grabbing a glass of champagne from a passing waiter as she went. She didn't usually drink at these events, but this evening she felt like a glass or two of vintage Cristal champagne, van der Linden's staple.

'Ah Caroline!' beamed the South African, visibly more relaxed now. The champagne probably had something to do with that, she thought. He was holding an empty glass in each hand, which was pretty good going, since he had only finished speaking a few minutes ago. He noticed her gaze and laughed.

'Not very elegant, eh?' he chuckled. 'I can tell you this though, I worked up quite a thirst out there tonight.'

He casually tossed the empty glasses into the fountain and relieved a passing waiter of two sparkling replacements. His companion clucked mischievously at these antics and followed suit, except that the glass he threw away was virtually full. Caroline recognised the older man. She'd seen his face in *Forbes* magazine, which had become her bible since joining Eleventh Hour. He was an oil baron who had become one of America's most celebrated industrialists. From memory, his personal fortune was north of $28 billion. The suit looked shabby up close. It was worn and shiny with a number of blotchy dark stains down the front. Definitely not what you'd expect the twenty-fifth richest man in the world to be wearing.

'Abe, this is Caroline Hartley, who has just joined the company to help me with my speeches. Caroline, Abe Gottlieb.'

Abe took her hand and sandwiched it between his own

as if it were something precious. They were dry, rough and sinewy, with the strength of someone who was no stranger to physical labour.

'Well done, young lady. Well done! You absolutely nailed it. I have been waiting for someone with the courage to say those things for a long time. But these days, you know how it is? Everyone's afraid of upsetting the liberals.'

His face was leathery and tanned, his skin bearing the deep furrows of age. Abe Gottlieb was well into his eighties and had clearly grafted hard during every one of those years because it showed on his face. His eyes were surprisingly young though, or at least they appeared so because of the way they sparkled with an energy that gave him the air of an aged television evangelist.

'You people give me hope, you know,' continued the old man, snaking a mahogany-coloured arm around van der Linden's waist.

'How's that?' Caroline asked, not really sure what they had done to please the old man to such an extent.

'Young lady, let me talk plainly, as that's the kind of guy I am. I've worked hard all my life. Through that work, and the Almighty's good grace, I've built one of this country's biggest business empires. What I manufacture in my factories is the best in the world and I defy anyone to say otherwise.' He broke off and looked around him, challenging them to disagree 'I'm mighty proud of what I've achieved. Problem is, no one buys American these days.'

He shook his head in disgust and drank deeply from his glass as if to cleanse himself of the thought.

'This once great country has been flooded with cheap,

inferior goods from sweatshops in the East,' he continued, 'and no one's doing a dang thing to stop it.'

He stabbed his finger in the air, beginning to get a bit worked up. Van der Linden said nothing and simply nodded approvingly. This encouraged the old man to continue.

'We're governed by appeasers, you see. Lily-livered, self-interested, shallow, wasters. Our so-called leaders want to be everyone's friend because they only care about one thing: re-election. And look where it's got us.'

He paused and looked hard at Caroline, as if assessing her worthiness to hear his words.

'Tell me, Miss Hartley. Do you understand economics?'

It was a patronising question. Caroline, already tiring of Abe's overbearing manner and wondering how she could best escape, answered without thinking.

'Well, yes, I used to work in investment banking before—'

'Oh sweet Jesus! You're one of them!' Abe exclaimed, dropping her hand as if she had something contagious.

'But we've saved her,' cut in van der Linden, putting a protective arm around Caroline. 'Abe, remember you have Caroline to thank for the speech today.'

'Well, I suppose so.'

Nevertheless, he continued to look at her suspiciously until his all-consuming desire to tell people his views got the better of him. He took her hand again. Caroline detected the mustiness of unlaundered clothes above his cologne as he pulled her nearer. He leant towards her, so close in fact that she could feel the heat of his rancid breath on her cheeks.

'People say 9/11 changed this country forever. Well it did, but not in the way they think. Al-Qaeda succeeded in bringing us to our knees, that's for sure, but they did it by accident.'

He paused momentarily to let this point sink in, a self-satisfied smile on his thin lips. He was obviously proud of this observation and Caroline could tell that this was a speech he had given many times before.

'The 9/11 abomination created the economic conditions that enabled the American people to spend freely. And spend they did. You see, money was cheap afterwards. Congress made sure of that because they couldn't risk a market crash, not since we were only just recovering from the Dotcom bubble, so they lowered interest rates. And this opened the door to the Chinese. And we soon learnt that there was no limit to what they could produce with their infinite supply of cheap labour. There was also no limit to what the American people were willing to spend. This consumer-fuelled credit binge, compounded by the sickening greed of your lot ...' he poked an accusing finger at Caroline as he said this '... lasted until we all came down to earth with a bump. Truth is, we have consumed ourselves.'

Another smile creased his cracked lips as he enjoyed the cleverness of his last observation. He now stood, with his hands outstretched, appealing to them for a reaction. Van der Linden didn't disappoint him.

'Well put, Abe,' he said, giving the old man the praise and affirmation he craved. 'I'd never actually thought of it like that. So, if I've got this right, what actually happened was that a virtually infinite supply of goods from the East simply soaked up money from the West and prices defied the usual economic rules and stayed benign.'

'Exactly! No inflation. No warning. The American people simply dug themselves deeper and deeper into debt. China built up a massive surplus and our deficit went into the stratosphere. Wealth was siphoned from the West to the East and no one seemed to notice and if they did, they didn't seem to care.'

Caroline found the whole lecture quite tedious, but noted how van der Linden massaged the old man's ego. He let him speak, gave encouragement when needed and showed great interest in what was being said. She wondered where all this was going and why he didn't move on and circulate amongst his other guests.

Unfortunately, Abe was encouraged by his words and launched into another monologue.

'I have to tell you,' he said, waving a crooked finger in the air, 'that this bankrupt nation is now facing its biggest challenge. And it's up to us all ...' He gestured at those around him '... to do something about it before it's too late.'

His voice was getting louder as the patriotic fervour rose. Caroline tried to think of a way to change the subject, but before she could do anything, Abe downed his drink. Following his host's earlier lead, he hurled the empty glass towards the fountain. His aim wasn't very good though and it glanced off a statue of a cherub and shattered noisily, sending a shower of glass splinters over the marble floor.

'Goddam!' he cursed.

Two waiters hurried over to clear up the mess, their

expressions tight with concern, as if the incident was the result of their personal failing. The conversation in the room died down momentarily and a few people started to drift over towards them, attracted by the commotion.

Meanwhile, van der Linden attempted to rescue the moment with a statement of generous intent.

'Abe, if we at Eleventh Hour can help in some way to restore the fortunes of this great country, I can assure you, we will.'

'Thank you, Edward. I think I'll take you up on that.'

Caroline remained silent. It seemed the best strategy as she disliked this crabby, bigoted old man and didn't share van der Linden's ability to mask her true feelings.

Abe wasn't finished with her though. She was starting to feel like his stooge.

'Tell me, girl, do you know how many people there are over there in Asia?'

'Well, I think in total there are about five billion—'

She wasn't allowed to finish her sentence.

'Too many,' interrupted Abe. 'Too goddam many.'

She could see where this was going and looked at her boss, hoping that he would do something to take the conversation down a different path.

But far from changing the subject, he seemed happy to egg Abe on.

'Well, there are certainly a lot of people over there. In fact, didn't I read somewhere that two-thirds of the world's population live in Asia?'

Abe rocked back on his heels and raised his eyes heavenward.

'You can talk all you like about there not being enough food in this world to go round, but I say there would be enough if there weren't so many goddam people.'

His voice had now risen to a squeal of indignation. Edward van der Linden didn't seem concerned at all, unlike Caroline, who was desperate to escape, but couldn't because Abe had hold of her arm.

'Let's talk about something else,' she said in desperation.

'Typical!' Abe exploded. 'You young people hate talking about these things, don't you? It offends your sensitivities. It's your world too, you know.'

She looked for support but none was forthcoming. Van der Linden just smiled at them both as Abe continued.

'Let me tell you this. The West is finished and the East will dominate. Soon they will be richer than us.'

'They already are,' said one of the new arrivals, a good-looking, young black man sporting a pair of large-framed glasses that made him look incredibly studious, which was no doubt the intention. His name was Bradley Nelson. He was the founder and majority shareholder in BNS Global, one of the largest hedge funds in the world.

'Abe, accept it, we're all swimming against the tide,' Nelson continued. 'You look at it from an industrial point of view. I see it in terms of capital. And I'll tell you this: the sovereign wealth funds of the emerging economies already own the world.'

'That's because you hedgys have teamed up with them,' replied the old man, unable to disguise his disdain. 'What an unholy alliance that is! You're on their side, young man.'

During her time at Montagu Steinhart, Caroline had witnessed at first-hand the lengths the banking and investment community went to in order to court business from the secretive sovereign wealth funds of countries such as China, Saudi Arabia, Kuwait and Singapore. They were the world's new investment superpowers with hundreds of billions, if not trillions, of dollars to invest. Unlike other market operators though, they chose to operate in absolute secrecy within what had become known as the 'shadow market'. Here, activities were unregulated, opaque and off the public radar.

Brad tapped the older man playfully on the arm and smiled down at him in good humour. He was here to have a good time, not to be lectured by a corporate dinosaur.

'Listen, Abe,' he continued, 'just accept that it's game over, OK? These guys already own most of Africa. China is currently hoovering up mining companies throughout the world. The Koreans own half the arable land in Madagascar and the Arabs have bought over forty percent of London's prime real estate. And those are just the bits we know about.'

'And you're helping them,' Abe said and stabbed an accusing finger in the younger man's face, coming close to knocking the huge spectacles from his nose.

Bradley Nelson held his hands up in mock submission.

'Whoa there, Abe! I'm just making an honest buck. I can assure you man, I make them pay for my services.'

'You're nothing but whores,' Abe snapped back.

Caroline looked at van der Linden in alarm. This was beginning to get out of hand again.

'Now guys,' he interjected, putting a massive hand on each of their shoulders, 'we're all friends in this room.'

Bradley Nelson had heard enough. He shook his head despairingly. With a surreptitious wink of solidarity in Caroline's direction – and a respectful 'Excuse me, gentlemen' to the others – he ambled over to join the nearest group of fellow billionaires.

'I'm sorry about that Edward,' Abe griped. 'It just makes me so mad that these fools are helping the enemy.'

'You're very passionate about this East / West thing, aren't you Abe?'

'You're right on the money there, Ed. I may be old, but I'm still alive and whilst there's breath in these lungs ...' He thumped his chest '... I'm not gonna let them beat us.'

'A true patriot,' said van der Linden patting his bony shoulder.

'It ain't over yet. I can make a difference, a big difference. They'll see.' Then he looked van der Linden in the eye. 'I'm right, aren't I?'

The Green Giant smiled a look of reassurance.

'Of course you are, Abe. We all have it in us to change the world. In fact, that's what Eleventh Hour is all about.'

He put his immense arm around the old man and gave a nod to Aleksei Lubov who was loitering nearby.

'Let's go outside and grab some air,' he said, steering Abe through the knot of people who had collected round them. As they disappeared out onto the balcony, Caroline was at last free to circulate.

*

Much later, when the hotel's staff had finished clearing away, Caroline was sitting in the lounge, nursing a steaming hot cup of coffee, when Edward van der Linden entered. He appeared in fine spirits.

'That was a great night. Did you have fun?'

'Well. It got better once you took Abe Gottlieb away.'

'Oh! Don't mind him. He's old and cranky. All he wants to do is make sure that when he dies his beloved America still dominates the world. That's his crusade.'

'Hmm!' Caroline said, choosing not to voice her true feelings about the old man.

'Caroline, we meet these people all the time. They are actually our best and most generous members, because they are passionate about their particular cause.'

'But Edward, he seemed more than just passionate, he was fanatical and ...' She paused, searching for the right words '... slightly unhinged.'

'Believe me, you don't build a business empire like his if you aren't in possession of all your marbles.'

He looked long and hard at her. 'You know Caroline, you'll have to develop a thicker skin if you are to continue meeting prospective members.'

She didn't like the way he phrased this. Was she messing things up for herself again?

'I'm sorry, Edward. It's just that I really care about all this and—'

'—you want it all to go as planned and for it all to be very ...' He paused, intentionally keeping her waiting before finishing his sentence '... *nice*. Well, these people are very rarely nice. They have battered and clawed their way to success.

You've heard the expression: "nice guys finish last"? Well, it's true. And these are the guys that have come first.'

Van der Linden was leaning towards her, his eyes locked on hers, filling her entire line of sight as he delivered this stern lecture.

She felt very small. He was right. She was a hopeless idealist, hamstrung by English middle-class sensitivities. These were people from vastly different backgrounds; driven, combative, powerful individuals who were used to getting their own way.

'Look, Caroline, you're doing a great job,' he said, his tone softer now. 'Keep doing what you're doing and leave the hard stuff to me.'

He was smiling now, obviously pleased that he had cleared the air. He rose, struggling a little to haul his immense frame from the low sofa and helped himself to a coffee from a tray on the sideboard.

'We did well today. I reckon we'll take over $200 million. Plus a new member on our advisory board.'

'Not Abe!' she exclaimed.

'Yup,' he replied, unable to stifle a satisfied chuckle.

He clearly knew she would be dismayed by the news. She had heard that there was a kind of inner circle of substantial donors who, in recognition for their generosity, were invited to become patrons of Eleventh Hour. Sue Baxter was one of them, although she, unlike others, chose to become operationally involved.

'I don't understand. Why him? What can he possibly bring? Apart from money, that is.'

'Caroline, Caroline,' he said in a tone usually reserved

for a tiresome and rather disappointing child. 'You still haven't grasped what fuels us.'

'Money,' she replied, slightly indignantly. 'That's obvious.'

'No, it isn't money. It's passion. The all-consuming desire to right wrongs, to change things, *whatever the cost*. Those people we entertained tonight all had their particular bugbears or causes they were passionate about. Like your Leo Brooks back at Montagu Steinhart, he cares about his fishing beyond almost anything else, which makes him an ideal champion of river preservation. You see?'

As he spoke, his eyes were alive with his own personal passion: his business, Eleventh Hour.

'But these people are not your average donors. They are used to getting their own way and expect to be able to buy anything they want without waiting for civil servants or governments to make their minds up (if indeed they ever do). They don't expect anything to stop them enjoying life. Our power and influence allows us to change things for them. And they are grateful. Very grateful!'

'Yes, I can see that. But someone like Abe—'

She wasn't allowed to finish her sentence.

'Abe,' the Green Giant exclaimed, holding his arms out in a gesture suggesting a eureka moment had been reached. 'Caroline, Brad Nelson and the others will donate ten or twenty million dollars each to help tackle their special interest problems. Abe, on the other hand, is that rare beast who is so consumed by a cause that he will give everything. Everything!' He paused and scrutinised her, no doubt to confirm that she fully understood what he had just said before saying very slowly. 'For that level of commitment, we give them a seat at the "high table". A fair exchange, don't you think?'

She understood. So that was why he was so elated. Eleventh Hour was twenty-eight billion dollars richer tonight.

Van der Linden tilted his head to one side as he gauged her reaction and then he snapped his fingers as an idea occurred to him.

'Look, I've invited Abe along on my trip tomorrow. Why don't you come along too? I know it's short notice but I'd like you to join us. It will be an opportunity for you two to bond.'

The offer took her by surprise. He was off to Guyana in South America. It was an exciting opportunity but she wondered whether she could stomach another dose of Abe Gottlieb's particular brand of diplomacy. But van der Linden didn't give her time to deliberate. He'd made *his* mind up.

'Right then, that's decided,' he said, clapping his hands. 'You may get a bit bored. We're visiting one of our research facilities. Board meeting, progress reports, that sort of thing. But I'll see if we can arrange a jungle excursion while we're there. It's one of the world's last unspoilt paradises.'

'Edward, it sounds wonderful and I'll try my hardest with "Mr Awkward". You have my word on it.'

He stood up to leave. As he did, she remembered that she hadn't broached the subject of Sue Baxter's department's ultra-security, as she had intended. Now was as good a time as any.

'Edward, one thing I have been meaning to ask.'

'Fire away,' he said, walking slowly towards the door.

'Sue Baxter.'

He stopped at the mention of the name and turned towards her. Caroline noted that apprehension seem to replace his gung-ho attitude of a moment earlier.

'What about her?' he said sharply.

'Is she on your advisory board?'

'Yes. She's been a patron from the start. But …' He hesitated, obviously in two minds about whether to say something. Caroline looked back enquiringly. 'But, she will probably be leaving us soon.' Immediately, he seemed to regret his candour. 'That's between the two of us. No one else should know.'

He placed his finger to his lips, urging silence.

'Why are you asking about her?'

There was now a definite suspicion in his voice.

'Well, I just wondered why her department operates behind locked doors, that's all.'

'Oh, that!' he said, relaxing. 'It's because of her obsession with personal security.'

'Really?'

'Yes. Because of the attack.'

'What attack?'

'Oh, didn't you know? Ten years ago, Sue was brutally attacked and beaten. They tried to strangle her and left her for dead. She actually died twice on the operating table but somehow pulled through. She's a stubborn old bird.'

Caroline was shocked.

'That's why she wears the jewellery, haven't you noticed? The chokers and scarves hide her scars.'

CHAPTER 27

With surprising speed, a rich October sunset melted away into a hollow, inky dusk, leaving the streets chilly and autumnal. Two lone figures – dressed in thick winter jackets, jeans and calf-coloured Doc Martin boots – were the only human presence. As they trudged along the road, they each tentatively scanned the shadowy doorways and dark alleyways. All the buildings in the narrow street were in darkness, most were unoccupied, some obviously derelict. This part of Bethnal Green was in desperate need of regeneration, being a mix of deprived residential and bankrupt commercial properties. Until then, it would continue to be the haunt of street gangs, drug dealers and vagrants.

They both felt decidedly less brave than they had a few hours earlier. Stuart Heyworth was definitely not the roving correspondent type. He had made his name writing caustic but well-informed tabloid exposés, not reporting live from the scene. So far in his career he had successfully avoided this kind of journalism, but his editor had insisted. It was his story after all. Ever since he had broken ranks with the rest of Fleet Street at the news conference, he had become the authority on the killings. Everyone wanted to know his take on events.

Stuart had never been popular, but he didn't really mind. He actually didn't like people very much, so it followed that they wouldn't care much for him in return. His first marriage had only lasted a year before his wife had moved out. She had nowhere to go, but had said afterwards that 'nowhere' was preferable to continuing to live with him. He'd been married twice since then, but had resolved not to go there again. It wouldn't work anyway. He lived for himself, not other people and he wasn't going to change.

The story was still providing headlines but it needed fresh impetus to keep it on the front page. There had been no further killings. All the available detail had been published, reviewed and analysed. The public – ever hungry for high drama – were getting bored with it now. One rival publication had even started to report that there were similar killings in France. His story was now in danger of being hijacked! That was why his editor had latched onto the idea of Stuart spending a night on the streets to report first-hand on how scared the people were and, of course, how let down they felt by the authorities. True to character as a notoriously objectionable specimen, Stuart had initially refused to play ball, citing personal safety grounds. But his editor had insisted and wouldn't back down. They both knew that there were hundreds of extra police roaming the streets but they were trying to cover London's entire area so were in reality pretty thinly spread.

So here he was, in a part of town he would never usually dream of straying into, with Big Phil, a twenty-three year-old rookie photographer. Conveniently though, Big Phil was also six foot five tall and eighteen stone and tonight Stuart was very pleased of his company. Who in their right mind would take him on?

As they rounded the bend at the bottom of the narrow street, they reached their destination: a large expanse of waste ground surrounded by disused warehouses and boarded-up homes. Recently, this had become a well-known meeting place for London's terrified street dwelling community who came here in ever increasing numbers. As he scanned the crowd Heyworth estimated that there must have been over fifty people there on this particular night. Some were already bedding down while others stood in tight huddles enjoying the security of companionship. At the centre of the open space burnt a large fire which sent showers of sparks into the greyness above.

'Bloody Nora!' fretted Heyworth, covering his face with his hands. 'What the hell am I doing here? Phil, just get your snaps and let's get outta here. I'll make up the story. No one will know and you better not let on to the gaffer. OK?'

Big Phil approached the nearest group of shadowy figures and started to flash away. Stuart stood back in the shadows muttering obscenities under his breath, already looking forward to a large tumbler of Chivas and soda – his favourite tipple – back at his flat in Pimlico, far away from this hell.

A figure approached him.

'Got everything you need, mate?' he whispered in a light, seductive voice. 'I've got some great gear on me.'

'Yes I have thanks, now bugger off!'

That's all he needed, some low-life drug dealer plying his trade in this godforsaken place. He looked around him. Where were the police? Surely he should be able to see at least one uniformed officer. Well, that was one thing he would be writing about. That's for sure!

Big Phil tapped him on the arm.

'Hey, look at that,' he was pointing towards a tall figure in a hood and full length cape.

'Dracula returns,' he chortled. Unlike Stuart, Phil seemed to be enjoying their little expedition.

People stepped aside to let the shrouded figure pass and as they continued to watch it drifted towards the wasteland in the centre of which stood the bonfire.

'Something's got them spooked,' remarked Phil noting movement in the crowd.

He was right. There was agitation all around as dark figures shuffled towards the light and the safety of the fire.

They both saw it at the same time. The hooded figure, now a matter of yards from the flames, hurled something into the bonfire. A second later, there was a blinding flash and three ear-splitting reports, like gunfire or small explosions. Someone screamed and there was pandemonium.

With the noise still resounding in his ears, Stuart took fright and legged it as fast as he could run back up the narrow street, the only route out of the square, closely followed by a stampede of fifty or so terrified, jostling, stumbling souls. He didn't care where he was going so long as he put as great a distance as possible between himself and whatever it was back there. Halfway up the street, Big Phil streaked past him; head down like an Olympic sprinter and showing surprising speed for someone of his build. So much for his bodyguard! He'd have words back at the office.

Then something strange happened. Phil's head jerked backwards and his whole body flew into the air. Stuart swerved to avoid him but he himself became suddenly airborne. He saw his own legs, kicking in front of him before he crashed hard to the ground. Winded and disoriented, he struggled for breath. All around him, he heard animalistic cries and screams as terrified people trampled over each other and over him. He lost consciousness.

He awoke, a short time later, to a chorus of unearthly groans and pathetic sobs. Someone was lying on top of him and he wriggled his torso in an effort to free himself from the dead weight, but couldn't muster enough strength. As he did this, his hand touched something solid. He grabbed hold of it. It was Phil's camera. Someone was approaching. He was safe. Someone was coming to help. He heard the drone of distant sirens. The police were minutes away. Everything hurt. Above him, he saw something reflecting the blue lights of the approaching police cars. It looked like a laser beam, but he couldn't think what it could be. It was in fact the filament of wire that had been stretched across the street – the wire that had virtually decapitated Phil and five others fleeing the scene and which had sliced open his own throat. Alongside the dead and dying and those crushed in the stampede, he lay patiently waiting to be saved.

Someone was above him now, coming to help. He feebly raised a hand to show he was still alive. A thin stiletto knife was then thrust deep into his chest, three times in quick succession, all the way to the hilt. In his death throes,

Stuart's hand clamped shut on the camera, gripping it hard and triggering a strobe of light. The last sight to be imprinted on his brain was of two eyes staring intently at him, alight with the cruel ecstasy of murder as his killer gouged two numbers deep into the flesh of his forehead.

CHAPTER 28

Helicopter travel isn't for everyone, but Caroline loved it. The Sikorsky C70 was moving at speed just above the green canopy of Guyana's pristine jungle, all but skimming the trees as it sped towards the Eleventh Hour research facility buried deep in the interior. It was a totally exhilarating experience.

The night before, after she had been invited on the trip, Caroline had immediately called Simon back in London. She had to tell someone, she was so excited. The Eleventh Hour tablet was proving to be very handy and had become a major part of both her working and social life. In fact, these days it was rarely more than an arm's length away, which was strange since she and technology didn't get on as a rule. The fact that she was essentially 'on call' to the company twenty-four hours a day didn't bother her. The pros of the device definitely outweighed the cons.

He had told her to watch out for the mosquitos, which was good advice as a quick scan of the internet had shown that malaria and dengue fever were endemic in the region.

'Why put a facility in such a remote place?' he had asked.

Caroline didn't know why, but at that moment she was

pleased that they had. She'd never been to South America and never visited a real jungle.

★

The majority of the population of the Commonwealth nation of Guyana live on a low coastal plain bordering the Atlantic Ocean with the remaining eighty percent of the country covered by dense forest. From Georgetown airport, the helicopter headed deep into the interior, speeding above the immense floodplain of the Rupununi River. This fertile country, known by Amerindians as 'the land of many waters' and the inspiration for Sir Arthur Conon Doyle's *The Lost World,* was little known beyond its immediate neighbours.

Van der Linden's private jet had taken less than four hours to reach Georgetown, the country's capital. Once on the ground, they had simply walked across the steaming tarmac from the plane into the waiting helicopter. Customs and immigration had come to them. A smiling Guyanan in a smart semi-military uniform with braided gold epaulets stamped their passports and processed them into the country with great enthusiasm, before gratefully joining them for refreshments of chilled orange cocktail laced with a twist of local rum.

Below them, the jungles of Guyana appeared dense and unspoilt.

'What a triumph,' declared van der Linden, following Caroline's lead as he crouched down to peer through the window at the vast verdant scene below.

'It just goes on and on,' she marvelled in awe and then she looked at him. 'But why do you say that?'

'Because, there's no burning of the jungle. Not a whiff of smoke as far as the eye can see. Look!' He gestured excitedly at the expanse below.

Caroline stared out of the window. Van der Linden was right, the air was clear all the way to the distant green horizon.

'Compare this to the Brazilian Amazon where logging and deforestation is still decimating the jungle.'

'So, what's so different in Guyana?'

'It's very interesting, actually. Ground-breaking, in fact. They have an agreement called the "Conservation Concession".'

Caroline looked back at him blankly, this meant nothing to her.

'Essentially, this country is paid not to deforest by a charitable foundation. So every year, the farmers receive money on the express understanding that they do not chop down their trees.'

'Incredible,' replied Caroline, 'they harvest an annual crop of... ...conservation.'

'Well put, that's it in a nutshell,' he laughed back. 'I think I'll use that expression myself sometime, if I may?'

'And are we involved?' she continued.

'No, remarkably not. They actually don't need us here. But I hope to replicate the model in other countries in the region.'

The helicopter banked steeply and executed a swooping descent with a deafening whirr that shocked a cloud of small birds from the treetops. Caroline and van der Linden returned to their seats and strapped themselves in. The change in trajectory was enough to wake Abe Gottlieb from his slumbers and he peered groggily with frog-like eyes as the ground raced towards them. He'd been asleep for most of the flight, much to Caroline's relief. On the plane ride from Newark, he'd been at his most vociferous and it soon became apparent that he didn't need an excess of alcohol to be opinionated, dogmatic and obnoxious. Caroline had only taken a sip of her coffee once the flight was underway before he started ranting on about the decline of America, his pet subject. She simply had no appetite for a re-run of last night's lecture so, the moment Abe was distracted, she had squeezed her eyes shut and pretended to be asleep for the remainder of the journey. That did the trick. She actually did drift off to sleep, which worked out very well, considering Abe had then slept soundly throughout the helicopter ride.

The Sikorsky C70 swooped down at speed and then slowed to a virtual stop as it hovered, with its nose raised, twenty feet above a large white H on the ground below. When the landing came, it was gentle to the point of being virtually unnoticeable. Aleksei Lubov threw open the side door, letting the South American sun stream in. Caroline was first out, followed by a wheezing Abe Gottlieb. It was blindingly bright and very hot. But this wasn't the dry heat of the Mediterranean, they were in the middle of a dense jungle with eighty percent humidity. The heat though was not the only thing that hit her as she hopped enthusiastically down the steps. The noises of the jungle were all around, clearly audible above the slow thump of the rapidly slowing rotor blades. The agitated chatter of monkeys and the screech of exotic birds, startled from the treetops by the helicopter's screaming descent, rose above the background cacophony of a million insects.

Polite applause rippled from a welcoming party, standing in neat lines outside the facility. Despite the fact that they were all dressed in white lab coats, it was obvious that the heat was taking its toll. Some were definitely wilting under the savage sun but, despite their discomfort, most were smiling and looked genuinely pleased to see them.

'Welcome,' said a tall figure of Eastern appearance at the head of the second line. Something about his manner suggested he was the senior man here. He looked over Caroline's head as the unmistakable frame of Edward van der Linden squeezed backwards through the narrow helicopter door.

'We are so pleased you have made the time to visit us here,' he continued in very precise English, then bowed his head to Caroline. 'I am sure you will find your stay very interesting. I have arranged a tour for you so that you may share in our exciting work.'

'Li Chun, great to see you,' boomed the Green Giant.

His shirt was already damp with sweat from the humidity even though he had walked a mere twenty yards. He slapped his arm once and then again.

'Bloody mosquitos!'

Li Chun bowed again, much lower though this time.

'So pleased to see you, Mr van der Linden, sir.' Then he looked around him. 'Yes, we have had a lot of rain recently and the insects are swarming. It's very bad! We will fog tomorrow.'

Caroline's pulse quickened as she remembered the

dangers. Had the visit been less spontaneous she would have had time to take anti-malaria tablets or at least coat herself in high Deet mosquito repellent. Looking around now though, she could see that the air was alive with insects of all sizes, some buzzing noisily whilst others hung ominously above the ground in shimmering swarms. Van der Linden slapped his wrist again as another insect landed on his bare flesh. He was clearly on her wavelength.

'Best we get indoors, otherwise we'll be eaten alive,' he said to the assembled community. Then, turning to Caroline and a rather lacklustre Abe Gottlieb, he added, 'Look guys, I'm not sure it would be such a good idea to go into the jungle today, what with all the mozzies. Sorry Caroline, I know that's why you were so keen to come down here with us.'

She was disappointed but also relieved. Anyway, just being there in that natural paradise with its raw beauty was a treat in itself. It certainly beat sitting at a desk in an office. Abe shrugged, obviously unconcerned by the cancellation of their excursion. He was beetroot red and sweating profusely. Caroline wondered why van der Linden had risked bringing an obviously unfit octogenarian into the heart of a tropical jungle. As she wondered this, she realised that in the excitement of being unexpectedly invited on the trip, she had not really stopped to question why they were coming here at all. She was just tagging along, but it now occurred to her that the visit must be very important for van der Linden to risk the health of his newest mega-donor.

Escorted by a phalanx of white-gowned workers, the party hurried towards a collection of flat roofed, military-style buildings fifty yards from the landing pad, which was to be their sanctuary from the ever-present flying peril that surrounded them.

Once inside, the majority of the workers disappeared, leaving Li Chun and a number of senior laboratory technicians to play host to the four Westerners at a buffet lunch.

'Let's get on with business now,' said van der Linden half an hour later as he downed the dregs of his coffee. 'We'll see you again soon Caroline,' he added, placing a consoling hand on her shoulder. 'Sorry, I really thought it would have been possible for you to explore the jungle but what can you do?' he paused and raised his arms in the air in a gesture of resignation before continuing: 'It seemed like a good idea back in New York, what with you being such a nature lover and all.'

'No, no,' Caroline replied sincerely. 'It's incredible. Just hearing the sounds all around is such an experience.'

She loved the smell and the atmosphere of the place. The view from the helicopter had given her a real sense of the forest's scale and denseness. Even now, it thrilled her to realise she was right in the middle of an ancient jungle. The buildings were prefabricated with thin plywood walls and she could hear the sound of untamed nature all around her.

'Well, perhaps another time,' van der Linden added, guiding Abe by his bony elbow towards the door.

'Make yourself at home here. I'm just going to show Abe round. We'll be back in an hour or so.' Then he waved a hand at Lubov, who was mumbling quietly into his mobile phone. 'Aleksei, make sure Miss Hartley is looked after and remains safe.'

It wasn't necessarily the words he used – although it was a slightly strange request given the evident safety of the facility – it was more the look he exchanged with the Russian that drew Caroline's attention. The eye contact was a fraction of a second too long and was clearly intended to convey an additional message of its own.

What was going on? And why was she not being shown around the facility like Abe? Once again she felt like an outsider, someone who worked for the company, but who was not yet fully trusted. But why? What was she not being allowed to see? Caroline was suddenly racked with anxiety and also an overwhelming curiosity.

CHAPTER 29

Sir Geoffrey's face had a grey hue and he didn't look his usual smart self. In fact, he looked ragged. His voice, like his uniform, had lost its crispness. His tone had become detached and self-pitying. This was definitely not the resolute and determined career policeman that John Cavey so respected. The man in front of him today bore all the hallmarks of surrender.

Cavey recognised the signs because he had seen them before. Ironically though, they were usually displayed by criminals he was questioning. In his experience, there was always that moment when they gave up and acknowledged defeat. Their eyes would take on a faraway stare, their shoulders would sag and they would shrink in stature. It saddened him to see his old friend in this state.

That morning, the country had awoken to news of a truly shocking series of events that had taken place the previous evening in a backstreet in Bethnal Green. With all the blood, guts, fire, darkness and chaos, Hollywood could hardly have staged the event better. And, humiliatingly, it had all occurred under the very noses of the Metropolitan Police.

People were angry, they wanted answers, but most of all they wanted protection. After all, that's why they paid their taxes. The press were baying for retribution, with one tabloid shrieking tastelessly that 'heads must roll'. In his professional life, Stuart Heyworth was an outcast and a pariah, but in death he had been transformed into a cherished member of the Fleet Street community, a fearless investigative reporter who crusaded for truth. A week ago, Heyworth's peers would have crossed the street to avoid him, but now he was one of them. Moreover, his brutal death had given journalists the kind of ownership that they loved. Now they were not just reporting on a story, they were part of it. All thanks to their new champion: Stuart Heyworth.

'I have a meeting with the Home Secretary in an hour,' said Sir Geoffrey in a dull, expressionless voice. 'Of course, it will be curtains for me. And you too, I'm afraid, John.'

Cavey cocked his head to one side, weighing up whether it was worth speaking to the Commissioner in his current frame of mind. He definitely had something to say and didn't want to waste his words. After pausing for a few second's deliberation he decided to go ahead anyway.

'Commissioner, we're close, very close. I know it.'

It was a simple statement of fact. Not a plea. Sir Geoffrey looked at him quizzically, but remained tight-lipped.

'Last night was different,' Cavey continued. 'Yes, it was daring – and we expect that now – but this time the killings were reckless, as if our murderer knows it's all coming to an end and is desperate to wreak as much havoc as possible before it's all over.'

'Murderer?' queried Sir Geoffrey.

'Yes, in this case we are sure it was just one killer acting alone,' Cavey replied.

'And what do you mean by "reckless"?'

The Commissioner was showing more interest now, which Cavey took as a positive sign.

'Last night, London was saturated with our men and the killer knew that. It was just bad luck that one of our officers wasn't close enough to the scene to apprehend them. You know sir; our nearest man was just two streets away. In fact, he says that when he and another officer arrived, they think they disturbed someone who was leaning over Heyworth's body before scuttling off down the street.

'We were that close?' asked Sir Geoffrey, a little more energetically.

They looked at one another without speaking, but Cavey saw the Commissioner's interest wain. None of this really mattered to him now. His very public sacking would be an ignominious end to an otherwise exemplary career and that was what weighed on his mind now.

'Shame you didn't catch them …'

The Commissioner's voice faded away and he bowed his head.

'Geoffrey,' said Cavey softly. 'We just need a little longer.'

The Commissioner turned to him sharply, a flash of anger in his eyes as his frustration boiled over.

'John, don't you understand? We haven't got any more time. You've had your chance and you didn't catch the killer. Now, as a direct consequence of that fact, in less than an hour's time, I will be fired and you will be booted off the case shortly thereafter to be replaced by that lickspittle Greg Simpson.'

Cavey didn't reply for a moment or two. He didn't like being spoken to like this, even by the man in charge of the entire Police Force. He was also a little surprised by Sir Geoffrey's unguarded remark about Greg Simpson. The Commissioner was usually so discreet. He nevertheless agreed with his sentiments. Simpson had a reputation for toadying up to people in authority and it was good to know his superiors saw him for what he was.

'But what if you give them what they want?'

'What do you mean?'

'I mean they won't replace you if you have an exciting new lead.'

'And what, pray, is this exciting new lead?'

As he spoke, he leant back in his chair and folded his arms tightly across his chest, challenging Cavey to convince him.

Cavey hesitated for a moment, then said tentatively. 'We may, just may, be able to identify the murderer.'

'What do you mean, "may"?' the Commissioner fired back.

'Well sir, ironic as it may be, Stuart Heyworth's final action on this Earth could be our salvation.'

'Go on,' said the Commissioner impatiently.

'Just before his death, he grasped hold of his dead colleague's camera and fired off a dozen or so shots.'

Sir Geoffrey looked incredulous. 'He took a picture of the killer? Why in God's name didn't you tell me this before?'

'Well, it's not as simple as that, Commissioner. The shots are blurred and most are virtually indistinguishable.'

Sir Geoffrey couldn't contain his disappointment. He thumped his hand down on the desk and rocked back in his chair, staring up at the ceiling for a few seconds.

'Damn! I thought you had something for a minute.'

'Just a second, Commissioner. It's not all lost.' A firmness had now crept into his tone. 'As we speak, the best photographic technicians in this country, aided by specialists from NASA, are working on the photos in an effort to enhance the images. Most of the pictures were massively overexposed because the flash setting was set for maximum distance and these were taken very close up. But you have to remember that these pictures are digital and not taken on old-fashioned bromide film so they can be computer enhanced.'

Sir Geoffrey wasn't convinced and it showed on his face.

'I'm very hopeful of one image in particular,' continued Cavey. 'The last to be shot as the camera fell to the ground. It caught the killer's reflection in a window opposite.'

'I'm not sure,' said Sir Geoffrey, visibly weighing up their options. 'Doesn't really sound enough to me. And what if you end up with nothing?'

Cavey's response was swift, his tone intentionally curt. This lack of fight was anathema to someone like him.

'Look, all you have to do is say that there has been a major breakthrough. We have a photograph and we hope to make an arrest very soon. If it comes to nothing, they will fire us. Well, they're going to do that anyway. Aren't they?'

Sir Geoffrey stood up from the desk and walked to the window, the stress obvious in his sudden movement. His office had a magnificent, panoramic view of St James' Park, but Cavey knew that his boss was not looking at the picturesque autumn scene below. His eyes were unseeing as he considered his next move.

'They won't do anything if they think we are about to solve the case.'

'But we're not, are we?' challenged the Commissioner.

Cavey didn't hesitate. 'We're closing in and the photo will clinch it. One of my team thinks he has located the survivor from the Vauxhall poisoning who gave us the slip at St Thomas'. He's evidently in the Portsmouth area.'

'Well, get someone down there,' replied the Commissioner, rediscovering his authority. 'A witness is just what we need for a prosecution.'

That's it, thought Cavey, noting that Sir Geoffrey was now thinking beyond the arrest of the suspect to the court case.

'We're already on it, sir. Actually, there's been a rather worrying development. It appears someone else has been asking about him down there.'

'What do you mean?'

'Well, we think the killer may be after him as well.'

'Good God! Look John, I want you to do whatever it takes to find this man before anything happens to him.'

'Will do, sir. You can be sure of that.'

'Good, good,' replied the Commissioner, almost back to his old self. 'Well, thank you, Chief Inspector. If that's all, I need to prepare for my meeting. I've certainly got a thing or two to say to the Home Secretary when I see him.'

Cavey didn't move from his seat. He sat calmly observing Sir Geoffrey.

'Yes? Is there something else?'

'With respect, Commissioner,' Cavey said in his characteristic monotone, 'wouldn't it be a better idea to announce this breakthrough *before* your meeting?'

'What do mean?' replied the older man a little indignantly.

'Hold a press conference.'

'What? In the next forty-five minutes?'

'As soon as possible. If you are correct that the Minister intends to replace you, he may still proceed as planned even after you tell him about the photograph at your meeting.'

'He wouldn't do that, surely ...'

The Commissioner's voice tailed off as he considered the Detective's words. He was right, of course. Politicians typically planned their actions meticulously in advance and were not generally very open to changing things once they had put matters in train. Sir Arthur would no doubt tell the PM of his intentions to fire him and would brief his civil servants and the Press Office before he even entered the room. Cavey was right. An unexpected, high-impact public announcement would wrong-foot the Minister and give Cavey's team the time they needed to make their arrests. It would be madness to replace a Commissioner who was on the verge of solving the biggest serial murder case in British history.

Cavey noted Sir Geoffrey's smile as he reached the inevitable conclusion and prodded a button on his desk intercom.

'Madeleine, please get hold of Simon McAlister as a matter of urgency.'

He had suddenly regained his energy. As if to prove it, he rose from the desk and stood ramrod straight with his arms behind his back.

'I want an emergency press conference in thirty minutes. Please ask Simon to come to my office immediately. Also, get onto the Home Secretary's office and cancel our meeting. Say something important has come up.'

Cavey raised his hand by way of farewell and headed for the door. Sir Geoffrey gave him a thumbs-up sign. He was a different man to the one Cavey had encountered some fifteen minutes ago.

CHAPTER 30

Aleksei Lubov had a nasty habit of snorting and sometimes he muttered to himself under his breath. He'd been reading emails and texting for the last thirty minutes with no attempt at conversation. Caroline was bored and distracted. Although she had little interest in making small talk with Lubov, the more she thought about it, the more annoyed she was that she had not been included on Abe's tour of the facility. Perhaps the Russian could shed some light on the matter.

'So, what actually goes on here?' she asked, trying to sound matter-of-fact.

The Russian didn't move, but his eyes flicked up from the device in his hand.

'Research,' he replied, before switching his attention back to his phone.

She could tell, though, that he wasn't really reading what was on the screen and was waiting to see if she continued her questioning.

'What kind of research?'

'All types.'

Caroline found Lubov's clumsy effort to say as little as

possible infuriating and it made her more determined than ever to push him for information.

'Like what, Aleksei? Research into the weather, animals, rocks, trees, the climate?'

'Just research, that's all.'

He got up from his seat and switched on a large television in the corner of the room. The BBC World News flashed up on the screen. The conversation, if that was what it was, was over.

'OK, I'll ask Edward about it when he gets back,' she said tartly to the back of his head as he fiddled with the channel controls. 'You can listen in if you like. It may be useful for you to know what the company does.'

She knew it was not a good idea to goad a man like Lubov. Her tone had turned priggish and immature, but her blood was up and she was becoming more and more resentful of her treatment with every passing moment. Had she known back in New York that she would end up locked in a room with this odious thug she would definitely have declined the trip.

The Russian turned around slowly to face her. As he did, he reached into his inside pocket for his cigarettes and lit up in front of her. He favoured an untipped Turkish brand with a distinctive strong aroma. Caroline instinctively looked around for a 'No Smoking' sign as he exhaled a cloud of pungent smoke, but then remembered where they were. For Lubov, cigarettes were an integral part of his make-up and he was rarely without one in his hand. He regarded her now through narrowed eyes as he took another long drag. Caroline noticed he was smiling, but the look on his face was cruel and humourless. He liked the fact that he had riled her. The smile melted away as he spoke.

'That won't be necessary. I know this company intimately,' he said, drawing the last word out syllable by syllable. A half smile flickered momentarily across his face as he added, 'In fact, I know it probably better even than you know your big security man boyfriend.'

Caroline turned away and stared at the television. Her mind was reeling. He'd been checking up on her, prying into her private life and perhaps even spying on her. Simon wasn't actually her boyfriend but somehow Lubov knew about him. How? she wondered. She would definitely report it to van der Linden. This kind of behaviour was totally unacceptable and he would no doubt agree.

A face flashed up on the television in front of her. It looked familiar, but she wasn't really focusing. Then she recognised the detective she and Kelly had met at West End Central police station. Lubov turned the sound up and moved closer to the set. It was strange standing there in the heart of a tropical jungle looking at the dark streets of London as the reporter recounted the gruesome details of the previous night. More murders.

After the report ended, they cut to a press conference that had just taken place in London. The police had a photograph of the killer and expected to make an arrest soon. Caroline heard a door slam behind her and realised Lubov had left the room. She was alone.

She slumped heavily into a chair after helping herself to a third cup of bitter-tasting coffee. Outside, through a large plate glass window, the tree line of the dense jungle was plainly visible thirty yards away. Parrots and other tropical birds were sailing effortlessly above the canopy before disappearing into the dense green backdrop. But Caroline wasn't really paying attention to this kaleidoscope of activity. Her mind was a maelstrom of thoughts and emotions.

On one level, she loved her new job. What she was doing was fascinating, exciting and, most of all, worthwhile. Edward van der Linden had treated her with kindness and respect ever since she had joined Eleventh Hour and he always made every effort to show her he appreciated her work. She couldn't ask for a more interesting, accommodating and generous boss. After all, she was here in this spectacular place because he was kind enough to invite her along.

But then there was the other side of the equation; the feeling of being an outsider under constant observation, who for some reason, was only allowed to see part of the total picture. She now knew beyond doubt that this was not her imagination. Aleksei Lubov had just confirmed it. And anyway, why would Eleventh Hour have a need for a man like Aleksei Lubov if everything was above board?

Where better to find her answers than here? It was time for action.

CHAPTER 31

Caroline followed Lubov's lead and found herself in a long corridor lined with anonymous doors on either side. She could clearly hear him stomping along the passageway some way ahead, so she slowed her pace. The doors were numbered sequentially and had small observation windows with wire mesh in the glass. As she stole past Room 51, she glimpsed white-coated figures huddled around laboratory work benches.

It went quiet up ahead. Lubov had stopped for some reason just around the next corner. Perhaps he had heard footsteps and was wondering who was following him. Caroline shrank against the side wall. Then, after a few seconds, she heard a strange whooshing noise and the footsteps started up again before disappearing altogether. She waited, listening intently for any sound. Perhaps he was doing the same, waiting for her to show herself. Caroline remained motionless, taking care to breathe as quietly as possible. Then, after two long minutes of total silence, she felt confident enough to move on again.

She shuffled hesitantly around the corner, half-expecting to be confronted by a triumphant Aleksei Lubov. But she was alone. The Russian had obviously moved beyond the smoked glass security door which now blocked her progress. She read a sign in large red letters: 'Restricted Area – Authorised Personnel Only'. The door was secure and could only be released with a security pass. Her expedition was beginning to seem like a waste of time when she heard a door slam in the corridor behind her. Footsteps rapidly approached. She looked around for somewhere to hide. There wasn't anywhere, she was trapped. The footsteps came nearer. Someone was about to round the corner.

The lab technician visibly started when he came upon Caroline standing with her back to the glass door. He looked familiar and Caroline half-remembered him as one of her lunchtime hosts.

'Miss Hartley. What are you doing here?' he asked in a clipped English accent.

His manner was friendly and he seemed to bear no trace of suspicion, so Caroline decided that bluff was the best course of action.

'I had to finish some work, so I missed the start of the tour.' She gave the young technician her most innocent smile. 'I was just trying to catch up with the others.'

'I'm sorry, but they will be some way ahead by now, Miss Hartley. Anyway, you need to be with someone with top security clearance to go beyond those doors.' A look of concern crossed his face. 'You will have missed most of the tour already, I'm afraid.'

'Oh, damn!' she exclaimed and folded her arms in a display of disappointment.

He studied her closely. She could see that he was deliberating. Then he spoke again.

'I could show you round quickly myself, if you like?'

'That would be fantastic. Do you think we can make it back in, say, fifteen or twenty minutes?'

She had no idea how long the others would be away but guessed that van der Linden would not have flown Abe two and a half thousand miles to give him a whistle-stop tour, so twenty minutes would probably give her enough time to see what she had to see and then return to the common room. The real danger was Lubov. She didn't know where he had gone or how long he would be.

Her escort waved a security pass at the sensor and the glass door slid open.

'Follow me, please Miss Hartley. By the way, my name is Hwang. Dr Hwang.'

A polite bow accompanied the introduction.

'Dr Hwang, I am so grateful to you for sparing me your time like this. I wonder, could you tell me firstly, what is the nature of the research being carried out here?'

He looked at her slightly quizzically, but he answered nevertheless.

'Our work is dedicated to the eradication of disease,' he said grandly.

'But why here? Why in the middle of the jungle?' she enquired.

Hwang smiled pleasantly as he answered. 'Eleventh Hour chose to locate the facility here due to safety fears and also because a great deal of our work involves the use of natural plant extracts. It is believed in these parts that the forests contain a cure for every one of man's ailments, including cancer.'

'Really,' replied Caroline. 'And is it all going well?'

Hwang turned to face her. 'Be patient, Miss Hartley, and I will be pleased to show you.'

They had stopped outside Room 68. Hwang knocked, then gently eased the door open and entered, beckoning Caroline to follow.

'This is Professor Herman Swannel, the world-renowned microbiologist and geneticist.'

Hwang said this with real reverence, gesturing towards a man who bounded enthusiastically towards them with his hand outstretched. He was tall, six foot at least, and sported two enormous greying lamb chop sideburns and a mop of tightly curled grey hair. He looked very happy to see them and he shook Caroline's hand warmly.

'Caroline Hartley,' she said, attempting to wrestle her hand free from his tight grip.

'Lovely to meet you. We don't have many visitors down here you know,' the professor boomed as if he was speaking for the benefit of an audience. 'Certainly none as pretty as you anyway, my love.'

Caroline smiled awkwardly. His accent was cut-glass English gent, so upper-class that it seemed almost exaggerated. His diction and pronunciation were reminiscent of the voiceover on a Second World War Pathé News bulletin. A pair of bifocal spectacles hung around his neck, secured crudely by a length of hairy twine and his top pocket was crammed full of biros of different colours which rounded off the whole 'eccentric scientist' image rather nicely, Caroline observed.

Dr Hwang saved Caroline further embarrassment.

'Mr Swannel, sir, perhaps you would be so kind as to give Miss Hartley a brief overview of your research?'

The scientist took Caroline's hand and gently led her towards the nearest work bench. The top of the bench was covered with rows of petri dishes and an assortment of flasks, beakers and miscellaneous other laboratory equipment. What caught Caroline's eye though was a large glass tank in the centre of the table. It contained hundreds of mosquitoes.

'Ah!' exclaimed Swannel, noticing the direction of her gaze. 'And that, Miss Hartley – or Caroline if I may? – is what we're all about: finding a way to rid the world of those little perishers.'

He gave the glass a sharp tap with his knuckle as he spoke, as if to remind the inhabitants that he was on their case.

'They,' he said, pointing an accusing finger, 'perform no useful function for man nor beast. All they do is cause death and spread pestilence. In fact, there is no reason that I can discern why the Almighty should have put them on this Earth in the first place. Your friend Abe, who was here earlier, is convinced that it is all a part of some kind of divine order designed to keep our numbers down.'

Caroline rolled her eyes at the mention of the old man.

'Quite, quite,' muttered the professor, throwing his arms in the air and shaking his head in disbelief. 'That's the sort of claptrap that Malthusians pedalled two centuries ago. They thought disease was a natural, self-regulating device that kicked in when population numbers exceeded a certain level.'

He drew close to Caroline, obviously enjoying the fact that he had such a willing listener.

'The reality though, Caroline, is that every creature on the planet is locked into its own individual battle for survival. And it's been that way since Adam was a boy. It's like a massive evolutionary chess game with each species developing in order to outmanoeuvre its enemies and to outsmart its prey.'

He was in full lecture mode now and when he gestured with a flourish of his arm towards a lab stool, Caroline sat down obediently.

'Take these nasty little creatures,' he continued, tapping the glass more aggressively than before. 'Unpleasant as they may be, they are actually a triumph of evolution. That's why they are so successful. A mosquito can land on its prey without being detected, even by the tiny hairs on our skin designed specifically for that purpose. When they bite they first of all inject an anaesthetic to mask the pain as they penetrate the tissue to drink our blood. Their saliva even contains an anti-coagulant to stop the blood clotting. The process is so efficient we don't usually even know it's happened. An absolute masterpiece of evolution. They are actually one step ahead of human counter-development.'

'Until now,' said Dr Hwang, beaming.

'Yes, yes. Now Hwang old chap, don't steal my thunder. I'm just setting the scene for our lovely guest here.'

He shot Dr Hwang a chastening glance, wagging a finger in the air to warn him against further interruption. Caroline was grateful for Hwang's efforts to hurry things along. She was becoming anxious and really didn't want to be missed by the others and have to explain why she'd been snooping around by herself. A shadow passed by the window in the door. She couldn't see who it was, but hoped it wasn't Lubov out looking for her.

'So, Caroline,' continued the professor. 'Do you know what has killed more human beings than all the battles and wars that have ever been fought in the entire history of *homo sapiens*?'

She knew this. 'Malaria,' she offered obligingly.

'Good girl! Would you like to have a stab at how many deaths per year this dreadful disease is responsible for?'

She didn't want to give an answer that was wide of the mark and made her look ignorant.

'I'm not exactly sure. You tell me, Professor Swannel.'

'Call me Herman, please Caroline,' he said smiling broadly and stroking her shoulder. Caroline took a step back. 'OK, I'll tell you,' he continued. 'Each year between 280 and 500 million people contract the disease and up to one million of these unfortunate souls will die of it. It's a massive problem and always has been.' For the first time since she had met him, the professor looked serious. 'But the world has woken up to it over the last few years. Governments have pledged millions to fund research into both prevention and potential immunisation and the World Health Authority and a number of Charity Foundations are now testing a very promising vaccine. So the race is on.'

He paused for a second and Caroline watched in surprise as a smile spread across his face. He then quite unexpectedly threw his arms in the air and exclaimed excitedly.

'Except that we have beaten everyone to it! We've won.

I, Professor Herman Jeremy Swannel, have come up with the solution.' He beamed proudly and then looked momentarily at the floor in an effort to compose himself. 'Sorry Caroline but it is still such a source of absolute joy to me. I just wish we could make an announcement but the "powers that be" here say "not yet". You know the way it is. Politics and all that.' He grumbled these last words unhappily but seemed generally resigned to the situation.

Caroline found herself carried away with the moment and even the poker-faced Mr Hwang gave a toothy smile.

'That's wonderful. So what exactly have you done?' she asked, keen to hear more. Swannel was visibly flattered at her interest and stood tall as he replied.

'Well, it's quite revolutionary actually, although not really what we set out to do. Put simply, we have found a way of eradicating the mosquito for good. So now we don't need a vaccine at all. Here, in this very laboratory, we created a virus that essentially sterilises the male of the species. And like so many great discoveries, our breakthrough was down to our old friend serendipity.'

Caroline said nothing but her look of puzzlement was enough to encourage Swannel to elaborate, if indeed he needed any such encouragement.

'Originally, like everyone else, we were trying to develop a vaccine. We were working with a virus called Adeno-associated virus or AAV, which we were using as a vector. Viruses, you see, are incredibly efficient at transporting genetic material around the body and into cells. It's called transduction.' The professor paused for a second. 'Not getting too technical, am I?'

'No, still with you Herman.'

Her use of his Christian name brought a smile to his face and made him look even more pleased with himself. Unfortunately, it seemed to encourage him in another way too. He paused and shamelessly ran his eyes up and down her body before he continued.

'So we tend to use viruses a great deal in immunology to actually transmit disease from one cell to another. Anyway, we didn't think that AAV, one of my particular favourites as it happens, caused any disease of its own and merely acted as a very efficient transporter of second-hand genetic material. We were wrong. The first sign that things were not as they should be was when we kept running out of mosquitos. For some unknown reason, we couldn't culture them in the lab and in the end we had to bring the little blighters in from the jungle. That got me thinking. It reminded me of an incident that was never really fully explained. After the Chernobyl disaster in 1986, many of the firemen became infertile. After painstaking research into their condition, geneticists finally concluded that the radiation had minutely altered their DNA and as a result had triggered a natural reaction in their bodies that prevented the tainted DNA from being passed on to future generations. Fascinating, isn't it? The human body is actually somehow programmed to avoid contamination of the human gene pool.'

Caroline nodded. This was all very interesting and she wanted to hear what happened next, but she was becoming concerned at the length of time she had already spent in the lab. They needed to get moving. There was no stopping Swannel, though.

'So I decided to subject AAV to more rigorous analysis and I discovered that the virus indeed caused DNA to mutate and these minute, almost indiscernible, changes directly affected fertility. I then gave the virus a few tweaks in the genetics lab and Bob's your uncle, we had the perfect solution to our problem.' He stopped talking for a second and cocked his fingers like a gun. 'So it's *arrivederci* plasmodium! That's the name of the nasty little parasite that causes the malaria disease, by the way.'

'Thank you, Professor Swannel, for sharing your marvellous triumph with us,' said Dr Hwang, showing signs of impatience now as he steered Caroline towards the door.

'Yes, thank you so much—'

Caroline stopped in mid-sentence and let out a yelp of surprise as she felt the professor's hand give her buttock a firm squeeze.

'Works even better on mammals, you know,' he said, as if nothing had happened.

She made it to the door well before Dr Hwang. Swannel was still talking as if it was perfectly normal to grope any female in close proximity to himself, which Caroline suspected was probably the case in his cloistered world deep in the jungle.

'... So we think it would be perfect to control rodent populations ...'

They were about to leave when the professor stopped them.

'Before you go Miss Hartley perhaps you could help me name my new drug. Not really my forte that kind of thing and you seem the creative type. Usually we go for simple numbers and letters, but I fancy something a little more, shall we say, interesting, this time.'

He handed Caroline his business card with a leering smile.

'Just email me if you have a moment of inspiration, or want a chat. If not, I suppose I'll simply be stuck with ZXK 214 or something like that!'

Dr Hwang opened the door and Caroline backed towards it, unwilling to present the professor with a tempting target. But as she turned to follow Hwang out of the room, she heard footsteps approaching down the corridor. Fast-moving footsteps. Lubov! It had to be!

She stopped in her tracks and looked round at Dr Hwang, who was readying to leave the room behind her.

'Just a second, Dr Hwang.' She held up her hand to keep him inside the room. 'I've thought of a name for the sterilisation drug.'

She positioned herself between her guide and the door so that she was hidden from view from anyone passing down the corridor. The footsteps drew closer.

'How about "E-rad-eX"? Written as capital "E", hyphen, then "rad", hyphen, "e", capital "X".'

Swannel paused for a second as he considered her suggestion. Then a broad smile lit up his face.

'Oh, yes, I like that.'

His eyes shone with enthusiasm as he scrawled the name down on a scrap of paper with a pen extracted from the multi-coloured clump in his top pocket. He wrote it again and then a third time, this time more slowly in much larger letters.

'It's clever. A shortened version of "eradicate" followed by an "eX" which can also mean … used to be or extinct.' He continued, as if she needed the name explaining to her. 'The "X" also keeps it sounding medical. For some reason there are hundreds of drugs ending in "X".'

The footsteps passed without stopping. She was safe for now.

Professor Swannel was still enthusing, oblivious to her anxiety. 'Capital suggestion. Swannel's E-rad-eX it is then!'

He said the word with relish as if he were announcing the numbers for a lottery. Outside, in the empty corridor, Dr Hwang hesitated.

'So sorry, Miss Hartley. Professor Swannel took up more time than I anticipated. We only have a little time left.'

'Please, don't apologise. It was absolutely fascinating. Perhaps we should go back now?'

'But there is so much more to see,' interrupted her guide with obvious disappointment. 'Perhaps if I quickly show you our most secure laboratory.'

'Oh, OK, if you like,' replied Caroline. The words 'most secure' pricked her curiosity and in any case she genuinely wanted to see more.

'It won't take long though, will it?' she continued.

She looked hard at her wristwatch to emphasise the point. They were already close to her self-imposed time limit.

To reach the laboratory, they had to walk outside in the blazing mid-afternoon sun. The heat and humidity were oppressive and their pace slowed noticeably as they approached an enclosure ringed by a tall razor wire fence.

At the entrance, Dr Hwang was nodded through by an armed guard in a sentry box, but then had to face a Perspex screen for a full iris scan before they were allowed into the building. As the door slid silently shut behind them, the chaos of the jungle was once again replaced by a sterile silence and the hum of air conditioning.

'Please follow,' said Dr Hwang, beckoning.

They approached a large smoked glass window, through which Caroline could see half a dozen figures dressed in what looked like spacesuits.

'We will not be able to enter today,' whispered Hwang. 'The area is restricted. Anyone entering the lab must wear a Positive Pressure Protective Suit or 'blue suit' as we call them with an independent air supply. Also, afterwards, everyone must pass through decontamination.'

He pointed to a room to the side of the main lab where Caroline could just make out a line of elaborate-looking showers.

'What's going on?' she asked in a hushed voice as if not to disturb the 'spacemen' on the other side of glass.

'This is our virology lab. Here we are working with the most dangerous diseases known to man.'

Caroline instinctively took a step back from the window.

'Anthrax, diphtheria, smallpox. All the old diseases and the new ones too. AIDS, Ebola, SARS and many types of flu virus.'

Four of the figures in protective suits were working with laboratory equipment on a large central table whilst the other two watched. Even from this distance, through the smoked glass, Caroline could recognise the immense frame of Edward van der Linden standing next to a smaller, stooped figure she took to be Abe. No sign of Aleksei Lubov though.

Dr Hwang continued his explanation in his quiet, precise voice as one of the heavily protected technicians in the room behind slowly poured liquid from a flask held at arm's length by a pair of extendable tongs. Everything seemed to be happening in slow motion, like a scene from a science fiction movie.

'Most of our work is on genetic mutation of influenza viruses,' Hwang said.

'Oh yes, swine flu and bird flu,' interjected Caroline. 'I think I read that they pose the greatest threat to mankind.'

'Maybe,' her guide replied with a slightly sceptical tone. 'Yes, a flu mutation could be very serious. The H7N9 and H5N1 bird flu strains are particularly worrying, although they're not airborne.' A smile crept across his face when he realised what he had just said. 'Not on their own, although I can't rule out the infection of an avian host capable of flying. So far, thankfully, they have affected only chickens.'

One of the 'spacemen' behind them – the big one that Caroline assumed was van der Linden – started to point towards a cabinet full of flasks. He was obviously explaining what was going on to Abe. The other figures stood back and watched, happy for the boss to do the talking. Although Caroline couldn't hear what he was saying, his passion was evident even from a distance and through a glass screen.

Reassured that the others were not yet ready to leave the lab, Caroline switched her attention back to Dr Hwang, who was still talking.

'Spanish Flu killed around fifty million people just after the First World War. But, believe it or not, that disease did proportionately less damage than the pandemics of the Middle Ages.'

Caroline raised her eyebrows in surprise.

'Oh yes, the Plague was terrifying and simply unstoppable. It was responsible for wiping out about sixty percent of Europe's population in the fourteenth century you know.'

'I had no idea it killed that many,' replied Caroline. 'It was spread by rats wasn't it?'

Dr Hwang smiled. Like so many academics, he enjoyed it when a layman attempted to show knowledge. It played into his hands. He nodded sagely and Caroline knew from his demeanour that a lecture was coming her way.

'That is the general belief, Miss Hartley. Yes, the Bubonic, Pneumonic and Septicemic Plagues were probably spread by fleas – *xenopsylla cheopis* to be precise – which were carried by rodents. But the Black Death, the ancient plague of Egypt and the Justinian Plague of the First Century AD, may all have been completely different and caused by something far more sinister.'

'Oh, I thought the Black Death *was* Bubonic Plague,' she replied, trying to remember her school history lessons.

'People think that,' said Hwang, 'but that's one of the things we're researching in there.' He pointed at the glass. 'Plagues are generally caused by the bacteria *yersinia pestis*, but we now believe that the Black Death may in fact have been a virus. An airborne virus. And that's why it was so lethal and spread so fast. People back then suspected as much and that is why they used to block up their windows on the side of the house that faced the prevailing wind.'

This was all very interesting from a research point of view, but Caroline was still a little unsure about the role of Eleventh Hour in all of this.

'So, what are these people trying to do?' she asked.

'They are working on vaccines. Vaccines and cures for all the planet's major diseases and any likely variants.'

'Variants?'

'Yes, bird flu, SARS, AIDS ... they're all the result of accidental genetic mutations. We have the ability to anticipate diseases that could pose a threat, rather than wait for them to happen. If they don't exist already, we make them.'

'You actually manufacture dangerous diseases?'

'Well yes, it's all perfectly safe. That's how we learn. We know for example a Black Death virus is possible—'

Caroline finished his sentence for him. 'Because you've created it!'

'Quite,' said the doctor, before adding proudly, 'you see, once you have the disease, then you can develop a vaccine.'

As he said these words, Caroline noticed van der Linden and Abe slowly making their way across the room. The scientist followed her gaze.

'Ah, they have finished. Decontamination will take about ten minutes. We still have plenty of time.'

'Thank you, Dr Hwang, this has been absolutely fascinating.'

Caroline worried that they had not seen Aleksei Lubov. She could just imagine him pacing the corridors searching for her and the thought of an ugly, unplanned encounter filled her with dread.

'Perhaps we can go back now?'

Hwang bowed politely. 'Of course, Miss Hartley. I am so pleased to have been of service.'

Next to the large, glass-fronted laboratory they'd been staring into, Caroline noticed a small room with a frontage of about three metres with a solid-looking door in the centre. It looked like a strong room of some sort. Hwang saw her gaze and stopped abruptly in front of it.

'Ah, yes,' he exclaimed, 'you will like this Miss Hartley. Don't worry; it won't take long for me to show you what's inside.'

And with that he pressed his security pass to a sensor and held his hand over a finger print reader to one side of the entrance. Caroline then watched as he grabbed hold of a large stainless steel wheel on the front and twirled it three full revolutions before pulling the heavy door open. There was a hiss of decompression followed by a cloud of white vapour.

'Refrigerated,' beamed Hwang. 'Everything is cooled to exactly 1.5 degrees Celsius, just above freezing.' A light flickered on automatically, bathing the interior in a dazzling white light. Caroline peered inside and saw row after row of small glass ampoules filled with liquids of different colour on tiered shelves running the length of the room. There were thousands of them.

'This is our vaccine store,' crowed Hwang proudly. 'Inside this room we have an effective vaccine for every disease known to man. And even some that are not known,' he added mischievously. 'One day, sickness will be a thing of the past thanks to Eleventh Hour.' He then closed the heavy door and they continued on their way.

The sounds and scents of the jungle once again invaded their senses as they left the silent, air-conditioned comfort behind them and walked back out into the blazing sunshine. Although the air was thick with insects, Caroline asked to return to the main building from outside rather than brave the corridors of the laboratory complex.

Hwang was still energised and talked animatedly about his laboratory's work and how Eleventh Hour would change the world.

'So where is home for you Dr Hwang?' asked Caroline, resorting to small-talk in an attempt to turn the conversation away from disease and pestilence, which she felt she had heard quite enough of for one day.

'I come from a small town called Miryang in South Chungeong, about one hundred kilometres from Seoul,' he replied and as he spoke a broad smile lit up his face. 'And I will be visiting there soon.'

'Oh that's nice,' she replied politely. 'Are you going on holiday?'

'The facility is closing for two weeks. We have all been given a vacation,' he announced excitedly. 'Mr van der Linden is rewarding us for good work. Eleventh Hour is even flying us all to our different countries and has chartered a plane especially.'

'That's incredible,' exclaimed Caroline, taken aback by the generosity of this gesture. She had already thought how difficult it must be for them all working in the middle of a dense jungle, thousands of miles from home. Obviously van der Linden appreciated this too. He certainly knew how to run a happy ship.

The logistics of the operation would be incredible though.

'How many countries will that involve?' she asked.

'Who knows?' said Hwang shrugging, 'I just hope South Korea is the first stop, although a night in Hong Kong or Bangkok would be fun.' He laughed out loud, before asking playfully, 'Do you like snakes, Miss Hartley?' They were skirting a small prefabricated building twenty yards from their destination. 'Or maybe spiders?' he added, then without waiting for an answer, opened the door to the building and beckoned her to follow.

It was another laboratory similar to the others they had visited, except in this room the walls were lined with aquarium-like glass tanks.

'Our Toxicology Department,' smiled her escort.

She looked closer at the tanks and realised that each one contained some kind of creature. She spied snakes and frogs, and massive spiders scratching at the glass in an effort to gain their freedom. Hwang chuckled when he saw her shiver and shrink back towards the door.

'It's perfectly safe, Miss Hartley. You have nothing to fear. Here we develop antivenoms. All of these creatures are potential killers. One bite from him ...' he pointed at a small black snake in a tank next to them '... and you wouldn't even make it to the door.'

Caroline turned to leave. As she did, she noticed a large

fish in an aquarium by the door. It was looking at her with huge, sad almost puppy-like eyes as it swam up and down the tank.

'Oh, meet Charlie,' said the scientist. 'We all love Charlie. He's our pet spiny puffer fish. Be nice though, because if you scare him, he'll inflate like a football.'

He tapped the glass and the fish responded by swimming towards his finger.

'Cute,' said Caroline, captivated by the creature, which at that moment seemed to be looking directly into her eyes.

'Yes, but deadly – like everything around here,' said Hwang as he led her from the building.

A few minutes later, he took his leave and hurried back in the direction of his laboratory. Caroline composed herself, took a deep breath and pushed open the door to the common room.

'Where you been?' barked Lubov, springing out of his chair and striding aggressively towards her.

'I decided to go for a walk,' she replied, meeting his gaze. 'There's no law against that, is there? Or am I your prisoner Aleksei?'

The door opened at the far end of the room and van der Linden entered, followed by a beaming Abe Gottlieb.

'What's going on?' he said to the Russian in a less affable tone than usual.

'Nothing, boss,' replied Lubov. 'She decided to go for a walkabout, alone.'

He jerked his thumb rudely in Caroline's direction.

Van der Linden looked at him sternly, slightly raising his eyebrows.

'Outside,' Lubov added.

Caroline was getting quite used to this form of unspoken communication and could easily interpret the meaning behind their glances. Van der Linden obviously wanted to know if she had been in the complex. His expression softened.

'Well, just so long as you came to no harm, that's fine.' Van der Linden turned to address her. 'It can get a little hairy out there. It is the jungle, after all.'

'We need to talk,' said the Russian, walking towards the far side of the room and gesturing for his boss to follow.

Caroline's pulse quickened. Was he going to complain about her and tell van der Linden about their argument? Then she remembered how Lubov had been prying into her private life. She was the one who should be complaining. It was outrageous!

The two of them went into a huddle, leaving Caroline prey to an excited and highly vociferous Abe Gottlieb.

'What a place this is,' drawled the old man. 'He's going to change the world you know. And I'm going to help him, yes sir. It was a lucky day when I met Teddy.'

'Really Abe?' replied Caroline less than enthusiastically.

She was actually trying to hear what was being said over the other side of the room, so didn't want to be drawn into another of Abe's monologues. She couldn't make out much of their conversation, but could tell by their expressions that they were discussing something highly contentious. Surely it wasn't about her? Cold dread gripped her. She might lose her job. Van der Linden raised his voice at one point, saying what sounded like 'enough'. Then she distinctly heard him say, 'She's had her last chance, she is jeopardising everything.' Her heart thumped in her chest.

Back in the helicopter, Lubov and the Green Giant kept themselves to themselves and on the return trip to New York they sat at the front of the plane in complete silence.

'Is something the matter?' Caroline asked her boss sheepishly when she could bear it no longer.

They were in the BA First Class Lounge at JFK. Abe had taken his leave a few minutes before and Lubov, ever restless, had wandered off somewhere.

'Sorry, Caroline,' said the big man, resting his hand on her shoulder. 'I haven't been particularly good company, have I? Look, it's nothing to worry about. And, hey, thanks for coming along. I know it was a bit of a disappointment for you.'

'No, it was great,' she protested.

And she meant it. What she wanted to say was that she knew about the amazing medical research he was undertaking and the strides he was making to eradicate malaria. But, of course, she couldn't. For some reason, he wanted the work in the jungle facility to remain a secret. This was disappointing, but at that moment she didn't care. What mattered was that she was not in trouble, wasn't going to be fired and could continue to work for Eleventh Hour.

CHAPTER 32

The café was clean but cried out for a lick of paint to cover the spattered mosaic of tea stains and food on the walls. Scuffed lino, laid bare to the floorboards, and a creaking door complete with an entry bell that pinged as it opened, finished off the 'greasy spoon' ambiance of Kev's Place. DC Hargreaves had been there for about ten minutes sipping a cup of sugary tea and wondering why it always tasted so good in places like this.

'Seen him love?' he asked the woman behind the counter, who'd been making eyes at him ever since he'd entered, holding aloft a dog-eared photo of Harold Butterworth. She was in her mid-thirties, a little on the plump side with heavy mascara and unfashionable blue eye shadow, but nevertheless, he had to admit she was quite pretty in a rather obvious way.

She leant over the table, intentionally displaying a large amount of cleavage underneath her white overall and squinted hard at the photo.

'You a copper then?'

'Detective,' replied Hargreaves.

'Ooh, I bet you look alright in yer uniform.'

Hargreaves didn't reply and just moved the photo closer to her face.

'What's 'e done, then?' she asked.

'Nothing. We just need to find him.'

She turned her head and let out a shrill cry. 'Kevin! Come in 'ere a mo, can yer?'

An older man poked his bald head through a hatchway at the back of the shop.

'What's up, Linda?' he shouted, looking put out. 'I'm doin' the sandwiches, aren't I?'

'Can you come in 'ere and 'av a butchers at this picture. 'E's a copper,' she added, nodding her head in the detective's direction.

A minute later, he waddled huffily into the room, wiped his hands down his stained apron, then took the photo from DC Hargreaves.

'I reckon it's the geezer you give a bun to the other day, Kev,' continued Linda.

'Yeah, you may be right there, girl,' he said holding the grainy picture in the air to catch a little more light.

'We get all sorts round 'ere mate: drunks, junkies, hookers, you name it. But 'e looked a decent enough sort. Reminded me of my old grandpa, as it 'appens. 'Cept for 'is hooter of course.' He made a gesture of elongation to his own nose. 'That was some Mary Rose, eh Lin?'

'Any idea where he may be now?' Hargreaves asked, watching Kevin rest his hand on Linda's ample backside as he contemplated his question.

'Last I saw of 'im, 'e was 'edding down the 'ill towards Jubilee Park.'

Hargreaves stood up to leave.

''E weren't in great shape you know, that's why I gave 'im the food. Not really with it, if you know what I mean.'

'Well, thanks for the information. It's been very helpful.'

With that, the detective headed for the door.

'Look, if you find 'im,' added Kevin, 'be sure to bring 'im back in 'ere. I'll stand the old bugger a five-star fry up, on the 'owse,' then he turned and headed back to the kitchen.

'Are you sure there isn't anything else I can do for you?' offered Linda, shamelessly batting her eyelashes.

'Leave the lad alone, you dirty cow,' yelled Kevin through the hatch. ''E's got a job to do, an' so 'ave you!'

★

Harold had been drifting in and out of consciousness for the last hour or so. *Dying wasn't that bad*, he thought. Then, through the haze of his failing vision, he saw two figures walking towards him. One, dressed in a green parka jacket, was small and plump, the other much taller. They'd come for him, he could tell. The adrenalin surge cleared his eyesight, but he was too weak to stand up. In fact, he was too weak to do anything but watch. They approached tentatively and when they were a few yards away they stopped and looked at him.

'It's him,' muttered the fat one.

'Positive?' replied the other, his hand sliding inside his jacket.

'Certain. Just do it.'

At that precise moment, Detective Constable Stephen

Hargreaves, entered the small park. Although he was still some distance away, he read the situation in an instant.

'Oi, you two!' he shouted. 'Stand away!'

The two figures spun round to face him. He'd hoped that they would turn tail and scarper, but they didn't. Instead they split up and started to circle him menacingly. Hargreaves felt a frisson of excitement as he realised that these were not a couple of opportunist thieves on their way back from the pub. They were in the park with one purpose: to kill Harold Butterworth. Outnumbered, with no help at hand, he toyed briefly with the idea of using his phone to call for assistance, but decided it would take too long. Anyway, he could see that one of his aggressors, the tall thin one, was edging closer, readying himself for an attack. Hargreaves had identified him as the main threat. He knew what he was doing, at that moment he was moving crab-like, with his legs apart to lower his centre of gravity. He was a pro. The detective adopted the same posture, working his feet into the soft grass, readying himself for the inevitable attack.

It was a mistake to discount the man in the green parka though. As Hargreaves focussed his attention on the tall thin one, he momentarily lost sight of the second man who seized his opportunity and rushed him from his blind side, cracking the policeman over the head with a cosh he'd surreptitiously slipped out of his coat pocket. Hargreaves saw the threat too late to avoid the blow, but nevertheless his sharp reflexes enabled him to deliver a savage jab with his elbow, which caught his attacker full in the face. He heard the nose pop and the fat man let out a squeal of pain as he scurried away up the footpath.

The blow to the head stunned the policeman and he momentarily lost his balance, going down on one knee. Thankfully, the other assailant didn't press home his advantage. He was distracted by his colleague's cowardly departure and watched him stumbling away into the gloom of dusk.

Hargreaves couldn't focus properly for a second or two. A sparkling constellation of flashing lights danced in front of his eyes. The thin man bent forward, ready to charge. The detective didn't actually see the stiletto in his hand, but something about the man's movements and posture alerted him to the danger. He was still groggy, but he somehow managed to avoid the blade as his attacker lunged at him. They circled each other and again his attacker jabbed at him. This time he wasn't quite quick enough and the blade pierced his coat, slicing deep into his left shoulder.

Blood was flowing freely down his forehead now from the livid wound caused by the cosh. He wiped his eyes, preparing for the next attack. His legs were growing heavy and his left arm was next to useless. The thin man closed in for the kill, but as he did, Harold let out a strange cry: half-wail, half-yell.

The noise disturbed the attacker's concentration, delaying his thrust by a split-second, which was enough to enable Hargreaves to block the assault and fling his full weight into the man. His unarmed combat training clicked in. In a move he had practised a hundred times, he simultaneously grabbed the knife arm and twisted the hand inwards. They tumbled onto the ground together.

Hargreaves rolled away and rose to his feet in a single action. He may have been wounded, but thankfully still had the vitality of youth on his side. His attacker wriggled a little at first but then fell still. As he tentatively approached, Hargreaves saw why, the knife was buried to the hilt in his chest. The thin man was dead.

*

Back in London, John Cavey's face was a mask of concern as he talked quietly into his mobile.

'Stay where you are lad. Help's on its way.'

Then he turned and shouted to his team who had stopped what they were doing and were watching him intently.

'Everyone, we've got a man down. Hargreaves is injured. Sergeant, you and Samuels get down there as fast as you can. He's found our man and taken out one of the killers as well by the sound of it.'

There was a flutter of excitement. Sergeant Noble already had his coat on and was hurrying from the room.

'Make sure you look after the boy,' Cavey said.

'I will, sir,' said the sergeant. 'You can depend on it.'

And Cavey knew he could. Noble had worked for Cavey for ten years now and his loyalty and reliability were beyond question. He was also well aware that the welfare of his team was always the Inspector's first concern.

Cavey spoke into the phone again.

'They're on their way. We're all proud of you, Stephen. You've done well.'

It was the first time he had ever used his Christian name. Down in Portsmouth, Hargreaves was slumped on the bench next to Harold. His first call had been to the emergency services and finally he could hear sirens in the distance.

Harold's eyes were leaden. He just wanted to sleep.

'You came back for me, son,' he muttered weakly.

'Course I did, mate,' replied the detective, clenching his teeth against the searing pain in his shoulder.

The blood was now soaking through his jacket.

'You never got to the punch line of that joke you started back in the hospital, so I had to come and find you!' Hargreaves joked, smiling through the pain, then added more seriously, 'I'm on your side, mate. We all are.'

'I thought you were a goner when he stuck you with the knife,' the old man continued, as if speaking in a dream.

'Me and you both, Harold. You didn't exactly jump up and help though, did you?'

Harold gave a chuckle.

Hargreaves knew he had to keep the old man talking. If he lapsed into unconsciousness, he may never wake up, but his own head was swimming and he felt his mind starting to fog. Someone laid a gentle hand on his shoulder and when he opened his eyes, he was surprised to see Linda from the café.

'Bloody hell, what you been up to dreamboat?' she said, taking out a white handkerchief and dabbing gently at the blood running into his eyes.

'Yer didn't mention that yer was Rambo. What a bloody mess.' Then she looked at the body lying in front of them on the grass. 'An' 'e don't look too 'elfy niver.'

Hargreaves grunted appreciatively through a thin smile.

'Keep the old man awake,' he said with some difficulty.

His speech was becoming slurred and the words caught at the back of his throat as he spoke. She shook the old man, but his eyes were closed. A police car rounded the corner and hurtled towards them followed by an ambulance.

'Here come the cavalry, Harold,' mumbled the policeman, but the old man couldn't hear him.

CHAPTER 33

The days were getting noticeably shorter. It was now November and the sun was barely above the horizon at half past seven in the morning. Caroline was sitting on a stool in her favourite coffee shop opposite the entrance to the Eleventh Hour offices, watching the chaos of the early morning Mayfair traffic. Usually she would have taken her coffee to her desk, but today she didn't much feel like going in to work.

She and Simon had been discussing things over the weekend and they both agreed that something was not quite right at Eleventh Hour but neither of them could work out what it was. Caroline was determined though to find out and had decided that she needed to be extra vigilant.

In the street outside the window, her attention was drawn to a figure in a dark coat wearing an unfashionable black furry hat. She'd walked past the shop three or four times already and now she was back, looking furtively across the road towards the Eleventh Hour building. This time, though, the figure darted into the coffee shop instead of walking past. Caroline put her coffee down and looked closer. Under the hat with its brim turned downwards, she could just make out the sharp features of Sue Baxter. She was wearing tinted glasses, but there was no doubting it was her. Perhaps this was a fortunate encounter, she thought – her opportunity to ask Sue what was going on at Eleventh Hour.

Sue perched on a free stool two down from Caroline. She didn't buy a coffee but just continued to watch the building across the road intently. What was she looking for? A place became free next to her and Caroline moved over and sat down by her side.

'Morning Sue,' she chirped.

Sue jumped in surprise. 'Jesus Christ! Caroline!'

Sue grabbed her arm, squeezing it so hard it hurt.

'You haven't seen me,' she said, drawing close.

'Ahh, OK!' stuttered Caroline.

The grip on her arm slowly loosened.

Sue looked wild. Her eyes were darting from side to side and her twitching head movements made her seem even more bird-like than usual.

'Tell no one you have seen me.' Then her voice rose in intensity. 'No one, OK?'

'Fine, yes. But what's happening, Sue?'

'I'm out. That's what. He called me up and that was it. Out on my ear!'

She stared angrily across the road. Then she turned back to Caroline.

'Look, will you do me a favour?'

'That all depends on what it is,' replied Caroline awkwardly.

'I've left my notebook and my diary in the office and

they are absolutely irreplaceable. Will you get them and bring them to me?'

Caroline paused for a second. This gave her useful bargaining power.

'OK,' she replied, before adding, 'but if I do this for you, you must tell me what's going on. Why all the secrets and—'

She didn't finish. Sue thrust her security pass into her hand.

'Access code's 3167. They're on my desk, two black Moleskines. Just nip in, grab them and leave. You can give them to me later.'

Caroline didn't reply but slipped the card into her pocket.

'Look, do this for me and I'll do what you want,' whispered Sue, 'I'll tell you all about *them*.'

She stabbed a finger in the direction of Eleventh Hour as she spoke.

'You're right, you need to know what you're getting involved in anyway. Meet me in the Queen's Head in Shadwell at nine o'clock tonight. Bring the books with you.'

Caroline nodded. 'OK,' she said, trying hard to stifle the smile of satisfaction. She felt a growing excitement at the prospect of finally getting some answers to her many questions. It was time she went on the offensive.

Sue was already on her feet preparing to leave. Before she did, though, she scanned the coffee shop, checking every face in the room.

'Nine o'clock then. And watch out for Lubov!'

CHAPTER 34

As she hurried along the barely lit basement corridor, Caroline realised that she hadn't really thought this through. Last time she was down here, the Direct Action Group was a hive of activity. How would she explain herself to Sue's team? Wouldn't they wonder what she was doing there?

It was too late to change her plan now so she decided she would just have to bluff her way around any awkward questions. She punched in the code and swiped the card before pushing open the door. The room was in darkness.

'They've all gone,' she muttered to herself in surprise as she dashed across the carpet-tiled floor to Sue's desk. The office was as it had been when she was down there before. Just like any working environment, there were papers stacked high on desks and waste bins overflowing with coffee cups. Everything looked normal, except there were no people.

The books were there. She grabbed them and rushed out of the room, taking care to slam the door shut behind her. She then ran to the lift, spooked by the silence and the oppressive gloom. As she reached out her finger to summon the lift she realised with a start that it was already on its way.

Someone was coming down to the basement. She panicked and bolted through the emergency door into the stairwell. The stairs would take her back to the third floor and safety.

She had just made it back to her desk and was still catching her breath from climbing four flights of stairs, when a breathless Aleksei Lubov ran into her office, accompanied by one of his men. He scanned the room.

'Have you seen Sue Baxter in the last few minutes?' he demanded.

'No. Why?'

Something about the way she replied must have been unconvincing as the Russian stopped looking around the office and scrutinised her intently.

'Sure?' he asked suspiciously.

Caroline looked down at her desk and started writing on her notepad as if his presence was of no consequence to her.

He stood watching her. After a while, when she could bear it no longer, she looked up. Her heart leapt. He wasn't staring at her; he was looking directly at the two black Moleskine books on her desk.

'Ah, little black books,' he said, as if talking to himself. 'You people love your secret contact lists, don't you?'

'They… they're just for personal use,' she stuttered, as innocently as she could manage. 'These days I actually keep all my contacts on my tablet.'

'Good. That's good. At Eleventh Hour, we share information,' he purred. 'Did you know we sweep your machines every day? We take all the information on your tablet into our central database. I bet we've even got Mama Hartley's number somewhere!'

He let out a cruel laugh, then left. As he hurried down the corridor outside, she heard the other security guard shout to him.

'We'll find her. She must still be in the building.'

Caroline looked at the shiny green electronic tablet on her desk. Staff were encouraged to use them for every aspect of their work. But she had no idea that the company had the ability to download all the information it wanted from the device. On top of that, it appeared that Lubov and his team were monitoring all staff movements via their security passes, hence their misguided belief that Sue was in the building.

The discovery left her feeling hollow. She needed to ask Sue about all of this tonight.

*

At exactly nine o'clock Caroline walked into the Queen's Head to keep her appointment. This was not a part of town she was familiar with and she had little doubt Sue had chosen it because it was situated in a rundown area in between Docklands and the City. Somewhere neither of them was likely to run into anyone they knew. The pub was dingy and smelt of stale beer. Like so many old English hostelries, it was a maze of alcoves and discreet corners underneath wooden beams adorned with the standard horse brasses, in an attempt to create atmosphere through the illusion of 'Olde Worlde' charm. She couldn't see Sue and walked around the place twice before she spotted her tucked away in the corner by the window. It was obvious that she'd been there a while. A plate of half-finished lasagne had been pushed aside to make way for a fresh glass of wine, her fourth judging by the empties.

Sue leapt to her feet when she saw Caroline, sweeping back her unkempt mane before enveloping her in an extravagant hug. Caroline sat down at the table. She felt uncomfortable, Sue was strange at the best of times, but in a state of high excitement and drunk, she was downright weird. There was no other word for it. Sue peered out of the window, then spoke with urgency in her voice.

'You weren't followed, were you?'

Her words were slurred and her eyes furtive. Caroline shook her head, toying with the idea of just giving her the books and leaving.

'Sure?'

'Yes, certain.'

'No one knows you are here?'

'No,' she lied (she had actually told Simon all about her planned meeting).

'We have to be careful. They'll stop at nothing.'

Sue stopped talking and gestured to a girl who was collecting empty glasses from another table, who came over and took Caroline's order.

'So,' said Caroline, in an effort to get the ball rolling. 'What's happening? A memo came round this afternoon saying that Direct Action has relocated to Berlin.'

Sue's eyes bulged and her mouth worked for a few seconds before she spoke.

'The lying bastards! They threw me out. Simple as that. Then they closed the unit down. Got rid of everyone.'

'But why?' asked Caroline.

'Because I didn't do what they wanted. I didn't curtail my work just because …' She stopped mid-sentence and looked out of the window again. 'You're sure no one could have followed you?'

Caroline nodded and took her drink from the waitress. Before Sue could continue, their attention was drawn to an old man moving from table to table, begging for loose change. Sue looked over at him and her eyes narrowed.

'Don't you dare come over here!' she shouted at him as he started to move in their direction.

He hesitated, giving them both a searching look, but when he saw Sue's expression, he stopped dead.

'Keep going, you filthy little man,' growled Sue menacingly.

Caroline looked on in shock, taken aback by the degree of malice in Sue's voice.

'Sue!' she exclaimed.

'What?' replied Sue, still bristling. 'Oh I see, you think we should all be nice to these vermin. Poor dears! They have such tough lives, don't they? They're harmless.' These last words were spat out with a mixture of sarcasm and real venom. 'Except they're not and I should know! Oh yes, I know all about street dwellers. Haven't you heard? Three of them jumped me one night near Old Street tube station. Imagine *that*, Caroline. Three filthy, smelly, drunken, toothless old men.'

Her voice rose progressively with every word as she relived the ordeal. The barman looked over enquiringly.

'When they'd finished, one of them ran me through with

a meat skewer whilst his mate tried to strangle me with a length of piano wire!'

'I'm so sorry,' was all Caroline could manage, in a voice little more than a whisper.

It seemed such an inadequate response. Sue fell silent for a moment, collecting herself.

'They left me for dead, but against the odds, I survived.'

A tear ran down her cheek, which she brushed away with an irritated swipe of her hand. Caroline reached over and rested her hand reassuringly on Sue's arm.

'Oh yes,' Sue continued. 'I know all about the filth that infest our streets and you know what?' She leant across the table, before answering her own question. 'I wish someone would do the same to them as they did to me.'

Her eyes glinted with anger.

They sat in awkward silence. Sue peered out of the window, whilst Caroline nervously toyed with her empty glass. She should go. But before she could move, Sue started up again.

'He's a genius, you know, our Edward. He recognised ages ago that the super-rich will pay anything to indulge their passions or assuage their fears and he's milked it for all its worth. Have you noticed how he zeroes in on certain people?'

So often Caroline had looked on as van der Linden had honed in on a particular individual in his audience and then spent a disproportionate amount of time with them, even to the point of neglecting his other guests. More often than not, he would then take them aside, accompanied by Aleksei Lubov.

'Yes I have,' she answered, 'what's that all about?

'Well,' continued Sue, more her old self again, 'it's because he has an excellent nose for fanatics and zealots. He sniffs out the people most likely to go beyond the stage of just supporting a cause. If they appear obsessive, that gets his interest and then he singles them out for special treatment. That's how he got me! He sensed my passion and simply reeled me in! Once he's got you hooked, he takes it a stage further and offers you a way of becoming personally involved. You can do whatever you want with his blessing and the company's resources. Eleventh Hour has billionaires helping to protect tigers in Sumatra, giving their millions much more willingly because they are involved and because they can experience the progress first hand.'

Caroline nodded, not wanting to interrupt Sue's flow, thinking now of the detestable Abe Gottlieb – Eleventh Hour's newest and most generous patron.

'What you won't know,' Sue continued, 'is that he gives the mega-donors free rein to do just about whatever they want, so long as they keep paying. That's really all he cares about. If it's the wrong side of the law, he doesn't really mind, he just uses the company's network to smooth things over. It helps, you see, if you can ask a favour of someone in a position of influence. Our membership includes senior police officers, politicians, judges and lawyers in every country throughout the world. And you'll not be surprised to learn that most of them are more than happy to help our illustrious leader if he asks them to do him a little favour. Never underestimate Eleventh Hour's influence Caroline. We are simply everywhere.'

Caroline noted her use of the first person plural. Sue was

obviously finding it difficult to come to terms with her status as an ex-employee.

'And don't think you can leave. Once you're in, you're in for life, no mistaking it. If you try to leave, Lubov and his men will hunt you down. Just like they did to poor David Whiting, one of the company's original founders. He worked out what was going on and he was found floating in the Thames a week later.'

Sue saw the look of terror on Caroline's face.

'Look, sit tight,' she continued, a softer tone in her voice. 'Things are moving fast there at the moment. Edward has called a meeting of the Controlling Board next week and he's going to announce that they are ready to kick things off.'

'What do you mean?' Caroline shot back.

'Put in train our master plan,' said Sue proudly. 'It's what Eleventh Hour has been working towards, where the money's gone. Billions of dollars. Most of the members don't know anything about it – poor suckers, he just takes their money to fund it – but those who do are on the Controlling Board, they share his vision and are part of his inner circle…as I was, until …'

Sue's voice petered out, as she became wistful that the company was going ahead without her.

'So you know what this master plan is, then?' Caroline continued, determined to push for information.

'I was Edward's Head of Strategy until that poisonous Russian turned him against me! Of course I know what's going on. I started it all. It's my plan,' she hissed. She stopped talking for a few moments as the anger and indignation overwhelmed her but her mouth continued to work.

'So what happened between you and Edward?'

Sue threw back her head and gulped down the last of her wine.

'He wanted me to stop my own work. Said it was getting in the way. Wanted me to concentrate on "the bigger picture", but I wasn't going to be pushed around. And then he set the Russian and his men on me.'

Sue stopped talking and cocked her head to one side as if listening for something. Then she turned and peered through the window. She started, stood up suddenly and then pressed her face close to the glass. Her eyes were wide and staring.

'Did you bring the books?'

Caroline felt a sudden wave of panic as she opened her bag and fumbled inside, Sue's skittish behaviour was infectious and she was beginning to feel genuinely afraid. The books were underneath the green tablet. Sue, who had been watching her closely, let out a squawk of disapproval when she saw it.

'Ah! You brought that thing with you,' she exclaimed, pointing at the device. 'They'll have tracked you here.'

She snatched the books and without uttering another word took off towards the rear of the pub, upturning a bar stool as she went.

Caroline's hands were shaking as she dialled Simon's number. Now she was scared. She knew she was in real danger.

'I need help Simon,' she gasped, struggling against the rising panic.

'What's happening?'

'Lubov and his men are outside. They're after Sue, but they know I'm here too.'

'You have to keep calm, Caroline,' he said in an even voice. 'I can't get to you. I'm still at work. Just stay put and let me think of what to do.'

She felt another wave of panic wash over her just as the line went dead.

The car park was in pitch darkness, but Caroline kept looking. After a while, her eyes adjusted to the gloom. At first, all she could see was the outline of vehicles parked out in front of the pub. Then she caught a glimpse of a figure, briefly illuminated by passing headlights, standing watching the front entrance. The bald head and squat physique were a giveaway. No one else was visible, but she assumed there were others watching the rear of the building. She wondered what had happened to Sue. Certainly, at this stage, there was nothing to indicate that she had been detected in her flight.

After five minutes, two figures joined Lubov at the front of the building. They went into a huddle. It looked like a change of tactics as all three then started to walk towards the building's entrance. Caroline leapt to her feet, knocking over the empties that littered the table in her haste. The barman looked over.

'Steady on there, love,' he shouted, scowling at her as he handed an overflowing pint to a waiting customer.

She ran over to him.

'Is there another way out of here?' she asked in her most helpless voice. 'It's just that my boyfriend is outside and I don't want him to see me.'

His craggy face broke into a smile.

'Man trouble, eh? Follow me, love.'

They went through a door marked 'Private' into what looked like staff quarters, then her chaperone ushered her through a side door which opened onto an alleyway.

'There you go, darlin',' he said paternally. 'He won't see you here. You hurry along now.'

She set off down the alley, stumbling and tripping in her heels, desperate to put distance between herself and the pub. Some way behind her, she heard a shout and the sound of running feet. They must have spotted her.

She sprinted down the road and soon found herself running through a warren of small streets and alleyways. No one was about. The buildings she passed were unlit and looked like small warehouses and commercial premises. All she could hear was the distant drone of traffic on the Old Kent Road and the yapping of a dog in a nearby lot which housed a row of lock-up garages. She saw a faint light down a narrow road up ahead and decided to head for it. Then she heard footsteps coming down the road behind her.

She took her shoes off and stole quietly down a side street, but the footsteps came nearer. She started to run. Still the footsteps followed. She then sprinted towards safety, no longer concerned with maintaining silence.

The light was coming from a small all-night convenience store at the bottom of the hill. Her sanctuary! Thirty seconds later, Caroline barrelled through the door, setting its entry chimes jangling madly. A startled Asian youth looked up from his magazine and regarded her with suspicious eyes as she edged further into the shop. She reversed slowly, staring fixedly at the door as she went, until her back was against a shelf, stacked with cereal packets and canned food. There was nowhere left to go. She was trapped. Her noisy entry had echoed out in the night's silence and undoubtedly alerted her pursuers. She continued to stare at the entrance, waiting. Nothing happened for what seemed like an age, but just when Caroline was beginning to think she was in the clear, the door opened slowly and a figure stepped over the threshold.

Standing before her was probably the last person she expected to see.

'I think you'd better come along with me Caroline, sharpish,' said Tom Beresford with a crooked smile.

CHAPTER 35

Cavey held the photograph at arm's length and tilted his head to one side to see if viewing it from a different angle made any difference. It didn't. The image was still a blur. The specialists at NASA had done their best. They had reconstructed the photo pixel by pixel, adding in the detail where it was missing, using advanced predictive imaging software to compensate for the bleaching effect of the flash, but still the features lacked clarity. It was useless and as he looked at it again Cavey was pretty sure that it would not prove to be the vital piece of evidence he had hoped it would be. Perhaps it had been a little unrealistic to hope for a picture of the killer. Life isn't usually that kind. Still, he reflected, the photo had provided him with a way of keeping Sir Geoffrey on side and had bought him vital breathing space.

'So, what do you think, Sergeant?' the Inspector asked the burly policeman who had brought him the package.

Sergeant Noble had only just returned from Portsmouth where he had taken personal charge of DC Hargreaves's welfare. The young detective had lost a lot of blood and needed ten stitches for a deep head wound, but was thankfully on the mend. Harold Butterworth on the other hand, had yet to regain consciousness.

'Not really sure, sir. Can't make it out at all. Looks like a face, but that's as far as it goes,' replied Noble.

He wrinkled up his craggy face to squint at the photograph. This wasn't his kind of thing really and Cavey knew it. He was more into the physical side of policing.

Cavey stared long and hard at the image. Slowly, after thirty seconds or so, the features of a face started to become more pronounced. It was just like a Magic Eye 3D puzzle where the eye and the brain combine to decode an image, cleverly discarding the irrelevant parts of the image and compensating for the absence of detail until a face was almost visible.

'It's a woman, sergeant,' said the Inspector. 'Definitely female. "The Angel of Death". That's what one of the tramps at Waterloo said.'

Cavey walked over to the window and stared out at the street below, deep in thought. Something about the face *was* familiar. He recognised it from somewhere, but couldn't quite place it. A young detective knocked on the door and entered without waiting for a reply.

'Sir, we've ID'd the guy Hargreaves took out.'

'And?'

'He's a German national named Otto Kengeter. Known to the German police. He has form: GBH, assault with a deadly weapon and affray. Not a very nice bloke by all accounts.'

'Job?'

'Not known. Previously ran a security firm, but no record of anything for the last two years.'

Cavey held up his hand.

'Keep looking. Thank you, Detective,' he said, dismissing the young policeman.

The detective hesitated. 'One last thing, sir.'

'Go on.'

'We've tracked his recent movements with the help of Interpol. He's been travelling around a lot over the last few months. Interestingly, he was in Paris a few weeks ago when the killings occurred in the Bois de Boulogne.'

'Good work, Constable.'

Cavey took out his mobile and punched in a number, then turned his back to the young man who was still hovering by the door.

'I'll share this information with Chazot's people at the Sûrété and get them to review all footage of our man entering and leaving the country. Let's see if they can find out where he stayed and, most importantly, who was with him.'

He dismissed the constable and turned his attention to the phone.

'*Bonjour*, Alain.'

CHAPTER 36

Back at the flat Caroline, Simon and Tom Beresford stood looking at each other in total silence. Caroline's mind was still spinning. Nothing made any sense. When they'd first arrived Simon had put a comradely arm around Caroline but she'd shrugged him off. Friend or no friend, he had some explaining to do! And for starters, she wanted to know what his connection was with Tom Beresford, beyond working together at Montagu Steinhart.

Tom had been uncharacteristically silent on the way back. His car had been parked a short distance from the convenience store and he had made little effort at conversation beyond asking if she was OK. He hadn't even asked for directions, just drove to her front door, apparently knowing exactly where she lived.

Only when they were back at the flat did Caroline finally feel able to speak.

'What's going on?' she demanded.

Simon said nothing and shot a glance at Tom Beresford.

'I suppose we have some explaining to do,' said Tom earnestly.

'Too right, you do!' she exploded.

'Sit down and I'll try to fill you in,' Tom said, then he turned to Simon. 'Can you rustle up a few drinks? I think we could all do with a little something. It's been quite a night!'

Simon looked across at Caroline enquiringly. It was her apartment, after all – she was glad to see he hadn't forgotten that.

When they were all settled, Tom took a huge gulp of scotch, closing his eyes momentarily as he savoured the burn of the liquid.

'Come on, then,' she started, impatiently. 'What's this all about?'

'OK, OK,' Tom replied, holding his hand aloft before starting to talk to himself rather theatrically. 'Where to begin, eh? Hhmm, yes I know…' Caroline tapped her foot irritably as she waited for him to start. She wasn't in the mood for histrionics.

'Well, my dear, first of all, I am not who you think I am,' he paused momentarily as he gauged her reaction. She said nothing but her studied look and slightly raised eyebrows invited him to explain. 'I am actually part of a top secret enquiry within the…' he paused here as he searched for the right words… 'let's call it Security Services.'

'You're a spy?' she blurted incredulously. The thought of this blundering buffoon being involved in espionage was quite ridiculous.

'If you like, in a manner of speaking,' he replied, seeming to weigh this up as if it were the first time it had occurred to him. 'Anyway, my particular project is actually more than just secret, it is off the scale in its secrecy. In fact, only six people in the entire Service know of its existence and two of them are in this room.'

Caroline stared at Simon.

'You work for him,' she said, jerking her thumb in Tom's direction.

Simon didn't answer.

'Yes he does,' continued Tom proudly. 'May I introduce Major Oliver Riley?'

Caroline couldn't believe this. 'You're not even called Simon!' she said accusingly. 'It was all a set-up! You were nice simply because you wanted to get close to me.'

Simon raised a hand in protest but Tom cut across him before he could speak.

'Whoa, whoa, whoa!' he shouted. 'Don't let's get emotional…'

'Fine for you to say,' she snapped back. 'You're not the one who has been lied to and…' She stopped in mid-sentence as the anger rose within her. Everything had been a fabrication, a con she had so readily fallen for.

'Look, I don't ask you to understand but at least hear me out,' interjected Tom, a steeliness stiffening his voice, 'but just remember, it was me who hauled your sweet little butt out of that supermarket. I could have left you there and then what?'

He was right. She was grateful for his unexpected intervention and shuddered as she remembered her desperate flight from Lubov and his men.

'Thank you,' he said, like a teacher who had just succeeded in chastising a petulant child. 'There'll be plenty of time for you two to talk things over.'

Caroline's cheeks burnt with rage as it dawned on her that Tom had been monitoring their every move as their friendship had developed. 'Simon' chose to look at his shoes rather than meet her eye.

'Anyway,' continued Tom, helping himself to another drink before making himself very comfortable once again on her couch. 'I, and a small team of operatives, have been in deep cover for the last two years. Our sole objective has been to investigate the Eleventh Hour Corporation.' He paused to allow Caroline time to take this on board.

Her mouth sagged open.

'The problem is, we can't find out what is happening there.' He paused and looked at her long and hard before continuing. 'We have suspected for some time that something deeply distasteful is going on under that veneer of benevolence. Our people in the field started to hear things, uncorroborated reports of all kinds of criminal activity from money laundering on a massive scale to incidents of intimidation and even murder. So we put a man into their Swiss office.'

Caroline put her hands to her ears, she didn't want to hear the end of the story, but she was too slow.

'...And we lost touch with him a few weeks later,' continued Tom. 'His body, or at least part of it – we've never found the head and arms – was discovered in a landfill site in Uzbekistan six months later. He'd been tortured before they killed and dismembered him.'

Simon put a comforting hand on her arm but she brushed it aside. *One problem at a time*, she thought.

Tom was still talking away as if to himself, but she knew

it was all really for her benefit. Her head was spinning. She was a pawn in all this. Had the detestable Tom Beresford somehow manoeuvred her into a job in which she'd unknowingly been risking her life?

'They're clever, you see. Underneath the façade of a standard company they operate a cell system, the same as is used by most terrorist organisations. This makes it almost impossible to track what is really happening in the organisation on the issues that matter, as there is no identifiable chain of command, just satellites around a central nucleus – Edward van der Linden. So, in reality, the only way to find out what is happening is to get close to him.'

'I see,' she said, though she didn't really.

'Our project is ultra-secret,' continued Tom, lowering his voice to emphasise his point, 'because we simply don't know who we can trust. So we trust no one.'

Trust no one, thought Caroline, *I know the feeling*. She wanted nothing more than to evict these two strangers from her home, where she couldn't help noticing they'd made themselves rather too comfortable. Beresford, or whoever he was, clearly had other ideas, and felt it imperative she hear more about his secret operation.

'Our friend Aleksei Lubov is ex-KGB. His father ran the Stasi in East Germany in the dark days of the old communist regime, so he's an instinctive intelligence professional, extremely unpleasant and highly dangerous.'

She gave a cold shiver. This confirmed something she had suspected all along and she realised now how foolish she had been to rile him.

'He has free rein to do whatever it takes to keep Eleventh Hour and its activities secure. And he has been very successful to date.'

All of a sudden she felt a desperate need for space. She had to end this. Get them out of her home so she could spend some time by herself and work out what to do next. Her second job in six months had just evaporated before her eyes and she needed time to think. Fascinating as all this was, Tom's diatribe terrified her because it was not a story, but real life. Her life.

'Look Tom,' she interrupted, 'I'm grateful for your help today, but I really don't want to hear any more of this. I'm just an ordinary girl, trying to make a living and all this cloak and dagger stuff, well, it's not my world ...' She stood up to emphasise the finality of what she was saying and to encourage them to leave but neither of her guests budged.

'Caroline, you misunderstand,' said Tom, clearly in no hurry. 'We can't just throw away months of work.'

She caught a furtiveness in his eyes and suddenly it all became clear. Her suspicions had been right.

'You bastard!' she exploded. 'It was you all along.'

'Now, now, don't go getting angry,' he entreated, but she wasn't interested.

'You made my life hell and got me fired,' she raged, 'and all the time you were grooming me to join Eleventh Hour.' In her mind, she replayed the events leading up to her dramatic departure from Montagu Steinhart, remembering how Tom was always somehow absent or indisposed for key meetings, forcing her to attend in his place. He'd been playing her all along. And worse, Simon had been in on the deception from the start. His job no doubt had been to keep her under close observation once she had left the bank.

She jumped to her feet and started for the door.

'Leave this house now and you're dead,' said Tom sternly. 'Whether you like it or not, the three of us are in this together and the sooner you accept it, the better. Caroline, Major Riley and I are the only people who can keep you alive.'

CHAPTER 37

The opaque darkness reluctantly gave way to an insipid grey dawn. She hadn't slept well and given the circumstances, this was not surprising. It was drizzling lightly as Caroline crossed the road from the underground station.

She scarcely had time to sit at her desk before the green tablet sprung to life. At Eleventh Hour, there was no other telephone system. All communication – emails, internal and external calls – was channelled through these devices. As she looked at the pad's illuminated screen, a flashing icon told her that it was Edward van der Linden calling. This was no surprise. Under Tom's stewardship, she had sent an email to her boss in the early hours of that morning requesting an urgent meeting.

'You go in there all outraged and resentful,' Tom had counselled after many hours of discussion. 'He'll already know about last night and he'll want to know why you met Sue Baxter and what she said. Just play ignorant. Say she ambushed you on your way to work and asked you to retrieve some books, that's all.'

It was almost the truth, and so Caroline had agreed to play the part. She really had no other option. She just hoped

Tom had been right when he'd said the very reasons he'd selected her after realising his original target, Leo Brooks, wasn't the man for the job – her apparent innocence and vulnerability – would give her more protection than any weapon ever could. Caroline knew there was no backing out now, especially after she had mentioned to Tom what Sue Baxter had said about the impending board meeting. That news had really pricked his interest.

★

'So, shoot,' invited the Green Giant with a smile, as he carefully eased the plunger down through a cafatier of rich-smelling coffee. In spite of all she now knew, Caroline still felt involuntary warmth towards him. His manner was infectiously friendly. For a moment, she even doubted the truth of what Tom had divulged to her.

'Well, I don't take kindly to being spied on by Aleksei.'

It was a good start. Van der Linden didn't respond beyond a slight raising of his eyebrows.

'Somehow he has found out details of my personal life and last night I think he may have followed me to a meeting with—'

'Sue Baxter,' interrupted van der Linden. 'Yes, I know all about that. Aleksei told me. Look Caroline, you shouldn't have got involved. I didn't really want the staff here to know, but ...' He paused and leant towards her in a secretive fashion '... I had to fire Sue.'

'Why?' asked Caroline, perhaps a little too quickly.

He said nothing for a few seconds. Caroline could see

him weighing the situation up as he decided whether he could trust her.

'She refused to obey company policy and she has been stealing from us.'

'But she's a millionaire,' Caroline exclaimed.

'Well, obviously it wasn't money. It was confidential information. Lists and so forth. You understand, I can't say anymore.'

He held up his hands as if to fend off further questioning. Caroline nodded, obeying her script. Tom had told her to say as little as possible. Van der Linden seemed disappointed and looked at her enquiringly, sizing her up and trying to read her thoughts.

'So, what did you two talk about last night?' he continued casually.

'Oh, nothing, really. She was terribly drunk and kept saying she hated Aleksei...'

'Nothing about the company then?'

'Actually, she skedaddled soon after I arrived because she thought she saw Aleksei and his men out of the window.'

'And did she?'

It was a clever question. He was asking her indirectly if she had actually seen them too.

'I don't know. She certainly spooked me though, and I left a few minutes afterwards.'

Van der Linden gave her another long and searching look.

'I'll have a word with Aleksei.' He leant over and put a paternal hand on her knee. 'I want you all to be friends, you know? After all, we're all on the same side, aren't we?'

Caroline could feel his eyes on her. The question was obviously not rhetorical.

'Quite,' she said.

Tom had told her to avoid answering 'yes' and 'no' whenever possible. Less familiar terms would make it more difficult to detect a lie.

'Good,' he said, emphatically.

She smiled and was about to stand up to leave when a thought occurred to her. Things had gone well. Better than expected in fact, so why didn't she do a little probing whilst she was there? After all, so far it had been plain sailing and van der Linden seemed in an extremely affable mood.

'Edward,' she started, employing her most innocent tone, 'is everything OK? It's just you seem…' and here she paused as if searching for the right word, before adding, 'troubled.'

He said nothing for a second or two and she felt his eyes scanning her face, looking for a tell-tale sign or inconsistency.

'Well yes. Everything's ….going to plan,' he said, with a slight hesitation in his speech pattern.

Caroline chose to say nothing but instead looked enquiringly into his face, inviting him to elaborate.

He held her gaze for a few seconds before his features clouded and took on an altogether different expression.

He looked perturbed and with a scowl he said: 'You know what we are doing here could well save mankind?'

Once again she stayed silent, not wanting to interrupt his flow.

'We write it in speeches every day, don't we? But you may not realise, it is absolutely true.'

Something in his manner suggested an inner turmoil. He wanted to open up to her but was resisting the urge. She decided to give him some help.

'What do you mean?' she asked softly. 'Can you explain?'

He leant back on his desk which creaked in protest under his weight.

'Tell me,' he started. 'Where do you stand on global warming? I mean, do you believe it is actually a threat to our existence?'

She paused before answering. 'Well yes, I think I do.'

'You think you do. But you're not sure!'

She was a taken aback by the vehement way he seized on her words.

'No, I *do* think it is, in fact I know it is,' she shot back more emphatically, trying to make up for her initial half-hearted response.

'Sorry, Caroline,' he apologised, running his hand through his hair. 'I'm not angry at you, but you see, that's typical of people's reaction these days. Governments have spent far more time and money promulgating the lie that the current rise in temperature is a cyclical factor rather than manmade, than they have on actually tackling the underlying problem. It's jokingly called a "greenwash" you know. But it's all bullshit!'

There was now fire in his eyes. Caroline hadn't seen this side of him before. He was usually so pleasant and full of bonhomie. As he continued to stare at her his eyes moved rapidly from side to side giving her the impression that he was wrestling with a dilemma – trying to decide whether to do something or not – and when he finally spoke she was left with the strong impression that he had made his decision.

'Sit down, Caroline,' he ordered, pointing to the sofa she had just vacated, 'and I'll tell you what's really going on. Then you'll be in no doubt as to what's in store for us all unless we take immediate action. OK?'

She nodded compliantly as he eased himself into the chair opposite. His eyes were stormy and his face tight with tension as he started speaking.

'The planet is heating up at an alarming rate; much faster than anyone anticipated. According to the IPPC, temperatures are the highest they have been for over 1,000 years and sea temperatures are higher than they have been for a million years. And the warming of the oceans is most pronounced in the Arctic which has the potential to be catastrophic. All that ice melting, you see,' he added, obviously keen to ensure she understood what he meant.

Caroline nodded, but she had heard this kind of thing before and remembered that some scientists claimed this temperature increase was an aberration.

'So what? ' continued the Green Giant, snapping at the words in indignation, obviously a little irritated that she had not shown a stronger reaction to this revelation. 'Well, I'll tell you why this is so serious,' he continued, inhaling deeply and seeming to swell in size as he held her eyes mesmerically.

'Already we are seeing the classic signs of global warming: the cycle of precipitation is speeding up, causing more ferocious storms, widespread flooding and unpredictably long monsoons. The Storm Intensity Index, which is used to monitor the destructiveness of cyclones and hurricanes, has actually doubled in the last thirty years. We've seen extremes in weather; both hot and cold, drought and inundation. And Caroline, no one is doing a damn thing about it. Instead the "powers that be" just question whether there is a problem at all, largely because they are in the pockets of big business and their powerful lobbying groups. Not forgetting, of course the fact that politicians as a rule have no backbone and would far prefer to avoid a difficult issue than tackle it. But this is not an issue that will go away. It will just get steadily worse.'

He sat immobile for a moment, quietly contemplating his own words. The monologue seemed somehow cathartic. He'd unburdened himself by telling her all of this and the anger was now gone, replaced instead by an air of self-assessment, as if he were talking to himself, or rehearsing a speech, rather than addressing her.

'Currently, nothing is serious enough to spur anyone to action,' he continued, 'but by the time they wake up, I assure you, it will be too late. We will be locked into a runaway cycle of such devastating proportion that it will threaten the very existence of mankind.'

Caroline looked suitably concerned at this candid assessment but remained silent.

'Here is what will happen,' he continued, leaning towards her and fixing her with a glassy stare. 'As temperatures rise, huge swathes of our planet will become uninhabitable; deserts will spread in a widening band around the equator. At the same time, coastal flooding will shrink the land mass dramatically as sea levels rise. Florida will go,

Holland, Bangladesh too, followed by the coastal lowlands in China and the eastern seaboard of the US. Eight billion people will be squeezed into a smaller and smaller space. Food will become scarce. People will die in their tens of millions from famine and disease. It will be like the ten plagues of Egypt over and over again, played on a loop that increases in speed. There will be savage wars throughout the globe as nations fight each other for inhabitable space. Strong nations will simply annex land from their weaker neighbours – friends will become foes simply because they both need territory that can sustain life, and one has got it whilst the other hasn't. Forget oil and gas. What they will all covet most is water, the one commodity that we all need to survive.'

He stood up abruptly and walked to his desk and seized hold of a thick document and held it in the air.

'It's all in here. This is a report compiled by our own scientists and climatologists. It explains the sequence of events in minute detail.' He sat down again and his expression softened a little as he adopted the air of a doctor about to impart bad news.

'Territorial wars, famine and pestilence won't be the end of it though. Ironically, the planet itself will finish us off. Which I suppose is fitting, given how we have abused it.' The storm clouds gathered in his expression again as he rose to his feet and paced the room once more.

This heartfelt speech had completely wrong-footed Caroline. The original plan had been for her to express her dissatisfaction with Lubov's behaviour and then to leave as soon as possible afterwards. This venting was highly unexpected. Whether it was designed to scare her into compliance or if van der Linden was somehow trying to test the strength of her conviction before inviting her to join his inner sanctum, was not clear. But Caroline was sure of one thing: the bottle was uncorked and she must do everything possible to encourage the big man to continue his revelations.

'Go on,' she said softly, but he needed little encouragement.

'If we continue to burn fossil fuels at the present rate our fate will be sealed. The fuse will be lit and we will be powerless to stop what follows.'

He paused once more, choosing his words carefully.

'As the temperature continues to rise, it will set in train a sequence of events that will in turn trigger the next irreversible cycle of global warming. Each phase being more extreme than the previous one and each taking us one step closer to the final, environmental apocalypse.'

He had her undivided attention. It was obvious that he believed every word and, as he continued to speak, she realised that so too did she.

'The ice sheets will melt completely. They are already well on the way anyway. We know, because we're monitoring them closely. Free from ice to reflect sunlight, the dark seas will attract the sun's rays to the planet, speeding up the process of global warming. When temperatures have risen by a further three or four degrees, vast quantities of carbon dioxide and methane hydrate will be unlocked from thawing peat bogs in the Arctic, where there are quite simply billions of tonnes of greenhouse gasses waiting to be liberated.'

He looked her squarely in the eyes as he rattled off these facts. 'Does this scare you, Caroline?'

'A little,' she replied, in a small voice.

'It should do. And more than a little!' He struggled back to his feet and strode over to the window. 'When we reach this stage, mankind is doomed. The lungs of the world, our rainforests, will by then have gone – combusted in the searing heat – fuelling the conditions for yet more atmospheric warming. Without the trees we will have to rely upon the sea to absorb carbon dioxide from the air.'

He stopped pacing up and down and looked down at her.

'Do you know what the most important plant resource on Earth is?'

'I thought it was trees?' she said meekly, suspecting though that this was incorrect.

'No, most people think that, but the answer is actually plankton. Or more correctly, phytoplankton. Remarkably, these minute organisms absorb half the carbon dioxide on the planet, billions of tonnes of the stuff, and they also provide us with much of the air we breathe.'

He stopped for a second and cocked his head to one side as he watched her taking this information on board.

'Plankton also provides the foundation for the planet's food chain. Take them out of the equation and every living creature will be affected. Catastrophically, increased ocean acidity and rising water temperatures will eradicate these, our most abundant bringers of life. And when the plankton are gone, where will our oxygen come from?'

As he uttered these words he raised his arms in the air

in an extravagant gesture and stared expectantly at her, appealing for an answer. But she didn't have one for him. Instead she tilted her gaze upwards as his huge frame loomed over her and watched him take another immense breath as he readied himself to deliver the dénouement of his doomsday speech.

'The end will then be upon us,' he boomed like an old fashioned fire and brimstone preacher. 'From the depths of the warm, acidic oceans, huge plumes of methane gas will start to shoot up to the surface and explode into our atmosphere. These great methane deposits have been lurking at the bottom of our oceans for millennia, frozen into the rotting sediment as methane hydrate. But once the seas warm above a certain, critical level these deposits will thaw, allowing methane gas to escape in simply gargantuan quantities. Massive methane clouds will then spread out over the remaining landmass, suffocating the planet in an invisible, toxic fog. Unlike other greenhouse gases though, methane is also highly combustible. Those poor, resilient wretches who have survived war, disease and food scarcity will be asphyxiated and then cremated.'

He stood stock still, staring ahead of him as if he could actually see this terrifying picture. Then in a voice barely above a whisper he said with finality: 'The end, Man's reign is over, and Mother Earth will be left barren and uninhabitable.'

He bowed his head and stood in silence as if mourning a great loss, his final words hanging in the air.

'But surely it won't come to that?'

Caroline had listened with mounting disquiet. In fact,

so absorbed was she that she had all but forgotten her mission.

'It will and probably in our lifetime,' he answered.

'No! Surely not so soon,' she exclaimed.

She had been thinking of a timescale of hundreds, if not thousands, of years. He threw the report down on the coffee table between them.

'It's all in there. Have a read if you like. Our fate is sealed unless something is done immediately.'

As he said this last word, he kicked the leg of his desk in frustration.

'Over the last thirty years, the planet has warmed by one degree. Even according to the IPCC's models – which are far more conservative and far less accurate than our own – temperatures will most likely rise by a further three degrees in the next fifty years. This will take us well beyond the point of runaway global warming. Beyond the much debated "tipping point".'

'But what can we do to avoid this happening?' asked Caroline.

'What indeed?' he replied. 'Well for starters, we need to cut global greenhouse emissions by eighty-five percent just to stop things getting any worse. Eighty-five percent,' he said, repeating the words slowly. 'It's not going to happen, is it?' He shook his head slowly. 'I ask you Caroline, are the Indians and Chinese going to tell their people they can't drive cars, own refrigerators and eat meat like their Western counterparts? Not a chance. Or will the US Senate pass legislation to curtail the nation's dependence on their greatest invention: the automobile?'

He smiled humourlessly and snorted at the absurdity of his own suggestion.

'Caroline. It's too difficult for governments. Look at the record. Kyoto, Copenhagen and every other gathering called to address this problem, has ended in dissension, procrastination and farce. No meaningful action is ever taken. So they've resorted to pretending that everything is fine and anyone who raises the issue is regarded as a naïve fantasist.'

Once again there was silence. Caroline remembered her objective. Rallying to the cause, she decided to egg him on.

'But you're going to do something about it, aren't you, Edward?' she asked, injecting a pleading tone to her voice.

'Yes,' he replied, 'I have to. It's my destiny. The fact is, I know that if nothing is done, runaway global warming is now a dead certainty. Just look what's happened in the last few years,' he continued indignantly. 'Japan and Germany have turned back to coal from nuclear power, whilst the US is hell-bent on exploiting filthy new fuels such as shale gas and tar sands. So, far from getting better, the situation is actually getting worse. They have forced my hand. I simply have to do something.' Then he put his enormous arm around her and pulled her towards him, bringing his face within a few inches of hers. His eyes were staring and desperate.

'Every day, Caroline, I live with this knowledge.' He pointed an accusing finger at the report lying in front of them. 'People come into this office agonising over the extinction of tigers, rhino, orang-utan, blue-fin tuna and a whole host of other endangered species. I listen sympathetically. I care, I really do.' His voice brimmed with sincerity as if he felt he needed to persuade her of his commitment to conservation. 'But all the time I know that when the Earth is burning, the sea has risen by twenty metres or more and the oceans are putrid and uninhabitable, those creatures will all be long gone and the people who are telling me how much they care will be fighting for their own survival.'

He looked tormented and wild. Then he put his head in his hands.

Caroline felt genuine sympathy for this troubled soul. The burden of this knowledge weighed heavily on him and it was obvious that he felt a huge sense of personal responsibility. He had been shown the future in all its horror.

'But you *are* going to do something aren't you?

The words seemed to chase away the self-pity. He sat up straight and fixed her with a look of determination.

'Yes,' he replied. 'Yes, I ... *we* are.'

She needed to keep pushing.

'But what exactly can you do?' she asked, with urgency in her voice.

He said nothing but instead, reached towards her and gently rested his hand on one of her shoulders. For a moment, Caroline even thought she saw a tear in his eye.

Then, with the measured tone of a lawyer he started. 'Regrettably, the solution to this extreme situation must by necessity be equally extreme—'

But he didn't finish his sentence. At that moment, the office door burst open noisily and in strode Aleksei Lubov. His head snapped around and he stared at them both, then at the report on the table. He said nothing, but puffed out his chest like a fighting cock when he met Caroline's icy glare.

'Ah, Aleksei,' said van der Linden, slipping back to his usual, congenial persona and releasing her from his grip. 'Let's chat again, Caroline.'

He then gently nudged her towards the door. Lubov's presence had transformed him from a close friend and confidant back to her employer. The spell was broken. Now he appeared slightly awkward, embarrassed even. Caroline was happy to leave though. Tom had told her to avoid contact with Lubov if at all possible. That advice suited her just fine at that moment.

Another twenty seconds and she was sure van der Linden would have told all. She walked thoughtfully back to her desk. That morning, she had been totally committed to discovering as much as possible so that Tom could then do what he had to do, which would enable her to reclaim something like a 'normal' life, or at least one free from fear. But the last half hour had changed all that. She now realised that van der Linden had taken it upon himself to do what world leaders were too timid to do. Not for the first time, he had beguiled her with his steadfast dedication to helping his fellow man. What was she to do? Help the duplicitous Tom Beresford stop Edward van der Linden from saving the world – or choose a different path?

CHAPTER 38

DCI Cavey picked up the photo again. What was it about the unclear image that was so familiar?

Outside, in the open-plan office, he heard a commotion. The odd hand-clap to start with, but then everyone stood up to applaud. He stuck his head round the door to find out what was happening. It was Hargreaves. The young detective constable was limping towards his office. His shoulder and his left arm were heavily strapped and he wore a thick wraparound bandage on his head.

'Oh, my hero,' joked WPC Jane Murray, the twenty-four-year-old office flirt.

The rookie policewoman batted her eyelids and planted a very noisy, theatrical kiss on the young detective's cheek, much to everyone's amusement. A fleeting smile passed across Cavey's face as he watched. He liked this kind of thing; it showed how close his team was. He then strode out of his office to greet the wounded policeman.

'Welcome back, lad,' he said, gently shaking the policeman's good hand and handing him a tissue to wipe off WPC Murray's smudged lipstick. 'Come into my office and sit down. The rest of you,' he said, addressing his assembled team, 'quieten down. Remember, we haven't nailed this one yet. We still have to find who's behind it. The guys in the park were just soldiers, bit players.'

He could see at a glance that the young detective was still weak.

'You should be at home resting,' he said, as he guided Hargreaves towards the armchair in his office.

'Any change with my old friend Harold?' asked Hargreaves, with genuine concern.

'Not really. He's showing signs of improvement, but he's still critical, mind you,' he continued, 'those two you took on would have done for him well and truly had you not been there. We found a length of wire, a ligature, on the ground near the body. They were executioners, that's pretty obvious now.'

'Really?' replied Hargreaves, 'I suppose that definitely links them to all the other killings then. The wire seems to be their weapon of choice. That and of course, a blade, a long sharp one,' he said, instinctively stroking his wounded arm as he spoke.

The words stirred something deep in Cavey's memory… an old case that had remained unsolved… a case he had worked on years ago.

He snatched up the photograph from his desk and scrutinised it anew. He still couldn't see the features of the face but nevertheless, at that moment he knew the killer's identity beyond doubt.

CHAPTER 39

Ever since Tom Beresford's surprise reappearance in her life, Caroline had been unable to think of much beyond what was happening at Eleventh Hour. At lunchtime, she decided to take a stroll in the fresh air to clear her head. As she crossed the road outside the office, deep in thought, her eye was drawn to the newspaper headline on a billboard at a news stand: 'Mystery Virus strikes Asia'. She bought a copy. Skimming through the article as she walked, she gleaned that an as-yet unidentified virus had killed ten people in Thailand and there were a further five suspected cases in the neighbouring countries of Vietnam and Cambodia. Her thoughts turned immediately to the Eleventh Hour laboratory facility deep in the jungles of Guyana. They would be able to help. They probably already had a cure for the disease, whatever it was. She pictured Dr Hwang's smiling face and thought of his pride in the work he was doing. Perhaps Edward van der Linden was indeed a force for good, she mused.

She was startled out of her thoughts as someone grabbed her roughly by the arm. She tried to pull free but they held her firm.

'Don't struggle, just come with me. We need to talk,' said

a familiar voice. Caroline's resistance evaporated when she saw who it was and she allowed herself to be led down a side street into a busy café.

She could hardly recognise the figure now sitting opposite her as the Jack Daniels she had once known; the fresh-faced, ever smiling, optimistic student she had dated for nearly two years. The man in front of her now had long tangled hair and looked as if he hadn't shaved for days, he was wearing a shabby calf-length coat over a grubby shirt with a pair of tatty baseball boots on his feet. He looked, and she couldn't help noticing, also smelt, like a tramp.

'What the hell's happened to you Jack?' she said in dismay.

He looked back through tired eyes that narrowed at her implied criticism.

'Don't judge me Caroline, this is all your doing.'

'What do you mean, "my doing"? I haven't seen or spoken to you for months,' she snapped back.

He looked around the café suspiciously and when he was satisfied no one was listening he continued.

'Remember you told me about the murders, the killing of street-dwellers throughout London?'

She nodded, still finding it difficult to accept that this dishevelled figure in front of her was her old boyfriend.

'Well Caroline, you were absolutely right. People were being slaughtered throughout the capital, from Cricklewood to Balham, from Stratford to Highgate – everywhere – and it was all being hushed up. I asked my news editor about it and he told me to leave it well alone. Can you believe it? A reporter not allowed to report!' He looked wild and angry as he recounted the story, his voice shrill with emotion. Caroline noticed people at other tables looking over at them, wondering what the problem was.

'OK Jack,' she said soothingly and placed her hand on his in an effort to calm him down.

'Anyway,' he continued, his tone still indignant, 'I wasn't about to drop the biggest story of my life and I told him so. Next day I was taken into a room and they told me my services were no longer required, evidently they were downsizing.'

'They sacked you?' exclaimed Caroline.

'Yup, and they dropped the Leo Brooks story as well. Someone got to them.' He then leant across the table, after a quick check over his shoulder to ensure no one was eavesdropping and added, 'A trusted contact has told me since – on the QT– that the orders came from the very top. Someone very powerful stopped that story.'

They both sat in silence, thinking about what Jack had just said. Caroline felt a sudden pang of guilt as her mind drifted back to her ill-fated video conference with Edward van der Linden, the conversation that had led to her leaving the bank, when she had implored him to do whatever he could to stop the story. Was she indirectly responsible for Jack's downfall? she wondered.

'I lost my job as well you know,' she offered meekly.

'Yes, I heard.'

'Well, thanks for your concern,' she replied, genuinely peeved that he had not been in touch, 'it's nice our friendship meant so much to you.'

'Sorry Caroline, it's just that ever since I got booted out,

I've been investigating the homeless killings myself, PA so to speak, and I haven't really been living a normal life.'

'Is that why you're dressed like that?' she asked, relieved that there was a logical reason for Jack's dishevelled appearance.

'Well yes, sort of,' said Jack, looking himself up and down with obvious embarrassment. 'I'm kind of undercover, blending in as best I can.' Then he added ruefully, 'Mind you I haven't been able to get a job since I left the paper so I'm not far off being one of them these days anyway.' Then he took on a more serious look as he added, 'But, you know, I really think I'm close to cracking it now.'

'What do you mean?'

He looked around the room again before replying in a hushed tone, 'I think I know what's going on. Who's behind it all. I was there a few weeks ago, when that reporter and the others were killed by the wire stretched across the road. I saw it all Caroline. Everything.'

Caroline reached across the table and gently grasped his wrist.

'You will be careful Jack, won't you?' she said tenderly.

Jack became reflective before looking up and asking, 'What about you? Where are you now?'

'I'm pretty happy, thanks. I work for Eleventh Hour.'

His expression changed instantly as she said the words.

'You're kidding me!' he exclaimed, incredulously.

'No I'm not, but why so surprised?'

But Jack didn't answer. His face suddenly took on an altogether different expression and he lowered his eyes and stared intently at the table top.

'What's up?' she asked.

'Don't look round, but I think someone's been following you,' he muttered, still keeping his eyes fixed on the table. 'They've been walking past every few minutes ever since we came in. He's looking directly at us and speaking to someone on the phone at the moment.'

Caroline turned her head slowly towards the counter and looked into the large mirror on the back wall. Jack was right. She could now plainly see the reflection of the face of her stalker. It was one of Aleksei Lubov's men, she recognised him immediately. Someone obviously wanted to keep tabs on her.

'I know him. It's someone from security at work. I'd better go,' she said hurriedly, standing up and sending her chair spinning sideways with a clatter.

She thrust her business card into his hand and turned to leave but he held onto her hand.

'What's going on Caroline?' he hissed.

'I'll call you,' she whispered, 'tell you everything.' Then she wriggled her hand free and turned for the door.

'Take care,' he muttered almost under his breath.

'You too Jack,' she said over her shoulder.

As she walked back to the office she felt unfamiliar warmth inside and something she hadn't experienced for some time, happiness. Her encounter with Jack had allowed a chink of light to shine into her dark world. It had reminded her that there was another world out there, a world beyond covert security operations and the dubious activities of an ultra-secret organisation. Although their meeting had been anything but normal, just being with someone she associated with happier times filled her with hope. They'd both get through this and be closer friends for it. This meeting had also crystallised her thoughts. She would call Jack tomorrow and tell him everything. As a minimum, it would probably help him get his job back. The thought of restoring his fortunes gladdened her heart. Perhaps, with his help, she could still win through.

In the Eleventh Hour foyer, she found Aleksei Lubov loitering.

'Call off your dogs, Aleksei,' she said without looking at him as she swiped her pass through the security turnstile. 'Or I'll have to have another little chat with Edward.'

The Russian could only manage a grunt as she swept past.

At the lifts, she waited for her hand to stop trembling. Since her very personal audience with van der Linden, the Russian had taken to shadowing their boss everywhere he went, no doubt to ensure he was not left alone with anyone again. Lubov had a sixth sense for human weaknesses. He understood van der Linden's vulnerability and it terrified her to think that perhaps he also suspected her intentions.

In the office, Caroline could find no evidence of the planned board meeting Tom was so interested in. Neither van der Linden's diary nor a thorough examination of all conference room bookings yielded the slightest hint of anything out of the ordinary. She was beginning to think that Sue had been wrong when a red icon flashed on both the homepage and also the mailbox of her tablet.

The memo, marked '*urgent, for immediate action*', advised staff that the Eleventh Hour headquarters were to be closed from 5.00pm on Wednesday the following week for 'environmental reasons'. A recent building inspection, it continued, had revealed the existence of potentially hazardous asbestos in some of the heating ducts and this needed to be investigated with the uttermost urgency. Staff were asked to ensure that they vacate the building by the allotted time and were not to return before 7.00am the next morning.

As Caroline slipped the tablet back into its velvet case she found herself wondering, not for the first time, who the members of the Controlling Board actually were. Beyond Edward van der Linden himself and of course Abe Gottlieb, she struggled to think of likely candidates. Faces flashed before her eyes as she remembered the events she had attended over the last few months. But of course, the majority would have already been in place before she joined.

*

'That's it,' exclaimed Tom excitedly as he read the memo on Caroline's tablet for a third time. 'Game on. Now we know when the meeting will take place.'

'So, what are you going to do?' asked Caroline.

'Me? Absolutely nothing,' he replied, looking across at Simon as if to say, '*Oh dear, she still doesn't get it, does she?*'

Caroline saw the exchange. 'What?' she said sharply.

'Well, Caroline, it's like this—' Tom started.

'No more!' she interrupted, the panic surging within her. 'You said all I had to do was help you find out about the meeting, and I've done that.'

'Well, yes, but we still don't know what they're up to, do we? Sorry old girl, but we're not there yet!'

'You promised!'

She was shrieking now. The pressure she had been suppressing now welled to the surface.

She looked at Simon for support but he just stared blankly back at her.

'Caroline, none of us is free from this until we find out what they plan to do. You must know that,' Tom continued, injecting a reasoning tone to his voice. 'Do you think they will just let you walk away, eh? No chance. That Russian and his acolytes would hunt you down and when they find you, and find you they would, he'd personally butcher you. And, you know what? He'd enjoy doing it. Caroline, I can't go up the line until I have better intelligence. Sorry, but the job's not done yet.'

She didn't move. She realised she had been naïve to think that they would allow her to opt out at this critical stage; deep down she had always known that Tom was simply toying with her. He would promise anything so long as she continued to be useful to him. She had been so willingly taken in by his lies because she was so desperate to regain her old life.

She heard the chinking of glass behind her. Tom seized her arm and thrust a drink in her hand.

'Get that down you,' he ordered. 'It's vodka and tonic. We've finished the gin. But it'll do the trick.' Then he added, 'Perhaps you can pick up some more booze at the offy tomorrow?'

The drink was strong. In fact, it tasted like neat vodka (which it probably was) and the fumes made her eyes water as she took a large gulp.

'So, what now?' she said dully.

The drink was doing its job. Her emotions were back in check. Desperation had been replaced by hollow resignation. She drained the glass, closing her eyes as she did so.

'Good girl,' said Tom, following suit. 'We need to hear what's said at that meeting. It would also be very helpful if we knew who was there.'

'But how are you going to do that? No one else is allowed in the building that evening. Remember?'

'Well, we may just have to disobey instructions. That's all.'

Sarcasm was heavy in his tone. *Back to the old Tom Beresford*, thought Caroline, irritated by his manner.

'You're just going to have to stay behind. That's all.'

'Me!' she squealed in dismay.

'Well yes, no one else can do it.'

'I don't understand. How can I possibly do that? They'll find me and anyway, what would it achieve? The meeting will be in the boardroom and—'

'Whoa! Just slow down there. We've obviously got some planning to do and no one's pretending it'll be easy. Major Riley can no doubt help with some electronic wizardry.'

He turned to Simon as he spoke. Simon nodded agreement, but his eyes were on Caroline, who was staring wide-eyed at them both.

'I won't do it,' she snapped.

She folded her arms stubbornly. She realised Tom had been planning this all along. He wouldn't release her until it was all finished one way or another. His plan relied on her. In fact, she *was* his plan.

Tom looked at her with a patronising expression, his head tilted to one side and his eyes rolling with exasperation.

'Now come on, Caroline. You know we have to do this. You heard what he said that day. They are going to take "extreme measures".' He stretched out the words. 'It's imperative we find out what that means. Heaven knows what they're capable of.'

Again, the memory of van der Linden's tormented face returned to her. Her instinct told her he wasn't mad, just totally dedicated. Whereas her present companions – Simon included – had proved to be dishonest, manipulative and most definitely not trustworthy.

They had all fallen silent.

'How's your mum?' asked Tom after a while, obviously searching for an uncontroversial subject to thaw relations.

'Fine. Happy and content.'

Actually, it was none of his business.

'Good, good.'

They fell silent again.

'No more dramas on the housing front then?'

'No. All sorted, thank you.' Then as an afterthought, she added, 'Thanks to Edward.'

'What do you mean, "thanks to Edward"?' replied Tom, rather annoyingly parroting her words back to her in an insultingly pathetic tone.

'Well, if you must know,' she fired back, her hackles rising, 'Edward pulled some strings and the whole matter was resolved in double-quick time.'

'Oh, really,' Tom replied sarcastically, 'and don't tell me, your late father's business partner, one Vernon Cartwright, was charged with fraud and the money they traced back to him paid off the debt on your mother's house! '

'Well actually, yes.' Then the penny dropped. 'It was you!' she exploded.

'Course it was bloody me. Don't you think Her Majesty's Government can handle a little matter like that! *I'm* your guardian angel, dear, not Mr Giant Greenfingers!'

If he thought this would make her feel indebted to him, he was wrong. Suddenly she saw it all clearly. He had wanted her to think it was Edward who had intervened on her behalf. Just another part of his cleverly crafted plan to shepherd and cajole her in the direction of Eleventh Hour.

Simon must have seen the look of disgust flash onto her face and he put his arm on her shoulder in an attempt to placate her.

'Don't you touch me,' she snapped. He withdrew his arm smartly. Simon was as much a part of this despicable business as Tom and she felt a sudden, bitter resentment towards him.

'Just get away from me,' she snarled. 'In fact, I'd like you out of my house and out of my life!'

Simon stood with a confused look on his face. Then, for a split second, his eyes darted in Tom's direction, as if he were awaiting instruction. This was too much for Caroline.

'Go, Simon… James, Oliver… or whatever your Goddam name is today!' she screamed. 'I never want to see you again.' Her anger was so intense that she clenched her fists by her sides with rage as she spoke. The two men looked at each other.

'I think you'd better do as she says, Major,' said Tom, 'I'll take it from here.'

A moment later, she heard the front door slam shut. Simon was gone.

Tom said nothing. He just raised his eyebrows as if to say, '*You've got what you wanted.*'

Caroline met his gaze. She was more composed now. She was glad Simon had left. It restored a sense of power to her and reminded her that however much they thought they were in control, it was she who held the trump card.

CHAPTER 40

Two hours before a grey autumn sunrise, Caroline gently eased the front door shut behind her. The catch made a metallic click, but apart from that, her departure was silent.

There was little traffic at that time in the morning. Virtually the only noise to be heard was the tapping of her heels on the pavement. She had packed a few clothes in an overnight bag which she slung over her shoulder, but no cohesive plan had emerged as she had lain awake the previous night. Escape was her primary objective. She knew that if she remained, Tom would force her to do his bidding and in the process, betray Edward van der Linden, which was something she had decided she was unwilling to do. In addition, she didn't see why she should place herself in danger. It wasn't as if she was a member of the Secret Service. If Tom needed someone to undertake a covert surveillance operation, he should look for someone with the requisite training, one of his own. Anyone in fact, but her.

When she reached Parsons Green underground station, she followed a handful of early morning commuters down the escalator to the platform below. There was comfort in this familiar routine. As she grabbed a free newspaper from its stand, she felt almost normal, as if she was on her way to work. She casually scanned the headlines as she waited for the next train.

The disease in Asia was now much more serious. It was spreading with alarming speed and the death toll had already exceeded one hundred. Shockingly, scientists had identified it as a new strain of an old killer: the Black Death. She went cold as she read the article. She'd learnt all about the virus from Dr Hwang. The thought of this ancient disease ravaging the modern population was terrifying. Surely though, Eleventh Hour would be able to help, she mused before blanking the thought from her mind. The company was no longer her concern! She was moving on.

The dull rumble of a train could be heard as it thundered down the line towards her. A few seconds later, it clattered into the station. The passengers alighted, the doors closed and it juddered noisily on its way again, leaving behind a solitary figure on the platform, sitting alone on a bench. An article at the bottom of page two had caught her eye. The body of a young man in his late twenties had been found in a backstreet in Stockwell. He had been badly beaten and there were signs of torture. The report stated that although the victim had been living rough, the police were not linking the incident with the recent spate of killings of homeless people in London. As she sat motionless, numb with shock she re-read the name of the deceased, just to make certain.

'You've missed your train,' said a voice by her shoulder. 'Not going, then?'

She didn't need to turn her head. She recognised Tom's

voice immediately. She didn't reply, but simply handed him the paper.

'They killed Jack,' she said, in a tiny voice after a brief pause. 'They killed him because they saw him talking to me.'

'I'm so sorry, Caroline,' replied Tom softly.

Caroline's mind flashed back to the last time she had seen Jack. They'd parted friends and he had told her to take care of herself. As she pictured his face, a tear ran down her cheek, followed swiftly by another, and then another. Tom handed her a crisp white handkerchief.

'Help us nail them, Caroline,' he whispered, 'if not for me, for Jack. Do it in his memory.'

CHAPTER 41

Scrawled on a whiteboard by the entrance, a handwritten message reminded staff that the offices had to be evacuated by 5.00pm that day. The method of notification was somewhat at odds with such a hi-tech organisation, thought Caroline, sensing the hand of Aleksei Lubov in the bluntness of the words and the crudeness of the communication medium.

The instruction was followed up by an email at midday and a bulletin on their tablets halfway through the afternoon. They were taking no chances that anyone might mistakenly remain in the building.

All afternoon, Caroline watched the clock on her office wall as the hour hand made glacial but inexorable progress towards the number five. Her heart-beat quickened as the hour approached. She could feel it pounding and was convinced that anyone passing by would surely hear it too.

She itched to check the tiny microphone Tom had given her, but he had been very firm on this point. 'You never know what kind of kit they've got,' he'd cautioned. 'It's quite possible that they may have trackers and anti-bugging detectors, so leave it till the last minute before you switch it on.' This particular discussion certainly hadn't helped shore up her fragile confidence.

From 4.30pm onwards, there was a steady stream of people leaving the building. No one wanted to be around when they started the potentially hazardous task of searching for and removing deadly blue asbestos. Caroline stayed put. At 4.45pm, Edward van der Linden walked casually by her office.

'Not off home yet, Caroline?' he asked, poking his massive head round the door.

'Just on my way,' she lied.

'A nice early night,' he beamed. 'You should do it more often. You work too hard, you know, Caroline.'

She smiled back at him, then stood up and took her coat from the stand and started to put it on.

'See you in the morning,' van der Linden said, as he strode off down the corridor. He sounded upbeat, almost excited, she noted.

But Caroline didn't leave. Instead, as planned, she stole quietly up to the fifth floor, avoiding the lifts and using the emergency stairs instead. The idea was that she would find a suitable place to hide the microphone and then she would leave. And the rest would be down to Tom. Her part in this whole affair would be over. The only complication to what should have been a simple exercise was that Tom expected Aleksei Lubov to sweep the building for hidden bugs beforehand, so they had agreed that she would wait until the meeting was about to start before activating the device. Then she would leave. She wasn't happy about this part of the plan but couldn't come up with any other satisfactory alternative.

She just consoled herself with one thought: once it was done, she'd be free.

No one was around. She stopped and listened before stealing tentatively along the corridor. When she was convinced she was alone, she darted over to the audio-visual room adjoining the company's boardroom and eased the door open. It creaked and her hand froze on the handle. She held her breath and listened. Nothing. So she yanked it open in a single, swift movement to minimise the squeak of the hinges. The room was small, probably eight feet by six in dimension and crammed with electronic equipment of all descriptions. She walked in and closed the door quietly; there was no key, so she slid the bolt into the 'locked' position.

A small camera portal opened onto the conference room next door. An ideal place to listen covertly to the proceedings, she thought as she peered through tentatively. No one had arrived yet, but the room was nevertheless fully illuminated. A neat presentation pack was positioned at each place around the massive conference table and jugs of fresh water were lined up at intervals down the centre. Everything was ready, they'd be here soon. She sat down on the floor and waited.

Twenty minutes passed. Thirty. Forty. Still nothing. Caroline's legs were beginning to feel numb as she sat with her back against the wall in the cramped room. As time passed and her anxiety increased, her heart-beat quickened and she wondered anew why she had ever agreed to such a foolish venture.

By six o'clock she was ready to call it a day but just as

she stretched out her hand to slide open the lock, she heard voices next door. She sat motionless, hardly daring to breathe. This was it. At first it was just two or three, but soon she could make out at least a dozen different people chatting loudly and excitedly. Once or twice, she thought she could make out the metallic drawl of Abe Gottlieb as well as another very familiar voice that she couldn't quite place. Who was it? she wondered. She really had to find out, so she moved slowly towards the opening and gently bent her knees before peering cautiously through the narrow slit to the brightly-lit room beyond. By now there was quite a throng. Nearly twenty people stood in the room, talking noisily and quaffing Cristal champagne. They were closer than she had anticipated, the nearest being a matter of feet away and she recoiled, instinctively seeking refuge in the shadows. She spotted some familiar faces amongst their number, one or two from the world of finance, a world-ranked tennis player and champion golfer, a well-known Hollywood actor, a racehorse owner, and there, in the centre, deep in conversation with an Arab sheik and a Greek shipping magnate, stood the owner of the voice she had recognised: Leo Brooks. Leo was one of them!

Just then the handle of the door rattled unexpectedly as if someone was trying to enter the room. She started then froze, expecting a knock on the door and a demand to be let in. But nothing happened. She waited. Perhaps one of the guests had taken a wrong turn. She held her breath. Now was the time to activate the microphone and leave, but how could she do that if someone was waiting outside?

Her thoughts were interrupted by the ringing sound of

a small hand-bell, which brought the assembled company to sudden silence. Edward van der Linden stood beaming at the head of the table and graciously invited them all to take their seats. Caroline slid slowly back down to the floor. She'd have to wait a little longer, until she was sure the danger lurking outside had passed. She took the tiny microphone from her pocket and flicked the on switch and set it down next to the portal. The device was activated and would now transmit all audible sound within a twenty-metre radius. Worryingly too, its signal could also now be detected. If it was, there was no escape for her.

'Welcome my friends,' van der Linden said, his voice rich and confident. 'This is a day you will remember for the rest of your lives. This is the day, I am happy to inform you, when your efforts and the money you have all generously entrusted to the Eleventh Hour Corporation, will save the planet.'

There was spontaneous applause followed by a murmur of excitement.

'You people in this room are not only our most committed donors, but each of you also shares a common vision. You know that mankind is finished unless decisive action is taken. You also know that those empowered to govern the peoples of the world will never take such actions. So it has been left to us here in this room, for we are the people who have the courage to do what is necessary.'

More applause. Caroline hoped the microphone was working properly, *she* could certainly hear his voice clearly enough.

'Friends, colleagues,' van der Linden continued, 'we have to be radical and we have to act now.'

Caroline's attention was again drawn to a noise in the corridor. She heard footsteps and saw the shadow of someone passing by in the gap at the bottom of the door. Someone was definitely outside, she was sure of it. She stared at the light under the door, looking for tell-tale signs.

'Our world is being throttled by the sheer number of people on the planet,' continued van der Linden. 'Every problem we have can be traced back to one simple factor: overpopulation. Pollution, climate change, deforestation, animal and plant extinction ... all of it has occurred because there are quite simply: too – many – people.'

There was a buzz of agreement, followed by another flutter of applause. Caroline was transfixed by the light under the door. There was someone there. As she stared in horror, the handle started to turn slowly, squeaking as it did. It stopped and all went quiet again. Panic gripped her. She was trapped there, cornered in that little room with no means of escape.

'We have used your funds wisely. Our laboratories and production facilities throughout the world have been working overtime and we are now ready.'

Caroline heard the sound of voices outside the room and rapid footsteps as two people ran past her hideaway.

Then she clearly heard the voice of Aleksei Lubov, talking to one of his men using a two-way radio. The device crackled with static as he passed by.

She was rooted to the spot in cold, paralysing terror. They had obviously tracked the microphone's signal! She had cleverly swiped her card at the exit turnstile a few hours ago but had not left the building, so it couldn't be her security pass that had given her away. No, it had to be the signal of the listening device she concluded.

She moved her hand to switch the microphone off, but hesitated as she heard what Edward van der Linden was now saying.

'Who here today knows about the rule of 72?'

'Me, I do,' volunteered Leo Brooks in his distinctive voice with its clipped speech pattern. 'It's a method of predicting the return from an investment.'

'Spot on Leo. It's a very clever little mathematical rule that tells you how long before something doubles in size. But it's not only used in finance, Leo. It can equally be applied to other things such as to predict population growth. When I was introduced to 72 it changed my life. This is how it works; quite simply, if you divide the number 72 by the annual rate of growth, you will find out how long it will be before the world population doubles in size. The formula is simple but irrefutable and the answer it yields is terrifying. People, you see, breed more people who in turn breed yet more people. The problem compounds and this growth is uncontrollable *and unsustainable*.

In 1804 there was only one billion people in the world. It took 123 years for this figure to double in size to two billion, then a mere thirty-three years for this number to increase by another billion. Then only fourteen years to grow by a further one billion.' Van der Linden paused to let these statistics make their mark. 'Since then, population growth has continued on its sharp upward trajectory, such that today we have over seven billion people on this planet and at the current rate this will reach eight billion by 2020.

Albert Einstein's rule of 72 brought the gravity of the situation home to me and allowed me to see into the future. In so doing, it defined my life's purpose. Population growth is currently exponential – how long before we reach fourteen billion? 72 can tell us that and the answer ladies and gentlemen is: *too soon!*' After delivering this warning he paused as a profound stillness took hold of the room.

'So what should we do?' he asked them in a quiet, almost secretive voice as if the choice was theirs and theirs alone. 'If you have a beautiful garden, what do you do if it becomes choked with weeds and brambles? You cut it back. You prune it hard and then you wait for the green shoots of recovery to appear. This new growth will be healthy and those green shoots will grow into strong plants that will guarantee the future health, vitality and beauty of your garden.'

They understood the analogy. He had them in his hand; the anticipation was palpable. Van der Linden continued, in a quieter voice still, drawing his audience yet closer. Caroline found herself involuntarily leaning towards the projector portal.

'Way back in the eighteen hundreds, people believed that there was a kind of natural self-regulating mechanism that would always somehow synchronise population and food resources. They thought that natural events such as drought, famine and disease would always keep our numbers to a level where the planet could continue to support its people. Well, they were wrong!' he snapped. 'No hand of fate, divine or otherwise, can be relied upon to do this for us. The rule of 72 prevails. Population *will* double, treble, quadruple in size. So, ladies and gentlemen we are going to have to solve the problem ourselves.'

This was it, thought Caroline, desperate to be on her way now that things had gone quiet outside in the corridor.

'I am sure you've all seen the latest news,' continued van der Linden. 'An outbreak of man's most feared disease, the Black Death, is ripping through the populations of Southeast Asia, as it did in Europe centuries ago.' He paused momentarily for effect before hitting them with the big news. 'It's not the plague of old though, but a man-made, genetically engineered variant, a viral strain of this ancient bacterial disease. They are finding that this super virus spreads very easily – it's airborne you see, with no need for an intermediary carrier, such as a rodent. Also, unlike the original plague, it's totally resilient to standard antibiotics and has no commercially available antidote. The illness is fatal in about two-thirds of cases and has an incubation period of three to five days. There are currently reported outbreaks in Vietnam, Cambodia, Indonesia, China and South Korea. But soon there will be cases in Western Europe and North America.'

There was silence in the room.

'You may think I know a lot about this disease. Well, I should do. You see, it's my virus. Or should I say *our* virus. This, my friends is the first stage of Eleventh Hour's bold project to save mankind. What we have all been working towards.'

The room erupted into rapturous applause. Someone even whooped, probably Abe Gottlieb, thought Caroline, as she stood alone in stunned silence.

At first she simply refused to believe what she had just heard, such was the enormity of the revelation. Then logic intervened and denial was replaced by reason. It was all true. Her mind looped back to the jungles of Guyana where Lubov had been so intent on stopping her exploration. So now she knew what this was all about and so long as the microphone had been working, so too did Tom. By his own confession, Edward van der Linden had intentionally unleashed on the world the most deadly virus his scientists could create, a disease designed to be as contagious and lethal as possible. Eleventh Hour, aided by its rich donors, had just embarked upon an exercise in global population control which would result in wholesale slaughter on a scale the world had never experienced before.

She had to get away, so she grabbed the microphone and stuffed it back in her pocket before seizing hold of the door handle ready to take flight.

The hinges grated, piercing the silence as she tentatively opened the door. Caroline shot an apprehensive look down the corridor, fully expecting to see Lubov and his cohorts but it was deserted and still. Behind her, she could hear van der Linden's voice, speaking now with greater excitement.

'So, this is phase one of our plan. We have an effective vaccine so don't worry, you will all be inoculated before you leave tonight. We have to preserve those we want to keep.'

It was now or never. Caroline closed the door quietly behind her and sprinted towards safety, his chilling words still resonating in her ears.

She reached the emergency stairwell, pushed open the door and hurried through. But she didn't get far. Someone was waiting on the other side and in her haste she barged straight into them. A hand grabbed her roughly round the neck and another clamped over her mouth. She tried to struggle free, but her captor was stronger. She battled harder but the vice-like grip tightened.

'Well, aren't we the dark horse, then?' said a very familiar voice.

Sue Baxter chuckled to herself as she whispered the words directly into Caroline's ear. She was so close Caroline could feel spittle shower her cheek as she spoke.

'I suppose it was you holed up in the projector room, eh? Completely screwed up my plans, I can tell you! I've had to hang around here instead.'

She loosened her grip, judging that it was now safe to release her quarry.

'What are you doing here, Sue?' panted Caroline, rubbing the side of her neck.

She shook herself free of the bigger woman's iron grasp. Then it dawned on her: Lubov had been chasing Sue, not her. They had obviously detected that she had entered the building and that was the reason for all the excitement.

'Let's just say I've a score to settle.'

'They know you're here, you realise that?'

'Yes, I do. I had to use an old pass round at the side entrance to get in. There was always the chance that that Russkie swine would spot it. And he did. Never underestimate the KGB, eh?' she let out a humourless cackle as she uttered these words. 'Not to worry. Just makes things a little more interesting, that's all.'

Sue stopped talking for a second and cocked her head to

one side, listening for the sound of approaching footsteps then turned back to Caroline and fixed her with a cold stare.

'So, now you know what they're up to. 72,' she added reflectively before continuing, 'it was me who told him about that rule you know. Me, I showed him. So it's my number, not his. I made it my calling card. That really hacked him off!' She let out another short laugh as she said this. Her eyes were wild and her features contorted as she tried to talk, listen and think all at the same time. 'Our code name for Eleventh Hour's whole project is 72, you know. And he hated it when I started using it on my little side-line. There's not so much difference between what I've been doing, and what he's planning, just a question of scale really. I just started mopping people up first… at the bottom, the very bottom.'

Sue put her hand to her mouth feigning surprise, like a young child who had inadvertently given away a secret. Caroline stared at her, not knowing what to say, her skin prickling into goose bumps.

'It was me. You may as well know it now. Me and my glorious, defunct team. We killed those low-life scumbags. All of them. And, you know what? I'd do it all over again if I could.'

Sue stopped talking for a second. Her eyes were blazing and her mouth worked, but no words came out.

'But it's all over now. *They* pulled the plug,' she said waving an arm disdainfully in the general direction of the boardroom. 'You know, at first they supported me,' she continued angrily, 'even helped me plan some of my little events. You see, Edward didn't much mind, so long as I stayed under the authorities' radar and he could continue to use my money. He's like that. Anyway, when we started to crank it up, industrialise the process if you like, they got cold feet and told me to stop. They didn't want the police sniffing round, you see. Not when the main event was about to start. But I wouldn't stop. Why should I? I hadn't finished.'

Sue's voice grew louder as she became more indignant. She wasn't even bothering to whisper anymore and as she raved on she drew a large stiletto knife from her pocket. Caroline's eyes widened with surprise which drew a derisory cackle from her captor.

'Don't worry sweetie, this isn't for you.' She stroked the blade lovingly before hissing, 'No, this is for the big man himself. Let's see how their little plan goes without *him.*'

Caroline had heard enough, Sue was patently insane and if she carried on talking in such a loud voice she would undoubtedly attract attention. She needed to get away. Sue was still raving though.

'He has no scruples. No loyalty. Even used his own people to implant the virus, you know.' She stopped abruptly, as if remembering something and gave Caroline a long searching look. A crooked smile then wrinkled her thin lips.

'Hmmm, but what about you? What about sweet, innocent Caroline? Don't you give me that little girl lost look. It doesn't wash anymore,' she snapped, abruptly changing persona. 'Now it's time for *you* to come clean. What are you up to and who are you working for?'

As she asked the question, she grabbed Caroline's arm with one of her bony hands and raised the knife level with her face.

Caroline didn't have the opportunity to answer though. They both heard it at the same time. People were running along the corridor towards them. Sue twitched and looked at the door, then switched her attention back to Caroline.

'We'll have to do this another time, sweetie. Right now, I think you need to make yourself scarce.' Then she drew her face within an inch of Caroline's and breathed, 'Otherwise some rather nasty men are going to snuff you out.'

Caroline didn't move.

'*Vamoose*!' She shrieked, pushing her roughly towards the stairs.

Caroline needed no further encouragement. Taking the steps in leaps and bounds, she hurtled towards the exit five floors below. As she reached the landing three floors down, she heard a commotion. Men's voices were shouting back up where she'd left Sue. Then she heard a scream and footsteps scuffling on the tiled floor. By the sound of it, Sue was now being chased down the steps behind her.

With only two floors to go, Caroline jumped and sprinted towards the safety of the building's emergency exit at the base of the stairwell. Seconds later, she crashed through the door. The street beyond was deserted. She slowed to a fast walking pace, heading for the shadows of the building opposite, and then ducked behind some large wheelie bins into a doorway.

A moment later, she saw two men run into the side street from around the front of the building. They had an official look about them and they moved in unison with urgency and purpose. At that precise moment, Sue burst through the exit, followed a few seconds later by Aleksei Lubov and two of his goons.

'Stay where you are,' one of the men yelled, dropping to one knee. 'Armed police!'

Sue turned towards them. Lubov was still in motion, not having been able to stop after barging through the door, his momentum carrying him forward a few paces towards Sue. With a look of satisfaction, Sue swivelled towards him, anticipating the collision.

With a balletic flourish, she swept her arm in an arc towards him. The stiletto in her hand slashed the Russian's throat clean through. He crumpled to the ground without making a sound, the surprised look on his podgy face the sole testament to his sudden realisation that his life was over. A second later, the night air was shattered by the sharp crackle of gunfire.

CHAPTER 42

The mood in the office was festive, however Detective Inspector John Cavey was not yet ready to celebrate. True, they'd nailed the ringleader behind the killings and there wouldn't be a messy show trial after the armed response officers had 'done the necessary' the previous night, but there were still too many unanswered questions. Cavey hated loose ends and this made him reluctant to accept the effusive congratulations that were coming his way from all quarters. He wasn't finished yet. The case was anything but closed.

'Good result sir,' said DC Hargreaves as Cavey approached a large table in the centre of the office around which most of his team were now assembled. WPC Jane Murray had been out to the local newsagents and brought back all the day's first editions which were now being enthusiastically reviewed by the team. One story dominated the headlines of every front page, temporarily relegating the Black Death outbreak to the inside pages.

'Thank you, Hargreaves,' Cavey replied. He appeared distracted and the young detective picked up on this immediately.

'Problem, sir?'

'Well yes. We're not there yet, lad,' replied Cavey, noting the detective's acute perception and sensitivity to mood as well as his verbal economy.

'But you got her, sir…'

'*We* got her,' corrected the Inspector, keen as always to recognise the value of team work. 'Everyone played their part in this. You as much as anyone.' He fell silent as his mind replayed the events of the previous evening for the umpteenth time since the shooting. Something wasn't right.

'There are still too many unanswered questions,' said Cavey. 'We still don't know what the number seventy-two means.

Hargreaves said nothing. He too had been wrestling with this conundrum and had concluded that Sue Baxter may have taken the answer to the grave.

'And also,' Cavey continued, 'why did Baxter sneak into the building through a side door and what was it she had been waiting for?' he said, speaking his thoughts out loud.

Hargreaves looked at his boss quizzically.

'Not sure what you mean, sir.'

'Well, she was there for a reason. She knew it was all over but she still stayed behind. She went AWOL until last night and it now transpires that she was actually holed up in the adjoining room to our surveillance team who were watching her employer's offices. We were looking for *her*, but what was *she* looking for?'

The young policeman now realised what Cavey was on about.

'Right, I get it,' he replied, 'why was she there at all? She knew we were closing in after the Portsmouth incident so why didn't she just make a run for it rather than checking into that hotel.'

'Exactly,' said Cavey, now starting to pace up and down his office as his mind sifted through the facts. 'She stayed behind because of unfinished business. We must find out what that business was.'

A thought occurred to him and he turned to the young DC, his eyes sparkling.

'Hargreaves, get me the video footage shot by our team at the hotel. They had a camera permanently on the front entrance looking for her. I want to see who else went into that building up to the point where Baxter was first spotted. If we know who was there last night it may give us the answer to why she sneaked into the building like she did.'

'I'm on it,' replied the detective, hurrying towards the door.

Cavey followed him out.

'OK, listen up everyone,' he shouted. 'Team meeting in the AV room in ten minutes. I want to run through every detail of what happened last night. And Sergeant Noble, see if you can contact the two SO19s who fired the shots. 'Phone the Yard and request their presence here. I'm sure their debrief session with the IPCC will have finished by now.'

*

As soon as the team was assembled in the Audio Visual room, the operator started to run the video. Cavey felt a tingle of excitement as he watched all the Eleventh Hour staff leaving the building.

'What's going on?' he asked.

'I think it was some sort of fire drill,' replied one of the officers from the surveillance team.

'But no one went back afterwards,' the inspector replied. 'Doesn't that seem strange to you?'

'A little, now you mention it sir, but we were there to look for the murder suspect, not observe the coming and goings of the building's employees,' replied the officer defensively.

Cavey cocked his eyebrow. He didn't like that answer.

'So, tell us what happened next, Detective Constable?' Cavey pressed.

'Well, nothing for a while, sir. Then a whole fleet of limos turned up.'

'Limos?' Cavey echoed. 'What do you mean?'

'Well, a load of top of the range chauffeur driven cars turned up and dropped people off.'

'Who did they "drop off"?' Cavey asked impatiently. 'Did you see?'

'Well, not really, sir. As I said, we were looking for the woman and there were only about three female passengers...' At this point, the officer turned to his colleague for support. 'That's right, Steve, isn't it?'

Steve nodded in reply. 'Only three women were dropped off, and none of them fitted the suspect's description. And then all the vehicles drove off; none of them waited behind.'

'How many people were there in total?' Cavey asked, acidly.

'Quite a few, sir, fifteen, perhaps twenty,' replied the officer. This was the kind of information Cavey expected to be told immediately. He had a rule: anything irregular should be reported without delay, they all knew that.

'So, let me get this clear,' continued the Inspector, biting his consonants as he spoke. 'First of all, every single member of staff unexpectedly leaves the building and then a fleet of cars delivers twenty mystery guests to the offices and you two don't think it's worth mentioning?'

The hapless officers looked at each other, desperate for an explanation that would placate their boss, but neither had one.

'Run the footage of the staff exodus again then fast forward to when the cars start arriving,' shouted Cavey to the video operator at the back of the room.

Half an hour later, the room was still humming with excited conversation. They had managed to name fourteen of the twenty guests.

'Bloody Hell, I hope they were well insured,' remarked Sergeant Noble who had surprised his colleagues by identifying two Global Hedge Fund managers and a Russian Oligarch in the remarkable procession of the super-rich delivered in quick succession to the Eleventh Hour offices.

Cavey said nothing. His mind was still trying to make sense of this development. He needed to know why Sue Baxter had been watching the building and he was certain that these visitors had something to do with it.

'OK, quieten down,' he said, killing the noise instantly. Then he continued, directing his words once again to the two surveillance officers.

'So, when exactly did you first see the suspect trying to enter the offices?'

The two officers flicked open their notebooks.

'At exactly 17:42,' said one of the officers, reading from his logbook, 'DC Rigby and myself saw the suspect crossing the road opposite the hotel where we were mounting our surveillance. It was just before the other people started to arrive.'

'Then what?' interrupted Cavey sharply.

'She skirted the building and entered via a side door in Harriet Street.'

The second officer now tentatively took up the account.

'Once we had positively identified her, we immediately called for armed backup and of course notified you, sir.' Cavey acknowledged the fact with a barely noticeable nod of his head. 'Then when officers Fenwick and Brady from firearms arrived, they took up a position between the main entrance and the side street whilst we continued our surveillance.'

'Go on,' ordered Cavey.

'Nothing occurred for some time,' continued the officer in a dull monotone. 'No one was observed entering or exiting the building. Then, at precisely 18:36, we saw someone leave by the side exit at speed and we immediately alerted the armed response team in the street.'

Cavey's gaze now switched to the firearms officers who, with no further invitation, took up the story.

'As we rounded the corner into the street, we observed two persons exit the building in quick succession. We—'

'Stop!' said Cavey, holding a hand aloft. 'How many people left the building?'

'Two,' said the armed response officers in unison.

'Three,' said one of the surveillance officers, looking over at his colleague for confirmation.

There was silence in the room.

'We only saw two,' continued the smaller of the two firearms officers. 'One female, who was later confirmed to be the suspect Sue Baxter and the other a Mr Aleksei Lubov, head of security at The Eleventh Hour. Both are now deceased.'

'So what happened to the other person?' asked Cavey, turning his gaze accusingly towards the hapless surveillance team.

There was silence as one looked intently at his logbook as if it would miraculously deliver the answer to the question, whilst his companion stared blankly at a dozen enquiring faces around the table. 'It all happened very quickly,' he offered lamely before his voice tailed off.

Cavey gave the pair a withering look before shouting again at the video operator, 'Run the film from 18:34.'

Everyone in the room stared intently at the screen. The angle was not ideal as the camera was trained on the main entrance at the front of the building and the footage was grainy due to the night-time gloom. The side of the building was visible but unfortunately the film quality was poor. It was good enough though to show a figure hurry from the building at exactly 18:36 and then move rapidly out of view seconds before Sue Baxter, followed closely by Aleksei Lubov, burst into view. The footage may not have been sharp, but those present could easily follow events as they unfolded.

When it was all over and the screen showed a confusion of figures circling two motionless bodies, Cavey was the first to speak.

'So, who was that?'

'Whoever it was, they were certainly in a hurry,' Sergeant Noble offered gruffly. 'Looked to me like they were being chased.'

'Female, I would say,' said someone else.

'Damn it!' cursed Cavey fractiously, 'If we'd known about this at the time we wouldn't be in this position.' He then directed an angry look at the two officers he held responsible for their present predicament. They both chose to look down at the table in front of them rather than meet their boss' gaze. 'Anyone got any bright ideas?'

'What about the building's CCTV?' It was Hargreaves. 'They're bound to have cameras at all the entrances,' he continued.

'Check it out immediately,' replied Cavey crisply. 'Call Eleventh Hour and tell them to make the footage available. We've got a meeting with their top man later today. We can take a look then.'

Cavey was reassured that his intuition had been correct but he was also irritated that he still didn't understand what was going on. Something significant had occurred in that building last night, he was now certain of the fact, and he was also sure that Sue Baxter had stayed behind instead of fleeing with the rest of her murderous team for a purpose. He wanted to know what that was.

CHAPTER 43

Caroline hadn't slept a wink. Whenever she closed her eyes, the vision of Sue's last moments were painted vividly on the canvas of her consciousness. In her mind's eye, she saw the smile of satisfaction over and over again, seconds before her final act of sweet revenge. Then she heard the spluttering of the bullets that had sent Sue's body dancing and wriggling to the ground. Her death had been instant. She'd twitched once as the armed officers crouched over her, but there was never really any doubt. She was dead.

It had taken a while longer for Lubov to depart this world. His fate was nevertheless sealed the moment the knife had slashed through his carotid artery. Seconds later, the area had been ablaze with orange and blue flashing lights, the still night air pierced by sirens of different pitches and frequencies and the crackling of police radios. A growing crowd of gawping onlookers, attracted by the commotion, massed behind the protective tape barrier, which gave Caroline the opportunity to leave the shadows and slip away unnoticed.

By dawn, the explosive story dominated UK news bulletins, but elsewhere in the world there was mounting panic as the plague epidemic continued to spread with alarming speed. Deaths were now being reported in twelve countries in Asia, with the terrifying disease having reached the Indian subcontinent and now well entrenched in nine of the twelve provinces of China. Over and above its inexorable progress through the most populous regions of the world, worrying reports were surfacing of suspected cases in New York, Los Angeles and three major cities in Canada.

'OK, Caroline it's all set,' said Tom breathlessly as he hurried into her living room carrying a scruffy Gladstone bag. 'I've contacted the Yanks and they want a meeting ASAP so I'm catching the 14:50 BA flight from Heathrow.'

'What did they say?' Caroline asked, her voice reflecting the excitement she now felt.

'Well, not a lot,' replied Tom as he continued to stuff clothes into the bag. 'I couldn't say much over an unsecure line but I have a meeting first thing tomorrow with my contact in the FBI. He wants a full briefing.'

'What about telling someone over here?'

'No can do,' he replied, 'we still don't know who we can trust and if we tell the wrong person we may stampede them into doing something that we can't undo. No, we have to keep our nerve and deliver the information to a trusted contact.'

'And then what?' asked Caroline, a little concerned that she and Tom were still the only people who knew the origin of the virus and the link with the Eleventh Hour Corporation.

'Then it's off to the US Army Medical Research Institute

of Infectious Diseases, the world's top bio-weaponry establishment. With their help we can escalate this thing fast to National Government level. The Feds and the MRIID will know how to do that and then we can move in on Mr Green bloody Giant and his crew! We have to be careful though as it's critical they're not alerted before we're ready to go.'

Caroline smiled. She liked the sound of this.

Tom squeezed her shoulder.

'You did it, just as I always knew you would.'

'Really, Tom?' she asked. Turning and fixing him with a searching look. 'But why, why did you choose me?'

He smiled and shook his head slowly.

'Still the self-doubt eh? Look Caroline, you're a lot tougher than you think. And in any case I thought he was most likely to open up to an innocent like you, everyone needs someone to confide in you know and it's not like our late Russian friend could have ever fulfilled that role.'

'And you were right, he almost did tell me everything.'

'Yep, *almost* but not quite,' he replied before adding reflectively, 'what about old Leo Brooks then? Who'd have thought he would have become one of them, eh? To think, I initially came to Montagu Steinhart to recruit him!'

'Leo, Edward, Sue… I still can't get my mind around the fact that I actually worked with people capable of … of… this thing,' said Caroline in a hushed voice, struggling for words to sum up their horrific intent. Tom wasn't really listening though.

'Oh by the way, tests by the scientists at Porton Down confirm that the virus has a very short incubation period, like he mentioned last night. It's what they call a 'hot virus', very hot as it happens. That's quite significant as they now predict the disease will burn itself out of its own accord well before it kills us all.'

Caroline had grown used to Tom's bluntness, but still she winced at his words.

'Oh, that's great news!' she replied, sarcastically. But Tom still wasn't listening.

'Strange, though, isn't it?' he continued. 'If their primary objective was to inflict maximum death and destruction, why did the scientists in their labs manufacture a disease that would burn out of its own accord, when they could have tweaked it to go on and on killing?'

He'd finished packing now and paused for a second or two as he reflected on his own words, then he shook his head before adding: 'Strange. Everything else has been meticulously planned … it doesn't add up. We've missed something.'

'Well, I hope it does burn out of its own accord,' replied Caroline, 'for all our sakes.'

'It's spread much further and faster than anyone anticipated,' Tom continued, 'they obviously designed it to be as contagious as possible but it's surprising how it took hold in multiple locations so quickly. I wonder how they managed that? I mean, how did they get it into all those countries simultaneously?'

Caroline's mind spooled back to the stairwell in the Eleventh Hour building and she heard an echo of Sue Baxter's voice.

'Sue said "he used his own people",' she exclaimed.

'*Used!* It was the laboratory technicians. He somehow infected them all then shipped them off home!'

Tom got there at the same time.

'My God! He walked it in using human vectors. Those poor souls probably never suspected…'

Caroline stared at him in dismay. In her mind's eye she could still picture the amiable Dr Hwang, his face beaming with joy at the thought of seeing his relatives.

'The first people they would have infected would have been their loved ones,' she gasped holding her hand to her mouth.

'No,' said Tom. 'If you remember, they were on a kind of trans-Asian shuttle; they would most likely have had to disembark at each destination for refuelling. They'd have gone shopping and had meals in the airport whilst they waited. And all the while they'd have been passing on the virus.'

'And that's why it has spread so rapidly,' finished Caroline.

'Quite. Each airport became the nucleus of the outbreak in that country and every passenger in or out became a potential carrier.'

'No wonder it went global so quickly. It's diabolical,' she gasped.

'It's also very clever, brilliant in fact,' added Tom.

They both fell silent for a few moments as they mulled over this latest development. It was Tom who spoke first:

'Even with it burning out of its own accord they still project a death toll in excess of a hundred million you know.'

At first Caroline thought she had misheard and turned

her head to face him directly, so she could hear his words more clearly.

'Sorry, did you say one hundred million?'

'Afraid so,' Tom fired back. 'Even with strict quarantine restrictions and a short incubation period, it's still likely to result in twice as many fatalities as the Spanish Flu epidemic last century. More people around today, you see.'

Caroline felt sick inside. All at once the full horror struck home to her. The intentional infection of millions of people with a deadly virus with one, sole purpose: mass extermination. She shrank inside at the thought that she could ever have had any sympathy for the man behind this abomination.

'A hundred million,' she repeated slowly.

'Yes, and remember that's with it fizzling out. He obviously intended that it would kill many, many more. What we need now is a vaccine, and fast.'

'My God,' shrieked Caroline, 'I thought there was one. Surely—' but Tom cut her off.

'Nope, not for this disease. Remember, this pathogen has been specially manufactured, so it's brand new. Virologists around the world have had to start from scratch. This Black Death variant is viral, not bacterial and will need to be approached like any new virus, which means a vaccine could be weeks or even months away.'

'*They* have one though!' she exclaimed excitedly. 'Last night, he said that everyone there would be inoculated against the disease. I actually saw all the vaccines for myself when I was at their laboratories in Guyana. They've definitely got one.'

'Well, maybe so,' replied Tom with a shrug. 'But how exactly do you propose we persuade them to share it with us?'

'Surely…' but Caroline didn't finish.

'Oh shit!' exclaimed Tom.

They'd left the television showing twenty-four-hour rolling news and Tom had just caught a few words of the latest bulletin. The screen showed scenes of panic buying and riot conditions in Asia. But what had attracted Tom's interest was the dramatic announcement that the first suspected cases of Black Death had been identified in London.

'It's here,' he said, gravely.

'Well go!' she cried, 'And hurry. Each second we delay costs lives.'

CHAPTER 44

The side street next to the Eleventh Hour offices was still cordoned off. There was 'Police Incident' tape everywhere and scores of blue flashing lights for good measure. DCI Cavey, with Detective Constable Hargreaves following closely behind, strode purposefully over to the area and stared at the chalked outlines of the two bodies on the road surface. A large brown stain was still clearly visible where Aleksei Lubov had met his brutal end.

'Anything new?' he asked one of the forensics, who was kneeling on the tarmacadam, sweeping it meticulously with a small brush.

'No, pretty straightforward really,' the man answered, without looking up.

Cavey stared towards the Emergency Exit. There was a CCTV camera on the wall to the left of the door. Hargreaves noted his gaze and gave a thumbs up sign. This was encouraging.

'Come on then,' said Cavey to the younger man. 'Let's see what they've got for us.'

Edward van der Linden was waiting at reception where he greeted the policemen cordially before showing them into a large bare-walled meeting room on the ground floor. He was confident and composed but not friendly. Everything about his manner seemed designed to remind the policemen of the fact that this was his domain, where he had absolute authority.

'What can I do for you, gentlemen?' he said grandly as he folded his huge arms over his chest and leant back in his chair, a gesture that made him look even more immense than usual.

Cavey said nothing for several seconds. The greeting may have been cordial, but it didn't chime with the guarded body language. The incongruity set him immediately on his guard.

'First of all, may I extend my condolences to you for your loss,' he started, his eyes locked on van der Linden's.

'Thank you, Detective Inspector. Aleksei will be sadly missed.'

'And Ms Baxter?' asked Cavey.

He glimpsed a momentary darkness in the big man's eyes before he rocked back in his chair once again and stared at the ceiling, breaking eye contact.

'It was a double tragedy,' continued van der Linden, back to his booming self. 'Heaven knows what demons were tormenting poor Sue.'

'Quite,' replied Cavey, his face expressionless. 'Whilst we're here, perhaps you could clarify something for me. Was she a full-time member of your staff here at Eleventh Hour?'

Van der Linden's expression became stern and a pained look replaced his thin smile.

'Regrettably, Inspector, we parted company with Sue a few weeks ago.'

'And why was that?'

'Shall we just say she became difficult to manage?'

'How so?'

Van der Linden hesitated before continuing. When he spoke again, his voice was quieter and he adopted the air of someone imparting very sensitive information.

'Sue ran our strategy unit, a very important role, and she was one of our most enthusiastic activists. She was passionate and totally committed but unfortunately a few weeks ago we discovered certain financial irregularities. I decided that it would be best for all concerned if we made a clean break of it and she left without a fuss.'

'And did she?'

'What?'

'Leave without a fuss.'

'Well, not exactly,' replied van der Linden, a little rattled. Cavey detected his discomfort and decided to use one of his favourite tactics: a sudden change of subject.

'Mr van der Linden, does the number seventy-two mean anything to you?'

The Green Giant's expression froze momentarily, then he shrugged his massive shoulders and said, 'Pass' as he shook his head innocently.

Cavey didn't dwell on the subject and moved on with his questioning.

'Could you tell me what exactly was going on here last night?'

The big man paused for a few seconds, blinked a few times then looked long and hard at the neat figure opposite him in an obvious attempt to assay the qualities of his opponent. When he finally spoke, his words were guarded.

'I'm not sure what you mean, Inspector.'

'Well, let me help you out, Mr van der Linden,' Cavey replied in a brisk, no-nonsense tone. 'Firstly, all your staff leave the building, then a fleet of cars deliver a host of VIPs to your front door and then an ex member of your staff murders one of your security staff. Not exactly a normal day at the office, I think you will agree.'

Van der Linden blanched. 'Aleksei was actually *Head* of Security and a great friend to me,' he replied, frostily.

Cavey stayed silent.

'Alright Inspector,' started van der Linden, allowing an edge of indignation to creep into his voice.'

'Detective Chief Inspector,' corrected Cavey.

'OK! Detective Chief Inspector,' van der Linden snapped back. 'I decided to close the offices temporarily in the light of the current plague epidemic. Staff left yesterday afternoon for a week's paid leave. The VIPs you mention are in actual fact the controlling board of this company, here for an important, scheduled meeting. And lastly, poor Sue was, as you have no doubt discovered for yourself, severely mentally disturbed. She made an unauthorised entry into our offices last night and fled when challenged by security, with the tragic consequences both of us are all too aware of.'

Cavey said nothing, and the two of them sat looking at each other until van der Linden's patience snapped.

'Well, if there's nothing else, Inspector, I have a great deal to attend to...' he said, tersely.

Then as he stood, signalling the end of the meeting, Cavey ventured, 'Of course, Mr van der Linden. If we could just have a copy of the CCTV footage from the side entrance, we will be on our way.'

'I'm sorry, Detective Chief Inspector, we've checked but unfortunately the camera wasn't working last night,' said van der Linden, shrugging his shoulders theatrically as he delivered the disappointing news.

Cavey nodded.

'Well, we'll just have to make do with what you have got. I assume the cameras at the front entrance were working, and also the one behind your reception desk?'

Van der Linden's hand hesitated as he reached for the door handle.

'Well, yes,' he stammered, 'but I can't imagine how they will be of any use to you.'

'We have to be thorough in these matters. This *is* a murder enquiry Mr van der Linden.'

'Well yes, of course, anything I can do to help…'

'Since you ask,' interrupted Cavey, 'you wouldn't happen to know who fled the building moments before Ms Baxter and Mr Lubov met their respective ends?'

Van der Linden was unable to conceal his surprise but said nothing so Cavey pushed harder.

'An unidentified person was seen running out of this building a matter of seconds before the other two. We want to know who it was.'

Van der Linden recovered his composure and pulled the door open before mustering a casual reply. 'I really have no idea Inspector. It's an emergency exit, so no one should be using it at all.' Then he added with unmistakable finality, 'Now if you'll excuse me, I really do have to get on.'

*

Only when Cavey and DC Hargreaves were safely in the car on the way back to the police station did the two policemen talk.

'So, what did you think?' ventured the young detective.

'He was lying,' replied his boss.

'About what?'

'Just about everything,' said the Inspector.

'So what now?'

'Well, first of all I want you to look through the security recordings,' said Cavey, tapping the video cassettes of CCTV footage they had been given so reluctantly. 'I want you to note down everyone that went into that building yesterday morning and tick them off when you see them leave later in the day. With a bit of luck you'll be left with just one by the end of the exercise.'

'Understood,' said Hargreaves.

'He hadn't realised someone else was there last night, you know,' Cavey added, furrowing his brow.

'We blew their cover then,' observed Hargreaves.

'Yes, that's right, lad, we did and that concerns me. So best we find out who it was, pronto They need our help!'

CHAPTER 45

After Tom had left for the airport, Caroline couldn't stop herself flicking through every news channel she had access to. Alarmingly, in the national news the story of the West End shooting was barely mentioned in the light of the escalating plague epidemic. Scenes of panic buying and near riot conditions were reported from cities throughout the world and the final film footage showed queues snaking for hundreds of yards outside supermarkets in West London and Birmingham. The UK was not yet descending into anarchy but these were the first signs that people were preparing for the worst. Caroline shuddered. *One hundred million people*, she thought. That's how many will die, murdered by the company she works for and a man she once so admired.

Just as she was about to watch the same footage for a third time, the phone rang. Caroline could tell her mother was in a state of high anxiety the moment she began talking.

'Isn't this disease frightful,' she wailed. 'Do you think it will reach us out here in the shires?'

'I'm sure everything will be fine,' she lied. 'Just go

down to the village store and buy water and non-perishable food.'

She hadn't intended it, but the suggestion caused instant panic.

'My goodness, are we all going to die?' her mother shrieked. 'If only your father was here, he'd know what to do…'

'Look, just stay calm, Mum,' Caroline interrupted, raising her voice and speaking a little more firmly than she had intended. Janet fell silent but Caroline could detect the occasional sob in the background.

'Mum, everything will be OK,' she repeated again, softly. 'We just have to be sensible and ride it out.'

'I want you here,' Janet said, in a voice barely above a whisper. 'We should be together at a time like this.'

She was right, thought Caroline, warming to the prospect of leaving London behind her and hiding away in the countryside. Tom could call her in Buckinghamshire just as easily as he could at her flat. She suddenly felt very guilty that she had not thought of her mother before. Of course they should be with each other in these circumstances.

'OK Mum, I'll pack up tonight and come home first thing in the morning,' she announced, feeling an unexpected elation at the prospect of getting away from it all. She was smiling to herself as she put down the phone. Yes, she needed to escape.

The apartment suddenly seemed oppressive and small and certainly didn't suit her current restless state, so she decided to go out for a walk to clear her head and get some exercise. The street outside was uncharacteristically quiet but otherwise seemed normal. However, as she rounded the bend at the bottom of her road she spied a small crowd gathered around a parked car. A man was shouting and then a woman started screaming. Suddenly the crowd moved away from the vehicle in unison as the car door opened.

'He's got it,' shouted one of them, 'look at him.'

A man staggered out of the car, his face was a livid red colour with a dark grey hue around eyes that stared in terror at the hostile faces all around him.

'Stay away!' screamed another woman, turning tail and running up the street towards Caroline. The others stayed where they were but kept a safe distance between themselves and the sick man.

Caroline noticed dark purple wields on his cheeks and his hands were shaking uncontrollably. He was gasping for breath and then without warning he bent double and vomited onto the pavement in front of him, three, four, five times.

'Help me,' he wheezed, falling slowly to one knee. But no one moved they just watched the pathetic figure in front of them crumple to the ground. A second later the silence was shattered by the squeal of sirens and a police car took the corner at speed and came to a screeching halt followed shortly afterwards by two army jeeps.

By now the man was lying on his back convulsing uncontrollably. The police didn't approach him but instead ushered the crowd further up the street. The soldiers started to erect a cordon and Caroline noticed that whilst four of them were carrying automatic weapons over their shoulders two were actually holding their guns and pointing them threateningly towards the crowd. They looked edgy and scared. Then one of them, obviously in command, raised a small megaphone and started to bark orders at the crowd.

'You must disperse now,' he shouted, 'we are empowered to disband any gathering that we believe will endanger life, by force.'

No one moved. The instruction didn't have the desired effect, so he tried a more direct approach.

'Move on, or we will open fire.'

This time the message got through and people scattered in all directions without the need for further encouragement.

Caroline felt the fear rise within her. Society was breaking down. This behaviour looked very much like a precursor to the formal imposition of Martial Law. The army had taken the lead and the police had just watched from the side-lines. As she reached the welcome sanctuary of her flat, it dawned on her that there had been no ambulance for the dying man and she realised the chilling significance of this fact: law and order was the priority and in future the sick would be left to die where they fell.

She went back to watching the news on the television where she was treated to a shocking, second by second account of the epidemic's progress around the globe. At 16:00 hours GMT the World Health Organisation declared the plague outbreak to be a global pandemic and made a direct appeal to governments throughout the world to share their research in order to find an effective vaccine.

Troops were on the streets in twenty-three capital cities globally. Borders were being closed. The world was seizing up.

★

Cavey placed a full stop very precisely at the end of a letter he had just written to Sir Geoffrey, thanking him for his forbearance and the faith he had placed in him. The Chief Commissioner had been a true and loyal friend. He then signed the bottom of the page in his slow but distinctive hand: *Gratefully, yours, John C*. All morning, messages had been arriving from well-wishers, many of whom had been standing in line twenty-four hours previously to humiliate him and have him removed from the case. But now all those politicians and sycophants were singing his praises in an effort to benefit in some way from his success. He certainly wouldn't be writing to them, though. The Detective Chief Inspector sat immobile, deep in thought and as he did his fingers fiddled with his cherished gold Yard O' Lead pen.

The telephone on his desk rang, interrupting his thoughts. It was DC Hargreaves.

'Bingo, sir,' said the young man excitedly. 'I think you should come down and see this for yourself.'

Cavey slipped into his tweed jacket and hurried down to the audio visual room in the basement.

'Shoot,' he instructed the young policeman as soon as he had taken up his position in front of a large VDU screen in the middle of the table.

'Two things, sir,' started a noticeably energised Stephen Hargreaves. 'First of all, you were right, he *was* lying.'

'Thought so.'

'If you remember, he told us specifically that he had given his staff a week's holiday because of the plague outbreak. Well, the CCTV footage clearly shows a sign in the building's reception reminding staff of a prescheduled evacuation that day at 17:00 hours. Not a holiday.'

Cavey raised his eyebrows. 'Interesting,' he said. 'Looks like he went to elaborate lengths to ensure the building was completely empty before his guests arrived. OK, so what else?'

'Well, I know who it was that left the building in such a hurry,' announced Hargreaves proudly.

'And?'

'Well, as we hoped, there was just one employee who entered the building that day who didn't leave by the main entrance.'

'Fantastic, who was it?' said Cavey impatiently.

Hargreaves hesitated before answering. 'No one well known or anything like that sir, but it's strange, I'm sure I've seen her before.'

'Really, where?' asked the Inspector.

'That's the weird thing, sir. I think it was here.'

Hargreaves' expert fingers danced over the computer keyboard and a moment later the image of a young woman flashed onto the screen in front of them.

'You know, I think you're absolutely right,' said Cavey, already flicking back through the pages of his logbook. Then he stopped and his finger traced the words on the page. He stared up at Hargreaves with a look of triumph.

'Caroline Hartley. That's who we're looking for. She came here with her friend Kelly Owen. I want to know everything about her and most of all where she lives.'

CHAPTER 46

Caroline awoke at around 8am and immediately checked her mobile for messages. There was no word from Tom. She'd slept fitfully after watching the news until the early hours as the situation had become graver by the minute. The disease had by now reached virtually every nation on earth with a rapidity that had taken scientists by surprise. Health experts couldn't understand how the virus was spreading so readily and with such speed. But, unlike Caroline and Tom, they were not aware that it was all meticulously planned. And that the plague was being deliberately and systematically introduced to country after country around the globe. All flights to the USA and Canada had been suspended and shortly after midnight it was announced that a state of Martial Law had been declared in every province of China and also in Thailand and Venezuela. They were burning victims openly in the streets of Nigeria and Egypt and shooting suspected carriers of the disease in a number of African and Middle Eastern countries.

Her case was packed and the temptation to flee to the countryside was almost overwhelming but she felt a growing disquiet at Tom's continued radio silence. She felt isolated and alone; still only the two of them knew all the facts and that concerned her greatly. What was he up to? she fretted. Surely his contacts in the US should have been spurred to action by now. Whatever was happening over there, she deserved to be kept informed, she thought indignantly. The plain fact was that she simply couldn't relax until she knew that Tom had passed on the information.

Things looked reassuringly normal out in the street as she gazed down from her sitting room window. People were still going about their daily business: travelling to work, walking their dogs and cars were still driving by. So for the moment, London appeared to be functioning as usual. Yesterday's shocking event out in the street seemed to be just an isolated incident. There were certainly no road blocks or signs of military action as she had feared there might be by now, bearing in mind the deteriorating global situation she had witnessed on the TV in the small hours.

Reassured, she decided to venture out to the convenience store around the corner to stock up on last minute essentials. It would be a good way of testing the water in any case, as she still found it difficult to believe that things were so calm.

Inside the shop, cans of food and bottles of water still lined the shelves. Caroline noticed though that people were not shopping. Instead, they were clustered around a small television set by the exit.

'What's up?' she asked the girl at the check-out.

'It's all over, thank God,' she answered gleefully, as she scanned through Caroline's shopping items.

'Some bloke's come up with a cure.'

'What!' exclaimed Caroline in surprise as she hurried

over to join the others, craning her head above a woman with a baby in a buggy to get a reasonable view of the small screen. On the set a female news reporter with a fixed smile and glossy red lips was outside a manufacturing facility or factory of some kind, talking in the characteristically animated way reporters do.

'What's she saying?' whispered Caroline to a girl of similar age, with closely cropped red hair and multiple ear piercings, standing just in front of her. The girl turned around and grinned,

'They've found a vaccine. Luckily that big giant guy, what's his name …?'

'Van der Linden?' shot back Caroline.

'Yea that's the fella. He evidently had it all along.'

Caroline was dumbstruck. What did it mean? She stared intently at the television, desperate to learn more about this wholly unexpected development.

The reporter was standing next to a large sign displaying a company's name in what looked like Chinese script. Caroline was transfixed. Although she couldn't read the sign, her eyes were immediately drawn to a picture in the bottom corner. A clock with its hands stuck at the eleven fifty-five position was plainly visible.

'And not for the first time,' cooed the anchor in a mid-Atlantic accent, 'it appears the world may have been be saved by billionaire philanthropist Edward van der Linden, or as we all know him, the "Green Giant".'

A picture of a beaming van der Linden flashed up on the screen. Caroline watched in bewilderment as the reporter continued.

'With the plague pandemic plunging countries into a state of near panic and the death toll from this deadly virus rising by the minute, scientists throughout the world have been engaged in a deadly race against time in a desperate search for a vaccine. Well, they need look no further. For we have been saved by the mighty Eleventh Hour Corporation, who have found one. And not a moment too soon!'

The report then cut to a production line with hundreds of boxes rolling smoothly along a series of conveyor belts, each stamped with the distinctive eleventh hour logo and the name of the drug: E-rad-eX.

'Here in this plant, and scores of others throughout the world,' explained the reporter enthusiastically, 'the company is producing millions of doses of a vaccine that we desperately need to save us from the scourge of this terrible disease.'

The reporter gave a saccharine smile and the camera panned across to the convoy of trucks behind her, each leaving the factory laden with boxes full of the life-saving drug.

The news report ended and a cheer rose from the ragtag audience.

'I'm gonna get me some of that medicine,' said a large man dressed in overalls with a distinctive Caribbean lilt to his voice. 'What's she say it's called?'

'E-rad-eX,' replied Caroline robotically. She should know, after all, she named the drug.

'What's going on?' she exclaimed out loud, not expecting an answer. The others drifted off, relieved that the global pandemic would most likely now not touch their lives.

Caroline started to walk slowly back to her apartment as if in a trance. She was totally bewildered by the news. Why, she wondered, would van der Linden intentionally introduce the disease only to inoculate the world's population against it? It simply didn't add up.

Once again her mind sped back to the jungles of Guyana. She'd actually been in the laboratory that had developed the virus, seen the amazing facilities behind its development, met the scientists there…

Then it hit her. She stood stock still in the middle of the pavement. She went cold. The whole thing now made perfect sense. She grabbed her phone and frantically dialled Tom's number. She had to tell him. Again there was no reply and the call went to voicemail.

'Tom, pick up!' she yelled in frustration, 'I know what's happening. It's not the virus Tom, that's just a foil to scare us. No, it's the vaccine that will do the damage. Tom, they're going to sterilise us all!'

E-rad-eX was Professor Swannel's drug.

The plan was so clever and would be utterly devastating. She remembered van der Linden's words as she had left the projector room: 'This is *the first stage* of our project …' If only she had stayed a little longer, or left the microphone behind as initially intended, then they would have learnt what else was intended. The first stage – the release of the deadly plague virus – was designed to set the scene for stage two – the wholesale inoculation of the world's population.

Tom's keen mind had seized on an inconsistency. Now Caroline saw that he had been right to question why the virus had been designed with such a short incubation period.

Quite rightly, he had been concerned by such an obvious flaw in this meticulously planned exercise. Although it would ultimately kill fewer people, with a short incubation period the disease would spread more quickly, with greater visibility. And that was what they intended. Van der Linden had undoubtedly chosen this particular virus because of its formidable reputation and its terrifying symptoms. He needed the outcry, the panic and the urgency of a virulent, fast-spreading disease to stampede world leaders into his open arms. Once they were desperate, they would readily accept what he had to offer – the only effective inoculation against New Variant Black Death. The clamour for a solution would ensure that testing would be 'lite-touch' to say the least. Not that there could be any doubt that the vaccine would work, it was, after all, his virus.

Caroline hurried back to her flat, her head light and her mind churning through a hundred different scenarios

'Where the hell are you, Tom?' she shouted out loud in frustration, as she flung open her front door and rushed up the stairs to her first floor flat. She was beginning to buckle under the burden of responsibility the discovery had placed on her shoulders. Outside the select members of the Eleventh Hour controlling board, she was the only person who knew the truth; the only person in the world who could yet scupper their plan. She desperately wanted to pass the baton to Tom, so the professionals could take it from here. But he was incommunicado, so it was all down to her.

As she watched the television, she felt an irresistible sense of urgency. She'd seen E-rad-eX rolling off the production line in Asia and now, on the latest news bulletin, shot at a factory in Pittsburgh in the US, there were hundreds more boxes being loaded onto a convoy of lorries. Not only did Eleventh Hour have the vaccine, they also possessed the manufacturing capacity to mass produce the drug on an industrial scale throughout the world. So, courtesy of Edward van der Linden's vast business empire, the vaccine could be manufactured, distributed and administered globally within a very short space of time. There was no time for delay.

Somewhat begrudgingly, Caroline couldn't help but admire the ingenuity of the strategy. It was all so meticulously planned. Dr Hwang and the eminent Professor Swannel had given her a very good grounding in both genetics and virology, enabling her to understand exactly how all the pieces of the jigsaw fitted together. The Black Death vaccine was intended to act like a kind of medical Trojan Horse. Swannel had laboured the point that viruses were good at transporting genetic material around the body and infecting host cells. Well, that is what the vaccine was intended to do. It would carry the practically undetectable sterilisation agent, SV40 around the body. Swannel himself had only discovered it by accident, so there was little chance that World Health Organisation scientists would notice that the E-rad-eX vaccine contained not one, but two, viruses. Once administered, the sterilisation gene would be imprinted on every host cell and thereafter the defective gene would prevent reproduction by anyone infected by the secret virus. Edward van der Linden was commencing a surreptitious mass sterilisation programme on the world's entire population.

Caroline paced up and down the room. What should she

do? What *could* she do? The production line in the factory in Pittsburgh was still in full swing on the television. She was only half watching but something caught her eye and she stopped in mid stride to look more closely. One of the factory workers was being interviewed and he was holding one of the boxes, plucked a moment before from a conveyor belt. Something wasn't quite the same though. The label looked different. It still showed the Eleventh Hour logo, but it was blue in colour and completely different in design to the red E-rad-eX labels she had seen previously. Caroline seized the remote control and froze the picture. There was no doubt about it. The label read 'Omnitorin 24' not 'E-rad-eX'. It was a different drug altogether. Why were they manufacturing two different vaccines? she wondered.

Her mind raced through the possibilities and a terrible conclusion slowly formed in her mind. Once the thought had occurred to her, she knew beyond doubt that she was correct. Omnitorin 24 would be comprised of a single vaccine: a vaccine that would prevent its recipient from contracting the new variant Black Death virus, a vaccine that did not include the hidden sterilisation agent. This vaccine would no doubt be administered to those specially selected by Eleventh Hour. Those the company had decided to allow to continue to procreate, whilst everyone else would be inoculated with the end of the line vaccine: E-rad-eX.

Caroline's mind raked through her experiences at Eleventh Hour. All the signs were there but she hadn't noticed them at the time. Why would she have? But now it all made sense and she knew exactly what he intended. The people in the emerging economies, a staggering two-thirds of the global population, would be neutered, whilst people in the developed world would be left to breed freely. Abe's dream of re-establishing global dominance for the Western economies would be fulfilled. No wonder he had been so elated on his return from the jungle laboratory; Edward van der Linden had just shown him how he was going to make his lifetime's ambition a reality.

She looked down at her phone which was still in her hand and cursed under her breath: Tom hadn't picked up the message yet. What was going on? In her current agitated state she found it difficult to stay still and she stalked over to the window and stared down at the street below. As she did so her eyes met those of someone sitting in a car directly opposite her flat. Someone was watching her; there was no doubt about it. She recoiled and stood with her back against the wall by the curtain, wondering what this meant. Who was it? But before she could find an answer, her thoughts were interrupted by an unfamiliar noise, like an old fashioned telephone. It rang three times, stopped then started the whole sequence again. She looked around the room in confusion. Just as a third ringing cycle started she located the source of the noise. It was coming from her green electronic tablet which she'd left lying on the coffee table. An orange light which she'd never seen before pulsed in time with each ring.

Caroline rushed over and picked up the device before it could ring again. An icon was flashing urgently. In its centre was a photo of the person calling. She let out a cry of relief as she stabbed her finger on a flashing picture of Tom Beresford. A second later, the screen was filled with a talking version of the caller.

'Hello Caroline,' he said as soon as the picture had fully loaded.

'Tom, Tom, thank God you've called,' she exclaimed to the shimmering screen. 'I've been trying to reach you, I know what's happening. They—'

But Tom showed no reaction and continued to talk, drowning out her words. 'This is a recording and it's absolutely imperative you listen to everything I say.'

Caroline threw her head back in frustration. She needed to talk to him in person, not listen to a pre-recorded message! What was he thinking?

The expression on Tom's face was uncharacteristically serious, with no trace of his usual humour or mischief.

'I'm sorry, Caroline, I've got bad news. If you are viewing this message, it is for one reason, and one reason alone; I am dead.'

She felt as if someone had punched her in the stomach as she took on board these unexpected words. Her head reeled in shock; she started to pant like someone emerging from deep under water and her eyes struggled to focus on the screen.

'My mobile has been programmed to call you on that green tablet thingy you always have with you, in the event my body temperature falls below thirty degrees. And that, regrettably, is what has happened.' He paused and when he started talking again his voice was softer as he adopted a more personal tone. 'Look Caroline, I know we've had our differences but believe me, you're the right person for this task. Just don't panic and you'll survive. You have to listen carefully now to what I have to say. Your life depends on it.'

She could hear the blood pounding in her temples. Tears welled in her eyes but she rubbed them away. This wasn't the time to get emotional, she told herself.

Meanwhile, Tom's message was still continuing: 'You know what's going on,' he said, sounding a little more like his usual self, 'and that makes you a prime target. I've been taken out of the game and you will undoubtedly be next on their hit list. Caroline, I'm depending on you to see this through, which means,' and here he laboured his speech as he said each word, 'you – must – stay – alive.' Caroline had been holding her breath and she now let out a loud gasp.

'Get out of that house immediately. Don't stop to pack, just leave. Now!'

Caroline suddenly remembered the face in the car parked opposite. They were already here! She rushed back to the window and stole a look through the side of the curtain. He was still there, watching. As she continued to peer through the gap she saw a large people carrier with heavily tinted windows draw up further down the road. The doors of the vehicle slid silently open and four people spilled out into the street. She recognised them immediately. They were Lubov's men. The driver was holding a compact-looking machine pistol and as Caroline watched with mounting horror, he silently directed the others into position. Two made for her front door, drawing handguns from inside their jackets as they ran with the fluidity of professionals. The third man crouched by the people-carrier, gun in hand, whilst the leader sped towards the flat's entrance. They were coming for her!

Caroline was still holding the tablet and as she watched

the scene below, she realised Tom was still talking, 'Good luck, Caroline, and look after yourself,' he said softly, with a note of finality. The image then faded away and he left her to her fate.

She looked around frantically, scarcely able to think straight. There wasn't a back entrance to the flat. There was no way out except at the front. She was trapped. Once her assailants were through the door at street level only a short staircase and a flimsy internal door would stand in their way. She had no plan; all she could do now was hope and pray for a miracle.

CHAPTER 47

Cavey's phone trilled. He was driving so he flicked on the hands free.

'Yes,' he snapped.

'Problem at the location,' started Hargreaves, he was speaking fast and his tone was urgent. 'Request armed backup. Four men, heavily armed, look like pros.' Cavey heard the distinct sound of glass shattering as the detective continued to speak.

'They're trying to break into the flat and they're almost in, sir,' exclaimed the young officer, his voice rising in intensity as he watched the action unfolding.

By now Cavey knew Hargreaves well enough to predict his likely response.

'Do not engage!' he shouted down the phone a second before he heard the explosive crackle of gunfire but he could do nothing to help his colleague. He was still five minutes away from the scene and their intended rendezvous.

'Stay where you are,' he shouted in a vain attempt to dissuade the young officer from becoming involved.

Caroline peered wide-eyed from behind the curtain. She saw the door open, saw the young man start to emerge from the car, seconds before it was peppered with bullets and the occupant sprang back across the front seats. The kneeling gunman then rose to his feet before carefully aiming his weapon in preparation to put his kill beyond doubt. Caroline raised her hand to her mouth and let out a shriek, but he didn't shoot. Instead, he stumbled drunkenly sideways before crumpling to the ground. Almost at the same moment one of his companions was hurled backwards as three shots thudded into his chest in quick succession and he was catapulted over a small wall into a front garden. A figure sprinted across the road and crouched momentarily beside the car. As he came to a halt he turned his head towards her.

'Simon!' she screamed.

Then he was off again, choosing to make himself a moving target. This drew a burst of automatic gunfire but Simon was too fast and surprisingly agile for a man of his size as he hurdled a car bonnet and disappeared from view. A second later, two shots rang out and the third gunman was sent spinning into a parked car before falling to the ground in an untidy tangle of arms and legs.

But the team leader was by now clambering through the broken front door. A moment later Caroline heard him thundering up the stairs and let out a gasp of terror. He'd be in the flat within seconds. She rushed towards the entrance grabbing a dining chair as she ran, opened the front door and hurled it down the stairs at her assailant. The unexpected action took him by surprise and the missile checked his progress. He stumbled momentarily, let off a burst of gunfire and clambered awkwardly over the obstacle. She'd delayed him a little but he was still coming to kill her. Caroline slammed the door shut, slid the lock into place, and then looked around the room for the best place to hide, before diving under the large rosewood dining table. A second later she heard the gunman throw his full weight against the door, splitting the surround on the second attempt before crashing noisily into the room. He loosed off a wild burst of gunfire as he entered the room. Then he stood for a moment, trying to work out where she had gone. She could sense him thinking. Panting with the exertion, he walked two paces towards the kitchen, then thought better of it and stood still again, listening. From where she was hiding she could just see his legs and she watched in horror as he started to move slowly towards her. He'd worked out that there was only one hiding place in the room. She held her breath and closed her eyes, ready for the end. A shot rang out, then a second. The gunman was slammed against the wall where he left a bloody smear as he slid lifeless to the floor.

Caroline struggled out from her hiding place just as Simon ran into the room. He was dressed in a tight fitting black windbreaker jacket and jeans, his face was unshaven and he wore a look of concern as he scanned the room. A smile broke onto his face when he caught sight of her. She took two steps towards him before falling into his open arms.

The silence was shattered less than a minute later as the police arrived with a cacophony of sirens, screeching tyres and slamming doors. Only when they heard the sound of heavy boots pounding up the stairs towards them did they release each other. Simon holstered his gun and held his hands out in front of him, palms first as three armed officers swarmed into the room, to be followed shortly afterwards by DCI Cavey and a slightly dazed but otherwise unscathed DC Hargreaves. They all stood in silence, weighing up the situation.

Simon was first to speak.

'Major Oliver Riley, special operations SIS,' he volunteered.

The SO19 squad relaxed visibly but Cavey held up a hand by way of caution.

'ID,' he snapped at Simon, his arm still raised.

Simon moved his hand slowly inside his jacket and as he did Caroline noticed the armed officers grip their weapons more tightly.

She stepped defensively in front of Simon, 'He's on our side,' she implored, looking directly at Cavey, who returned her stare without blinking.

'Move aside!' he ordered.

Simon flicked open a small wallet containing his official ID card and held it at head height, pivoting slowly around from one side to the other so everyone could see it.

Cavey nodded acknowledgement and gestured for the armed officers to lower their weapons. The tension in the room evaporated.

'What's this all about?' he asked, staring intently at Simon.

'Miss Hartley has been helping us to infiltrate a corrupt international organisation, the Eleventh Hour Corporation,' started Simon. At the mention of the company's name, Cavey darted a look in Hargreaves' direction.

The name triggered something in Caroline too,

information and facts she had learnt but a matter of minutes before came flooding back into her conscious mind. She turned to Simon.

'Tom's dead,' she said in a faint voice as if waking from a dream.

'I know,' he replied putting a reassuring hand on her shoulder.

'The vaccine!' she blurted urgently. 'What about the vaccine?'

But she didn't continue; she was interrupted by a loud ringing noise. She knew what it was immediately and one look at the screen told her who was calling. With a flourish she bent down and swept the device off the table top and answered the call with a stab of her finger.

'Edward,' she said as his face filled the screen.

'Caroline. Er, how nice. How… how are you?' he asked in a far less confident voice than usual.

'Fine, thank you Edward,' she replied in a clipped voice, before adding, 'still very much alive, as you can see.'

She could see his mind working as he ran through the implication of what she had just said.

'Caroline. There's so much you don't know,' he simpered, employing his most appealing tone.

'No Edward,' she replied frostily. 'On the contrary, there's so much *you* don't know. Like for instance, who came up with the name for your vaccine. Well, it was me!' she declared triumphantly. 'You didn't know that did you? I also met the scientist who developed it, when I was looking round your complex in the jungle. Of course, he's dead now,' she added, 'you saw to that.'

Van der Linden said nothing.

'And I also know about the rule of 72,' continued Caroline, watching his reactions carefully as she made the revelation.

Cavey and Hargreaves exchanged glances whilst the Green Giant's eyes opened wide as full realisation dawned on him. Then his expression changed; his lips narrowed and his eyes became cold and malevolent as Caroline delivered her coup de grace.

'You see, I know what you're up to, Edward. I know exactly what's in E-rad-eX. Your secret is out!'

He stared at her for a few seconds without speaking, his face stormy and mean before his rage boiled over.

'You'll ruin everything you treacherous bitch,' he screamed. 'Everything— '

Cavey gently eased the tablet from Caroline's hand and held the device up in front of his own face.

'Hello again, Mr van der Linden,' he said, staring icily at the image on the screen. 'It sounds to me like it's time we had another little chat. So just you sit tight; my men will be with you imminently.'

Van der Linden sat immobile, his face frozen in shock, he had obviously assumed Caroline was alone when they had been talking and the policeman's sudden appearance was a complete surprise to him. He didn't utter another word before cutting the connection.

Cavey flicked open his phone and punched a number on the speed dial.

'Arrest Edward van der Linden at the Eleventh Hour offices immediately,' he commanded.

As he turned to Caroline, his expression changed. The sternness that characterised his whole demeanour was replaced by a softer, more sympathetic expression and his eyes were alight with a look of intense satisfaction. Cavey permitted himself a rare smile – the case was solved. Now he had all the answers, bar one.

'Miss Hartley,' he said politely. 'What exactly is the rule of 72?'

But Caroline held up a hand to stop him. This wasn't the time. She still had an urgent matter to attend to.

'I'll tell you in a minute but first of all we need to save mankind,' she said, without a hint of irony.

EPILOGUE

Even after a mass inoculation program concentrated in the worst affected areas of the globe, it took over six weeks before the pandemic was brought fully under control. Three months after the disease first appeared, there were still isolated cases reported to the World Health Organisation as the virus stubbornly refused to acquiesce to man's efforts to stamp it out. Official estimates place the total death toll in excess of one million people, a massive loss of life, but far short of where it would have been had a vaccine not been available.

The man in the street was not told about the nefarious activities of Eleventh Hour or of the existence of a vaccine with a hidden sterilisation agent. This information was kept secret and officially classified by the G8 nations – the only countries entrusted with the full facts on the matter. The confiscation and subsequent destruction of vast quantities of E-rad-eX vaccine in parts of Asia did not go unnoticed and caused widespread consternation in the region, with rioting breaking out in a number of capitals as people accused the authorities of intentionally depriving them of life-saving medicine. Even when the substitute vaccine was liberally distributed, commentators still speculated on why the E-rad-eX drug had been so hastily withdrawn. One popular internet blogger even postulated that the action was driven by a conscious desire by Western countries to reduce the number of people in the most populous nations by allowing the plague to run unchecked.

However, despite the rumours of dark ulterior motives, the mass immunisation program earned a place in history as the first truly universal, global health initiative.

A body discovered in a small boutique hotel in New York was later identified as that of Tom Beresford, a businessman from London who worked for International Investment bank, Montagu Steinhart. The cause of death was not immediately apparent and only after a second post mortem (at the insistence of the Foreign Office) was it discovered that he had been poisoned. Detailed analysis of the toxin used, revealed it to be a rare lipophilic alkaloid poison extracted from the dart frog of Columbia, traditionally used by indigenous Indian tribes on the tips of their arrows. Secretly, Tom Beresford was posthumously awarded the Distinguished Conduct Medal for bravery, the highest military honour after the Victoria Cross.

No official record exists of a Caroline Hartley from the village of Oakdene in Buckinghamshire.

Harold Butterworth survived his ordeal and was placed in sheltered accommodation in the Bournemouth area where he lives comfortably on a small pension and receives the occasional visit from a young Detective Constable who is a rising star in the Met's Murder Squad.

All Eleventh Hour offices throughout the world were

discreetly closed down and the company's assets – a staggering US$45 billion – confiscated and then distributed amongst leading environmental charities. None of those who served on the company's controlling board holds any public office and half are now in prison for a variety of crimes ranging from racketeering to money laundering. Leo Brooks stepped down from the CEO position of Montagu Steinhart. His current location is unknown.

Edward van der Linden had fled his offices when police arrived to arrest him. Mystery surrounds his current whereabouts but it is widely suspected that he continues to benefit from the patronage and help of a cadre of billionaires who conspire to keep him hidden.

Detective Chief Inspector Cavey is on the case and has assured his superiors that he will not rest until Edward van der Linden is brought to justice.

POSTSCRIPT

BBC News June 3 2013

"The secretive **Bilderberg Group** *held its annual meeting in a luxury hotel in the English countryside today. The people who are invited to the meetings, and the topics discussed, are official secrets which the media is forbidden from reporting. Bilderberg is effectively an elite secret society ruling the world from behind closed doors and outside the democratic framework. To be admitted to this elite club you have to be immensely wealthy, run a multinational bank, a giant corporation or a country."*

ACKNOWLEDGEMENTS

It is said that writing a novel is like swimming the Channel; you have to do all the hard work yourself but throughout the process you rely on others to keep you going and, most of all, to confirm that you are still going in the right direction.

With these sentiments in mind I must acknowledge the help and guidance I have received from so many quarters.

As a first time novelist it was invaluable for me to receive positive feedback and encouragement from experienced literary editor Ben Evans who reviewed my first and last drafts. His words of encouragement sustained me through numerous plot refinements and the endless 'polishing' exercise. Equally helpful was my daughter Emily who, having worked in literary PR, knows a thing or two about books. Her natural positivity and refreshing enthusiasm was a potent antidote to self doubt. My other two children, Becky and Elliot, were also a great help and full of useful suggestions.

I also owe a debt of gratitude to all those who have read and critiqued the novel. A number of the suggestions proffered by these readers have made a real difference to the finished article. Thank you to avid crime novel enthusiast

Duncan Ponikwer, ace consistency checkers Elaine and Steve Cook and helicopter consultant Philip Homan.

Lastly, my ever supportive wife Julia has lived with this project for a number of years now and has steadfastly kept me on track. Her common sense approach to life and incredible eye for detail have also helped ensure that the characters in the novel are true to life and the story line has remained realistic.

RESEARCH ATTRIBUTIONS

In writing a novel of this kind I have had to conduct a great deal of research into virology, environmental issues and in particular Global Warming. The following works should be acknowledged in this respect:

'*Storms of My Grandchildren: The Truth About the Coming Climate Catastrophe and Our Last Chance to Save Humanity*' by James Hansen.

'*Hell and High Water*' by Alistair McIntosh.

'*Six Degrees (our future on a hotter planet*)' by Mark Lynas.

'*Our Final Century*' by Martin Rees.

'*Requiem for a species*' by Clive Hamilton.

'*The China Syndrome (the 21st Century's first great epidemic)*' by Karl Greenfeld.